PRAISE FOR RACH

T0029225

"A fresh voice in crime fiction."

—Lee Child

"Devilishly clever . . . Hall's writing sizzles and pops."

—Meg Gardiner

"Hall slips from funny to darkly frightening with elegant ease."

—*Publishers Weekly*

PRAISE FOR *WHAT NEVER HAPPENED*

"Rachel Howzell Hall does it again. *What Never Happened* blends blade-sharp writing and indelible characters with a suspenseful story that pulls you in and won't let go, as a seeming paradise grows dark with storms, suspicion, and murder. I couldn't put it down."

—Meg Gardiner, #1 *New York Times* bestselling author

"*What Never Happened* opens with a gut punch and doesn't let up from there. Rachel Howzell Hall's twist on the you-can't-go-home-again story is smart, dizzying, and thrilling. She not only handles the mystery elements expertly, but she honors the grief and rage of our past and present."

—Paul Tremblay, bestselling author of *The Cabin at the End of the World* and *The Pallbearers Club*

"Rachel Howzell Hall has crafted her own genre of slow-boiling, powerfully emotional thrillers. Her realistic characters are ordinary people, haunted by past horrors that won't stay buried, forcing them to face pure evil to find their own redemption."

—Lee Goldberg, #1 *New York Times* bestselling author

"In *What Never Happened*, Rachel Howzell Hall seamlessly weaves together the past and the present, decorating her breakneck plot with dark secrets and unexpected reveals that glitter like jewels. I couldn't turn the pages fast enough."

—Jess Lourey, Amazon Charts bestselling author of *The Quarry Girls*

"*What Never Happened* is superb. Beautifully and smartly written, it is an engrossing thriller with an ending that will leave your head spinning. It is deliciously creepy and perfectly crafted. In a word, stunning! Don't miss this one!"

—Lisa Regan, *USA Today* and *Wall Street Journal* bestselling author

"Rachel Howzell Hall's *What Never Happened* is a spine-tingling twist of a roller coaster that keeps you on the edge of your seat to the very last page and will have you saying 'Thanks a lot, Rachel, for my lack of sleep.'"

—Yasmin Angoe, award-winning author of the critically acclaimed Nena Knight series, *Her Name Is Knight* and *They Come at Knight*

PRAISE FOR *WE LIE HERE*

"*We Lie Here* is another fast and surprisingly funny thriller from Rachel Howzell Hall. I was on the edge of my seat through all the revelations, twists, and turns in a fast-paced third act. Get this book and relax with the knowledge that you are in the hands of a fantastic crime novelist."

—Adrian McKinty, Edgar Award–winning author of the Sean Duffy series

"In *We Lie Here*, Rachel Howzell Hall gives us a tight, lean, eye-level look at the Gibson family—flawed, normal, abnormal, and each affected by a deadly secret left buried for years—while weaving a page-turning tapestry of dread, cold-blooded murder, and nail-biting tension. What a ride. What a wonderful writer. More, please."

—Tracy Clark, author of the Chicago Mystery series

"Rachel Howzell Hall continues to shatter the boundaries of crime fiction through the sheer force of her indomitable talent."

—S. A. Cosby, author of *Blacktop Wasteland*

"*We Lie Here* is definitive proof that it's impossible to be disappointed by Rachel Howzell Hall, who just gets better and better with each book. She has tools and tricks to spare as she pulls you to the edge of your seat with her razor-sharp plotting and keen eye for the darker side of human behavior that's too easily obscured by the California sunshine."

—Ivy Pochoda, author of *These Women*, a *New York Times* Best Thriller of 2020

"Loaded with surprises and shocking secrets, and propelled by Rachel Howzell Hall's magnificent prose, *We Lie Here* is a captivating thriller that I couldn't put down. It's very clear to me that Hall is one of the best crime writers working today, and she keeps getting better. *We Lie Here* is a can't-miss book."

—Alex Segura, acclaimed author of *Secret Identity*, *Star Wars Poe Dameron: Free Fall*, and *Blackout*

"Rachel Howzell Hall continues to prove why she's one of crime fiction's leading writers. *We Lie Here* is a psychological-suspense fan's dream with both a heroine you'll want to root for and a story you'll want to keep reading late into the night. A must read!"

—Kellye Garrett, Agatha, Anthony, and Lefty Award–winning author of *Like a Sister*

PRAISE FOR *THESE TOXIC THINGS*

An Amazon Best Book of the Month: Mystery, Thriller & Suspense

"This cleverly plotted, surprise-filled novel offers well-drawn and original characters, lively dialogue, and a refreshing take on the serial killer theme. Hall continues to impress."

—*Publishers Weekly* (starred review)

"A mystery/thriller/coming-of-age story you won't be able to put down till the final revelation."

—*Kirkus Reviews*

"Tense and pacey, with an appealing central character, this is a coming-of-age story as well as a gripping mystery."

—*The Guardian*

"The mystery plots are twisty and grabby, but also worth noting is the realistic rendering of a Black LA neighborhood locked in a battle over gentrification."

—*Los Angeles Times*

"Rachel Howzell Hall . . . just gets better and better with each book."

—CrimeReads

"Rachel Howzell Hall continues to shatter the boundaries of crime fiction through the sheer force of her indomitable talent. *These Toxic Things* is a master class in tension and suspense. You think you are ready for it. But. You. Are. Not."

—S. A. Cosby, author of *Blacktop Wasteland*

"*These Toxic Things* is taut and terrifying, packed with page-turning suspense and breathtaking reveals. But what I loved most is the mother-daughter relationship at the heart of this gripping thriller. Plan on reading it twice: once because you won't be able to stop, and the second time to savor the razor's edge balance of plot and poetry that only Rachel Howzell Hall can pull off."

—Jess Lourey, Amazon Charts bestselling author of *Unspeakable Things*

"The brilliant Rachel Howzell Hall becomes the queen of mind games with this twisty and thought-provoking cat-and-mouse thriller. Where memories are weaponized, keepsakes are deadly, and the past gets ugly when you disturb it. As original, compelling, and sinister as a story can be, with a message that will haunt you long after you race through the pages."

—Hank Phillippi Ryan, *USA Today* bestselling author of *Her Perfect Life*

PRAISE FOR *AND NOW SHE'S GONE*

"It's a feat to keep high humor and crushing sorrow in plausible equilibrium in a mystery novel, and few writers are as adept at it as Rachel Howzell Hall."

—*Washington Post*

"Hall once again proves to be an accomplished maestro who has composed a symphony of increasing tension and near-unbearable suspense. Rachel brilliantly reveals the bone and soul of our shared humanity and the struggle to contain the nightmares of human faults and failings. I am a fan, pure and simple."

—Stephen Mack Jones, award-winning author of the August Snow thrillers

"Heartfelt and gripping . . . I'm a perennial member of the Rachel Howzell Hall fan club, and her latest is a winning display of her wit and compassion and mastery of suspense."

—Steph Cha, award-winning author of *Your House Will Pay*

"An entertainingly twisty plot, a rich and layered sense of place, and most of all a main character who pops off the page. Gray Sykes is hugely engaging and deeply complex, a descendant of Philip Marlowe and Easy Rawlins who is also definitely, absolutely her own woman."

—Lou Berney, award-winning author of *November Road*

"A deeply human protagonist, an intricate and twisty plot, and sentences that make me swoon with jealousy . . . Rachel Howzell Hall will flip every expectation you have—this is a magic trick of a book."

—Rob Hart, author of *The Warehouse*

"*And Now She's Gone* has all the mystery of a classic whodunit, with an undeniably fresh and clever voice. Hall exemplifies the best of the modern PI novel."

—Alafair Burke, *New York Times* bestselling author

PRAISE FOR *THEY ALL FALL DOWN*

"A riotous and wild ride."

—Attica Locke

"Dramatic, thrilling, and even compulsive."

—James Patterson

"An intense, feverish novel with riveting plot twists."

—Sara Paretsky

"Hall is beyond able and ready to take her place among the ranks of contemporary crime fiction's best and brightest."

—*Strand Magazine*

WHAT

NEVER

HAPPENED

OTHER TITLES BY RACHEL HOWZELL HALL

WHAT NEVER HAPPENED

A THRILLER

RACHEL HOWZELL HALL

THOMAS & MERCER

Published by Thomas & Mercer, Seattle

www.apub.com

Amazon, the Amazon logo, and Thomas & Mercer are trademarks of Amazon.com, Inc., or its affiliates.

ISBN-13: 9781662504150 (hardcover)
ISBN-13: 9781662504136 (paperback)
ISBN-13: 9781662504143 (digital)

Cover design by Caroline Teagle Johnson
Cover images: © Naturfoto Honal, © svrid79, © cowii, © oxygen / Getty Images

Printed in the United States of America

First edition

For Lucky, my favorite golden girl.

There is nothing like returning to a place that remains unchanged to find the ways in which you yourself have altered.

—*Nelson Mandela,* Long Walk to Freedom

The Obituary of
Colette Sienna Weber

Colette Sienna Weber of Los Angeles, California, is no more. She left this world on Sunday, March 22, 2020. The woman didn't heed any of our previous warnings. That is why Colette was taken to the highest point on Santa Catalina and shot in her fingers, toes, and then knees, living agonizingly long enough to suffer until one final bullet between the eyes ended her for good.

We warned you, Colette.

You fucked around—and you found out.

Saturday, June 23, 2001

All Colette wanted was to be kissed at the end of the pier, to hold hands sticky from cotton candy, to have a guy with pretty eyes and great hair win her a stuffed unicorn after knocking over all the milk jars. All she'd wanted was to hear that guy say, "You complete me," or . . . something.

The island had quieted and was now resetting. Tourists would wake up to clean sidewalks and empty trash cans, the stink of spilled beer and rank suntan lotion replaced by the aromas of funnel cakes and french fries.

Her stomach alley-ooped again. She staggered to the bushes and vomited nachos and wine coolers and Michelob and someone's mother's peach schnapps. Tonight she'd opened her new bottle of Tommy Girl and used a new foundation powder that didn't make her skin look like desert rocks. The bronzer on her cheeks burst like sparkles and summer sun. At sixteen, she was already over drinking, over "being bad." This night had not turned into the evening she'd risked it all for. "You guys act like little kids over here," she'd announced after someone brought a carton of eggs from the store to throw.

"Y'all don't dance or play video games . . . ?" she'd asked after someone pulled out a joint. "This is so boring, and it totally fits into the stereotype of—"

"*You're* boring," the freckle-faced girl pronounced.

"I thought Black people partied," the dark-haired slouch said.

Heart thudding in her ears, Colette had bit her tongue and kept quiet, and she'd told herself, *Whatever.*

Freckle Face said, "You're never gonna fit in here. Your dad doesn't, and he's been our teacher for, like, three years."

The only Black people these island kids knew lived on TV. Sassy Moesha and wise auntie Oprah. The perfect Huxtable family and you-so-crazy Martin. Colette's family was none of that and all of that. Shifty and smart, aloof and in your face. Boring-ass party people.

Stupid island kids. What did *they* know? Absolutely nothing. Seven hundred grapes went into that bottle of cheap wine they were drinking—they didn't know that. No one on the *real* Apollo 13 said, "Houston, we have a problem"—they didn't know that, either, until she told them an hour ago.

"You're pretty," the blond boy had said, "but I didn't think you were a . . ."

Nerd.

Whatever.

No holding hands with the floppy-haired blond boy during *Shrek.* No stuffed unicorn. *Whatever.* Instead, the island kids had gone on without her to vandalize golf carts. *Whatever.* She'd passed out on the beach and had awakened to a deer licking her face.

Alone.

Boats bumped against their moorings. Water splashed against the sand.

They'd ditched her. Not "whatever." More like . . .

Oh shit.

And now, she stumbled along the dark streets, feeling like the most boring piece of trash—a used napkin or juice-can tab—with only the fancy-pants hotel on the hill as a guiding light. The entire island seemed to tilt up, up, up without modern streetlights or helpful adults who could direct her to safety.

You know they don't give a damn about you. That was what her father would say.

All this for a stupid white boy who didn't even buy you an ice-cream cone? You got your ass in trouble for that? That was what her mother would say.

Hey, can I wear your Lakers Starter jacket since you're grounded and you ain't going nowhere ever again? Her brother would say that.

Her parents didn't understand. They never let her live, they never let her just *be*. If they allowed her to just *be*, she wouldn't have snuck out and guzzled *schnapps* and . . . and . . .

Her best friends, Melody and Bella, were also honor roll geeks. Never been kissed, study and church and college prep courses even in the summer. Colette also lived life by the books—brush and floss, homework and extra credit completed, never spending a penny more, no slammed doors, *yessir* and *no ma'am*. She wanted to stay smart but also be kissed, become a Bruin and the most beautiful girl in the world. Why couldn't she have it all?

She'd told the cute blond boy about her family's argument tonight, about moving from LA to Avalon, about her fear of not fitting in. He'd complained about being a rich kid who wanted more than money, but also adventure and . . . She'd listened to him intently, without interruption, and hoped that he noticed her deep interest in his desire to run with the bulls, to climb Everest and fly to the moon.

Didn't matter because he'd ditched her.

And now, she lurched to the roadside cactus and hurled more of that nasty Michelob–wine cooler–schnapps concoction into the dirt.

The world seesawed and dimmed at its edges. Once her view stopped boogying, she found the inn sitting high upon the hill, bright and green roofed. Her family's rental—until they moved into the house—was located on a street below the inn. But where, exactly?

Her head pounded, and her feet burned while rubbing against the insides of her Vans. *I'll never drink again, I swear. Just let me be with my family again.*

The boring-ass Webers.

So weird sneaking out. She rarely disobeyed, mostly because her mother, three years of being a cancer survivor, deserved quiet and respect.

Tonight, if Colette failed and got caught? Disrespectful. There'd be more noise in *that* argument than the arguments earlier that day.

Right now, she *yearned* to be boring. To step into the shower, brush her teeth and tongue—*ugh, schnapps*—and then climb into bed. Maybe sleep on the couch in Langston's room. Listen to him breathe. Or maybe she'd camp outside her parents' room. Listen to her mother snore. Listen to her father roam the house and check the locks one last time.

All she wanted was for her heart to slow down and not pop.

A deer bounded across the street.

She yelped. Her pulse boomed.

A cat darted from one bush to the next.

She yelped again.

This was not helping her booming heart.

No golf carts puttered past her. No drunken posse of bridesmaids singing Madonna or Bon Jovi stumbled in the middle of the street.

Follow the light . . . Follow the light . . . Follow—

I know that golf cart!

And that porch light.

And those wind chimes.

The rental's street number—she didn't know that or even the street name. But she knew those wind chimes. That tinkling had always annoyed her. Now, though . . .

Home. Kind of. Whatever.

No lights burned on the front porch or anywhere in the house. Dad wasn't sitting in the cranberry-colored golf cart, ready to search for her. Mom wasn't pacing before the large plate glass windows, full lips set in a hard line.

Did they know that she wasn't home?

No—they would've left on a light.

Success!

Tomorrow, she'd tell Bella and Melody about tonight's adventures, downplaying, of course, this incredibly disappointing ending of her now wobbling to the side of the house, slipping on leaves and her own drunken feet.

Had Langston left the kitchen door unlocked as she'd asked?

Where are you going?

To mind my business. Leave the kitchen door unlocked.

What you gon' give me?

He wanted her fifty-dollar gift certificate to Foot Locker. Deal.

She'd brought Langston a caramel apple because he loved caramel apples. But when she woke up on that beach (*alone!*), there was nothing but a white stick and a happy deer. She'd buy her brother another apple, and she'd clean the kitchen and the dining room without her mom asking. And she would wash the patios for Dad. And *maybe* she'd do something for her aunt. She'd do anything to keep Mom from canceling her spot in the journalism summer camp at UCLA next week.

As Colette twisted the doorknob, she heard . . . nothing. Unlocked. *Love you, El.* In his last checks of locks and windows, Dad had missed this door. Weird—he never missed doors back in LA. Each entrance had a sensor with a computerized voice that announced, "Door. Open."

Their Realtor, Sandy, always made a big fuss about the island's safety, that everyone here left their doors unlocked.

Mom had smirked, not buying it. If there was a T-shirt saying, "So Safe We Don't Lock Our Doors," Dad would've bought one in every color.

The kitchen was dark except for the night-light above the range top. The microwave clock said that it was 2:48 a.m.

The house was thick quiet. Like . . . "before the lights popped on and your friends shouted, 'Surprise!' and threw confetti into your face" kind of quiet.

Colette pulled off her Vans and sighed with relief as her bare toes wriggled freely. She left the shoes beneath the kitchen table and padded into the—

Whoosh.

She slipped and bumped her head against the breakfast bar.

Someone had spilled and hadn't wiped—

Liquid on her hands . . . even in the dark, she saw that the ick wasn't clear like water. And it felt heavy, thicker than milk.

She knew the sticky smell of spilled alcohol. But this whatever-it-was on the floor, this wasn't beer or wine coolers or schnapps.

In that weird range-top light, she saw that this . . . that this was . . .

Blood.

Her pulse kicked in her chest, and she swayed on her knees and hands.

Over by the breakfast bar . . .

A black Nike flip-flop.

Dad's flip-flop.

A bare foot.

A large body collapsed on the kitchen's granite floor.

"Daddy?" Colette crab-walked over to the big man now staring at the ceiling, unblinking.

She shook her father's meaty shoulder. The neckline of his basketball jersey was no longer Clippers white but the same heavy color of the gore beneath his head. "Daddy, what's wrong? Daddy, wake up. I'll get Mom."

He didn't respond. He didn't tell her to calm down, to chill out like he always did.

Her feet melted as she careened past her father and through the dining room. Dizzy still from the wine coolers, beer, and schnapps, she wondered if she were dreaming this, if she were still passed out on that beach.

Let me be dreaming. Please.

She started up the stairs, then stopped.

A flashlight beam danced against the wall outside her parents' bedroom.

The power wasn't out. Her mother wouldn't need a flashlight unless . . .

Colette tiptoed back down the staircase and crept to Langston's bedroom.

The television was still on. A DVD menu for *Bad Boys* bounced across the screen.

Beside her brother's bed, a raised hand rested against the wall. That hand connected to a muscular arm. On the wrist: a puka-shell bracelet with a painted name: L BOOGIE.

Langston!

Colette launched herself across the bed, ready to whisper, "Dad's hurt." But she never whispered those words. The black carpet beneath her brother had been beige carpet when she'd snuck out the bedroom window hours ago. Langston's white football jersey was now as dark as their father's, and his head hung to the side, barely connected and as floppy as a dog's favorite rag doll.

Someone's footsteps scuffed down the steps, their breathing too heavy for a woman.

Oh no.

Colette snuck into the bedroom closet, closed the slatted door, then crawled behind a giant suitcase. She was only five two, happy for the first time that she'd been skipped over in height.

A stranger entered the bedroom.

Black jeans.

Black sweatshirt.

Dark hands.

Long knife in the right hand.

Colette blinked and tried to see past the slats and past the shadows made by the DVD's bouncing menu. Her stomach gurgled.

Did the stranger hear that? Did the stranger hear her hard breathing and the contained hysteria of the little girl she truly was?

Where was her mother? Strong Mom, who'd battled a disease no one could see without machines, who didn't back down from anything. Was she okay? Was she . . . alive?

Colette wanted to vomit again—because of the alcohol, because of the smell of drying blood on her hands and knees. She wouldn't dare—she'd drown first.

The stranger stood over her brother and then left the bedroom.

Colette's muscles cramped from holding in screams now twisting around her guts.

But she waited . . . and she waited . . .

The tracks on the patio door squeaked as that door rumbled open. And then, the door squeaked as it rumbled closed.

But she waited . . . and she waited . . .

Those twisting screams cut through her heart, and those sharp twin blades of hurt and fear struck her most tender parts.

So quiet.

Too quiet.

Crypt quiet.

But she waited . . . and she waited . . .

Until finally the sun traced a path of light across the bedroom carpet. That was when she dared to move. That was when she tumbled out of the closet and into the bedroom, and that was when she screamed and screamed.

1.

Monday, March 9, 2020

The man with the unkind eyes receives my gifts: a can of ginger ale and two packets of saltine crackers. His honey-brown skin (now tinted the pea green of nausea) glimmers—not from the light rain now drifting from the sky and pebbling against our jackets but from the barely there sway of this express ferry racing from Long Beach across the Pacific Ocean to Santa Catalina Island.

He reminds me of another man with unkind eyes and honey-brown skin.

But this seasick passenger is not Micah, although at first glance my breath had caught in my chest and I'd shrunk, a habit formed after living with someone in need of the spotlight.

Superman was allergic to kryptonite.

Micah is allergic to the dark.

"You work here?" the sick man mumbles.

I shake my head. "Just a concerned citizen."

His girlfriend, all spiral curls and swirling tattoos on her hands and neck, smiles at me. "I tol' him to take a Dramamine. He don't ever listen to me."

I can't say, "I have one at home." That would set this guy off, being ganged up on.

The sick man rolls the cold, sweating can of ginger ale against his forehead and cheeks. He closes his eyes as he pulls back the tab. He takes long pulls from the open can, burping every third glug.

He still hasn't said thank you.

The girlfriend coos encouragement—*It's gonna pass. You'll be okay. Drink all of it*—and scratches her turquoise-painted stiletto nails behind his ear.

He ignores her and me, and glares at his Air Jordans while chomping saltines.

The girlfriend sighs and shrugs—she knows he's an asshole. Somewhere in the contract, though, there is a clause that states that the kinder significant other must offer excuses like . . .

"He's just sick." She bites her lip, then adds, "Probably scared to open his mouth."

I flick my hand. "No biggie. Glad I could help. Oh—the best place to sit when you're seasick is at the back of the boat."

The sick man's eyebrows furrow as his skin resets to its usual color.

Prideful. Stubborn. Handsome. Probably expects her to manage his life. Probably trolls her with, *I hate telling people what to do,* while telling her what to do.

Just like Micah.

Except that Micah would *never* be on this ferry to Catalina Island. *I don't have time, Coco,* he'd say. *What if a job comes in last minute, and I'm all the way across the world on a freaking island?*

A *job*? He's not worried about a *job*. No, that bitch is scared of the waves, of the blue, of the awesome uncertainty that is the ocean.

Still, I would've explained to Micah that Catalina Island is just twenty-six miles from the Port of Long Beach. That the express ferry ride is an hour long, that if we lived in Rancho Palos Verdes in the South Bay like he'd wanted, the commute to any movie or TV set in Los Angeles County would've taken him longer on most days.

Micah would've glared at me and said, *You're not making sense again, Coco,* and *I'm trying, okay? No need to do the condescending thing,* then sank on the couch to glare at me for the rest of the day while I wrote, cooked, or breathed. Those judgmental blue eyes of his would burn my back because, somehow, I had kept the phone from ringing, and I had somehow blocked opportunities that would've resulted in him becoming the next Denzel Washington. Then, I would've apologized because a trip to Catalina Island *was* illogical and because I *did* tend to do the "condescending thing."

But Micah's not here, thank the stars.

The corpse-gray, frothy ocean sinks and swells around me. Corpse-gray clouds spit misty rain that tries to slip past every fiber of clothing to chill my bones until I shiver to death. This leaden sky, as flat as a Nebraska prairie, is so different from the tangerine LA sky filled with fire, flirt, and flair.

My phone hasn't buzzed in an hour—no reception out here between Long Beach and Catalina Island. Still, I pull it out to look again at the bright-white split-level ranch house on Beacon Street and its sparkling windows that bring sunlight and offer breathtaking views of the island and ocean. All that lush greenery and those multicolored brick walkways. That white board fence that embraces all that charm.

I love it, I just love it.

My chest warms, then clenches, and one side of my mouth quirks upward.

"Appreciate it, concerned citizen," a man shouts.

I look up from my phone.

The seasick man is still sitting out here in the misty rain. Guess he's endured one too many nudges, elbow pokes, and pleadings from his girl to *just be nice, damn.*

I smile at him. "Hope you feel better." Then, I duck into the warmth of the ferry's near-empty cabin.

Yeah. He's just like Micah.

◆ ◆ ◆

Running away.

That's *not* what I'm doing.

Yes, I'm miles away from that fourplex on Curson Avenue, near the farmers' market and the Grove. Yes, I turned in my house key and surrendered the security deposit. And, okay, all my bags are packed, all random things either stored in some unit near the fourplex or already in boxes on the island.

There is unsigned paperwork curled right now in my duffel bag. The words "No fault" are a total lie because this dissolution of marriage is *his* fault. *He's* the one who left our home and our marriage for some frizzy-haired key grip who keeps a horse out in Encino, a woman who's a distant relative of director Michael Mann or Reginald Hudlin or somebody. All Micah wants is spousal support and the diamond-and-ruby ring willed to us by his acting coach, Edith Reeve, who'd claimed to be one of the many, *many* mistresses of J. Paul Getty. After a consultation in his shop, an appraiser ballparked the value of the ring at $500,000.

I didn't know that Micah was *gone* gone until I found two letters that he'd left for me.

First, I opened the letter taped to the bathroom mirror.

> Dearest Colette,
>
> Let me say this: I love you. From the moment I sent over that green apple martini and you sent it back to me with a note (Make it a Pellegrino and we'll talk), I fell for you like a man wearing two left shoes.
>
> But things have changed. You know it. I know it. You've been unhappy for a very long time now, and this is more than the basic, "Micah, why didn't you pay the phone bill?" and "Micah, why didn't you take

out the trash?" kind of unhappiness. All that drama that happened a long time ago? It's seeped into our marriage and it's poisoned the well. There are pieces of you that I'll never be able to fix. I know I told you that I'd help you with that, but I can't.

You keep pushing me away and it's hurting me and I know you love me and would never in your heart want me to hurt. So, I'm taking myself out of the equation.

You are SO STRONG and you have SO MUCH LOVE TO GIVE. But to be strong and to love fully, you need to figure some things out and be willing to fix yourself first. You can do it!

You've survived the worst.

Now become the best.

Always yours,

Micah

In the six months Micah and I have lived apart, I've rage-fucked the equivalent of the starting lineup of the Los Angeles Lakers, season 2018 to mid-2019—and I didn't have to bake a cake or do laundry afterward. *You're gettin' it* all *in,* my college friend Maddy once cackled over brunch.

I didn't love my ho-ish ways, and for the longest time, I felt like I was dishonoring my husband and my family . . . even though I knew that I didn't have either a husband or a family, not really.

On that day Micah left, and after I found that first letter, my hands were shaking, everything quaking, my eyes wild in the mirror's reflection. "No. *What?*" I kept saying that—*No, what? No, what?*—as I bounced across the apartment in search of my cell phone.

Become the best?

I was *already* the best.

From acting as his secretary to managing his bookings and using my family's money to pay for his classes and photographs. I laughed even though his jokes weren't funny, and I clapped even though no one else did. I ignored his bragging about his acting and his bragging about *my* writing even though he thought writing obituaries was morbid and creepy.

Become the best? *You fucking kidding me, Micah?*

Once I found my phone that afternoon, I called him. "Pick up, pick up, pick up."

He never picked up.

I left a voice mail. "I just read your note. What do you mean, you're taking yourself out of the equation? I'm so confused right now. Call me back, please. *Please?*"

I paced enough that morning that I closed the movement goal on my Apple watch without ever leaving the house. The light changed from marigold to dusty gray in the living room. The neighbor's French bulldog, Lars, barked, ready for his six-o'clock walk. The aromas of onions and coriander wafted from the apartment next door. Dinnertime.

Micah didn't call me back that day.

Was this it? As I waited for that answer, I took lovers, traveled with friends, joined a wine club, and wrote the obituaries of the famous and not-so famous.

After I left a threatening voice mail—*I'm calling the police if you don't respond*—Micah's brother, Ezekiel, reached out to assure me that Micah was alive, that he was also heartbroken, that I'd never supported his brother's dreams, that maybe Micah would change his mind about us and return to our marriage. *Just leave him alone,* Ezekiel counseled. *If it's meant to be, it'll be.*

But was he truly gone? Did he *really* leave me?

Sometimes, the room that I'm in feels heavy, and some object I've used is moved from its spot—the TV remote control from the arm of the couch, my coffee cup on the end table. The doors and floors creak, and drafts sweep past that smell like his cologne. Bare spaces on my neck prickle, and the roots of my hair tighten as though Micah is watching me.

Once, I came home to overturned tables, pulled-out drawers, and a discombobulated laundry hamper. But then, on my Ring security camera, I saw the video of Micah entering our unit. He was looking for his acting coach's diamond-and-ruby ring.

Yeah, he's asked for a divorce, but the joke is on him. On our wedding day, I never signed the official marriage certificate required by the State of California, only the ceremonial one. In fact, I still have that marriage certificate—it's signed by Pastor Timothy Cullen and by Micah Joseph Patton. It's in my box of important things. Maybe I unconsciously balked—I loved him, but signing a declaration to legally profess that . . . "I'll sign it tomorrow" turned to "I'll sign it this weekend," to "Yeah, I should probably sign that," to "Yeah, I'm good."

Once Micah discovers that the last six years of our lives together aren't considered legal matrimony . . . What will he do?

As for the diamond-and-ruby ring . . .

I've hidden it in the stuffed unicorn Micah won for me on our first date. We'd had dinner at Geoffrey's in Malibu, and he didn't even flinch after I ordered lobster bisque, grilled lobster for my entrée, and some random dessert that cost nearly twenty dollars that I didn't even finish. Afterward, we'd hopped in his Acura, then zipped down to Santa Monica. We made out on the Ferris wheel. We made out in the photo booth. We shared cotton candy and secrets. He hugged me as I cried, then won me a stuffed unicorn by knocking over milk jars. I named that unicorn Moe.

A week ago, I shipped Moe the Unicorn to Catalina Island with the rest of my things.

If he wants it, he'll have to catch me first.

And catching me means boarding a ferry and crossing the Pacific Ocean, and then finding me on an island that murdered my family twenty years ago.

2.

Nothing at the Avalon Pier has changed since I was last here on July 3, 2001, including the vibrant tiled sign that separates the dock from the parking lot.

WELCOME TO THE ISLAND VALLEY OF AVALON

The dingy, sea-green day lockers waiting to store tired bags and sweaters haven't changed.

The pods of visitors wearing caps and suburban-mom capris and sneakers haven't changed, although everyone's bundled up since it's March and off-season with flat gray clouds and misty rain.

Fishing boats and kayaks bob on the water. Golf carts zip up and down the narrow road. Passengers pull rolling suitcases and take big gulps of salty air heavy with rain, golf-cart exhaust fumes, and the soft rot of dead fish.

I pull my phone from my pocket. I don't have many people to text that I've arrived.

To my college friend and new boss, Maddy: I crossed the river Styx and I'm now standing on the banks of Hell! Will check in with you later!

To Gwen: Hey auntie! Made it to Avalon. See you soon!

No other members of my extended family on Mom's or Dad's side care or even *know* that I've temporarily relocated to Catalina Island. After my family's funerals, they returned to Baltimore or Atlanta, their own daily dramas swirling like grit around them and blocking their view of the orphaned teen girl all the way in California. *Gwen's got it,* my father's aunt Odelia always said. *We ain't worried. But, Coco, if you need something, just call. I promise I'll be there in a jiffy.*

I needed plenty, and I reached out once, leaving a message on Aunt Odie's answering machine. Almost two decades have passed, and she has yet to return my call. That was my last plea for help—if I needed something, I'd find a way to get it myself.

Because promises are potato chips. They're cheap. Easy to break. Too many hurt your heart.

I don't see the man with the unkind eyes disembark. Maybe his spiral-curled girlfriend pushed him into the sea, Jonah-style. The waves *did* calm some as the island came into view.

My phone rings and vibrates in my hand.

It's Andrea Liszl.

Crap.

I was supposed to join the literary agent on a conference call with Stan Breckenridge, an editor at . . . *which house?* . . . fifteen minutes ago. The one-thirty call would focus on packaging the true story of the 2001 Avalon slaughter written by me, the sole survivor.

I didn't know anything about this project until I returned a voice mail a year ago and listened in awe as Andrea Liszl talked about the Weber family and the horror and IP this and IP that and the proposal that she'd emailed the week before that I'd signed off on . . .

I hadn't signed off on a proposal. *What* proposal?

"We need money," Micah had complained, "and so I reached out—"

"And sold a story that wasn't yours to sell?" I shrieked back. "A story that I'm not ready to tell?"

"You have to do something to keep us afloat," he said, "now that you've been fired."

"Laid off. There's a difference." I'd received a six-month severance package from the *Los Angeles Times*. Micah left me at month seven.

I agreed to talk to Andrea and Stan, but I've canceled our talk twice now. And Micah—in this instance, *me*—was a year late on delivering a simple outline.

"Need a taxi?" A red-faced man sitting behind the wheel of a cart waves at me. A TAXI flag hangs from his left-side mirror.

I slip the phone into my pocket and pull my bags toward the cart. "Thank you," I say. "I was just wondering how all this works with no real, like . . . cars."

He tips his blue golf cap. "Just like LA, but smaller."

I help him stack my bags on the back bench and watch as he secures all of it with bungee cords. He slips into the driver's seat and taps the steering wheel. The index and pinkie fingers on his left hand end at the knuckles. "Name's Frank. Welcome to Avalon. First time on the island?"

I shake my head. "Haven't been back in about twenty years."

He turns the ignition. "Still lovely. Still safe. Still paradise."

My heart trembles at "still safe," and I droop in my seat.

He tosses me a grin, says, "Let's get you where you need to go," then jams the gas pedal.

And we're off!

Mom and Dad always drank too much at that yellow restaurant over there . . .

Langston and I ate so much ice cream at that shop over there . . .

We took family pictures at that railing over there . . .

And now, my trembling heart crumples, and I let out a soft, "Wow."

"Yeah," Frank says, beaming. "'Wow' is right. We call this part 'the Flats.'"

Behind the shop, bright-colored houses cram together, their carts and Smart cars parked at the curbs. Some of the houses' paint has dulled from sun and mist, time and neglect.

"I guess it's a good thing folks are buying up these old houses," he says, "slapping on a new coat of paint and renting them out for visitors. We can't have houses sit empty for too long because the squatters come, and bad things happen. Investors and B and B–ers keep the island vibrant, I guess."

I cock an eyebrow at him. "You don't sound thrilled about it."

Frank shrugs. "Changes the character of the island, in my opinion. Some property owners care more about accommodating tourists instead of keeping the rents low and islanders housed. Comes down to the mighty dollar, just like every other place in the world. But what do I know? I'm just an old man driving a taxi cart. Avalon's still safe. I'm still safe. We're *all* safe. Don't let people tell you otherwise."

"And why would folks say otherwise?"

He shrugs. "Stupid rumors going around to make Avalon more exotic than it is. Making hay outa blades of grass." He tosses me a smile. "How long you here for?"

My grip tightens on the duffel bag on my lap. "Not sure."

He laughs. "What's the problem? It's too perfect for you?"

"I'm dealing with a lot of . . . *uncertainty* right now."

"Like?" He winks at me. "I was a priest and a bartender in my former life."

"Ha. Same old, same old. Job change. Relationship change. Family stuff."

"Any resolution for any of them?"

I laugh. "No, which is why I'm here."

"To resolve."

"To hide, and let it all work itself out."

An old blonde driving a bright-yellow cart toots at us. Frank toots back and waves.

"I want to do *that* more," I say. "Smile and wave and really mean it."

"That didn't just happen overnight for me, young lady. I had to leave what I thought was my calling. And then, I had to put down the bottle and stop doing things that led to—" He waves his injured hand. "You have to stop and face your demons before you can win the game. You may get a little bloody, even lose a limb—or a few fingers—but know this." At a stop sign, he looks over to me. "Running ain't gonna make it go away."

I haven't lost fingers or a limb. No. I've lost so much more. Twenty years ago, my family and I moved from our home in View Park—the heart of Black Los Angeles—just so that 75 percent of us could be murdered on an island that has more bison living on it than Black people. I'm only alive today because I'd snuck out that night. But I won't say this to Frank. I'll let him enjoy his illusion here in Mayberry by the Sea.

Last Christmas, Gwen got lost on the island and drove her golf cart damn near into the harbor. The Department of Adult Protective Services got involved, and a social worker called me. "This was her second time nearly crashing into the harbor," Pam Robins told me. "You need to either bring her to live with you in Los Angeles or I'll have to place her in a safe environment outside of her home."

"Y'all not putting me in some death farm," Gwen spat over the phone.

"I don't want to do that," I said, "but Pam's not fucking around on this, Auntie."

"I zoned out," Gwen said. "Everybody zones out once in a while. You've done it a few times dealing with Micah's ass, and every time you snap out of it, you find blood beneath your fingernails."

I said, "True, but—"

"And if you think I'm leaving Avalon," she continued, "you more stupid than I already thought you were. I left my island to take care of you twenty summers ago, and I'm not leaving again. You gon' have to drag my dead body off this piece of rock."

With no one to look after her—Gwen never married, and her friends are also old—I told Pam Robins that I'd temporarily move to Avalon and help care for my aunt. I'd stay a year, long enough to unravel my own personal messes and to also sell the house on Beacon Street. Then, I'd return to LA with a clear head, money in my wallet, and Aunt Gwen's dead body, if that's how she wanted it. In other words, my aunt would have no choice except to leave Avalon.

At Beacon Street, Frank turns right, passing the Pepto-pink Hotel St. Lauren. He whistles as the cart slows on this tree-lined street. He turns around at the dead end and parks at the curb. "Here we are."

Here.

This is not the murder house up on Middle Terrace, just a mile away. No, *here* is the house my parents bought—the house we were moving into the summer of 2001.

From the cart, I enjoy the extraordinary view of the Pacific Ocean, now a part of the sky. But the house itself . . . the brick-laid walkway shines with falling mist. The white paint now looks seasick with its chips and bald spots. The overgrown yard rambles past the white slatted fence. A green water hose is half-curled, half-collapsed around its stand. The two flights of stairs leading up to the front door will convert to toothpicks any day now.

There is an empty, wooded double lot behind the house and only one other house to its right. I can't hear the chugs and burps of golf carts, nor can I hear the chatter and woo-hoos of tourists. Secluded and quiet, the house on Beacon Street is still a jewel.

After we place my bags on the sidewalk, Frank putters back to the harbor.

I turn to gaze at those flights of rickety stairs.

Shit, Colette.

From the corner of my eye, I spot movement in the side yard's wild grass. I creep closer, breath in my chest.

A man is hunched near the water meter, pliers in his gloved hand.

"Excuse me," I say. "May I help you?"

He twists back to look at me. His pockmarked face reddens, and his thick salt-and-pepper eyebrows furrow above his dark-blue eyes. "May I help *you*?"

I square my shoulders and step forward. "I *live* here."

"Doubt that." He gives me the up-and-down. "Never seen you here before, and I know pretty much everybody on this island. You have ID?"

I snort. "Do *you* have ID? You're trespassing."

He chuckles without humor. "I'd say the same goes for you, young lady."

We glare at each other, neither giving in.

He nods to the house. "Who lives here? You answer right, I'll drop the interrogation."

Blood roars in my ears. "Gwen is my aunt. I'm staying with her."

No, Colette. Gwen is your aunt and she's staying with you because this house is yours.

"That's all you gotta say." He grins but his eyes stay flat. "I guess Gwen's last crash into the harbor brought you here. About time you swooped in to take care of business."

I don't even try to smile. "And you are . . . ? I always like to know the name of people trying to mind my business."

He blinks, and his eyelids move sideways, chameleonlike. He holds up the pliers. "I'm just the handyman. We watch out for each other on this island, pitching in to help the oldsters."

"Well, thank you . . ."

"Call me Handy Andy."

"Thanks, Handy Andy." I point to the overgrown bushes, some heavy with purple berries the size of cherry tomatoes. "What kind of plants are these? Does Gwen have a gardener to do some cutting back, or can I—"

"*You* don't wanna just go hacking plants around here. That there is solanum wallacei, also known as Catalina nightshade."

I gape. "As in *deadly* poison nightshade? Why is it in my backyard?"

He frowns. "This is its home—it *belongs* here. The flowers come in April, May . . . they're beautiful. I'll handle the yard work, okay?"

"Got it and thank you." I point to an opening that leads to the crawl space beneath the house. "Please tell me that you're fixing that?"

"Yep." He runs a hand through his damp silver hair. "Cats have been getting under there, so I'm replacing the screen."

My bladder presses against my abdomen, urging me to keep it moving.

"I'll need help from you to fix a few things," I say, moving back to the curb and my luggage. "We're gonna need more than a new grating and a few patch jobs. Hope you're ready to wear out your tools."

He blushes, clears his throat.

I roll my eyes and smile. "That came out weird."

He grins, and this time, his eyes crinkle at the corners. "I'm gonna finish up here and head home. Gwen has my number."

I grab the handles of my two suitcases, miffed some that Handy Andy hasn't offered to help. I start the climb up the stairs. Overheating, I drop the bags at the first landing and shake out my arms. Sweat rolls down my back—my body is a bog.

I return to the curb for the remaining suitcase and the duffel bag. My pulse bangs between my eyes, and my poor bladder bobs around my torso, and I promise myself that I'll never do this again.

A mahogany glass-paned door sits as the prize at the top of the second landing. I'll need to change this door. Someone can break one of these panes, reach in, and turn the doorknob.

Worrying about this is absurd, though. No one needs to break anything, because the door is cracked open, and they can *walk right in*. Unless this cracked door isn't a regular thing—maybe Gwen doesn't feel like getting up every time Handy Andy needs to enter the house.

"Colette," my aunt shouts, "you out there?"

With the toe of my sneaker, I push open the door. "Hey, Auntie! I'm home."

A half flight of stairs leads up, and another half flight of stairs leads down.

I close the front door and note the simple single lock and janky slide chain.

Up in the living room, the monstrous brick fireplace nearly overwhelms the space. Dusty yellow curtains block nearly all the light, and the light that *does* survive is weak and gray. The couch is a mismatched mess of upholstered red-and-purple lower cushions and faded blue corduroy back pillows. Boxes line the walls, only separated by that fireplace.

Gwen, dirty martini in hand, is a tiny thing in her big green La-Z-Boy. Sections of her white hair are wrapped around a handful of pink sponge curlers. She's wearing a pink-and-blue silk kimono too big for her body. With those long sleeves and droopy neck, the robe was sewn for a larger woman.

Which bigger woman wore it first?

The TV tray beside the armchair holds a large Holy Bible and a large platter of her favorite snack: vienna sausages, Ritz crackers, and yellow mustard. The television plays *Family Feud* from its rolling cart.

She's watching a new episode, living in the present.

Good.

Gwen's eyes flick at me, then widen. "That *is* you!" She aims the remote control at the TV to pause the show, then takes a quick sip of her martini. Fortified by vodka and olive juice, she wriggles out of her recliner, then gathers the kimono around her body.

We hug—she feels like a construction of silk and Popsicle sticks. Gwen plants kisses all over my face with rice-paper lips, then holds my face in her hands. She frowns. "Look at you."

My complexion is clear, unwrinkled, and sable brown. My eyes are big chestnuts just like my father's (and Gwen's brother).

Her eyes stop at my hair. "Guess you gonna keep sailing over to LA to keep that weave nice. Ain't nobody over here can do that."

I chuckle. "You don't do hair on the side anymore?"

"Yeah, I can shampoo, press, and curl. But all that beneath all that hair?" She flaps her hand at my head, then gives me a raspberry.

"Guess I'm going back to LA once a month."

"Prayer and bobby pins in between?"

"Yes, ma'am."

Her eyes keep pecking at me.

What is she looking for?

"For real, Auntie," I say. "I'm good, and I'm *so* happy to be here." I point at the TV. "Don't tell me that's all you've being doing today. Sitting here and watching TV and drinking."

Gwen's jaw tightens and her eyes narrow. The sponge curlers vibrate around her head.

I go purple from holding my breath, not that there's any air left to breathe. Cheeks hot, I force a smile. "Sorry. Just joking, Auntie. I'm jealous. You're hashtag goals." As though my seventy-eight-year-old aunt knows what the hell *that* means.

Gwen smirks, then sips from her martini glass.

I tap the Bible. "Is this real, or do you store vodka and cocktail onions in it?" Gwen has hidden alcohol in a hollow Bible before. One summer, she attended tent revivals only because she was sleeping with the married organist. She told me that he'd play certain hymns just for her. "Abide with Me" and "Give Me Oil in My Lamp."

And now, Gwen says, "I don't do that no more. I actually *read* this book. Even attend the church down the street. I'm done with my sinful ways."

My eyes skip past boxes too soggy and dusty to be mine. "My stuff get here yet?"

"Downstairs," Gwen says.

"I brought you some coffee table books and a few prints from Art Walk—everything's in those boxes." The unicorn is also in one of those boxes—I didn't want to carry it with me in the event Micah confronted me on the way out of our apartment. Just like Gwen with her hollowed-out Bible, I've previously stowed keepsakes in random places—and my soon-to-be ex knows that.

Gwen's frown deepens. "You totally free from Micah now?"

"No. It's . . . whatever at this point." I shrug, waggle my head, and smile. "It's all good."

She pinches my cheek. "Such a little people pleaser. It's *not* all good. You ain't breaking my heart by lying to me."

My brain searches for the best response.

Auntie, I'm not a people pleaser cuz I like pleasing people.

Just trying not to catch any smoke—from you or anyone else, Auntie.

Keeping my head above water . . . trying not to make any waves when I can.

Gwen plops back into the recliner and stares at frozen Steve Harvey on the TV screen. "I know why you're *really* here. To kick me out." She futzes with the silver charm dangling from a thick chain around her neck. Her thumb pushes the hidden button on the charm's backside.

My phone vibrates—I've just received a text that shares Gwen's exact GPS location. The senior alert mobile app also sends alerts and provides high-level timelines of her movement around the island.

"There you go, jumping to the end of the story." I smile and crouch beside Gwen's recliner. "I'm not kicking you out, Auntie. I'm here to help both of us."

Gwen aims the remote at the TV again. "You're here for more than *that*. I'm not dumb, Colette. You're Reggie's child through and through. Pleasant and all smiles on the outside, judgy assholes on the inside, where it matters." She presses PLAY on the DVR remote. "You didn't need to move here. I zoned out is all. If I was in LA, they'd call it a fender bender."

"But you're not in—"

"I'm not an invalid," she snaps. "If anybody's feeble brained in this house, it's you."

Gwen's sharp anger is a punch in the nose.

"Well, I'm here now, and I'm the only niece you have, and now, Pam Robins can report to the county that you're being looked after, which means you can stay here in Avalon. You're welcome." I stand, body tight, skin hot. "Want me to make you another martini?"

"No. Hush now."

And Steve Harvey asks: "Name a house you never want to be in."

This house, Steve.

Gwen spears a soft pink sausage with a tiny fork, then smashes it between two crackers.

"Dee Dee is supposed to be having a little get-together," Gwen says between bites. "I don't feel like going, but I don't want Dee to think that since you're here now, I don't have time for her, so . . ."

I hold up my hands. "Please. Hang out with your bestie. Not like I'm going anywhere."

"You don't need a babysitter anymore," Gwen says, stuffing her mouth.

"No, ma'am, I don't. I'm about to be thirty-five years old."

And since I'm Reggie's daughter, I add:

"So, yes . . . I *do* want the house now. I've been paying property taxes all this time, and my parents' insurance paid the note off a while ago. Even if I take this job at Maddy's paper, it won't pay enough for rent in a decent place *and* to pay all my bills on top of that.

"But you're staying here, just like I said, just like I told Pam Robins. Nothing's changed, not really. Well . . . it *is* my house and . . ." My voice trails off and lands in the pool of mustard on my aunt's plate. My emotions spray across my insides like graffiti. "It's not like I'm ecstatic being here but . . . it *is* my . . ."

Wanting to cry, I sit back on my butt and cross my legs.

Gwen's staring at the television, not moving.

I touch her foot. "Auntie?"

Gwen blinks at me. "You say something? I zoned out a little."

Nah. I saw her lips tighten, her eyebrow lift in contempt. She held her breath, even if it was for a second or two. Gwen heard every word I said.

Now, though, she turns her attention to *Family Feud* playing on the TV and says, "Haunted house, Steve."

Number one answer.

Outhouse.

Doghouse.

Big house.

No "house on Beacon Street" because that wouldn't be true. I *do* want to be here. This house *is* mine, after all. And once I sell the mistress's diamond-and-ruby ring, I'll have enough money to make it the house my father had loved enough to sacrifice his life for—along with his wife's and son's lives, too.

The front door creaks open, and a slice of bright light shines past that crack.

Maybe Gwen didn't intentionally leave the door open. Maybe she "zoned out" again.

I'll have Handy Andy buy new dead bolts and a sturdier door.

I won't tolerate another alien invasion. Not again.

3.

A framed picture of my family (including Gwen) sits on the fireplace mantel. It was taken that last summer we were all together, and it's the last picture I'd taken with them. It's also the picture I selected for their funeral. That Wednesday, back in July 2001, hundreds of people attended—islanders who worked with Dad at the high school, his UC Irvine college friends, people who'd worked with Mom at her law firm, her college friends and sorority sisters from UC Berkeley, Langston's friends and teammates, my friends, teachers, distant family members.

After the burials in the valley, Gwen and I drove back over the hill to our house on Fairland in View Park. Located in the largest National Register historic district in California—and the largest in the nation based on Black history—my family's four-bedroom, three-bathroom home had its original hearth, a kitchen with its original tiled ceiling and walls, and views of downtown Los Angeles. It sold for $1.7 million, money that had helped pay the mortgage for the house on Beacon Street.

Despite the new owners' sorrow for me, they wouldn't cancel their purchase. Owen and Everett promised, though, to continue restoring and upgrading this gem of a home.

The house on Beacon Street was mine, but I'd refused to live on an island that had killed my family. Gwen found us a two-bedroom town house in Culver City, just four miles away. It was smaller than anything I'd ever lived in. But a million dollars wasn't infinite—college, bills, attorney fees, private investigators, and living in Los Angeles.

The house on Beacon Street sat empty, with Gwen taking trips over once a quarter to run the water, collect mail, and keep the house alive.

Once I enrolled at UCLA, Gwen moved back to Catalina Island—and into the house.

Back then, I didn't care about the Avalon property.

Micah—he was the one who forced me to care. *That's just money sittin' and Gwen's getting over on you.*

I know he wants half of the house, but he has no rights—we weren't married for ten years. Hell, we weren't married.

Win the game, Colette.

How? I don't know the rules. Hell, I don't *know* the game. What am I supposed to do?

◆　◆　◆

I've been standing in the hallway for nearly five minutes now.

This house on Beacon Street is not the murder house—my mother, father, and brother were not killed here. This house, though, still feels . . . *haunted*. Our future here died, and I see my father's ghost rushing from room to room, holding Mom's hand, wide smile on his face, shouting about a new life, more opportunities. I see my brother's ghost, arms crossed, glaring out the large windows and thinking about all that he'd soon lose by transferring from Crenshaw High School to Avalon School, a place not known for its football or AP chemistry programs.

The door to the bedroom that would've been mine twenty years ago is closed.

The door to Langston's room is closed, too.

The door to Mom and Dad's room is also closed.

The only open door belongs to Gwen, and her bedroom is filled with boxes of things and scarves and a large four-poster bed. Silk robes of every color hang on those bedposts. A wrought iron fireplace poker leans against the nightstand.

Does my bedroom still face those hillsides filled with deer? Is that pineapple-patterned wallpaper that dared me to lick it still hanging on the walls? Is the glossy floor still slick enough that I can slide across it like Tom Cruise in *Risky Business*? By the manic way my pulse revs and kicks, I won't know the answers to those questions today because I'm not opening this or any of these bedroom doors.

I take steps back . . . back . . . back . . . too much of a coward to turn away from those doors.

We asked one hundred people . . . name something associated with ghosts.

That house on Beacon Street, Steve, the one whose dead family was supposed to live.

I leave the gray-lighted upper floor for the ground level. Only one bedroom down here, but there is a small sitting room with a red couch. Surprisingly, there's an empty storage closet, a full bathroom with plants hanging from ceiling hooks and spilling over themselves. There are multicolored flouncy curtains stitched with peacocks and blue moose, cross-legged deities, and purple elephants.

I can't see the ocean from any of these windows. Just Beacon Street and golf carts parked at the curbs. Just overgrown grass and teeming bushes that could be hiding anything. There's a giant clay pot out there filled with dirt, water, and two different types of plants that produce tiny-petaled yellow and orange flowers. The rain makes the long grass bend, and the rim of the clay pot wobbles with water. A deflated beach ball brightens the white fence.

Down here, the air is thick, cold, and swollen with dust motes. Some of those motes have stuffed themselves into that red couch—the cushions look too big to be healthy.

But look at this space! There's enough room for a better, healthier couch. Room for a few bookcases and maybe even a massage chair and a Peloton.

I roll my suitcases to the bedroom.

The mattress—no box spring—sits on the floor and is almost hidden beneath round pillows and square pillows that are blue, yellow, cranberry striped, and batik printed. Floor rugs of dizzying patterns cover every inch of hardwood. A desk lamp with a red shade burns on a round side table crammed with a potted minicactus and frog figurines. Paintings, sundials, and random poster prints of Josephine Baker hang on the walls. A potted plant with wild vines hangs in the middle of the only window—there are no curtains.

Beyond this window, though, and beyond those clouds, there is bright-blue sky, and just a mile or two away, there is a brighter-blue ocean. There are ice cream–colored houses and cute golf carts that toot and happy people wearing shorts and sunscreen and . . .

Holy hell.

Boxes filled with random crap take up space in the bedroom closet, and I paw through tangled necklaces and brooches. Chipped ceramic rabbits. Motorolas and Nokias and Ericsson mobile phones from the late 1990s to the early 2000s.

My nose can't take any more, and I sneeze, then sneeze again.

There isn't tissue in the bathroom, but there is a small Persian rug and a phallic-shaped cactus on the windowsill.

Looking past the eclectic . . . *beauty* of my living quarters, I see a worrisome water patch in the ceiling. I note the single-paned windows that don't protect anything or anyone from the cold. The lights flicker, and one glance at my phone tells me there is no Wi-Fi. In addition to a bed headboard and box spring, I need new electricity and internet wiring down here.

"And I need TV," I say, my eyes skipping to spaces where a television would sit.

While there is no TV, there *are* creaking stairs, peeling caulk in the bathrooms, and zero smoke alarms. Figuring out how to fix all these things will keep me entertained.

How in the hell am I gonna buy a Peloton if I can't pay to fix the plumbing?

In all the clutter, I spot one moving box. BEDROOM written by me in black marker. The unicorn is in a box marked JUNK, and if that $500,000 ring hadn't been shoved in its ass, the unicorn *would* be junk—just like the watch that loses time and the letter opener, too dull to open mail, and all the other shit Micah gifted me over our six years together.

Micah had considered the unicorn as junk, too, because he trampled it when he snuck back into the apartment and turned over every container and pulled out every drawer in his search for the ring.

I kneel beside the mattress and dump the contents of my purse onto the comforter. Swiss Army knife, tissue pack, pens, condom, earbuds, and this check. On the State of California Controller's website, I'd discovered a checking account that Mom had opened on a whim and immediately forgot existed. She had a balance of $3,823.64, and now, I have a check for that amount. It will be enough to pay for a little pipe work.

My phone vibrates: a text from Micah.

I won't read it now, but it's as hot as ghost pepper and lava and the surface of the sun. Heat waves roll off my phone, and I don't have the strength to deal right now.

The phone rings.

I yelp.

His number and face burn the screen.

I hold my breath in case he feels me breathing on the other end.

One last ring and then . . . silence.

I exhale and close my eyes.

I'd wanted to be the "good wife." Not necessarily pot roast and sex every night, but cacio e pepe pasta and sex every three days or so. Okay, maybe I didn't want to be *Micah's* "good wife," which is why I found myself beating his Acura with a titanium driver. That night, he'd said something to me like . . . *You take shit too seriously* or *This is your fault* or *Hey, Colette* and I just . . . *zoned out*, as Gwen says, only coming to in the back of a patrol unit.

My phone rings again.

This isn't Micah calling. The face on my phone has a square jaw and a *Mona Lisa* smile. Dr. Tiffany Tamaguchi is calling . . . calling . . . calling . . .

I hold my breath again and stare at the green answer button.

Calling . . . calling . . .

I clench, willing the phone into silence, not daring to touch Decline because somehow Dr. Tamaguchi will know that she's been manually sent to voice mail.

"You gon' answer that?" Gwen is making her way down the stairs.

"No," I shout back. "It's just my therapist. I'll call her later, after I . . ." I push my hair back and sigh. "After I settle in."

Gwen clucks her tongue and scans the room. "I'm a nasty house-keeper—that's what you're thinking, ain't it?"

I cock my head. "Not at all. It's crowded, not filthy. And it takes a lot of money to maintain a house." I smile at her. "You've cleaned other people's messes your entire life, and I don't expect you to spend your golden years with a broom in your hand."

She clucks her tongue again, then sets her hands on her thin hips. "Glad you're still talking to somebody. It's important, getting it all out? Grief's gotta go somewhere, Colette, and other than me, you got more grief than anybody I know. But at least you're moving forward."

Moving forward. Like a snail with a broken shell.

"Micah's an asshole," Gwen spits.

"True, but I was a wreck before we got together." I make a face. "I just hope he doesn't come here, trying to start shit."

"Why would he do that?"

My cheeks warm. "I have something that he believes belongs to him."

Gwen's neck swerves. "Wish he would step foot on this island. I'm old but I'll still cut a bitch. I know people—they old, too, but they got sons and daughters happy to start some shit."

"Ha!" I throw my head back and laugh. "Maybe *you* should be my shrink."

She flaps that compliment away.

"No." My eyes skip from the rugs to the plants to the posters. "This space definitely has *many* vibes."

Gwen straightens the pillows on the couch. "It reflects my emotional journey."

I nod. "And all the posters?"

Gwen taps the graphic poster showing mocha skin and bright-pink lips, gold earrings, and a lock of hair. "Josephine was authentic and fascinating, and she did not give one single damn about boundaries." Gwen smiles. "We would've been best friends if we ever met."

We both study the poster.

Gwen's phone chimes in her robe pocket. She pulls it out along with a pair of readers and squints at the screen. "Just Dee Dee telling me what to get for her little dinner party." She holds the phone out and uses one finger to text back to her best friend.

Cute.

After what feels like an hour, Gwen pushes out a breath, then shuffles back to the staircase. "She wants me to bring a dish. How about . . . Chinese? Mrs. T's. You can get some dinner and pick up something for me to take. Get me some of that mushroom chicken, some pot stickers, and beignets."

"Beignets?"

"It's a bakery, too. And stop by the post office while you're out. I got you a PO box key—it's on my ring. Box 378. They still got your other boxes."

"Sounds good," I say. "Gotta stop by the paper first."

"Don't go wandering off by yourself," she says, waggling her finger at me. "People's dogs been disappearing."

"Coyotes?"

"Ain't no coyotes on this island. Plenty crazy people, though." Gwen shuffles up the stairs and shouts back at me one last time. "Call your therapist. Keep getting your head right."

Because my head isn't right.

"And I'm gonna come up with a plan to redo the house," I shout up to her. "You're gonna have a lovely home again to share with your friends."

Gwen turns around. "What makes you think that I don't do that already."

I bite my lip—she's right.

I'd assumed.

No wandering. Beware of crazy people who steal dogs. Got it.

My phone vibrates.

Dr. Tamaguchi has left a voice mail.

Something scratches and rustles outside my window.

I gasp and listen to the scratching, to the rustling. I don't move. I become cold-blooded, blending in just like I'd done while hiding in the closet so many years ago . . .

The crunching and rustling gets louder, closer.

I slowly drop to my knees, and my mind clicks and chitters.

Green flannel shirt . . . tan Dickies . . .

Oh.

Yeah.

Handy Andy handymanning.

Crap.

Running away ain't gonna make it go away. That's what Golf Cart Frank told me less than an hour ago. He was wrong, though. Running and hiding *will* keep me alive. It did before and I survived.

And isn't surviving the point of the game?

4.

My scratch-paper home-repair to-do list is ready for Handy Andy. By the time I leave the house, though, he's no longer scooting around the yard. The wire grate is completely gone, and anyone can crawl beneath the house and live there, if they want.

Handy Andy needs to come back and fix that and a million other things.

Once upon a time, this house was the diva on the block, a Mariah Carey in a neighborhood of *American Idol* semifinalists. That has changed.

The owners of the brown house across the street need to clean their yellow awnings of bird poop, but at least that house doesn't look like it will collapse any minute now beneath the weight of two people. The green house next to it has weird-shaped windows, but someone's grilling, and the aroma rides on damp air. There are no smells like sizzling beef at my house, and now, my stomach growls.

My phone vibrates in my hand; then the Cardi B ringtone plays.

"Maddy!" I shout into the phone.

"Blame Flynn," she shouts. "We were supposed to meet you at the ferry with signs and balloons and flowers, but Flynn's ass . . . I'm gonna miss going to heaven fucking around with him."

I laugh. "It's okay."

"No," she says, "it's not. Apologies. You'd think at our age, he could stop playing Madden for an hour and do grown-up things."

My heart lifts. "Really: it's not a problem."

"But something could've happened to you—"

"Dude, this ain't the Oregon trail, it's Catalina Island. And I got to the house without any ax murderers or ambushes."

She cackles.

At our dorm in our first year of college at UCLA:

Madeline Swenson stood before me in her tight little T-shirt and khaki shorts. "Your hair looks like you've been living on a plantation."

I shouted, "And you're a fucking racist," before bursting into tears.

Gwen didn't have time between her three jobs to handle my hair. And I thought paying attention to my appearance when my family had been murdered years before was vain and shallow.

Overnight, Madeline somehow learned about my family situation, and she drove me to a salon in Beverly Hills that weekend. Hooked me up with a stylist who did Tyra Banks's hair. "I'm not a racist," she explained as we tooled around in her Jeep. "And I apologize for using that word. As a journalism major, I should know better." Since then, she's helped care for my heart and has helped me to heal.

Where is Handy Andy?

I wander back to the driveway and to Gwen's parked golf cart, a sweet ride back in the day. In Los Angeles, Gwen drove a cherry-red Mustang, and since she couldn't bring it here, she bought a custom golf cart with a fire-engine-red body, white flames on its sides, white leather seats with red trim, and bright chrome rims.

"I don't half step," she'd always brag, chin high. "I got style and panache, sweetie. Even when I'm cleaning other people's toilets." Tourists would take pictures in front of her cart. She even rented it during the summers.

Our last week together, I drove Langston into town in that bright-ass cart, its radio blasting Biggie and Destiny's Child.

Today, that fire-engine-red paint looks mud-hut orange, and there's space where that radio used to be. The white flame decals are peeling or altogether missing. The chrome rims are also gone, and the leather seats are dingy, faded, and ripped. The side mirrors hang on with silver duct tape. The front bumper is dented and also hanging on with duct tape.

Gussying up Gwen's cart will go on my Fix-It spreadsheet.

And anyway, according to Maps, *Avalon Breeze* is just a three-minute walk away.

Walk? Sure!

The annoying misty rain has stopped, and now, the sun plays peekaboo behind lighter clouds. Silver mist hugs the hilltops that make up the island's interior and coast. Soon the tapping of my sneakers against wet pavement is overpowered by the putter of golf carts, the squeal of children in backyards, and the clink of dishes in cafés. Every window in every third house displays a FOR RENT and CUTE VACATION RENTAL sign. Every fifth telephone pole has been stapled with HAVE YOU SEEN MY DOG? and MISSING posters for a schnauzer, a Chihuahua, and Amy the Friendliest Mutt in Avalon. Also weird: I have yet to see one Black person power walking or sweeping their front porch.

A part of me wants to visit the murder house up on Middle Terrace again.

A bigger part yells, *Beware, there be monsters up there. Enjoy the quiet.*

I listen to that bigger part and remain down in the Flats.

Life moves slower here—just me walking proves that. If the island were music, Avalon would be Jimmy Buffett to LA's Guns N' Roses, Perry Como vs. Post Malone.

Since 1914, *Avalon Breeze*, Catalina Island's local newspaper, has published once a week every Friday. The paper captures all the goings-on among the island's four thousand residents. My aforementioned college friend, Maddy, who's also the paper's editor in chief, offered me a job as the obituary and community events editor. "I'd be a fool not to hire an award-winning journalist," she said last week. "And I'm many things, but I'm not a fool."

I'm not getting paid nearly as much as I did at the *Los Angeles Times*—I worked there for nearly fifteen years and always in Obituaries. I'd worked my way up from intern to entry-level staff writer and assistant editor until I was just a fingertip away from the editor position. But they hired another reporter (not even an obituary writer!) to head the desk. We were a team of six full-time obituary writers, tapping reporters at other desks to write obituaries as needed.

Avalon Breeze is not the *Times*, but something is always better than nothing. I'll continue freelance writing for funeral homes, and since I no longer pay rent or mortgage for the house, I don't need as much money to live on as before. And then, there's the ring and the book deal.

Book deal. Crap. I need to call Andrea Liszl.

Later.

The newsroom of *Avalon Breeze* sits in the middle of Metropole Avenue. The newsroom is also two doors down from Catalina Cable TV—another to-do item on my list of making the house on Beacon Street livable. The Catalina Museum for Art & History is across the street.

I will visit that museum and see if my family's murders made the history books or if we've been erased like we were in those summer 2001 issues of the *Breeze*.

Two minutes into the newsroom office tour, I worry about the state of my smile. In my heart, the slash across my face feels wobbly—too weak to snap, too strong to bend.

Maddy Swenson, the tallest blonde on the island, is too focused on showing off her domain, the pride in her eyes oblivious of my purgatory smile.

"And this is the break room." Maddy waves at the well-lit space with its shiny linoleum, its couch upholstered in gold and red, a Keurig coffee machine, and a flat-screen television.

A muscular redhead is tinkering with the garbage disposal beneath the sink.

"Babe," Maddy coos, "look who's here."

Flynn Nilsen leans away from his plumbing project and beams at me. "Coco! You're here. Now Maddy can quit worrying that you'll change your mind. Oh: sorry about this afternoon. I had an appointment that I couldn't reschedule."

Maddy snorts and rolls her eyes.

Flynn reminds me of the actor cast as the head Wildling in *Game of Thrones*. Tormund Giantsbane, Catalina Island–style, no beard, though, but wavy red hair combed away from his face.

"I was just giving Coco a tour," Maddy says. "Showing her all the fancy new things like our coffee machine and the TV . . ." She turns to me. "Not that you'll be watching TV. No. *You'll* be honoring our dead and celebrating our milestones with words."

This time, Flynn and I roll our eyes.

"Doing that thing that you do," Maddy continues, unbothered. "Making us an award-winning paper cuz you write award-winning pieces for the living *and* the dead."

Last year, I won a Grimmy from the Society of Professional Obituary Writers—for writing the Best Obit of an Ordinary Joe/Jane. "Pie Lady" Alice King died in her bakery located on the corner of Crenshaw and Jefferson, but she lived long enough to crawl to the kitchen and turn off the oven. *Alice's custard was like the curls on her head: tight and bright. Her crust never burned, because she filled each pie with love.*

And now, I've brought my Grimmy-winning ass to the island's community paper.

"It's pretty dead around here," I say. "It's the quietest newsroom I've ever visited."

"That's because nothing happens here," Flynn says.

"No, that's not true," Maddy says, her face flushing. "It's quiet because it's Monday."

"If you say so," Flynn says with a playful smirk.

"I say so because I know so," Maddy says with a decisive nod.

They're cute.

The island's journalists, the Swensons have lived here since the 1930s. The paper has passed down from son to son to son and, now, to daughter, each dedicated to telling the hard truths about vandalized park benches, upcoming fun runs, and the pet of the week. The obituaries are the typical, straightforward, and rote ones found in nearly every newspaper—*Jack Jones passed away peacefully . . . Jill Jones was a graduate of Cal State Long Beach . . . Karen Smith's childhood was spent dancing . . .*

Gets the job done.

A notification brightens the phone in my friend's hand. She peers at the screen and scrunches her eyebrows. "I'm already sick of these virus stories. Why is the *Times* wasting so much ink . . . ? Whatever. So . . ."

Flynn points to the sink. "May I go back to the job you assigned?"

"Absolutely." She shoves the phone into her jeans pocket, then threads her arm through mine. "Let's walk."

We leave the kitchen and turtle toward the front office.

"So," Maddy says. "You asked about my strategic plan. Well, for starters, I'm transforming this paper from a family-run business to a true communications enterprise—from traditional paper to mobile, podcasts, and documentary series. We may live on an island, but we're not yokels. I went to freakin' UCLA for a communications degree, and damn it, I'm gonna use that expensive paper to shake shit up." She raises her hand for a high five.

"Shake it up, girl," I say, slapping her palm.

The *Times* has a daily readership of nearly 1.5 million along with a wall filled with nearly fifty Pulitzer Prizes. But you shoot for the stars, sweetheart.

"I've landed a benefactor," Maddy says. "He lives up in the hills and wants to become Avalon's Patrick Soon-Shiong. He's throwing me crazy amounts of cash to put us on the map."

"You're going balls to the wall for a circulation of six thousand?" My eyes peck at the in-window air conditioner, the broken wall clock, and the wood-paneled walls. "Who *is* this tycoon–cum–aspirational newsman?"

Maddy narrows her eyes. "He wants to keep a low profile. And I'm expanding our circulation. I've already digitalized our archives, updated the server, and . . . hired *you*."

I nod. "Just in the nick of time, too. Thanks again." I try out that purgatory smile. Feels like lettuce wilted and died on my face.

Maddy cants her head. "You sign the divorce papers yet?"

I sigh and blink at the wreath of corks hanging on the men's bathroom door.

If I sign, I'd be breaking the law, right? Cuz Micah and I aren't married, so there can't be a divorce. This goes through my head as Maddy squeezes my hand and says, "At least he's not being an asshole about it."

"People fall out of love," I say now. "That's the way love goes, as Janet Jackson says."

Maddy snorts. "And you're okay with that? After six years?"

"I'm not gonna force him to be with me."

"He gets what he gives, then. The universe will handle it." Maddy squeezes my hand. "*That's* why he's only landed roles in cable movies that come on random Thursday nights."

Micah's played Black Ops Doctor in a knockoff of *Clear and Present Danger*.

Ferrari Driver in a knockoff of *The Fast and the Furious*.

Jake's Brother in a knockoff of *Nightmare on Elm Street*.

Rinse. Repeat.

Bryan Cranston landed Malcolm in the Middle *when he was forty-four,* Micah would always say. *And Morgan Freeman was fifty-two when he landed* Driving Miss Daisy.

Both Cranston and Freeman can *act*, and Micah . . . looks good.

"Fuck Micah, wherever the hell he is." Maddy points at me. "I warned you about him." She beckons me down the hall. "Next up: bathrooms."

The squeak of my sneakers against the linoleum matches Maddy's pace. Eyes burning, I try to grin, but any Micah-adjacent conversation pulls me into a cry-cloud of *near tears*. That has been my status since waking up that morning to an empty apartment. Those first weeks without Micah are blurs of weeping and vomiting. Maddy ferried over and spent the night long enough for me to snap out of it to say, *I'm fine*, as though I banked ten grand every time I muttered those words. But then, hours passed, and I'd slip, inch, creep back to *near tears* again until my friend pulled me from the cry-cloud once I was strong enough to say, *I'm fine*, again.

But I'm *not* fine, even now. I wanna combust as I tour my new workplace. Yeah, I wanna combust and sweep my ashes into a cannon and shoot myself into space.

Maybe if I'd been more supportive of Micah . . .

Maybe if I'd actually *signed* the marriage certificate . . .

Maybe, maybe, maybe.

We cross the hall and return to the kitchen.

Maddy turns to me and says, "The hearing?"

For the second time, Harper Hemphill has been granted an appeal hearing. Harper's attorney, Isaac Pierce, continued to work on the case even as Harper sat in jail. Pierce eventually reached out to the Innocence Project and had the physical evidence tested again for DNA. Results from my mother's nightgown and Langston's football jersey came back inconclusive. Then, Pierce and the Innocence Project attorneys came into the possession of the ten-inch hunting knife that had allegedly been used in the murders but had been misplaced all this time. There were no fingerprints found on the knife, but there was blood. Harper's attorneys immediately submitted the knife for DNA testing.

"Still waiting on results from the forensics tests," I say, "but . . ." I shake my head and find interest in the packets of tea. "Ooh, green matcha!"

"You don't wanna talk about it," Maddy says, "but let me know as soon as you hear."

I offer a strained smile. "Yep."

"And you're starting here . . . when?"

"Now, I guess. Gimme access to the calendars and the inbox and the archives and yeah . . . How much do we charge for obits?"

"Four hundred."

I gape at Maddy. "The *Times* charges two hundred and five dollars for five lines."

"And now, we have the *Times*'s obituary writer." Maddy cocks her chin. "And she's one of my dearest friends. I'm lucky to have you in my life again."

That first year at UCLA, after she basically called me a pickaninny, Maddy realized that we lived on the same dorm floor. Once we became friends, we did Jell-O shots together. Took all the required comms classes and interned together every summer in the *Times* training program. Our friendship never sputtered over boys—Maddy liked moody redheads named Phoenix, Orin, Winter, and Basil.

No. We sputtered out over ambition—battling to be a staff writer for the *Times*. Oscar the hiring editor loved my portfolio, which included stories I'd published as a *Times* intern, as an intern for the South Los Angeles paper *Sentinel*, and as the crime editor for UCLA's campus newspaper, *Daily Bruin*. Several articles focused on the murder case surrounding my family. Maddy's portfolio showcased articles on neighborhood council meetings and changes in UCLA's enrollment system. Strong but not *Los Angeles Times* strong.

But Maddy's father, Ronan, played squash with Oscar once a week. Maddy landed the job.

No sense in holding grudges—Maddy was my girl, and a bridesmaid in my wedding. My only grudge? I learned from a friend of a friend that Maddy was engaged to Flynn. On top of *that*, she didn't ask me to be a bridesmaid in her wedding.

Oscar eventually hired me, and my beat was death: obituaries. *Not for long, though,* Oscar promised.

Fifteen years later . . .

"Listen . . ." Maddy clears her throat now, then bites her lip. "I've been wanting to apologize for the longest time . . . I'm sorry."

I blink at her. "For . . . ?"

"Everything. I mean . . . this must be weird for you. All that . . . *drama* from a long time ago has been hanging over our friendship, and I just wanna say sorry for, y'know, all the nepotism. You were more talented, but . . ." She slips her hands into her jeans pockets. "The world is rarely fair. But I'll make it up to you, okay? You stay for a month, and I'll make you assistant editor in chief, and I'll get you a raise because it's expensive living here. Okay?"

"Okay."

"I'm gonna prove to all my haters that I *am* a good newspaperwoman. This paper is gonna be successful. By any means necessary."

Maddy lifts her hand for another high five. "Let's bring home a Pulitzer, baby!"

"Hear, hear."

We hug and a smile wriggles across my face.

"And I'm finding you a good man," she says. "And you're gonna live happily ever after."

"Yay."

"I'm so happy you're here, Coco." Maddy pats my back. "We're gonna rule the world, you and me."

I smile and follow Maddy to her office.

Ha. This bitch really thinks I trust her.

5.

Of course I don't trust her.

Hell, I don't trust *anyone* (yet another reason I've been in therapy for twenty years).

But I'll never let Maddy know that I still think she and most of the citizens of Earth are folklore scorpions asking for a ride across the river.

Sting me once, never again.

Since I have a strong phone signal in the newsroom, I deposit Mom's check via mobile banking app, then hightail it to Mrs. T's Chinese Kitchen. A mingle of tangy sauces, stir-fried veggies, yeast, and sugar envelops me. So many smells. After pondering the quotations around "hot" beignets, I order food for Gwen and me, select a dozen doughnuts, then hit fresh air again with bags of food.

The post office is located in the same three-story building as the *Breeze*. The customer service windows are closed—I'll need to come back tomorrow with the golf cart. At least the unicorn is safe.

I find the gold-and-red box 378, and it's stuffed with envelopes and catalogs.

I dump the mail into the food bags and head home. This was the easiest errand run ever.

The misty rain lightens to a drizzle. Out past the harbor, catamarans skim across the ocean's gray surface like Jesus bugs. A dollop of contentment fills me, and I'm almost convinced that this is how the world can be. Post office, Chinese food, and "hot" beignets.

I grumble some more and start my walk home.

Televisions glow behind windows just steps away from the couch. Shadows of humans perch on living room couches or stand in brightly lit kitchens. A black cat with a white nose greets me with a *meow*, then slips over to a paper plate left out on the grass strip by the gods.

Footsteps that aren't mine tap behind me.

I look back over my shoulder.

No one's there.

The house on Beacon Street sits just a block away. The lights in my room and Gwen's room burn, but the front porch is lost in shadow.

I pick up my pace.

I hear a stranger's footsteps again, quicker now.

Unless the sounds I hear are echoes of my own steps.

I dare myself to look back again.

Those steps aren't echoes.

The stranger wears a hoodie and a baseball cap.

I can't see their face.

My keys are in my hand, and one key sticks out from my knuckles.

I quicken my pace.

The walker quickens their pace, too.

My pulse explodes.

Fuck it.

I run.

The walker runs, too.

I don't want to lead the stranger to my house, but there's nowhere else to go.

At the cottage ahead, TV light shines, and someone's sitting on the couch in front of it.

There! I'll run—

Boom!

The air feels loose around me.

Are they shooting at me?

I reach that cottage.

No one's sitting on that couch—it's just a large teddy bear.

Pain spikes through my lower back. A current sizzles up my side and slows my running . . . but I don't stop, even as tears fill my eyes.

I've lived in the rough parts of Los Angeles. Walked alone across the campus of UCLA. Visited strangers in their homes. Survived a massacre.

Why am I so scared?

The house—*my house*—is right there.

Go, go, go!

I jam up the stairs, and each step feels like I'm pushing down knives. I reach the landing and spot a crowbar in the corner. I grab it and swing . . .

No one's behind me on the steps.

No one's down on the street.

I shove my key into the lock and rush inside.

Up in the living room, *Matlock* plays on the TV.

I hurry downstairs and take off my shirt to stand before the mirror. I search my reflection, turning this way, turning that way. No blood. No gunshot wounds. But my eyes are bloodshot and bright with fear.

The pain spikes again, and the muscles in my back and right side spasm beneath my skin.

Outside my window, branches swish and crackle.

Is that light shining in?

I grab my phone and press the side button, ready to call 9-1-1.

I tiptoe over to the window, take a deep breath and hold it, then slowly . . . peek . . . past the curtains . . . into the dark, overgrown garden.

The grass moves.

The nightshade rustles.

Is that a man out there?

Or is that a monster?

I don't move. I just hold my breath, and I wait for the creature to emerge.

I wait . . .

And I wait . . .

Any minute now . . .

I can't feel my hands.

Feels like bricks have been stacked on my chest.

I can't take a deep breath . . .

Breathe . . .

I can't breathe . . .

I know I'm having a panic attack, that I'm seeing things that aren't there. This feeling—my limbs frozen but my mind spiraling—I've experienced this before.

In that closet on the night my family was killed.

In the hotel on the night before I testified against Harper Hemphill.

On the morning I was supposed to go to jail for destroying Micah's Ducati after learning he'd changed our banking account passwords, but I didn't go to jail because Ted Archer knew one of the most powerful defense attorneys in Los Angeles.

I can't blame this irrational fear on alcohol. But I *have* been thinking a lot about death and murder.

Too much and not enough. The recipe for panic attacks.

Acknowledging this, though, doesn't keep my heart from scrambling in my chest or the room from spinning all around me.

Phone. I need to . . . Dr. Tamaguchi . . . where . . . my phone?

I empty my purse onto the bed, and I push through the junk . . . not here . . . phone not . . .

Where is . . . ?

I reach to touch my sweaty forehead, and something cold bangs against my skin.

My phone . . . I've been holding it all this time.

I tap Dr. Tamaguchi's number.

The line rings . . . rings . . .

My stomach cramps.

She isn't picking up. Why isn't she picking up? Is she about to board that flight to Tokyo? How many days ago did she leave? *Has* she left?

I drop her a brief message—*It's Colette, I'm having a hard time, please call me*—then stumble to the bathroom sink. I turn the cold tap and hold my wrists beneath the shocking, chilly water. My mind snaps to attention, and I take deep breaths in . . . out . . . in . . . out . . .

Okay. I'm okay.

Back to my bedroom.

With a shaky hand, I light a lavender candle, grab a pillow, and lie back in bed, breathing in . . . breathing out . . . as the flame flickers and dances and makes shadows against the ceiling. The knot in my belly loosens, and the clanging in my mind softens.

There's nothing outside my window except deer, trees, shrubs, and the ocean a mile away.

There's no one trying to kill me. No one kills anyone here, not anymore.

I breathe in through my nose . . .

I push out through my mouth . . .

In . . . out . . .

In . . . out . . .

. . .

◆ ◆ ◆

I calm down enough to wobble up to the living room.

Aunt Gwen, wearing a sparkly sweater, flutters from the kitchen to her armchair. She is a cloud of Opium with red-painted lips and earlobes bright with diamonds. "There you are," she says, smiling. "Ooh, that smells so *good*."

"You look fancy," I say. "Diamonds from a lover or . . . ?"

Gwen smirks. "Guests of Room 311 at Hotel Vista Del Mar."

My eyebrows lift. "Racist?"

"Not directly. Mr. Camden didn't pay his workers, and Mrs. Camden stole silverware from the restaurant." She taps a stud. "She left these babies on the bathroom counter, and so, when I cleaned the room, I liberated them from her evil clutches."

"So many villains, so little time," I say. "And the sweater?"

"Ross."

"A vacationing family or the store?"

She laughs, waggles her head.

"You're not driving to Dee Dee's, are you?"

Gwen's smile dims. "I move around this island just fine." She pauses, then adds, "Jackie's picking me up."

No idea who Jackie is. I nod, though, and set the food on the dining room table.

Gwen points at the couch—she wants me to sit. "You talk to Ted yet?"

Theodore Archer, Esq., represented Gwen and me during this murder trial journey. I've attended the first appeal hearing and one probation hearing—and I left both times satisfied in knowing that Harper Hemphill would never experience freedom again.

I check for voice mail messages. "Nothing from Ted. He call about the hearing?"

Gwen takes a deep breath. "Harper's getting out of jail."

"What?"

Gwen shakes her head. "The tests came back. His DNA doesn't match the DNA on that knife."

There was my family's blood on the knife and handle. There was also blood from a stranger: the murderer. And none of it belonged to Harper Hemphill, the man arrested and convicted of the murders.

Harper Hemphill didn't kill my family. *Why would he?* His defense attorney asked that question all throughout the trial. The prosecutor had arrived at a theory involving obsession and revenge—Harper stalked my mother, she rejected him, he couldn't let that go and followed her around Los Angeles and, then, to Catalina. That June, he snuck into the house on Middle Terrace Road and shot, stabbed my family because of that obsession.

Harper had admitted to being at our rental. *Just to visit my friends, the Webers,* had been his explanation. My parents hadn't been there to confirm or deny this friendship. I told the officers and the prosecutors that I didn't know Harper Hemphill—and that had been the truth. The first time I saw him was that night on the patio.

Hemphill had stalked women before—it's in his police record.

Hemphill had a history of violence—from domestic to public—it's in his police record.

And now, he's been vindicated by DNA found on the knife blade used to end my family's lives.

But that knife blade had been missing for nearly twenty years until it mysteriously reappeared months ago.

My mouth moves but no words come. No air can make its way through my nostrils or my lips. I will die any minute now.

Gwen stares at the carpet. "I don't know *what* to believe. But if they say he didn't do it, then . . ." She shrugs. "Can't keep a man in jail for a crime he didn't commit."

Any other time, I would've wholeheartedly agreed—Innocence Project donor here.

But now, I snap my fingers. "Just like that, he's out?"

Gwen nods.

Science has now freed the man convicted of killing Reginald Weber, Alyson Weber, and Langston Weber at our vacation rental on June 23, 2001.

I sag on the couch, suddenly fatigued.

All this time—hating Harper Hemphill, hating courtrooms and attorneys, holding my breath, taking a breath, going to therapy because I feared that he'd find me and finish me . . . all this time, and he didn't *do it*?

I'll be paying Dr. Tamaguchi forever because *all this time*?

"Ted said that they're processing him now for release," Gwen says. *"Already?"*

Aunt Gwen places her hand on my knee. "The man's been in jail for twenty years. He didn't do it. He didn't kill our people."

A realization shrieks like a missile from the sky and hits my head. "But if he didn't do it, who did?"

Gwen's eyes widen before they silver with tears. "I don't know, Coco. We'll probably never know."

That Chinese food–post office serenity splinters and cracks, and life becomes rubble again. And now, I'll never wear Langston's puka-shell bracelet or receive any of my family's things (my Vans, Dad's flip-flops, Mom's diamond studs) kept in those evidence boxes. The case isn't over, not anymore.

"Harper wasn't a good man," I whisper, overheating now, sweat bubbling over every inch of my skin. "He was a drug dealer. A thief. A thug."

"But he's not a murderer."

And yet, I still hate him. *Can* I still hate him?

I push out a breath, then squint at my aunt. "Why aren't you upset?"

Gwen's lips tremble. "I . . . I . . ."

I sense relief in Gwen. Because the case is over or because Harper Hemphill is free?

The house creaks in complaint. The people who would've loved it, maintained its pipes and electrical systems and the yard and the paint, were stolen away, and now, it barely stands.

Gwen shambles to the dining room table and separates her food from mine. "Thank you for getting the mail. They couldn't find your boxes?" She sorts through the envelopes.

That's that?

That's that.

"The office was closed," I say.

That *can't* be that. Who's gonna fight for us? Who's gonna make sure justice is served? What tangible goal can I work toward now that the biggest obstacle that keeps me from living fully—moving beyond the murders of my family—has just widened from Colorado River size to the Grand Canyon on the dark side of the moon?

Aunt Gwen holds out an envelope. "This is for you."

A letter from Micah.

Crap.

All feeling leaves my face.

I don't need this now.

A million minutes click by as I stand here. He's mailed letters to me before, with declarations that swing from hysterical and angry to hysterical and frightened. Finally, I tear the flap as my heart knocks like an old water heater.

> Colette.
> This isn't a letter of apology or a plea for you to take me back.
>
> My life has improved since our separation, and reuniting would only shatter all of that. I want what's mine. That's why I'm writing you. You stole that ring from me. Edith willed it to me. She told me that.
>
> The will is inaccurate. And who's to say that you didn't pressure her to change it? You spent a lot of time alone with her. You're a liar. You've always been a liar.
>
> I'm coming over there, Colette, and I'm taking back what you stole from me.

If you get hurt in the process, that's on you.
YOU'VE BEEN WARNED!!!
Always,
Micah

The black ink shimmies on the page, freeing itself and wriggling into my skin. Those words slice and swirl, and spread through my blood to poison my heart.

Fear flickers in my chest—from Micah's threat but also . . .

The monster who killed three people—*my family*—has escaped justice all this time. And that monster is still walking free.

That can't be, can it?

And now, here I am, living on this island, possibly next door to that monster.

And back in Los Angeles, my angry ex is waiting to pay me back for taking something from him.

I'm screwed.

Did I really believe that my days were gonna be filled with writing obituaries and graduation announcements?

The outside steps groan, pulling my attention from Micah's letter to the front door. A photograph has been slid beneath the landing strip.

I peek out the door's glass pane—no one's there. I snap up the picture . . .

. . . of sixteen-year-old me, wearing a Popsicle-colored bikini top and white jean shorts, biting into a candy apple as the blue ocean sparkles behind me.

There's handwriting on the back of the picture.

To the one who survived

WELCOME HOME

6.

On the night she was supposed to die, the old woman stumbled through chaparral and sagebrush, her eyes glazed and lips and chin tacky with vomit. Fog and fast-moving clouds moved all around her, and the mist saturated her buffalo-print pajama bottoms. Her beige T-shirt stuck to her, a second skin.

With the fog moving like that, and the moon no longer visible, she couldn't see her hands, she couldn't see the space up ahead, she couldn't see.

Running blind.

Don't let me die here, not tonight.

The old woman cried out as her ankle twisted over a wet root. The brush snagged her left house slipper as a souvenir. Second shoe gone.

She couldn't see it, but she could feel it.

Death, coming hard for her, rumbling beneath her two bare feet. Death's steps rumbled differently than the bison's hooves thundering toward her.

At this time of night, there shouldn't be thundering hooves—the herd should be asleep.

Someone disturbed them.

The monster now slow chasing her through the interior?

Yes, slow chasing because at seventy-eight years old, she trotted, never cantered, never raced. Except now, her heart raced and was moments away from bursting.

The herd rumbled closer. She could hear their lowing and snuffling—sounded like a lion's roar and a bear's growl combined.

Maybe they'll kill me first.

She'd cared for and counted bison since coming to the island—her ancestral land—more than seventy years ago to live with her grandmother, her mother's mother, her neshuuk. Later, she met islander Danny, the whitest man on Catalina, her people said. Ah, but love. He saw her even as some said she and her mother's people weren't "real," that her mother's people were extinct.

Danny had traveled beside her in the Autoette, a wad of mint gum in his cheek, his gray eyes twinkling. He'd carried his hunting rifle as a last resort, just in case the relocation efforts failed and a bison charged. After pleading and begging from the tribes, the people in charge had stopped using guns to manage the herd and, instead, partnered with the Lakota, the Sioux, and the Tongva to return some of the bison back to the Great Plains, their ancestral land.

Back then, there'd been more than five hundred bison freely roaming the back country. Some even wandered into town.

The ones who stayed on the island got birth control shots. She'd aimed her air-powered rifle at female bison rumps and winced in sympathy as the darts of PZP sank into their targets. Once the vaccines hit their marks, the orange darts fell to the ground, and she and Danny would round those up, too. Birth control had been a little too effective, and no bison calves had been born in seven years. Only one hundred bison now wandered the backcountry.

Her stomach twisted, and she slowed in her step. Crème de bananes, Kahlúa, and half-and-half burned her throat and soured her tongue. Her eyelids drooped as she shambled. She stopped, not knowing if she stood on a trail, off a trail, in the brush. Though her cut feet no longer distinguished the type of earth, she still felt the vibrations of a herd on the move.

She closed her eyes and listened . . .

The bison's craggy bellows.

Soft rain falling.

The everlasting roar of the Pacific Ocean pounding at rocks and eating away the shore.

A truck's whirring engine.

Her limbs quivered as poison swirled through her veins.

"You are one tough bird," the monster said.

Nauseated, she sank to the soft ground. "Huutokre."

Saying that word . . . I see you . . . made her gasp for air.

She peered into the monster's face. Even with blurred vision, she knew that smirk, those flat eyes. All sociopaths in that family. Destroy land. Destroy people. Forget about heritage. Forget about respect. Bones are for museums—only the strong survive. Not as crass as that huckster back in the 1950s but just as evil. Not selling giants but selling another lie: this island was Paradise.

Her knees gave, and her cheek sank into the mud.

I've done nothing to deserve this.

Did she say that aloud or . . . ?

Get up, girl.

That was Danny. He was here. If you lie there, you're gonna die for sure. That ain't a good look for a Tongva warrior, right? Get the fuck up. Get UP!

Danny, dead now for a month, hadn't talked to her all this time. This was the moment he chose to show up? Always late to every—

Her body shuddered against the earth.

Arms—can't feel 'em.

Legs—President Bush.

Corn cakes make the best pillows.

"Just close your eyes," the monster cooed, "and let the medicine work. That's it. Be a good girl."

She moved her mouth, whispering words now. "Turkeys you course."

"Say that again?" The monster moved closer.

She could see that smirk and those dead, flat eyes up close. Of course it's you.

Something inside her knew exactly where she was. That fucker. *The clearest thought she'd had all night.*

Tears warmer than the rain rolled across the bridge of her nose and joined the mud. She smiled, forced herself to lift one hand to touch the monster's wet cheek. So soft, so . . .

She scraped her fingernails along the monster's neck.

"Damn it!" the monster roared back.

The rumble of the herd vibrated against her body. They were just over the ridge now and would trample her to death if she didn't move.

The truck's engine revved, and the mud-stuck tires whirred. The smell of exhaust mixed with the earthy aroma of wet brush and wet fur.

The bison bellowed, grunted, and snorted.

She could almost feel their hot breath against her face.

Eyes closed, she willed her left heel to dig into the earth.

Just a nudge . . . just a scoot . . .

The strongest male always led the herd, and she heard his high-pitched grunts now. Taamet—"sun" in her great-grandmother's tongue. She'd known Taamet now for all his life, knew him by the question-mark scar on his woolly forehead. His picture graced her soaked T-shirt. Her bi-SON. Her bi-SUN.

Hyaa'mo pakooro taamet. The sun is going to set now.

She wanted to see it. All she needed . . . just . . . nudge . . . and scoot . . . just . . . nudge.

7.

I want to use the slide chain on the front door, but Gwen still isn't home. Should I wait up for her? Is she nearby?

The pink dot that represents my aunt's geolocation hasn't moved from Dee Dee's house all night. Sometimes the dot moves away from that spot but then stops and returns to that spot.

What are old people doing at 11:15 on a rainy Monday night?

Not sitting on a mattress staring at an old photograph, that's for sure.

To the one who survived

WELCOME HOME

I take a picture of the picture, then send it to Maddy with a text message. Someone just sent me this.

No immediate response from my friend.

Since the words have burned into my mind, I slip that old picture of me into the crumpled manila envelope that contains my bank statements, severance documents, and expired passport. Micah's letter will soon join these artifacts, but it's less than twenty-four hours old, and so it lives in the depths of my purse.

I stand at the window and peer into the dark garden, but I can see only my reflection. If I squint hard enough, I can see the backyard, and that wild Catalina nightshade, and a single yellow flower that is somehow standing against the pounding rain. The one who survived . . .

After showering, I return to that mattress on the floor. In the second window, a single streetlight as bright as Venus burns in the dark and shines directly in my face. The toilet hisses and the pipes clank and clang.

This light . . .

That picture . . .

Those words . . .

I rearrange the pillows—they smell like dust and fabric softener. I grab my phone—it's 11:45 p.m., and the person who murdered my family is out there, watching me. Maybe.

I sit up.

Moths now flit around the streetlight.

My eyes burn, and my exhausted body sags. I don't have the strength to trudge upstairs, find the remote control, and fall asleep on the couch while watching old *Law & Order* reruns. I must learn how to sleep alone—and without a TV.

I throw myself against the mattress and yank the blankets over my head.

That light, hidden now, still burns in my mind's eye.

Hello, insomnia, my old friend.

To the one who survived . . .

On the day that picture was taken, our parents let Langston and me wander the island alone. My brother—six one and two hundred pounds, smooth dark skin, a smile as bright as the gold chain around his neck—wore one of his Crenshaw High School football jerseys. Wearing my favorite Popsicle-colored bikini top and white jean shorts, I'd been a teenage show horse with an easy smile and a fresh press and flat-iron. (That had been the last time I wore that bikini top—the string got caught around the lint tray and tore.)

Langston and I had fifty dollars and decided to spend the bulk of it at the arcade. We started at the air hockey tables, then moved over to timed basketball free throws. A few kids competed against us, and they lost. El and I were the bomb.

After video games, we bought slices of pepperoni pizza and bottles of Mountain Dew.

As we ate on a low wall near the pier, we both lamented moving here—Catalina Island sucked monkey balls, my brother said. We had *plans*, man. Being a teenager in Los Angeles during the summer was exquisite. There were days spent at Magic Mountain from sunrise to almost midnight. Hanging out at the Santa Monica Pier and Third Street Promenade. Just driving up and down Crenshaw Boulevard, being fly in Mom's convertible Audi TT. He told me about this cute girl named Stephanie that he planned to ask to the homecoming dance. I told him about Kenneth, the cute freshman intern at Mom's law firm, where I'd been working as a seasonal file clerk. Kenneth kissed with his teeth, and his mouth always tasted like pickles.

Langston and I vowed to get in some Magic Mountain–Audi time before our move here was complete. That afternoon, we bought matching puka-shell bracelets with our nicknames—COCO and L BOOGIE. Then, we bought candy apples and sat back on that wall overlooking the harbor. The wind tousled my thick hair as I pointed at the yachts I'd buy after selling my bestselling self-help book that had been chosen by Oprah, who then gave me my own talk show, *Coco* or simply *Colette*.

Someone had been watching us that afternoon and had taken my picture. Whoever that was knew that I had just returned to Avalon . . .

Leaving the picture behind—was that a threat, a warning?

To the one who survived . . .

Or is "*WELCOME HOME*" a sincere salutation and greeting?

The stranger had slipped the picture beneath the door without a "how do you do," though.

That says "threat" to me, but moths bigger than a popcorn kernel are also threats to me.

What do I do?

I text Maddy again.

Hey!

Me, again

Don't trip out but . . .

Having second thoughts especially with this picture

Maybe I'm not ready to be here

My hands shake.

Should I go back to LA and get my old apartment back?

Come back after I've made progress in therapy?

This time, Maddy responds with: No!

                    Sorry for not answering earlier!

                    That picture is weird okay but

DO NOT LEAVE!!!

And therapy is forever anyway!!

Your new life is here in Avalon

With me & Flynn & Gwen & all the friends you're gonna make!

And Micah's a total drama bitch right now

You'll end up doing something stupid again!

Like burning him alive

Or running over him

Poisoning him for real this time

If you go back there somebody's gonna die

Tuesday, March 10, 2020

As the sky brightens from a new sun, I order three sets of bed linens online. The delivery estimate: a week from today. "Next Day" doesn't work well when you're living on an island.

The theme song of *Family Feud* circa 2000 drifts downstairs. Louie Anderson announces, "It's . . . the *Weber* family!" Louie banters with Dad, calls him "Reggie." In his deep baritone, Dad introduces his gorgeous and crazy-smart wife, Alyson; his lovely and witty daughter, Colette; his brilliant and beautiful mother, Victoria; and his sister,

Gwen, no adjectives. We won that episode and three more episodes after that. Though we didn't win the maximum $100,000, we did win $80,000—enough money to add to the down payment for this house that now stinks of mystery meat and sick timber.

Gwen is poking through my moving box. She has papers in her hand, and the pockets of her robe look bulky.

What the hell?

I clear my throat, then say, "Looking for something, Auntie?"

Gwen's head bobbles and she offers a weak smile. "Just cleaning out junk I don't need."

I squint at her. "Those are my boxes."

She squints back at me. "Come again?"

"They don't belong to you. They're mine." I take the papers she's holding—the contract from selling my car back to Honda—and make a note to check the robe pockets after she's taken it off.

She chuckles, then wanders to her armchair. "No wonder I didn't recognize nothing."

I watch her for a moment, not believing that she's as discombobulated as she's acting, then scan the contents of the box. No clue what she swiped. But my face burns—shame for suspecting my aunt of stealing from me. I close the box, then retreat to the kitchen to make breakfast: yesterday's doughnuts, bacon, and eggs.

As I prepare two plates, I call Gwen's social worker, Pam Robins. Since she's not answering, I leave a voice mail message. "I'm here in Avalon now. You'll be happy to know that Gwen's doing great. Fixing her breakfast now. I'll be driving her wherever she needs to go, so you won't have to worry about late-night skinny-dips in the ocean, ha ha."

By the time I sit on the living room couch, Gwen has switched to live television. We don't talk as she flips from channel to channel between sips of coffee and nibbles of doughnuts.

She has basic cable on this TV set, so we're not totally cut off from the catty housewives, the worst cooks, and the ax-wielding competitions.

Gwen settles on a cooking show, with two people competing against each other to ultimately beat chef Bobby Flay. She's wearing someone else's robe this morning, a cranberry-colored one with white cranes. Gorgeous, but the sleeves fall over her hands, sweeping eggs from the plate onto the tray. Still, she's better dressed than me—no one will write a song about the woman in ankle boots and army-green skinny jeans.

"How was the party?" I ask my aunt.

Her hands dance around her head as she tells me about mah-jongg and the special cocktails and back in the day and bison in the backyard. "Haven't had such a good time in ages," Gwen says, her eyes twinkling. "I always feel bad for feeling good and . . ." Her lips clamp, and her mouth twists.

I place my hand on her wrist. "I know. No need to explain."

She swallows, tries to smile. "I asked folks to remember, to think of who could've done that to Reggie, to Alyson and El."

I sit up straighter. "And?"

She shakes her head. "I'm not gonna stop asking, though."

And I'm gonna figure it out, too.

I've decided not to show her the picture of sixteen-year-old me. Can't have the both of us freaked out.

"What she makin'?" Gwen snarks.

My gaze now settles on the cooking show even though my mind churns, anxious about someone—*the monster?*—watching me.

"That mess looks like dog shit," Gwen says. Her phone vibrates on the TV tray, and she picks it up, squints at the screen, then taps out a message. She sets the phone back on the tray, then says, "Y'know, I cut my finger on a mandoline once. I stole it, so I guess the universe said, 'Bitch, please.'"

I pull at the skin on my bottom lip as I think and lick at the tiny dot of blood from my torn skin. But blood doesn't stop me from pulling, nor does it ease my anxiety.

Maybe I can hire a PI to help me figure this out. That takes money, though. I have ten thousand in the bank, and some of that *must* go to making this house livable. If I stay here a year, Maddy will give me a pay raise. *Allegedly*. And the book deal, there's that, but . . . *ugh*. Oh yeah, there's the ring—I'll sell it. Maybe Ted the Attorney knows a detective who'll work for a song.

I bite at my injured lip and rock on the couch as I think . . . and think . . .

Even if I hire a PI, that person will still need to start from the beginning. Meanwhile, the monster has me—*the one who survived*—in their crosshairs.

My stomach hurts now, and I rub my face with numb hands.

And then, there's this riddle: How do I get Gwen on a ferry back to Los Angeles? Maybe there are papers she needs to sign. Maybe there's money she needs to claim in person. And when she thinks it's time to go back, I'll tell her then that there *is* no going back. Yeah, money will . . .

A breeze drifts across my sweaty face. Light slips into the living room through the crack in the front door. The *open* front door.

"We have to change out this door." I hop up from the couch, hurry down the steps to close the door and to pull the slide chain across its slot.

"You got front-door money?" Gwen says to me as she changes to *The Price Is Right*.

"I do . . ."

But I'm going back to Los Angeles any day now—and you're joining me. I don't like the way my heart races here. It's too quiet in some ways, and too loud with all the chugging golf carts. And too unpredictable with bison just . . . *chillin'* this close to people and a murderer possibly living a block over . . .

I hustle to the bathroom and run cold water over my wrists.

Breathe in . . .

Push breath out . . .

In . . .

Out . . .

Aunt Gwen will be pissed. I'll sell the house and buy a nice condo with a security guard and a swimming pool since my aunt likes being near water. Since grocery stores now deliver, I'll never have to leave my unit. Maybe I'll buy a gun, and if Micah decides to break in, I'll shoot him.

Breathe in . . .

Out . . .

A jury will have compassion—I'm the one who survived—and maybe the judge will sentence me to house arrest. No problem. All I do anyway is write and shop, sleep with men I barely know, and I could get them online, too.

I'd have a better outcome over there than staying on this island in a house surrounded by poison that can't even keep its doors closed.

Okay. *It will be okay*—that's what I tell my reflection in the bathroom mirror.

On my to-do list: make a *real* to-do list for Handy Andy. I can't sell the house with a janky door. If he can't do it, I'll buy the damn door myself and hire a day laborer to install it. Then, I bounce. Back in Los Angeles before sunrise tomorrow.

The misty morning air smells honeysuckle sweet, though a weird haze sits over Avalon and mutes all the colors. I can't hear my footsteps . . . which means I can't hear someone else's footsteps, either.

My blood gallops through my veins.

It's okay. You're okay. It's all good.

The world reveals more of itself the closer I get to town, and now I hear those carts rumbling, and I hear water running, and I hear a bell tolling. It is 9:45 in Avalon.

The post office is still holding my boxes. Fine. I'll be shipping them back to LA anyway.

I hurry past the *Avalon Breeze* and speed-walk until I reach the Catalina Express ticket window. Behind me, the ferry slips lack ferries. Gulls perch on wooden posts, and, like me, they wonder where the people are.

The ticket agent behind the plexiglass says, "No boats today. The weather."

I squint at the sky. "But it's not that—"

Raindrops the size of marbles hit the concrete, pounding so hard and heavy that I can't hear my breath. Even the gulls shriek and flap off.

The woman behind the glass laughs. "See? Weather. No boats coming in or going out. Tomorrow should be better, but don't count on it."

8.

Should I stay or should I go?

    Doesn't matter since right now I'm trapped.

    My phone vibrates with a text from Maddy.

> Ready to write your first obit?

> Yay yay yay!!!

> BTW was that you walking past the office this morning?

My lips numb—I *am* being watched. There aren't many (hell, I can almost say "any") young Black women living here. I need to remember that. According to nearly every modern-day census taken on Santa Catalina Island, there are approximately three Black people out of four thousand living full-time in Avalon at any time. If my family had survived, that would've taken the count to seven.

    Ha, I text Maddy back. Yes getting coffee

> I've attached the form

For the obit

Daughter wants to meet in person

Deceased is Paula Paulsen

878 Clarissa Ave

Might as well head there since you're close!

A nine-minute walk from here—*That's close?*—and almost in a straight line. If anything, I'll become healthier from all this walking. My phone vibrates again with another text from Maddy.

If you think Gwen's house is a mess JUST YOU WAIT!

Umm . . . How does Maddy know Gwen's house is a mess? And umm . . . the house on Beacon Street is *my* house. *My* house is a mess. Words matter.

Paula Paulsen's house sits on the corner of Clarissa Avenue and Tremont Avenue. The dusty yellow two-story was the Linda Evangelista of houses back in the day. Splintered wood and peeling yellow and white paint cracks across the facade. Two sick potted palms flank the porch steps, and wet spiderwebs droop like soggy pantyhose between the fronds. The second story boasts a patio with wicker chairs and a filled damp ashtray that I can smell from street level. Wind chimes hang from any place they can hang, which means they hang everywhere.

Over the privacy wall, I spot a hoard of storage tubs, sagging boxes, fishing poles, and dresser shelves. Modelo boxes and Sapporo boxes. Pink plastic shopping bags filled with who-knows. White plastic shopping bags filled with who-knows. Milk jugs and PVC pipes and cinder blocks, oh my.

The woman answering the door introduces herself as, "Heidi, I'm Pep's daughter. Come in. Excuse the mess."

The mess: layers of brittle plastic bags and brittle holiday face towels, yellowed plastic bottles and newspapers, dresses on hangers, and mugs, figurines, vinyl album covers, ukuleles, and chessboards. There is a heavy oak sideboard, there is a china cabinet. A framed and cobwebbed Jackson Pollock painting, a Steinway piano, and a full-size harp. Seagull art—metalwork, stuffed, stained glass, and beaded—takes the best places on walls and mantels.

Heidi leads me to a patch of decluttered space in the kitchen. "Water?"

"Sure."

"Tea? Coffee? It's freezing out there." She hands me a bottled water.

"No, thank you."

Heidi, a twinkle of a woman with sparkly blue eyes, shows me a picture of Paula, a woman with short silver hair and those same Caribbean blue eyes accented with shimmery turquoise eye shadow. The woman in this picture drinks lots of brown liquor and has a sandpaper laugh. She smells of crushed roses and Pall Malls.

"This feels . . ." Heidi shivers. "I don't like talking about Momma in past tense."

My eyes skip around in search of a place to land. "It's completely normal to feel that way." My gaze finally settles on the woman before me, and I smile. "It's in her nickname: Pep. I can tell she was a vibrant woman for nearly eighty years. The single day that death occurred shouldn't define her."

Heidi's eyes brighten with tears. "I'm so glad you said that."

During my walk here, I googled Paula Ellen Paulsen, a.k.a. Pep. She ran Pacific Treasures, the island's only thrift store. She'd been quoted in the *Avalon Breeze* as talk of demolishing the minigolf course overheated. "New folks hate the old things and want to tear it down. Us islanders cherish old things. They need to go back to LA, destructive sons of guns."

"Let's talk about that," I say.

Heidi finds a yellowed and framed newspaper article on the crowded dining room table. "She hated the developers and the real estate types. She led marches to protest the building of all the apartments that house workers. They were kicking people out of their houses and making them vacation rentals, so into apartments they went. Once she couldn't march anymore, she resisted another way."

I scribble and smile. "How?"

Heidi touches her brow. "Not sure if this should go in but . . . just like Momma collected junk? She collected secrets, too. Who was sleeping with who. Who ripped off who. And she let folks know that she knew."

My smile dims. "A dangerous trade, especially on a small island."

"Yeah. I wonder . . ." She rubs her temples, her eyes bouncing from thought to thought.

I wait.

She waggles her head a bit, then says, "She gave the most thoughtful gifts. She could tell what people would like and appreciate." She considers me. "Momma would get you . . . leather cubbies because you seem very organized."

I laugh. "I'd *love* leather cubbies."

I *am* organized, and the house on Beacon Street is an affront to my nature. No wonder I couldn't sleep last night.

"Is this the photo you'd like to use?" I ask.

Heidi is staring at me. She has the same floppy cheeks as her mother. Her eyes aren't rimmed in thick black liner and frosted eye shadow, but give her ten years. By then, her fingers will also shine with seagull-inspired costume jewelry just like the woman in this picture.

"Sorry for staring," Heidi says. "I remember you. It's been twenty years, but . . . I can't forget such a lovely face."

My cheeks flush. "Yes, I'm back. For now."

Our vacation rental is not too far from this house. So, yeah. Heidi would remember the one who survived.

"Momma thought it was the most evil thing that's ever happened here," Heidi says, "and that was the moment she wanted to leave this place."

My lips struggle—the purgatory smile returns—and I now want to end this interview.

"Momma reached out to you," Heidi says. "Did you know that?"

I frown, shake my head.

"She sent you little trinkets—a bracelet, a leather journal, and a pen . . . she didn't want you to think that we were all evil white people over here. And that's still very much true."

I stare at Heidi, then blink. A single hot teardrop plops from my eye and lands on the back of my hand. My stomach yaws from the stink of old and dead things, sweet and sour things, tangy things that smell of fetid cheese, macerated flowers, and chewed wood.

"Let's complete the form," I say.

Heidi answers the simplest questions first: length of residence in Avalon and schooling. She smiles as she remembers, then retrieves photo albums kept safe in the pantry. Light finds its way back into my heart as we flip through the albums. There's Pep, dressed as a sexy Mrs. Santa Claus. There's Pep, standing at the just-opened Pacific Treasures. Here are pictures of antique jars and a mink stole, a piggy bank made of crystal . . .

"I like your mom's eclectic collection," I say. "She and your dad look happy on these . . ."

"Antiquing trips," Heidi says, nodding. "England, Germany . . . Luxembourg once. She hated Luxembourg—it's a landlocked country. She enjoyed sea air. She loved living in a place with no traffic lights, no big-box stores, no smog."

Heidi squeezes her hands as she talks about Sunday mornings with her parents. They'd bicker about the store, then kiss and make up during Mutual of Omaha's *Wild Kingdom*.

"The hoarding got worse after Daddy died from a heart attack," Heidi shares. "At first, Momma refused to throw away his things, and then, *all* things became *his* things. I think she wanted to make the house ugly so that people couldn't make comps."

She pauses, then adds, "Momma knew what people were saying about her . . ." She stares at the tabletop, then sighs, shakes it off. "Anyway, you may have realized that renovations are even more expensive over here. We have a lumberyard, but it's small. Everything comes over on barges. Twenty years ago, the Flats were mostly residents who grew up here. Now, though, the houses are mostly vacation rentals.

"Mom's last protest was at a city council meeting. She wanted these Airbnb places restricted, but the city mothers and fathers think that less vacation rentals mean fewer tourists, and our saying here? 'Don't bite the visitors—they feed the locals.'"

"Not that I'm for this," I say, "but . . . why not build more?"

"Can't—island's protected. *And* there's a water problem. Limited access to fresh water. In other words, we were never supposed to be living on this piece of rock."

"Which is why *you* left," I say, nodding.

"Yeah." She goes back to rubbing her temples.

"We should complete the form," I say again, turning a page in my notepad.

Full name of deceased, birth date and death date, children, grandchildren.

Then: "How did your mother die?" I ask.

Heidi dabs at her eyes with a knuckle, then pushes out air. "After dinner back on last Friday, Momma took her evening hike over to the botanical garden, which she always does, and . . ." She splays her fingers across her chest. "She sat on that little stone bench by this ringed stone garden and . . . that's it. Hikers found her the next morning. She was dead."

"What happened?"

"The death certificate says, 'heart attack,' but she didn't *have* cardiac disease. I mean . . . your heart just doesn't *explode* without warning, right?"

My pen pauses. "No idea." Back to the form: "Was the garden her favorite place?"

"One of them. She loved going to the Casino Theater, but they closed it last year. It wasn't making a lot of money." Heidi taps her chin, shakes her head. "She'd been feeling good, y'know? The chemo was kinda kicking her ass, but she'd drink her concoctions, and she'd spend time out on the balcony . . . she tried to make the best of it."

"May I ask—what type of cancer?"

"Liver." Heidi wrings her hands and stares at the stiff curtains and the mounds of termite dust on the windowsill. "When Daddy died ten years ago, everything around here just went to shit. I begged her to sell and move overtown to Rancho Palos Verdes with me. It's still right by the ocean, and it's *nice*, y'know? She wouldn't have to worry about the city writing her citations about the trash. But no."

"She loved living here," I say. "It's a privilege to live on the island."

Heidi cocks an eyebrow. "Funny hearing you say that. After what this place did to you, what it *took* from you."

I chew the inside of my cheek, then say, "Fortunately, everyone's experience here is not like mine."

"And you've forgiven this place?" Heidi asks, squinting at me.

I open my mouth to say yes, but that isn't altogether true. Saying no isn't accurate because here I am. Instead, I say the truth. "Depends on the day and how lonely I'm feeling. Anyway. Your mom went for a walk. About what time was that?"

Heidi shrugs. "I talked to her around four. She told me that she and a friend were having dinner at five. I called her back at six thirty, but she texted that she was out walking and that she'd call me later." Tears shine in her eyes. "She never called."

I apologize again. "Anyone else you'd like me to talk to? For a quote or anecdote?"

Heidi, still in that rock garden with her mother, shakes her head.

"Going back to what you said about your mom collecting gossip. Did she . . . ?" My tongue twists and I force out my question. "Do you think she had a theory about what happened that night with my family . . . ?"

Heidi holds my gaze. "She kept a scrapbook." She looks over her shoulder at the mess beyond the kitchen nook. "It's somewhere out there . . ." Her shoulders sag. "Momma used to brag about this place being virtually crime-free, but then . . . she started locking her doors after that night. And she never believed that man they arrested was the murderer. She'd always say, 'Why would a Black man come to the whitest place in LA County to kill other Black people?' She'd say that a lot, and the wrong people heard that and didn't like her saying it. That's another reason she started hoarding."

"To protect herself," I say.

"You can't kill someone if you can't find them." Heidi pauses, then adds, "You know that firsthand."

After she signs the obituary request form, Heidi leads me to the front door.

"Did you request an autopsy, especially since she didn't have heart disease?" I ask.

Heidi's eyebrows meet. "No. I mean . . . she was old, y'know? What happens . . . it's God's will. And ultimately, I think it's a blessing."

"What will you do with the house?" I ask.

"The barbarians are at the gates. I'll give 'em what they want."

"And what about the store?"

Heidi shrugs, then chuckles. "Does Gwen want it? She's a magpie, too. She steals all the shiny shit, but then again, so do most museums, y'know?"

She touches the doorframe and taps a seagull wind chime. "Something good will come after all is said and done. It's a treasure, this old house. I know it's gonna bring some family visiting from Kentucky so much joy."

9.

So much to process, from Paula's interest in my family's ending to land grabs on an island of just four thousand people. Even back in Los Angeles, I'd heard people grumbling about investors buying houses, fixing them up, and converting them into Airbnb rentals, basically pricing people out of their own neighborhoods.

I'd love to read anything Heidi finds about that night in June. Sometimes I think I imagined it all, that I'm in a dream, my own *Inception* or *Matrix*, and my parents are standing over my bed right now, worried that I'll never make my way back to them.

Heidi said something else that's stayed with me.

You can't kill someone if you can't find them.

Hiding. Being too scared to . . .

What, Colette? Fight a murderer? You were a child.

Guilt is irrational, Dr. Tamaguchi has told me several times. Guilt demands ransom even though you're broke, and it demands that you keep it company even though it's fused to every molecule in your body. Guilt makes you scream, "What more do you want?" even though it's already taken everything, including your happily ever after.

In the end, hiding didn't work for Paula. She hoarded herself into a fortress, and death still found her. And her house will be rented out to that vacationing family from Kentucky.

Before then, though: How many junk-hauling trucks and plastic trash bags will they need to make that house make sense again? And once the trash is gone, what will Heidi find? Buckled walls held up by three sets of *Encyclopedia Britannica*? Rotten carpet hiding rotten floorboards and petrified rats? She said something good will come of it, but I'm not sure about that.

◆　◆　◆

It's refreshing to be out in the cold, wet air even though the streets are eerie and deserted.

Soggy tourists huddle in restaurants or wander from souvenir shops to pastry shop, muttering, "It's so dead here" and "We should've drove to Palm Springs," as they fumble with umbrellas and jackets.

I push open the front door to the newsroom. The TV across from my desk is on and turned to CNN. The chyrons beneath John King's head all relate to this strange flu bubbling across continents and landing in Washington State.

I settle at my desk. It's solid oak with drawers already stocked with pens, paper clips, legal pads, and bottles of Wite-Out. Maddy has also provided me with a docking station and monitor for my laptop. Multicolored pushpins on the corkboard hanging on the wall to the right of me spell WELCOME. From my bag, I pull out a small desk calendar of Shakespearean insults and a framed picture of my family and me parasailing over Cancun during the summer of 2000.

Does this mean that I'm staying?

I lean back in the rickety chair and push out a breath.

The last edition of the *Avalon Breeze* sits on my desk.

From "Continued Debate on the Avalon Housing Crisis" and "Runners Prep for Catalina Island Conservancy Marathon" to "Lancers Prepare for Season Starter with Bolsa Grande" and the ferry schedule on the last page.

The heater rattles above me. The rain patters against the windows. These are the sounds of a peaceful life.

Am I staying?

Without a ferry, do I have a choice?

I grab my notepad, then log on to my computer, ready to write my first obituary for *Avalon Breeze*.

Paula Ellen Paulsen—"Pep" to her friends—looks like she'd tell you a hella funny yet inappropriate joke about a rabbi and a hooker meeting at a bris. Then, she'd bake all the pies for the middle-school carnival.

My pen creeps across the legal pad—I haven't written an obituary in months. Between sips of coffee and peeks at the silent television, I write three drafts by hand, retype a fourth, then email the final draft to Maddy for approval.

And for a moment, I feel . . . normal, healthy, less troubled than last week.

My phone chimes—the *Jaws* theme.

Micah.

U don't think I see you?

I know what you're doing

I have people EVERYWHERE

You will never be alone

I snort, then text, Uh huh.

What infomercial audience member will you be playing today?

85

I'm not doing this with you Micah

Watch your back Colette

I respond with 👍.

I stare at my thumbs-up emoji and wait for his response. Micah rarely lets me have the last text. Nothing shits up my screen, though, and my mind creaks a little. Does he really mean that? People everywhere? Never being alone? I mutter, "I hate that man," then toss my phone to the desk.

Heavy rain still falls on the world past the newsroom's plate glass window.

I stare at the lock on the front door.

Do I have the right to lock that door?

Something's scratching in the supply room.

The motor of the copier whirs.

My heart jolts and I sit up in the chair. "Maddy?"

All this time, I thought I was alone.

On shaky legs, I tiptoe down the hallway.

Paper hits the copier tray.

Who's here?

Holding my breath, I peek into the supply room.

No one claims the sheets of paper piling in the tray.

Behind me, something *pops.*

I look back over my shoulder.

The TV's turned off.

My desk is now lost in the shadows.

Something is still scratching in this supply room.

To my right, golden light spills into the hallway.

"Maddy, is that you?" I move toward that light, following a trail of waterdrops dotting the hardwood floor.

Whispers—*jzzsh, jzzsh, jzzsh*—get louder as I move closer to the light.

Jzzsh, jzzsh, jzzsh.

I step into the room.

Maddy, with her earbuds in, works the handlebars of an elliptical machine. *Jzzsh, jzzsh, jzzsh.* Her mouth moves to whatever song's playing in her ears.

I exhale and sag with relief against the doorframe.

Maddy shouts, "Something wrong?"

"No," I shout back, tossing her a smile and a wave.

I return to my desk.

My pulse jumps.

My coffee cup is gone. The pens I just used are gone, too. The small waste can that was filled with three discarded drafts of Paula Paulsen's obituary has been emptied.

What the *hell*?

I have people EVERYWHERE. That's what Micah had texted moments ago.

I click on the desk lamp and open the drawer to grab another pen.

A folded map of Catalina Island.

Someone's written on a sticky note and stuck it to the map.

For the new girl. Open please.

I spread the map across my desk.

Bird Park and the botanical gardens are circled in black. And there's a third circle . . .

What do these markings signify?

And who left this map?

I hate anonymity. Say what you need to say instead of pussyfooting around.

"What's that?" Maddy peers over my shoulder. She smells of Icy Hot and sweat.

"No idea, but . . ." I tap the botanical gardens. "Mrs. Paulsen died here at the rock garden. This other site . . . no clue."

"Ah." Maddy dabs at her sweaty face with a paper towel, then checks her phone.

"You're not curious?" I ask.

Maddy's eyebrow quirks. "About?"

"Uhh . . ." I point at the map.

"Should I be?"

"What does it all mean?"

Maddy crumples the damp paper towel and drops it into my waste can. "No offense, but . . . I don't care."

I'm annoyed—by her funky trash and the way she's dismissed my curiosity.

"Two things," she says. "First, the kite festival and marathon are Saturday. Attend both, por favor. Take pictures and write two very short articles. That cool?"

"Got it." I enter the events into my calendar.

"Second thing," she says. "I'm on a smoothie run. Want me to bring something back?"

I shake my head. "Thanks, though."

Moving to the door, she turns back to say, "If you change your mind about a smoothie or a coffee or whatever, just text, okay?"

I give her a thumbs-up.

She leaves without a raincoat or an umbrella, wearing only workout clothes.

I turn back to the map and that third circle.

A house on Middle Terrace.

That's the house where my family—

"Excuse me?" A woman's voice.

I yelp and spin around in my chair, once again thinking that I was alone.

A young Latina with long curly hair pushes up her glasses and glances at the map in my hands. She's holding a spray bottle and a dustrag. "Didn't mean to scare you. Miss Maddy doesn't like seeing trash, so I'm always emptying the wastebaskets."

I exhale, then grin. So the sudden clean desk wasn't a supernatural act. "I'm Coco. I just started working here today."

The young woman glances toward the front door. "Yes, I know."

"And you are . . . ?"

"Yesenia Duran. I work here, too. Cleaning."

"I'm the new reporter. Well, I write the obituaries and events stuff."

Her eyes brighten behind her glasses. "So you *are* gonna write about them?"

My smile falters. "Write about . . . *who*?"

"The old women. No one's talking about them. Seems like every other week, someone else dies. He hacks them up, and he eats them. That's what I heard. The sheriffs aren't doing anything about it, either."

"You're saying . . ." I squint at her. "That there's a cannibal killer in Avalon?"

She blinks at me. "Maybe. But that's your job, right? Writing about the dead women?"

I chuckle. "I'm writing about dead folks, but I'm not *investigating* their deaths. That's not my beat. *But!* If you want an obituary or a piece written about an upcoming community event, then . . ." I point at my chest, then pull fake suspenders. "I'm your girl."

Yesenia doesn't laugh. "Just . . . be careful, and please look out for Gwen. They say—"

"*Who* says?"

"People. They say he only does it in the rain."

"Does *what* in the—"

"Success!" Maddy pops into the newsroom with two purple smoothies. "Dude, I totally forgot that it's raining. I brought you one just in case you changed your mind."

Yesenia wipes down the desk across from mine. She avoids my eyes.

Maddy's talking about the ferry, the rain, the canceled fun run for the elementary school.

I nod and say, "Got it," and "Wow," even though I'm thinking about Yesenia's warning.

Look out for Gwen?

And . . . *He eats them.*

And . . . *He only does it in the rain.*

Does *what* in the—

Maddy snaps her fingers in my face. "Hello, hello, hello?" When I blink at her, she snorts. "Coco's distracted again."

I snort. "Excuse me?"

She sips her smoothie. "You and your little fugues—you blank out and then wake up with a broken mug and Micah's blood all over your hands."

I laugh and roll my eyes. "Mug mayhem only happens on Fridays."

"I'm just concerned. Don't want you . . . *disappearing* on me." Already the color of cranberries, she's darkening to match the color of her smoothie.

I force myself to smile. "I'm good. I'm here, and I appreciate your care. A lot is going on right now. This weird map and Paula Paulsen's house and Micah's newest threat—"

"*What?*"

I show her Micah's text messages. "*And* Harper Hemphill is out of jail."

Maddy gasps. "Oh no."

"The blood on that knife wasn't his. He didn't do it."

Maddy gapes at me and tugs the neck of her wet T-shirt. "That means . . ."

"The monster's still out there. Yeah. I'm . . . gonna keep it together, though. I'm gonna figure it out." I clear my throat and offer her a weak smile.

Her shoulders droop. "I'm so sorry. I'm here for you, okay?"

"I know." My eyes shift to the latest draft of Paula Paulsen's obituary. An effective distraction from Harper Hemphill and his newfound freedom.

Yesenia's anxiety about old women dying on the island seems . . . *weird?* Death comes for the sick, for the old, for the sick and old who decide to hike three miles and find rest in a rock garden. Denial—that's what Yesenia's experiencing, and that's part of the grieving process.

I think of all the interviews I've conducted. Loved ones left behind always say, *She was healthy,* and *He had a target on his back,* and *She shouldn't have died like that.* Page after page of denial held together by a single weary stapler.

Seems like every other week, someone else dies.

He eats them.

But Paula Paulsen wasn't eaten. Heidi would've mentioned that.

Still . . .

Who are these old women?

Maddy's still talking about being there for me when I notice a man standing in front of the plate glass window.

He's wearing soggy jeans and a hoodie, and his hands are cupped at both sides of his face as he peers into the office. He's looking right at me.

Panic rips through my heart.

He backs away from the window, points at me, then makes gun fingers at his temple. He laughs, then shambles east toward the harbor.

Without thinking, I dart to the front door and out into the street.

Maddy calls out, "What's wrong?"

But the man is gone now, melted away like spun sugar in heavy rain.

10.

How would Micah know where to send one of his "people"?

Well . . . there's only one paper on the island, and, therefore, my most likely employer. He could've called Gwen or our landlord, who has my new address. And who are his "people"? Fellow bit actors who play crazy on TV and now have the chance to play crazy in real life? He pushed me enough, gaslighted me enough, that I played crazy in real life, too.

Like . . . the time I sat in a pile of trash I'd dumped on our bed.

Like . . . the time I bought bags of cat food and wept about losing the cat. (We didn't have a cat.)

Like . . . not speaking—not one word—to anyone for a week.

All to freak Micah out.

All to push him away for good.

And playing crazy worked . . . he freaked out, and he left for good, and my playing crazy landed me in court-appointed therapy.

Ha ha, joke was on you, Judge Cramer. I was already *in* therapy. Poor Dr. Tamaguchi will have to deal with me until she retires. Which means . . . poor *rich* Dr. Tamaguchi.

Anyway, whoever this man at the window was, he's long gone.

Maddy blinks at me as I settle back at my desk. "You good?"

I dry my face with a bunch of tissues. "He wants me to lose my mind."

"He . . . ?"

"Micah." I tap the space bar on my laptop. "He's just being . . . Micah."

I'm not scared of him. I've faced the worst and survived.

Maddy slurps her smoothie, then says, "I looked at Pep's obituary. Good job. Send it to Heidi for final approval."

I do, and then, I check the paper's general inbox for emails.

Almost time for Avalon kindergarten registration—Maddy will want me to take that one.

Time for Avalon school sports spring season—I'll take that one, too.

Public hearing . . . public hearing . . . citation appeal hearing . . . knitting club meeting . . .

Sheriff's log.

I pause and cock my head at this weekly report from the Avalon Sheriff's Station. Maddy curates this section of the paper.

Narcotics warrant . . . child neglect . . . overturned golf cart . . . missing dogs . . .

I click onto the *Breeze's* website and find From the Blotter, the column that lists these crimes around Avalon. Were the murders of my family mentioned?

Nope. The logs go back only to 2012.

"Sea Eyes" had been the island's previous public safety section and captured only water-related incidents. In the June–July 2001 archives, there are no mentions of the Weber family slaughter. The entire island heard about it midday the next day. The shocking news story then played on West Coast television for weeks, and the crime became a blemish on the island paradise's sheriff's department blotter typically filled with overturned golf carts, DUIs, and domestic assaults.

Before leaving the newsroom for the day, I look around for Yesenia.

She isn't wiping down the elliptical machine, nor is she washing the coffeepot. She needs to do some explaining. She can't tell me to "watch out for Gwen" and effin' *bounce.*

But that's exactly what she's done.

The map of the island now lives in my bag, and as I stroll down Metropole Avenue through the misty rain, my fingers tug at the map's corners. Those black-marker circles—I know why the rock garden is circled. I know why the house on Middle Terrace is circled, too. But not Bird Park.

What happened at Bird Park?

The mix of ocean and golf-cart gas fumes makes me queasy. Laughter drifts from back porches and side yards, and I smell grilled meat and baking cakes. My stomach rumbles since I've eaten nothing more solid for lunch than cream in my coffee.

Micah would hate living here.

Too many tourists.

This place is so boring.

Why does everything cost so much?

But then, he also hated our apartment in Beverly Grove.

Why is everything so expensive?

It's so loud on this block.

What happened to you?

You used to be fun.

Why did you make me move here?

As though I forced him to sign the lease at gunpoint.

It was my fault that he parked his car on the street despite the warnings—and someone broke into that car and stole his favorite jacket.

It was also my fault that someone stole his jeans and shirts out of the laundry room dryer.

According to Micah, his star hasn't ascended across Hollywood's sky because *I* convinced the one showrunner friend I have that Micah can't act his way out of a soap bubble.

Toward the end of our relationship, I apologized for every calamity he faced just to make him shut up, just to make him move on, just to let us . . . *be*. But then, guilt bubbled on my back like a tortoise's shell, and I moved just as slow.

Now, I'm breathing heavy, and I'm walking faster, damn near running.

Micah thoughts.

The pink Hotel St. Lauren, with its white trim and wrought iron balconies, brightens as I move closer. The scent of warm vanilla urges me to stop into a café, any café, grab the menu, and order every third dessert listed.

I don't stop—but I *do* smile.

If I stay in Avalon, I'll take this vanilla-scented walk every day. Yeah, pastry-scented living with more walks and trips outside and breathing cleaner air and . . .

Footsteps tap behind me.

I look over my shoulder.

A man with stringy hair walks with his eyes on his phone.

Up ahead, another man leans against a raggedy golf cart, lighting a cigarette.

Either could pass for the man who'd stood in the *Breeze*'s window.

Just in case, I grip the Swiss Army knife in my pocket and cross the street.

The man near the cart says something that I can't hear over my hammering heart.

Dr. Tamaguchi's voice plays in my mind. *Stand your ground, Colette.*

But the survivor in me—her voice is louder. *Run, girl, run!*

I compromise and pop into the bright-pink hotel. Stepping into the St. Lauren is like stepping back into 1978. The oak check-in desk, gold-framed hotel art, and rose-print upholstery remind me of a church mother's room. From the entrance, I see the ocean, and most important, the empty streets. No one loiters or lurks, waiting for me on the corner.

I catch my breath and return to Beacon Street.

Alone. Again.

No need to pull out my little knife.

Let's keep it that way, Avalon.

◆　◆　◆

The front door is closed and locked today.

Wonderful. Never been so happy to use a key.

With my breath a shallow puddle in my chest, I charge into the house.

Up in the living room, an actress talks about the power of Tide Pods.

I take the stairs going down and pull out my phone.

The line to Dr. Tamaguchi rings . . . and rings . . .

A woman answers, but her voice is too high and too young to be my therapist.

"May I speak with Dr. Tamaguchi, please? It's Colette Weber."

"Just to let you know," the receptionist says, "Dr. Tamaguchi's about to board a plane to Tokyo in about an hour."

That's a twelve-hour flight. She won't be reachable until almost three tomorrow morning.

"Do you need to talk to someone else?" the receptionist asks. "You in crisis right now?"

The phone carves into my hand because I'm holding it so tight.

"Hello? Miss Weber?"

"Yes. Umm . . . I need to talk to *her*."

"I'll try. Maybe she has a moment. Please hold."

I exhale through clenched teeth.

My phone vibrates. A text from Chase, some guy I'd hooked up with after *Hamilton* at the hotel club across the street from the Pantages.

Let's meet up again

I thought I'd blocked him.

I clench the phone even tighter.

"Colette," Dr. Tamaguchi says out of nowhere.

I block Chase, then say, "Dr. Tamaguchi, hi!" I sound more cheerful than I feel.

"I didn't see you at our regular time back on Friday."

"Oh. Yeah. Well . . ." I rub my damp hand on my jeans, then settle onto the lumpy couch.

"You know you can't miss too many sessions," she says. "Judge Cramer won't be happy—"

"I had a few things to do," I say.

"She already thinks you're trying to pull one over on her."

"I'm not," I say. "I moved to Avalon, just as we discussed. So I'm not avoiding you. I just got caught up in packing."

"Oh, congratulations. I think that's a brave step. How's the sleeping?"

"Okay." A smile cracks the edges of my mouth. "No random men have found their way into my bed. I didn't sleep well last night, though, but it was my first night on the island since 2001, and the conditions of this house are not . . . *ideal*. And then, there are other things."

Dr. Tamaguchi says, "And those other things?"

"Harper Hemphill has been freed from prison."

"It wasn't his blood."

"No, and Micah—I think he knows now. About our marriage certificate."

Her breath sharpens. "And his reaction?"

"A little threatening, but I still feel in control. For now."

Something in my voice, though, makes Dr. Tamaguchi sigh. "Oh, Colette."

"I think my aunt and I are safer together. But I need to decide something. Maybe you can help." As I pace the small living room, I tell her that I'm stuck between staying on the island with a possible murderer or returning to Los Angeles.

"Your gut's telling you . . . what?" she asks. "Then, weigh that against the facts."

Silence crackles through the line.

I frown. "That's . . . *it*?"

"Do what makes you feel safest," Dr. Tamaguchi adds. "Even if that means moving to Atlanta or Colorado, somewhere without a threat of violence, from you or from him."

"Which 'him'? The murderer or Micah?"

"Either, Colette. Both."

This isn't helpful. "I need to go feed my aunt now," I say, underwhelmed.

"Colette," Dr. Tamaguchi says, "we need to talk more about Micah. If he gets to Avalon somehow, what will you do?"

"If Gwen doesn't eat," I say, "she can't take her medications."

"Let's unpack this," she says. "After I hang up, I'm on a twelve-hour flight to Tokyo."

"Have a great trip. We'll talk when you get back." I press END CALL and toss the phone on the couch.

Hopefully, when she's back in the States, I'll still be a free woman . . . and alive.

My life right now resembles Paula Paulsen's house—junky and speckled with treasures lost in piles of useless and priceless crap. The old woman also experienced great loss; then she'd started collecting everything, throwing nothing away so that she could fill those empty spaces in her heart.

I've filled my own empty spaces with words, men, and guilt.

Maybe Paula Paulsen's solution works better.

My mind wanders to my family, and to the detective in charge of our case.

Martin Gaines had kept me in the loop during that first year but was then transferred to another unit after he'd been caught falsifying evidence.

Who replaced him?

Gwen sits in her armchair, watching *Family Feud* and pawing through a tub of scarves.

"Auntie?"

On TV, Steve Harvey asks, "Tell me a word that rhymes with 'election.'"

"Erection," Gwen says.

"Erection," blushing Brian of the Klosky clan says.

Gwen cackles and waves a green-and-yellow scarf at the TV.

"Auntie," I say louder, "where are your case files?"

"Somewhere over there." Gwen points at boxes stacked beneath a hanging dream catcher. "Perfection. Somebody say 'perfection.'"

"That's a big collection," I say, nodding at the scarves.

"Ooh, collection! That rhymes, too." She pulls a pink-and-green scarf from the tub. "This one's from one of your snooty sorority sisters who called me 'ghetto' and 'low class.' And this one"—a jewel-colored Hermès—"came from some bitch who accused me of stealing her scarf."

I point to the scarf. "Stealing *that* scarf?"

Gwen laughs and throws the Hermès scarf into the air.

"I visited with Paula Paulsen's daughter, Heidi," I say.

"For what?" Gwen's back to sorting through the tub.

"Paula died."

Gwen pauses, then says, "Some of that crap in the house finally fall on her?"

I tell her about Paula's last evening alive. "Heidi mentioned that her mother had sent me care packages back then."

Gwen cocks her head. "I don't remember that. But who knows? It was a crazy time back then. I was trying to keep both of us together."

I say, "Yeah," doubtful that she's unable to remember. Doubtful that she tried to keep us together, since I'd overheard a phone call to Aunt Odie about me moving in with my Southern relatives. "You know how I feel about all this," Aunt Gwen said, "about raising a teenager I don't even *like*." But then, Gwen didn't like *any* teenagers, she explained once she found me crying in bed. "I didn't like *me* growing up," she'd said, laughing.

Years later, I turn to the boxes beneath the dream catcher and find familiar-looking documents that our attorney, Ted, shared long ago.

Summary sheets from the medical examiner for each slain member of my family.

Weber, Reginald Age: 44 years old

Findings—

I flip past that.

Radio Traffic Transcript

Officer (17): That him?

Officer (?): Not sure if it's him or not. But he's just standing there. Stand by.

Officer (17): Black male wearing a blue shirt. That's gotta be him.

I remember this . . .

Crime Laboratory Analysis Report—7/1/2001

VICTIM: Weber, Alyson

Specimen Q1

Description: Victim Weber's pink T-shirt with reddish-brown stains throughout and several apparent holes.

Narrative: Examination disclosed the presence of blood. A swabbing (Q1-1) of the nonstained areas was retained for trace.

I flip to the last page.

ALSO SUBMITTED

Sealed evidence envelope containing paper bag from suspect Hemphill's left hand

Sealed evidence envelope containing paper bag from suspect Hemphill's right hand

Swabs, fingernail clippings . . .

Where's the sheet listing the knife?

My skin turns to gooseflesh as I remember these days and months after the murders. Going back to church with Gwen and feeling nothing as people seated on the pews around me sang about a merciful

God, the mighty fortress that He is, the watchful Shepherd. I'd become the embodiment of sorrow for my church family, a representation of "the worst it could get," until two planes crashed into the World Trade Center two months after my family's murders.

I flip through the pages and then turn to the box, in search of that piece of evidence that was lost but then found months ago. But I find only old bank statements, tax returns, junk mail, school announcements, and menus from our favorite Thai restaurants and barbecue joints back in Los Angeles.

"Gwen," I say, "how did they find the knife? Where had it been all that time?"

The old woman is now snoring lightly.

Who took over the case after Gaines was booted?

I close my eyes and search my mental Rolodex for a name, for a face . . . olive skinned . . . name ended with a vowel . . . tacos . . . I open my eyes. "Delveccio. Alan Delveccio." During the trial, I'd always think "Del Taco" anytime he said his name. He'd worn mirrored sunglasses and a lot of cologne, chewed gum as he talked, and talked fast.

We're gonna nail this guy, the detective promised Gwen during our first meeting with him. *I'll work this case till it drops his ass onto that padded table up in San Quentin. Swear it on my mother's grave.*

A quick internet search tells me that he retired last year and now runs a gym in Manhattan Beach. I call the number listed, and the receptionist puts me on hold.

Seven minutes later, the line clicks, and a man says, "Delveccio here."

I introduce myself, then remind him that he handled my family's case twenty years ago, that there'd been movement on the case, and that Harper Hemphill had been freed from prison.

"Oh yeah," Detective Delveccio says. "I remember you now. You're the Webster girl, right? You hid in the closet. *You* told us it was Hemphill."

"*Weber*. Actually, I didn't *say* it was Hemphill. I said Hemphill was on the *patio*."

The former detective snorts. "Sure. Okay." He snorts again, then adds a chuckle. I tell him that no one's ass is on a padded table at San Quentin.

"Yeah," he says now. "Sucks about Hemphill. Damn shame. All that work we did down the toilet."

"Down the toilet" because Hemphill was released or because he was wrongly convicted?

Delveccio pauses, then asks, "You doing okay, though? Still seeing that shrink?"

"Dr. T? Now and forever." I clear my throat, then ask, "Who has the case now?"

"What case— Hey, you wanna not drop the weights like that?" He covers the phone with his hand. Muffled words—he's talking to someone else. Then: "Sorry. What case?"

"My family's. If the murderer is still free, the case reopens, yes?"

Delveccio says nothing for a long time, and then, "Sure."

"So what happens now?" I ask, tugging at him through the phone. "Because technically, it's a cold case. Justice still needs to be served."

"Right. Hey—" More muffled conversation with someone other than me.

"Could you tell me how I'd find that detective?" I squeeze my eyes closed to keep the dragon within me tamed.

"No idea. Everybody I worked with is gone. Guess you could talk to someone at the Avalon station. I wouldn't get your hopes up, though. You all made the island look bad back then. Kicking up dirt again— that's not gonna fly, I can tell you that right now, especially with social media making shit viral. There's no murder in Paradise."

But there *is* a serpent.

"Hey," the retired detective says, "I gotta go. Thanks for checking in, Miss Webster."

"*Weber.* One more question—"

He hangs up.

Silence.

He doesn't care. He can't even get my name right. He has no burning need to right wrongs and to seek justice, to answer the questions:

Who killed my family? Have they killed since then?

Maybe they have, but no one's connected those murders to my family. Maybe if I looked into these recent deaths around the island—*every other week, someone else dies*—I can figure out if there's a connection. Maybe the monster who's allegedly *eating* people and dognapping schnauzers has blended on the island for so long that no one suspects them.

Maybe this is the worst idea I've had since spraying pepper spray into the dirt, only for it to bounce back into my eyes.

I don't know . . .

I have to do *something*.

Because I've already lived my adult life clenched—and that was when I thought the killer was behind bars. But now that I know he's not? That I may still be in danger? I've become an armadillo ball again, holding like that for so long that I can't enjoy sunshine, can't eat, can't love. I'm just waiting for the threat to pass.

So yeah: I *must* do something. And if shit gets crazy, I'll freakin' . . . *swim* back to LA and live in one Residence Inn after the other. As for Micah, if he decides to come for me, then . . .

I don't know . . . again. But I do know this:

Right now, I'm the only one who cares about the Weber family murders.

Fate is working now—there's a reason I can't buy a ticket to return to Los Angeles.

I'm the one who survived, and that must count for something . . .

Right?

The Obituary of
Paula Ellen Paulsen

January 3, 1941–March 6, 2020

If you believe that the heel of a loaf of bread is tasteless, or that beef shank is good only for soup, stop for a moment and think of Paula Ellen Paulsen. Known as "Pep," the longtime resident of Avalon loved tough bread and tough meat. Her favorite saying: "Give it some love and it'll fill your belly and get you through life's bullshit."

Pep gave many throwaway items much-needed love. The handmade Navajo eagle dancer she found in a dumpster now sits on her Steinway piano. The tarnished gold miniature diving helmet key chain left on a park bench at the botanical gardens forty years ago still holds the keys to her house and storage units. Herman "Manny" Paulsen—she found him on a wintry December in 1963. He'd finished a tour in Vietnam, and his then girlfriend (and ride home from the bus station) didn't show up. Pep had come to pick up her brother, who was returning home from the war. But she also had room in the car for his now-deserted best buddy Manny. After that day, Pep gave Manny plenty of love until his death on September 22, 2010. Together for forty-seven years, they got through life's bullshit, including the death of their first child, Richard;

the birth of their twins, Heidi and Harold; the opening of her thrift shop, Pacific Treasures; and the construction of their house in Avalon.

After the devastating Catalina fire in 2007, Pep sought to give love to many throwaway things. Antique skeleton keys. Silver pocket watches. Vintage caviar pillboxes hand-painted in France. Amber bracelets. Framed butterflies.

Her smallest collection: children and grandchildren. Heidi (Lars and son, Timothy) and Harold (Kathleen and daughters, Jenna and Molly). After several courses of chemotherapy to treat her liver cancer, Pep suffered a heart attack at her favorite place on the island and has now reunited with Manny. Rumor has it that she's resumed her acquisition of heavenly collectibles.

On Thursday, March 12, friends can visit with Pep's family at VFW Island Outpost on 180 Pebbly Beach Road. Mass of the Christian Burial will be celebrated at 11:00 a.m., Friday, March 13, at Saint Catherine of Alexandria. Bring your least favorite canned food for the food drive to benefit the Lord's Cupboard Food Pantry.

11.

So. We're gonna stay.

I log off the Catalina Express website since I no longer need to know the ferry's schedule. We won't leave immediately, not anymore. And even though I know only two people here—Maddy and Aunt Gwen—folks seem friendly.

This *is* my house, after all, and yeah, it's drafty, and it's rattly, and it's slowly disappearing each day into a vortex of chaos and crazy, *but!* I'm young, and I'm smart, and I can read instructions, and I can watch home-repair videos. I'll work at the *Avalon Breeze*, and maybe do some kind of side hustle—obit writing for the funeral home here. I will retrieve the boxes from the post office, grab the diamond ring out of the unicorn's ass, sell that ring, send a third to Micah (maybe he'll leave me alone then), and use the rest for projects, including *zhuzhing* up Gwen's cart. I'll have enough money to turn this house back into the beauty that it used to be. My parents would want that.

So, yeah. I'm staying here for them, too.

I grill hamburgers for dinner. The meaty smoke mixes with the damp air, and I mean . . . When was the last time I *grilled*? Better living already.

The wire grate that Handy Andy was supposed to fix is still open. If he doesn't fix it tomorrow, then I will. There must be a YouTube video somewhere on fixing crawl spaces.

◆ ◆ ◆

Gwen looks dignified in her yellow tracksuit. The FRIENDS OF AVALON name tag she wears catches light, and for a moment I'm proud of my civic-minded aunt. But my pride immediately shifts to suspicion, and I wonder if she's hiding a stolen Beverly Jenkins romance in her bra.

She isn't saying much right now. Just takes apart her burger, then nibbles the bacon. Finally: "Okay."

I blink at her. "That's it?"

She chews as she stares at me. "And what will you do when you find the killer?"

I grin. "You obviously have confidence in me because you just said, 'when' and not 'if.' Thanks, Auntie!"

Her eyes flare with anger. "Be serious for once."

My smile becomes a scowl, and I swallow the fire burning up my throat. "I'm not gonna do any citizen's arrest or nothing crazy like that. I'm gonna partner with whoever's the captain here, and I'll let *them* do all that. I'll just focus on the investigatory work. I can't just . . . *sit* here and do *nothing*."

"Hmph." She bites into her beef patty without joy.

"Where are the other boxes with the case files?" I ask. "You had three or four."

"They're in your parents' bedroom," Aunt Gwen says.

That's the primary suite at the end of the hallway. One of the closed doors that I've yet to open. If I'm gonna find the murderer, though, I'll have to open *that* door, at least.

Tomorrow.

"Don't cross anybody," she says. "I'm not tryin' to die in this house."

"I'm not trying to die in this house, neither." My scowl tightens, and my breath comes hot through my nose. "You really have a gift, Auntie." A virtuoso at making me feel like crap.

She mutters something, then takes her plate over to the armchair and TV tray. She aims the remote at the television and finds *Wheel of Fortune*. She snatches her phone from the tray and taps out a text message like a sullen teenager. What is she texting to Dee Dee? OMG I hate her sooooooo much grrrrr!!!!!

"Do you need anything else?" I ask.

She ignores me and focuses on the puzzle. It's a phrase:

$$\_\,\_\,Y\,\_\,N$$

$$\_\,\_\,D$$

$$\_\,\_\,\_\,\_\,U\,\_$$

"Day in and day out." I ignore Gwen's glare and take my burger and seltzer water out to the front porch and settle on the wet wood.

Fog drifts along Beacon Street. Out on the ocean, lights from marine vessels blink. Somewhere in Avalon, a monster is brushing his teeth or making a bologna-and-cheese sandwich for his loved ones . . .

Somewhere on the mainland, my ex paces on a beach, gnashing his teeth and snarling his snarls, his plans to destroy me foiled by the biggest body of water on the planet.

Thick splinters from the deck stick through my leggings to prick the backs of my thighs. But that's how I know that I'm alive.

"Okay, so I'm not a cop or anything," I tell Dr. Tamaguchi's voice mail. "Nor do I know this island. But somebody's gotta find out what happened the night they were taken from—"

The voice mail beeps and the recorded voice says, "Thank you."

My phone chatters.

How's it going? Maddy texts.
I'm good, I text back.

Healthy

Still keeping it together

Look at me

I send her a selfie of me sitting on the porch along with a video of
dark Beacon Street.
Is this a good thing or a depressing thing? she asks.
Yes! I text back, laughing.

You know what's missing from this picture?

You are vulgar—and yes

Gimme time tho

Only been here a full day

What's his face from Hamilton texted me

You forgot to block him???

I did forget but then I hit that BLOCK

Anybody on this island do weaves?

Gwen braids but she doesn't do the weaving part

Don't let Gwen braid your hair!!

She used to light your scalp on fire!

Gwen *did* have a heavy hand, and my braids would yank at my scalp.

She just didn't want them falling out, I text Maddy.

Sure. Okay.

I just won't go swimming

The weight of water will weaken my tracks then I'll have to explain weaves to whatever white boy I'll soon victimize lol

Back in the house, Gwen turns the shower knobs. I can hear the bathroom pipes rumble as hot water travels through the house.

Maybe I'll record my progress—a real-time home-improvement project combined with a personal journey and search for the killer. Maybe there's a book in there somewhere.

There's a book on the table already.

Oh. Yeah. I haven't called the agent back. It's not like I *have* to—I didn't reach out to her in the first place, nor have I taken any money yet.

I find Andrea Liszl's number, and her line rings until voice mail takes over. "Hi, Andrea. It's Colette Weber. Let's talk about this project this week. I've been thinking a lot about it, and now that I'm back in Avalon, I think there's great promise in it. Looking forward to chatting."

This will be hard—staying here, living with Gwen, working a full-time job, finding the monster who changed my life . . .

So many pebbles to turn over just to make sense of it all.

But I have time.

12.

My phone's clock says that it's now ten minutes after one, but that can't be right, because the lamp shines bright, and a pen is in my hand, and there are sticky notes on the wall in the crude order of which house repairs to do myself and which house repairs deserve the expertise of Handy Andy.

Sticky Note 1: *pipes (H.A.)*
Sticky Note 2: *electrical (H.A.)*
Sticky Note 3: *woodwork (H.A.)*
Sticky Note 4: *painting (me and H.A.)*

Other task-related sticky notes: throw out expired food, throw out nasty linens and towels, buy new sconces and area rugs, light switches and a better broom, a hammer, nails, curtains. Buy a bed headboard. Buy good art and matching silverware and fruit fly traps . . .

Mom also made lists, and after I went through her things years after her death, I found a few in her favorite tote bag: steno pad sheet of Christmas-card recipients (*Gwen wasn't listed*), a torn-out notepad listing ingredients that could've made a bomb (*hydrogen peroxide, duct tape, and white vinegar*), and a sticky note bulleting someone's personality quirks (*too stubborn, prideful, stops listening after three seconds*).

Was Mom writing about Dad? Gwen?

And did *Gwen* intentionally braid my hair too tight? And what would Maddy know about Black hair care anyway?

The hardwood floor beneath my feet creaks now as I walk back and forth, adding notes and moving notes.

My eyes burn since I haven't been able to close them.

At two thirty, I turn off the lamp and fall back onto the mattress. Sleep is a cobweb in the highest part of a cathedral ceiling. I can reach it . . . I'm almost . . . there . . .

Plip . . . plip . . . plip . . . right outside the garden-facing window.

Right now, that plipping is the loudest sound in the world.

I peek into the garden.

Its tawny head lowered, a deer drinks from a puddle. The drizzle wets her coat and makes her shimmer, makes her magic.

I watch her for a moment before crawling back to the mattress. I take a deep breath and close my eyes.

There is no television in my bedroom because there is no cable box down here. There is no internet, so there is no streaming on my computer unless I use my phone's hot spot. But my phone isn't charging because the electrical system in this house is *old as fuck*.

I could go on a walk through the neighborhood . . . the dark, dark neighborhood . . . the cold and dark neighborhood haunted by strangers, deer, and possibly my ex-husband, who was never legally my husband, haunted by the monster who murdered my family . . .

Plip . . . plip . . . plip . . .

Is that deer still drinking?

I crawl back over to the garden window and peek out again.

She's gone.

Plip . . . plip . . . plip . . .

I try to squint past the halo of white streetlight.

What's out there in the darkness?

Who's out there in the darkness?

◆ ◆ ◆

After making oatmeal for Aunt Gwen, I find Handy Andy's phone number written on a slip of paper beneath a Caesars Palace refrigerator magnet. The ink has almost faded—if I breathe too hard on the paper, the number will disappear. So I hold my breath and resolve to call him at a reasonable hour.

There's a voice mail on my phone left by Pam Robins. Guess she'd called as I showered. *"Thanks for your message. I'm glad to hear everything's okay. Let's check in later this week."*

I find Gwen in her armchair, and I kiss the top of her head. "I need to take your cart—I'm picking up some of my boxes from the post office."

She opens her big Bible to Ezekiel, then pulls on glasses too big for her face. "Extra key is in the knife drawer." She grabs my hand. "Don't ever take a fence down until you know why it was put up."

I squint at her. "Wow. Yours?"

She sucks her teeth. "Girl, that's Robert Frost." Then, she aims the remote at the TV and finds a rerun of the original *Let's Make a Deal.*

What does she mean by this, though? I'm not making major changes to the house or altering the way she's lived. But then, she and Dad quoted random things all the time, their favorite being, "Use your enemy's hand to catch a snake."

After wiping off dust, cobwebs, and dead leaves, I slide into the driver's seat of Gwen's cart and turn the ignition.

To my surprise, the engine purrs. The cart's not as beat up as it looks.

There is no big-box store like Home Depot or Lowe's on Catalina Island. Chet's Hardware is open, and its inventory of appliances, home-improvement tools, and cleaning supplies makes my bleary eyes happy. I drag myself from aisle to aisle—hammers and nails there, and trash bags and mops and brooms there. Dad didn't do much home repair, so I know almost nothing about building or fixing. I grab interior-decorating magazines for inspiration, and then, I grab caulk, a screwdriver, and air freshener. I snag three lavender candles to combat the headache banging above my eyebrows.

In line in front of me, a tall man wearing a jogging suit pushes a basket filled with face masks, latex gloves, six cans of Lysol spray, industrial-size jugs of bleach, and Mr. Clean.

Did he just cut up his girlfriend in his bathroom?

A man wearing paint-splattered whites snorts as he also scrutinizes Clean Freak's shopping cart. "You really falling for this virus nonsense?"

"This nonsense is real," Clean Freak says. "My cousin up in Spokane? You met him last year at the parade? He says the hospital beds in Washington are full. That it looks just like the movies."

The painter rolls his eyes. "Fake news, my friend."

The news stories I've seen have shown researchers wearing bunny suits peering into microscopes, and physicians wearing bunny suits peering into patients' throats, and all of it looks like a Hollywood movie, like the one starring Dustin Hoffman or the other one with Gwyneth Paltrow. I hop out of line and grab the last can of Lysol spray along with a pack of gloves and face masks. Can never be too careful.

No one's in line at the post office, and ten minutes later, six of my boxes mailed from Los Angeles are stacked into the cart.

It takes me another ten minutes to carry each up the steps, then down to my bedroom. My knees burn. Sweat streams down my back. I'm reminded to find a gym or fitness class sooner rather than later.

I find the unicorn in the bottom of the "Coco's Junk" box. I tear away the loosely sewn stitch in her ass, then pull out the diamond-and-ruby ring.

I whisper, "Gorgeous," as it sparkles in the light. How much will I get for it?

Back into the unicorn's ass it goes.

I pull from the hardware store bag the most expensive purchase from this morning: a hot spot that allows me to connect to ten devices. Paying for data by the month will cost a lot, but then I'll be able to work at home while the house gets rewired.

I pluck that "Get hot spot" sticky note off the wall, then rush out of the house to start my second full day at *Avalon Breeze*.

Rain clouds still sit over Paradise. Puddles are growing into lakes, some with purple oily sheens that spin and kaleidoscope with the reflection of the heavy sky.

A woman with a closed fist for a face sits at the reception desk. Phone to her ear, she tells the caller, "That GD flipper came back this morning, askin' to buy my house. Why? So that some asshole from Miami can dig up the ferns? I worked hard on those ding-dang ferns."

The office smells of fresh-brewed coffee and Icy Hot. Maddy's been working out on the elliptical machine again. I follow her voice down the hallway to her office. She's on the phone. An acai bowl sits untouched before her, but the berry smoothie is almost gone. She smiles and waves at me.

I settle at my desk behind the receptionist and pop an Advil chased by a pull of coffee. Now on the road to wellness, I check my email. No email.

Does Maddy have an onboarding process with sessions on time off, piracy, and sexual harassment? Do I need to complete a W-9? Show proof of identity to work in the US? She hasn't asked for my Social Security number. How often is payday?

I check the calendar of events. Across the street at the museum, there's an ongoing exhibit featuring Esther Williams, "The Swimming Queen of the Silver Screen." There's also naturalist training at the conservancy.

Exciting stuff.

I text Handy Andy.

Good morning!

Would you mind stopping by around 3:00 today?

I have THE LIST!

Would love to get started ASAP

I'll pay whatever you need!

Let me know

This is the one time I don't mind sounding desperate.
My inbox chimes—my first official email.
The sender: Heidi Paulsen.

> Miss Weber, this is such a lovely obituary. Approved. Thank you so much. I stayed up all night thinking. It's strange that Momma went out late like that. It's really been bothering me, to be honest, especially since I still don't know who she had dinner with. I talked to her friend Yvonne, and it wasn't her. I wish I had time to talk to the others but I'm trying to finish up funeral arrangements. Anyway, I hope to see you at the services—she really loved reading the Breeze. I've counted 335 copies of it so far, ha ha.

My stomach feels slick, like one of those oil-sheened puddles on the sidewalk.

Who are the other people? I email back. I can ask them, and if they have special anecdotes about your mom, maybe I can write a follow-up profile. I don't mind.

I turn in my chair, waiting for her reply. Okay, so it *is* crazy for a very sick and very old woman to be out and about in the rain. Avalon has its own rules, so I'd just figured . . .

A response from Heidi.

June Oliver

Clarence St. Joseph

Loretta Tucker

Heidi has provided phone numbers for each of her friends.

I call June Oliver first.

"And who are you again?" the old woman shouts into the phone. She sounds like a tuba and a "pack of Pall Malls a day" smoker.

I repeat my name and that I write for the *Avalon Breeze*. "Heidi Paulsen thought I should call you," I shout.

The fist-faced receptionist turns around and shushes me.

I hiss back, "She's old and deaf. Patience, please."

"I don't know you," June Oliver shouts. "How do you know Pep? She's dead, y'know. Damn shame." A pause, then, "Are you selling subscriptions? Pep loved the *Breeze*, y'know."

I try Clarence St. Joseph next. No one answers. No voice mail takes over.

I dial Loretta Tucker's number, but her daughter, Loretta Junior, answers. "Mom's at church, taking care of the priest's robes." The woman sighs, then adds, "Are you calling about Paula?"

"I am," I say. "Heidi suggested I call a few of Paula's friends."

Loretta Junior grunts. "Poor Pep. Heidi should've forced her to move overtown once the city threatened to take the house."

"Do you know if Pep and your mom had dinner together back on Friday night?"

"Mom was at church on Friday night," Loretta Junior says. "Mom's always at church. She attends Saint Catherine. She survives off communion wafers and the blood of Christ."

I find directions to Saint Catherine. On Beacon Street, it's just a five-minute walk from here, in the opposite direction of my—

Someone taps my shoulder.

I smile and spin around, expecting to see Maddy.

But it's not Maddy.

He's tall, tanned, and blue eyed. He smells rich: sunscreen, wood chips, and fresh fifty-dollar bills. His clothes are classic Americana with the blue sweatshirt over the white T-shirt and relaxed jeans. There's a small compass pendant around his neck. He has the square jaw and straight spine of "legacy," and his vibe is "total fuckup," with the crooked smile and battered high-top Vans worn by other rich, hot total fuckups.

"Welcome," he says with the drawl of a California white boy born by the sea.

I blink at him, and my head goes wobble-wobble.

He points at me. "You must be Colette."

My tongue butts against my teeth like a robot vacuum cleaner against a wall.

He offers me his hand. "Noah Bancroft, your coworker."

"Ah. Hi." *Victory!* "Colette. Hey. Thanks."

We shake hands.

One of his fingers feels crooked in my grasp—broken a long time ago. His palms are calloused in some places—boat hands. There's an angry welt between his thumb and index finger—what or *who* was he doing to be scratched like that? He wears no rings, nor are there tan lines of rings from a once-upon-a-time love affair. My pulse jumps as I imagine this hand casually draped across my thigh.

"So," he says, "where are you staying, Colette?"

"Call me Coco. And I'm living with my aunt. We have a house on Beacon Street."

"And your husband?"

I frown. "My . . . *what?*"

He *Mona Lisa* smiles like a man who knows how to make women forsake their spouses. He lifts my left hand so that I can see, oh yeah, my wedding ring. A cheap gold band that Micah promised to replace once he "hit it big." The only thing he hit big was our neighbor's chonky cat, Weezer. And on his biggest payday, Micah bought a Ducati motorbike. *For my image,* he explained.

And now, I shrug as Noah holds my hand, and I say, "Oh. That. Means nothing now."

He chuckles. "Lemme guess. You're trying to figure out your marriage, and you've come to this beautiful island to learn life lessons, to sleep with a compassionate stranger, and to discover your truth in this stranger's bed, which you'll sneak out of as the new day starts. Then, you'll sail back to . . ."

"LA," I say.

"LA," he says, "where your husband surprises you at the dock with a bouquet of . . ." He squints at me. "Purple roses."

"Nice."

"And over there, at the docks, he'll apologize as you hold the roses to your nose. Your eyes will glisten, but with happy tears this time. He'll get on one knee and propose, presenting you with a solitaire the size of the moon. Bystanders will stop whatever they're doing to shout, 'Marry him, honey!' Overcome with emotion, you'll nod and say 'yes, I'll marry you,' and you'll kiss him, and he'll pick you up, and he'll twirl you around, and together, you'll live happily ever after, for *real* this time, the end." He holds out his hands, *ta-da*, and takes a sweeping bow.

My smile lingers a moment before I say, "My husband's . . . dead."

And now, that cocksure grin cracks and his jaw drops. He blushes and stutters, "Oh, oh, crap. I'm so sorry. I—I—I . . . didn't . . . I didn't know."

I smile. "He's not *dead* dead. Just dead to me. It's complicated."

He runs a hand over his hair. "Ha. Good one."

"Corny story, by the way," I say, smiling. "You must've majored in econ."

He throws his head back and laughs.

The fist-faced receptionist has yet to shush *him*.

"I *am* a writer," he says, "and I majored in English, to my father's chagrin. Obviously he was right—I am a lead-worded hack." He takes another sweeping bow.

I flush and my belly swirls.

Noah points to the desk on the other side of the office. "That's me, although I don't come in very often." There are no desktop framed photographs of him cuddled up with a perky blonde or a silky brunette. Just pictures of him on sailboats with an older woman with his blue eyes and an older man with his square jaw.

He offers me his jar of gummy bears. "Maddy's a total fan. After reading some of your obituaries, I can see why. The pie lady was pretty good, but I liked the one about the old porn star. You wrote something like . . . 'Fenton successfully passed as a Gentile and landed bit parts in low-budget films—Cowboy No. 2 and Lead Hoodlum. However, the director for *Cherry's Sexy Secret*—notorious for his blurry close-up shots and his antisemitism—discovered that Fenton was Jewish the moment the actor pulled down his plaid boxers. Alas, Robert Fenton, born Avnar Fingerhut, did not land the lead role in that skin flick starring two Presbyterians and a Mormon.'" He throws his head back and laughs. "Awesome."

I blush and pluck a few gummies from the jar. "Just words on a page."

He searches for red bears like a surgeon searching for a tumor. "How'd you ever get into writing obits?"

"Another long story."

"How about you share it with me," he says, popping three chewies into his mouth. "Maddy wants me to drive you around the island. Orientation."

I smile. "I'd like that."

He taps at his computer keyboard, then beckons me over. "You'll want to add these sites to your bookmarks."

Los Angeles Sheriff's Department Incident Reports for Avalon and Two Harbors. Lots of, "Victim reported that someone stole his camera from his cart," "Deputies responded to a call about a man who was passed out drunk . . ." and ". . . suspicion of being under the influence . . ." No "found partially eaten head at the casino" or "discovered partially mutilated corpse near the minigolf course."

"I know you're not the crime reporter," Noah says, "but it'll just give you good background info. And then, there's . . ." He clicks over to Facebook and the Catalina Island public discussion group. "Events around the community, some gossip, missing pets, job alerts . . ."

"Good to know, thanks." I bookmark both sites on my laptop's browser.

And then, I wonder: Does his mouth taste like cherry gummy bears?

He leads me outside and to a shiny black golf cart with red seats.

"Lemme guess," I say. "You went to Stanford."

He cocks his head. "How'd you know?"

I slip into the passenger seat. "Your cart's Stanford colors. Also the big red *S* hanging from the rearview mirror."

"And I hear that you're a Bruin," he says. "Some of my worst friends are Bruins."

I ask him how to get a cart. "Not that I like being in these things," I say. "I feel so . . . *vulnerable*. Someone can just . . . yank you out—"

"And then, what?" he asks.

I shrug. "Beat you up? Steal your cart?"

He chuckles. "And then, what?"

I blink at him.

"My point is this: it's pointless. You'll get caught, arrested, and charged. And for what?"

My eyebrow cocks. "No petty crime in utopia?"

"There is, but . . ." His turn to shrug. "Here's hoping someone tries to carjack me. I'd love to see what I'd do." He tosses me a grin. "I didn't answer your original question. Only one cart per household. Full-size cars are limited here, and the waiting list to get one is fourteen years long. Most folks ride bikes, motorcycles, scooters, and get this: we *walk*."

"Walk? Bike?" I snort. "Heathens. I worship at the temple of Honda." I couldn't bear to sell my Civic to strangers. Instead, I sold it to my neighbor.

Also: Noah's profile view is as good as his front view, and that causes electric tingles to popcorn all over my body, even my knees. A good sign that I am alive on this eleventh day of March, and that, yeah, I could have any man that I want, that they cloud around me like gnats, and I can choose them like a kid with an Advent calendar. A Morris Chestnut on the first day. A Chris Evans on the twelfth. I am Beyoncé in Target, rich enough to buy all the things, rich enough to hitch the entire store to the bumper of my Lamborghini SUV.

We pass the pink Hotel St. Lauren and roll past houses with front porches right there on the sidewalks. There are Smart cars and golf carts as far as my eye can see.

"Carts can't be longer than one hundred twenty inches," Noah tells me. "People usually leave their keys in the ignition."

I look at him with bugged eyes.

"What's the worst that can happen?"

"It gets stolen."

"And where are they going with it? We're on an island twenty-six miles long. Everybody basically knows everybody else. It's not worth it."

We drive up, up, up, with Noah pointing at the eucalyptus trees—not native. "They're called widow-makers over here. The dry limbs fall and kill people."

Firebreaks scar the hillsides. "A lot more made after the big fire in 2007," he says.

Wrigley Memorial and Botanical Garden. "William Wrigley's not buried there anymore," Noah shares. "When Pearl Harbor was bombed, the family feared Catalina could be bombed, too, and so they moved him."

"Overtown" is the mainland. "The Flats" are the lower half of Avalon, where the brightly painted houses are, and "the Hills," that's the island's interior. "Islanders" are the people born and raised here, like him, like Maddy, although no babies are actually *delivered* here. "You take a fifteen-minute ride overtown on a medevac," he says.

"So plan accordingly," I say.

Gwen is a "local," and I eventually will be, too.

Noah grins, slowing the cart as we roll behind a bare-chested redhead jogging up the block. He toots his horn. "I know this guy."

Flynn looks back at us and smiles. "What's up!"

"Hey," I shout back.

"Just taking her around the island," Noah says.

Flynn gives us a thumbs-up. Noah and I toss him another wave and speed away.

Here I am, waving just like Frank the taxi cart driver.

"The barge comes six times a week during the summers." Noah slows at a lookout point. "In winter, it comes as weather allows, so—"

"Plan accordingly," I say.

We roll on, going up, up, up. This time, he parks the cart at another vista point. "Welcome home."

Even a gray day in Avalon is a beautiful day. Gray clouds soldier over the Flats and the Hills. Bright houses still twinkle, and the greens still shine, and it's all so cluttered and perfect. Here and there, I see a fancy whitewashed house with a red clay tile roof—I want to buy that house over there. I want to write in that house, and make babies in that house, and bring those babies back from overtown via medevac to that house over there.

One day.

I inhale and hold that breath. I smell and taste eucalyptus and pine and the sea, and smoke and chaparral and Noah's cologne.

Micah's wedding ring feels so loose right now that if I sneeze, it will slip off and roll down this hill, into the sea.

"Be prepared for boredom," Noah says. "I was an asshole growing up cuz I was bored."

"An asshole?" I smirk. "You? Get out of here."

He snorts. "Ha. Yeah. And I'm still an asshole. Anyway, we'd run out of things to do, so we'd throw firecrackers at the bison."

My frown is deep and wide.

He blushes. "Maybe I should've confessed that one later."

I say, "I've read that men who hurt animals turn into serial killers."

He grins at me. "Or CEOs or presidents of the United States."

"You're not a president. You don't run nothing except your mouth. So . . ."

He laughs. "Do me a favor: start a list of things that make you swipe left on a guy."

"Terrorizing bison, that's for sure," I say, squinting at him.

He holds up both hands. "That was a long time ago. I've been redeemed. Today I believe in Jane Goodall, and I'd follow Sir David Attenborough to the ends of the earth. Swear."

We hop back into the cart and drive up, up, up, passing the golf course and football field, the nature center, and Hermit Gulch Campground with tents as bright as the houses back in the Flats. Up, up, up until the air chills even more and denser fog rolls across the dirt trail. We leave the cart again and stand in the clouds next to a sign that says, "Garden to Sky Summit—YOU MADE IT!"

He points down into the canyon. "Look."

I forget that my teeth are chattering, that goose bumps are crowding my skin, and I gape at the bison, those bulky figures that represent the American West.

My heart hurts from all this joy. It's not built to handle all this joy.

And oh my lord, Noah Bancroft is such a ho—and I am here for his ho-ish ways.

He grabs a puffy jacket from the cart's storage compartment and drapes it around my shoulders. "The bison roam everywhere, so be careful. Don't take any selfies with them. They'll charge if they feel threatened. If they *do* charge, look for something to hide behind. Throw something to make them look the other way. Pray."

"You're actually cautious around the bison?" I ask.

He smiles to himself. "The correct answer is, 'Yes, I am.'"

I take a step closer to take a picture, and I notice that my phone has no bars. "No reception up here." I turn to see that his eyes are on my ass.

Behold, dude, and wonder.

"So, Maddy?" I say.

"Needs a hit," he says. "Her father basically broke the paper's back, promoting his friends, which *never* sells papers. No one cares about the *Breeze*. The publication's a joke." He pulls a black vape pen from his pocket. The red tip glows, and vapor that smells like raspberry slushy billows from his mouth.

I cock an eyebrow. "And yet, you work for it."

"And yet, I work for it." He offers me the pen.

I decline.

"For shits and giggles, though. I write for *Vice* and *Wired*. My last piece was about the Keystone Pipeline protests. I stayed with the Standing Rock Sioux Tribe for about three months. I'll probably go back this summer. I've also traveled to an island in the Andaman Sea, where members of the highly isolated Sentinelese shot arrows at me. What else? I joined activists in Pamplona protesting bullfights—"

I point at him. "Ooh, I read that series."

"And?"

I hold his gaze. "You don't need me blowing up your head even more."

"You'd be surprised by what I need." He holds *his* gaze.

I don't blink.

It's a tie.

He draws from his pen again and blows out a raspberry-scented cloud.

Smoke gets in my eyes.

"Speaking of needs," he says, grinning, "with only one grocery store on the island and with whatever's happening now with this weird virus, you should probably stock up on some things. Make a trip before the aisles are bare. Again, in weather like this, the barge comes when it comes."

"Good to know." I'll go later today since I don't wanna be left with bottles of nasty, flat club soda in Gwen's pantry or those emergency purse condoms that slip off and smell like science. "So you're writing for the *Breeze* . . . ? Why?"

"Because Maddy needed help," he says. "Because she promised that I could write whatever I wanted as long as it guaranteed eyes and didn't make the paper look bad. *But . . .*"

"But?"

"Nothing happens here."

All these old women are dying for no reason.

"Oh," Noah says, "the receptionist Harriet? She's useless. She doesn't type fast, can't do research, knows jack about social media. Don't rely on her for one effing thing you need in a hurry or done right. I think she's Maddy's godmother or some—" He glances at his watch, then says, "Crap."

"Need to get back?" I ask, my heart dipping back toward Earth.

He stretches, and his long limbs click. "Yep."

We climb back into his cart and leave the clouds as though we've been away for decades. My phone vibrates with messages that have been waiting for my descent—including literary agent Andrea Liszl.

Noah pulls in front of the newsroom. "I'm glad you're here, Colette."

"I'm glad I'm here, too." I slip off his puffer jacket and leave it on the passenger seat. My chest opens, my armadillo ball a little looser. "Thanks so much for the tour. I learned a lot."

Please stay.

But he tosses me a wave and hits the gas, U-turning to go the direction we just came.

I pull out my phone and send my fingers flying across the digital keyboard.

MADELINE!!

COLETTE!!

Let me guess.

Not in my crisper yet, I text, but in the basket omgomgomg

It's almost four o'clock now, and Aunt Gwen has requested blackened mahi-mahi and cheese curds from Lobster Trap. I call Clarence St. Joseph's number again—no one answers—but I'm no longer in the mood to visit the church and talk to Loretta Tucker.

In my inbox, there are two obituary request forms: Herbert Lane (ninety-eight) and Mae Green (ninety). I'll handle them later. I dash over to the restaurant, breathing cold air that stings my nostrils, trying to ignore the sensation of being watched. But that sensation burns between my shoulder blades, so much so that I look up and down the street. Alas, there's no golden boy with sailor's hands watching me. The diners at the Mexican restaurant across the street sip Coronas and margaritas, flirt and laugh.

Hmm . . .

As I read the menu in the window, though, the hair on the back of my neck stands. Fear pops and pops around my stomach and between my ears.

Breathe, Colette.

Wind and rain stir my hair as my eyes shift from the empty shuttle stop to the empty parking lot . . . no one's walking by. No one putters past in their golf cart.

As far as places go, Catalina Island is the safest.

Except that one time for my family . . .

13.

No callback from Handy Andy—and the wire grate is still open.

Well, damn.

I pull out my phone and type into Google, *repair wire grate crawl space*, and find a video that's *only four minutes long*. But the man in the video starts talking about needle-nose pliers and metal louvers—I'm a woman who just electric-taped a bedsheet to her window.

Pliers? *Louvers?*

This can wait for now.

Aunt Gwen hasn't been outside recently because there's a note rubber-banded around the front doorknob.

WILL BE BY LATER TO START MAKING THINGS RIGHT AGAIN

Yay!

While Handy Andy works on the big things, I will start minor projects like . . .

Cleaning out the downstairs bathroom cabinets.

Like . . .

Using lime and rust cleaner on the shower tile and chrome fixtures.

Like . . .

Changing out the petrified shower curtain for a new one with lemons and dairy cows.

Bursts of window cleaner make the bathroom mirrors useful again. My reflection now shows a woman who wasn't as exhausted as the prior mirror had led her to believe.

The hardware store didn't have a large color variety of bath mats, but if I squint and believe hard enough, the purple mats kinda complement the lemons-and-dairy-cow brightness.

Okay. So my space looks far from the staged brilliance in the shiny pages I tore out of those home-improvement magazines and taped to the closet door. Nor does this space resemble the lemon-clean split-level house from 2001.

Life is a marathon, honey.

I unpack a few of my boxes—my favorite comforter that is way too big for this full mattress; my desk set, but I have no place to put this stapler, hundreds of pens, and blotter; and a wardrobe that ranges from Old Navy to AllSaints, cotton to cashmere.

I hang my framed Grimmy Award over my mattress as a reminder that I'm a winner. I pluck Moe the Unicorn from her box and squeeze her ass. If I didn't know, I'd think the nugget of hardness is cheap plastic or a sound box that no longer works.

A quick internet search tells me that there are no pawn shops or *real* jewelers in Avalon.

Hmm . . .

Selling this ring will take some effort.

Five filled garbage bags show my work—old towels, ancient bars of Ivory and Lava soaps, cotton swabs, metallic curlers, red eyeliner pencils, papyrus that used to be rolls of toilet paper, empty tubes of bubble bath, and sanitary napkins thick enough to take a bullet. In one unopened bag that had already been placed in the bin, I spot important-looking papers. House-related papers. Title. Loan agreements. For this house. *My* house.

I didn't throw them away, which means Gwen threw them away. Does she think that destroying evidence of my ownership makes me . . . *not the owner?*

With shaky hands, I snatch the papers from the trash bag—my Social Security number and other identifying pieces of information live throughout these documents—then, drag this bag and all the other bags down the porch steps to the trash bin.

Bins from other houses sit at the curbs.

Tomorrow must be trash day.

I try to smile as I push the recycle and regular trash bins to the sidewalk. Gwen will not win, for I am now the Lady of the House on Beacon Street.

◆　◆　◆

The hot spot works.

Internet results for *Noah Bancroft* immediately load on my laptop.

These Protestors Take No Bull

In this piece, Noah witnessed bullfighting season firsthand. He watched a bull gore a matador, and another bull trample men wearing white. He sprained his ankle in a melee of protestors and bullfighting fanatics. He fell in love with a matador's daughter, who was also training to be a matadora.

Hollywood bought the rights to this series, and Scott Eastwood, son of Clint, is supposed to star.

Another result: a feature in *Los Angeles* magazine. Noah stands between Elle Bancroft, a platinum-blonde beauty with delicate bones and blue eyes that flare like solar storms, and Sidney Bancroft, the kind of man who plays on Saturday, prays on Sunday, and preys every day in between, because look at that jawline and that head of beautiful hair and those strong hands, and you will give him all that he wants. He is a Master of the Universe.

A philanthropic family, the Bancrofts give millions to charities on the island, to Stanford University (they have an endowed research fund there), and to the Music Center in downtown Los Angeles. They own land—from houses and apartments to parking lots in Avalon and LA. They're partial owners of a basketball team in Italy. Throughout California, they own boutique hotels originally built in the 1940s and 1950s that have been painstakingly restored to their razzmatazz-bebop days. Sidney Bancroft has also been under investigation a few times—for shady land deals that involved encroachments on protected wetlands and enlisting local politicians to pressure homeowners to sell to him as well as two DUIs while zooming down PCH in a rented Ferrari.

"So . . . Noah's *rich* rich," I say to the laptop.

And Noah's gorgeous.

And Noah's single.

What's wrong with him, then? Other than a crook for a father, something's gotta be wrong with him.

"Noah Bancroft" doesn't come up in my search through sheriff's incident reports. Not that rich people allow their sons to be charged with drunk and disorderlies or sexual assaults.

I find his social media pages.

Adventures in Thailand. Adventures in Peru. Sunsets over the water. Drinks with Indigenous peoples. Shirtless while adventuring. A busted and swollen toe. A gorgeous woman sunbathing on a yacht wearing a bikini. Another gorgeous woman sipping a frozen cocktail on a patio on stilts above the clearest blue water. Bros around a bonfire raising bottles of beer.

I could be wrong but . . . looking at these pictures, it seems that I'm the only Black American he's spent more than an hour with. Looking at these pictures, it seems that he observes the Other but doesn't have relationships—platonic or otherwise—with the Other.

Noted.

My heart sinks. On an island with basically no Black people, this—being the Black friend—will become my every day.

I click over to the *Avalon Breeze*'s digital archives, which start in 1925.

Back in the day, the last page of the paper was dedicated to ads—Linen Sale at Haywood's! Arden Milk with the Famous 27 Flavorseal Cap! Loans to Build! Apartments for Rent—Women Only! House for Sale—Charming with Six Bedrooms, Only $6,500! The last page also featured HIT YOUR FUNNY BONE, a collection of jokes like . . . "A Negro was offered a ride with a speed demon . . . the Negro climbed out and said to the driver, 'Tank you, guvnor, for dem two rides . . . mah first and mah last.'"

Sprinkled throughout are editorials on the phenomenal success of "colored" athletes due to the tendons in their feet being longer and stronger than a white man's as well as racial pride in competing with white people on an equal basis.

There's a Did You Know column—this day's column states that the rural South seems to be the best place for the Negro because there are sixty-six deaths to one hundred births compared to 116 deaths to one hundred in the north.

And this paper has always been in Maddy's family, huh?

Says a lot. *Too* much.

I grit my teeth and close out of the archives.

I log on to the Avalon community page and scroll through the posts.

I'd planned to search on Paula Paulsen as well as any stories written about my family—their deaths or even my father's life on the island as a teacher and coach. This trip down this particular memory lane, though, makes blood crackle through my—

Looking for a year-round rental . . .

Is someone missing a cat?

Pebbly Road is still closed due to fallen rocks.

There's a picture of the man who'd gestured to me in the window yesterday. The post calls him "Louis," and he's been arrested "yet again" for indecent exposure.

"He's always been a perv," according to poster Diane.

"Deputy Santos is a very patient man, but he's starting to lose it with Creepy Lou," posted Eileen.

So the man in the window isn't a friend of Micah's. He's just the island flasher. Eww, but yay. I worried for nothing.

Upstairs, glass shatters.

My phone also rings, and a number that I don't know lights the screen.

I ignore the call and rush up the steps. "Auntie?"

Gwen's not seated in her armchair.

"Aunt Gwen?" I shout.

"I'm in the kitchen," she shouts back.

She's standing by the back door.

A grid of glass from the door window is gone, and fresh, moist air sweeps freely through the open space, lifting my aunt's thin gray bangs.

Gwen is holding a broom.

"Ohmigod, what happened?" I ease her away from the sharp glass on the linoleum floor.

"I saw a big spider." Gwen settles into a rickety, metal-legged chair by the fridge.

"You kill it?"

"No, he got away."

I find a heavy metal dustpan in the pantry. "It's okay—I'll clean up."

Downstairs, my phone keeps ringing.

I tap the green phone icon on my Apple watch and spit, "Hello?"

A woman's voice tries to push through the clank and the swish of the broom sweeping glass into a dustpan, and Aunt Gwen nattering about the missing spider. "This is Andrea Liszl."

The literary agent in New York.

It is impossible right now to have a meaningful conversation via watch.

I say, "Hi—" and the call drops.

Gwen points to the broken windowpane. "I'll have somebody fix that."

"Andy was supposed to come today," I say. "I'll just put this at the top of the list. Having this open is gonna worry me. Someone could just stick their hand in and turn the doorknob." I swipe at the sweat now bubbling across my forehead. "Do you have a better number for him? I found a number on the fridge, and it was pretty old. Maybe that number's disconnected? Anyway, I should call him—maybe he can do something now."

"He who?"

"Andy."

She blinks at me.

"For now . . ." I search the pantry and find a few wood planks that could've been shelves. I retrieve the hammer and nails I purchased this morning.

Gwen frowns. "Why you doing that?"

I toss her a smile as I nail the boards across the lower half of the window. "We can't have an open window right above the doorknob, Auntie."

She mutters something, then asks, "You having dinner?"

"We ate. Lobster Trap, remember?"

The wood around the door is weak—termites—but it'll do for now.

"You don't need to worry about that," Gwen says. "Ain't nobody comin' off in here."

"I'd blame myself for *not* doing this, though, if someone tried." I survey my simple solution. "I can't sleep as is. I don't need this on my mind, too."

Downstairs, my phone rings . . . and rings . . . and the anger I've boarded in my soul's basement awakens and lifts its shaggy head.

I run down to grab my ringing cell phone from the sitting room couch. "Yes, hi, Andrea. Sorry, I'm trying to care for my aunt right now."

There's silent surprise from my abrupt greeting. Then: "With whom am I speaking?" A man's voice, older, white.

"With whom are you trying to reach?" I ask, irritated.

"I'm trying to reach *you*. I'm calling about the house on Beacon Street."

"What about the house on Beacon Street?" Past my windows, the fog has rolled in, and I can see only my reflection in the glass.

"I'm interested in buying it," the man says. "Such a great property, but it needs work, and the owner . . . well, it's obvious she can no longer afford the upkeep and—"

"No, thank you," I say.

Upstairs, something thumps.

Did Gwen just fall?

Did that spider return?

"You haven't even heard my offer," the man says.

The floorboards above me creak.

My eyes scan the ceiling. "I don't need to hear your offer, sir. I'm not interested—"

He snorts. "It's really not your call to make, though, is it?"

Another thump upstairs and the heaviest penny in the universe rolls across the floor.

I follow that rolling until I'm standing at the window. "*You* called me, so I'm—"

"Six hundred thousand dollars. Cash."

I suck my teeth. "This house is worth over a million—"

"What are you doing right now?"

I back away from the window and return to the foot of the staircase. "I'm hanging up—"

"What a nice hoodie you're wearing, Colette. Is that a tiger print on the front?"

I spin back to face the window.

That fog keeps me from seeing outside.

I end the call and scurry forward to scan the bushes, the parked carts, the empty sidewalks. I look for anything strange, but I've lived here for only two days—I don't know what is strange or who doesn't belong. And strange? *I* don't belong. *I* have a diamond ring up a unicorn's ass. *I'm* the strange one.

I close the curtains even though they're sheer. My heart bangs in my chest as dust motes and cobweb strands from those ancient sheer curtains dance around me.

How did that man get my number? How does he know my name?

My phone rings again. That anger living in my soul's basement spikes, and I tap ANSWER. "Look—"

"No, *you* look, you uppity nigger."

"*Whoa*—"

"If you don't let go of that house," he shouts, "I'll burn it down myself with you and the other bitch in it! You hear me? You understand me?"

My breathing bumbles in my chest and . . . I've stopped breathing.

"Fucking bitch," he spits. "Go back to the ghetto."

A click. Then, silence.

My hand cramps from holding the phone tight. My body twitches. I'm shaking.

"Coco," Aunt Gwen shouts.

My mind snatches at the frayed nerves around my body, gathers them like daisies, and holds them in a tight bouquet. I force out a breath, then rub my numb face. "Okay. Okay."

Upstairs in the kitchen, a vodka bottle sits in a puddle of booze. The tart scent of olives hangs in the air.

Gwen says, "I spilled all over the floor. I'm just a mess today. I'm sorry."

"It's okay, Auntie. I'll clean it." I grab the roll of paper towels from the counter.

Aunt Gwen's phone chimes from her housecoat pocket. She sips her cocktail and watches me clean, and for a second I wonder if she's doing this on purpose.

The phone keeps ringing.

"Auntie, you gonna answer that?" I snap.

Gwen startles out of her fog. "Oh! Yes." Then: "Hello?"

A man's voice spikes from the speaker.

"Who *is* this?" Gwen asks, eyes wild.

I pluck the phone from her hand and listen:

"—gimme what's mine."

It's the same guy who'd just threatened to burn down the house.

I hit END CALL.

"Who *was* that?" Gwen's shaking hands make the martini glass wobble. Vodka splashes everywhere.

"Wrong number." I wipe up the new spills.

She has high blood pressure and heart disease. Gwen shouldn't be fretting.

I keep her phone and settle her into the armchair. "Ooh, look!" I say, remote control pointing at the TV. "*M*A*S*H* is on."

"I love Alan Alda," she says.

I find her pill case and hand her the medication for WED PM even though she's drinking vodka. Fuck it all.

Gwen's phone rings again.

DECLINE.

BLOCK.

My phone rings again.

DECLINE.

BLOCK.

My eyes skip to the wooden planks nailed over that broken door pane. In my hand, my phone rings for less than a second before Apple's operating system kicks in and blocks the caller.

Twenty years ago, I escaped Avalon in fear of my life. Since returning, my heart has seesawed from slush-filled lake to peaceful valley. Good and bad electricity has zigzagged around my body.

I will *not* play this game. The crazies will *not* take my aunt.

The crazies will *not* take me.

And *that's* a promise.

14.

Before tonight, she had never feared this rugged country. In the summer, yes—there was no shadow, and there were poisonous plants, and being out in the open could be dangerous. The bison sometimes charged. The high places were high, but the trails were more like dirt roads. There was water in plastic jugs at the campgrounds and here at the reservoir. So not that dangerous. Before tonight, this pond had been her favorite place. That was before tonight.

She couldn't move, and the red bench was hard against her back.

Cold.

Rain.

Water slipped into every space.

"Buenas noches," the driver whispered.

Frogs croaked . . . and croaked . . . so much frog song.

An engine rumbled. Tires spun in mud and skidded against slippery rocks.

She blinked as water slipped into her eyes and nose.

Move un poquito. Un brazo. Un dedo. Algo.

But her arms, her fingers . . . nothing would move.

She squinted into the darkness. Nothing to see. Just the night sky lost in white.

The world was so heavy.

And she was so sleepy, so floaty that she hovered above this city island of lights. Casino there, the pier there, her house there.

Her mouth was thick and fuzzy as her hearing.

So cold.

So hot.

A yip. A snort. A grunt.

Fox. Bison. Deer.

Too cold for snakes.

Sticky skin. Stinky clothes. Bananas and acid and cancer. Vomit burned her throat and lips. She couldn't take a full breath—she'd already filled her body with too much air, except she hadn't. She hadn't enjoyed the cool sensation of new air sweep past her nostrils since . . . forever.

¿Me estoy muriendo? ¿Aquí? ¿En mi lugar favorito?

Would she die here in her favorite place all because she'd refused to sign her life away?

What if she changed her mind? What would happen if she said yes? Was it too late to say yes?

They waited until she was alone, when she was vulnerable.

And now, she mewed like a kitten—her mouth was broken.

Please, por favor, one more chance, I say yes.

She closed her eyes and remembered . . .

Balancing bottles on her head.

The red full skirt.

Dancing all night.

Roberto.

Carlos.

Rides on the back of Esteban's scooter. Dancing with little Socorro, mi amor, mi estrella.

And then, after the Lord took her love and her light, the troubles came . . .

Only eighty years young.

The world thundered.

¿Helicóptero? In this weather? Maybe the pilot—Michael, her favorite—will spot her down here at the pond.

No lights. No sound. That was no helicopter.

Death had arrived, and now, all she heard was her body's crackling and dull thuds. All she heard now was her own pleading.

Cambié de opinión.

No vale la pena morir for nada.

I changed my mind.

Nothing is worth dying. I don't need things. I want to live.

Drinking . . . taking from others. Her people were bad people, awful pendejos who'd spit at you rather than talk.

So much anger. People blamed her as though she could control them.

Agua que no has de beber, déjala correr.

That was what her mother always told her. Water that you must not drink, let it run.

She tried to keep away from them, to let them run, but they followed her here.

And now, she was living with the results out here on this bench.

She would give it all back if she could. She would be a better disciplinarian, put her foot down more, dole out punishment with one hand and love in the other. Just for another chance.

Cambié de opinión.

I changed my mind.

But the driver, the demon, has gone. There was nothing left to do except blink out into the darkness and listen to the frog song and think about little Socorro, mi amor, mi estrella.

This city of lights, this island of lights . . .

So beautiful tonight.

So beautiful.

15.

It's two fifteen, I can't sleep—and there's no Scott, Chase, or Kenny (a.k.a. Mother Nature's sleep aid) to call. Instead, I try to find the name behind the phone number of the angry man who'd threatened Gwen and me. No Google results, though.

Go back to the ghetto?

Uppity?

That word?

That word is always spat out by racists who can't get what they want.

In this case: my house.

Maybe I'll stand in front of my house and watch out for racist men glowering at me.

The glow behind the bedsheet burns as bright as a neon sign and a supernova combined. All that light is making the Catalina nightshade grow even wilder, so wild that soon it will cover this house, and I will be trapped, and no one will cut it back to save me, because the nightshade belongs here, and I do not.

Every time I blink, my eyes crackle, and as I lie in bed, I play a game. *How many times can I make my jaw creak?*

. . . twelve . . . thirteen . . . seventeen . . .

Upstairs, Gwen sleeps. How does she sleep so well here?

Outside, rain pounds against the earth. Sounds like I'm trapped behind a waterfall.

. . . twenty-three . . . twenty-four . . . twenty-eight . . .

Right after the murders, the doctor in charge of my care prescribed me Valium, one a night. I'd run out of sedatives by night fifteen. Gwen told me that I had to have been doubling up sometimes. But she always slept so well . . .

Did she pop my Valium sometimes? She could've asked for her own prescription.

Anyway, I would sleep well the first half of the month, and then, I wouldn't sleep well at all the second half.

Tonight feels like March 25.

I push away the comforter and crawl over to the plastic bin filled with stapled and banana-clipped papers and envelopes—important documents, including real estate papers, tax statements, and . . . *This!*

> **Living Trust . . . Gwyneth Weber, trustee . . . Langston Weber and Colette Weber, beneficiaries . . .**

After her cancer diagnosis and treatment, Mom hired an estate attorney to do estate planning. She and Dad named Gwen a trustee in the event they died while Langston and I were still minors. The house was part of their modest estate as well as a mortgage protection insurance policy. That policy kicked in a month after their murders. Gwen became trustee since I was too young to live in this house alone. After I turned twenty-five, I collected all the papers needed to transfer ownership to me. Then, I signed more papers and, weeks later, received a new deed bearing my name. And *only* my name.

As payback, Gwen didn't speak to me for over a year—and when she did speak, she said that I'd regret my decision to kick her off the deed. (Not that she was ever on the deed.) She vowed that even if it took until the end of her life, she'd make me see the errors of my ways. Then, she quoted a Dutch proverb—"A handful of patience is worth more than a bushel of brains"—and presented me with an iced lemon birthday cake.

The words on this title are too small to read this late at night, but I want to see only the most important parts—"Colette Sienna Weber" and "215 Beacon Street" and "owner."

I bring the document to bed and place it beside me, draping an arm over it like a lover.

Gwen blinks at the deed, blinks at me, then shifts her gaze to the bowl of oatmeal on the table before her.

The house creaks around us as rain continues to flood the world.

"Any plans today?" I ask. "Didn't you say you're going to—"

"Don't change the subject," she snaps.

I take back the sheaf of papers.

"I'm not stupid," she spits. "I know this is your house. You weren't ever interested in it."

I grip my spoon and push the oatmeal around my bowl. "Can you really blame me?"

She smirks. "Do I need to move out so you can *have your house*?"

I ignore her tone by killing it softly with a smile. "Of course not. You're staying. Especially after . . ." I smile wider. "I just wanted to see the deed again, and to show it to you since yes, I am now interested in the house."

She stares at me as she spoons oatmeal into her mouth. Game recognizes game. "So thoughtful of you to share it with me. Since this is your house."

I nod and eat another spoonful of oatmeal. The warm cereal tastes like sweet snot.

As I wash breakfast dishes, I spot Handy Andy drifting around the backyard.

Yay!

"Gwen is showering," I say, inviting him in. "Volunteer hours at the library. She's gotta get there for a school trip this morning, so I'll show you that bathroom later."

He smells like wet flannel and damp cigarettes. No tool belt hangs around his waist. Was he planning to do any work today?

I lead him to the front door. "I'd like to change out this door. It feels flimsy, and the locks are weak. And, of course, the kitchen door, especially now with the broken window."

"Yep." He knocks on the doorjamb. "This needs new framing."

"That's fine. Whatever's needed." I point out the flickering lights, then stop talking so that he can hear the creaking and rumbling.

He chuckles, shakes his head. "This house is in worse shape than I thought."

I cock an eyebrow. "Weren't you doing repairs all this time?"

His neck reddens. "A patch here, a patch there. Nothing too expensive."

"Gwen tried to keep it up."

He turns to face me. "Did she, though?"

I hate nodding in agreement, but he's right. "Well, I'm gonna make her all pretty again. With your help, thank you very much."

He smiles, but his eyes flare at this wreck of a house. "Good that you're trying. It's obvious this place means more to you than it does to Gwen."

We wander back to the kitchen.

My eyes burn, and I chew my bottom lip to keep from crying. "Yeah. It's economics, too, but yeah. Maybe." I push out air, then force out more anxiety by wriggling my fingers. "How's two hundred to start?"

He toes a piece of glass that I missed in sweeping last night. "Sounds good. I'll start on the easy stuff first. By that, I mean your doors."

I walk Handy Andy down the slick porch steps, then look up at the heavy sky. "You can work in this weather?"

"I can do the doors, yeah, but we gotta wait for a break in the rain before we do the serious stuff. Good to see what I'm about to get into."

I wave back and watch him until my phone vibrates from my back pocket.

A text message from Noah!

Let me show you the island at night

Work related of course

An un-date lol

I smile and type, Sounds good

BTW working at home today

He responds with, Meet you at the Naughty Fox 6pm

What should I wear on this un-date?

After dumping clothes out of my suitcases, I grab a pair of distressed jeans, a sexy black slouchy sweater, black leather high-top Vans, and a red puffer jacket. I gently gather my hair into a loose ponytail—the thread on one of my extensions has loosened some. I'll need to ferry back to LA sooner that I thought.

As I change the studs in my ears, news notifications blanket my phone's screen.

US to Suspend Most Travel from Europe . . . Dow Ends 11-Year Bull Market . . . Singer Billie Eilish Postpones Tour Dates . . .

Worry rises in my belly like smoke. All of this sounds like *The Stand.* "They'll figure it out," I tell my reflection in the mirror.

Tonight, on this episode of *Nightlife in Avalon,* maybe I'll giggle and shimmy to music and bite my lip, and maybe Noah will understand that it is all for him. Maybe I will share the story of my life after leaving this place as an orphan and how I still managed to thrive, and maybe I will grow three sizes bigger, become a sunflower for a change instead of baby's breath.

In the mirror's reflection, I see a woman who's been missing for two years. This chick has glowing skin; big, clear eyes; and a smile that used to break hearts and open wallets.

"She's ba-ack," I say, with a wink.

Even as water gurgles through the pipes above me and rotting wood creaks beneath my sneakers, I am Naomi Campbell, and this house is a Tuscan villa, and I know that I can fly.

Located in the whitewashed boutique Bellanca Hotel and across the street from the Avalon harbor, the Naughty Fox bubbles with chatter and the aromas of garlic and burning wood. There aren't many diners sitting in the restaurant's lime-green chairs. There aren't many patrons sitting at the bar, watching basketball and soccer games on the two televisions. Noah hasn't arrived yet, but the hostess seats me anyway at a window table and leaves behind two dinner menus.

Outside, the nighttime island twinkles—from the fairy lights strung around palm trees and across the cobblestone streets to the far-off shimmer of boat lights and hillside homes. The rain slides over it all.

"You look great." Noah's suddenly standing over me. He's wearing a sweater and jeans. His hair is damp, and a bead of candied blood shines on his neck.

I stand and reach to hug him. "Hey!"

He startles, dodges me, then catches himself and goes in for the hug. "Hey."

I frown, confused with his reaction.

He squeezes my hand. "You just caught me off guard. I don't hug." He winces. "My parents are Episcopal."

I say, "Ha. I come from African Methodist Episcopals. Total huggers."

"Great table." He sits across from me, then leans forward. "I won't have to worry about people overhearing me."

I rest my chin on my hand. "Yeah? What won't they hear?"

"That they're all boring compared to you."

"Aww." My face warms. "You're such a bullshitter."

His eyes twinkle. "You didn't buy that?"

"For a second but only because it's true."

We laugh.

"Noah, Noah, Noah." A late-sixties willowy brunette with cotton-candy-pink lips and matching fingernails drapes her hand on top of Noah's shoulder. "How's Elle? I hear she's been experiencing a few health challenges."

Noah blushes, says, "Haven't we all?" and then, "Helen, this is—"

"I know Colette," she says, pivoting to me with a smile.

I sit up. "You do?"

She thrusts out her hand. "Helen Nilsen. Flynn's mother. We met at their wedding."

I accept her handshake. "Ah. Yes. Nice to see you again." *Again?* I don't remember the first time.

Her eyes flick across my landscape, and she nods, pleased with what she sees. "I heard you were back. If you ever need my services, please reach out immediately. To *me*. No one else." She waggles her finger. "Promise me, dearest."

I waggle my head. "Promise. What services—"

"Gotta go, babies." She pecks Noah on both cheeks, then gives my shoulder a squeeze before launching herself through the restaurant and to the exit.

"What does she do?" I ask Noah.

He snorts. "Acts like a Realtor. Minds everybody's business. Gin-and-tonic lunches. Usual rich lady stuff."

Over lobster sushi rolls, macaroni and cheese, and french fries, Noah tells me more about the struggling *Avalon Breeze*. "Maddy's in a fucked-up situation—she and Flynn? They sank money into this thing, but like I said earlier: there's no compelling news here."

"But she has this big-time anonymous donor," I say.

He snorts, rolls his eyes. "A.k.a. *Flynn*? Sure. Got it. Next."

"I read about a drug bust a few weeks ago," I say. "The woman they arrested—she had a warrant, right?"

He nods. "That was rare." He slides a french fry through a ketchup puddle. "The fire in 2007—another rare thing. You wanna know what happens here?"

"Looking in the newspaper archives, racism?"

His eyebrows scrunch, and he slows his chewing.

"The jokes pages from the past are filled with 'Negro this' and Uncle Remus dialect and 'yes suh' and the Negro problem. Facts." I lean forward on my elbows. "Did you know that there was some kind of Avalon community committee meeting right after World War II, in 1946, discussing ways to keep Blacks, excuse me, *Negroes* out of Avalon. They wanted property owners to sign an agreement to not sell to Negroes."

I also wanna tell him about last night's phone calls, but I've swung at his head already.

And now, he gapes at me, then remembers to close his mouth and chew. "No, I didn't know that." He blushes. "I was just gonna say . . .

people get drunk and they hit each other. They steal headphones from golf carts. Golf carts turn over. And folks have been coming lately to sell fake gold jewelry."

"Ah."

"See the guy in the blue polo eating with the redhead?"

Yes—they're sharing calamari and sipping each other's cocktails.

"The Schwartzes," Noah says. "He's sleeping with her sister, and she's sleeping with his mother."

I cough, nearly choking on a macaroni noodle.

Noah nods toward two older women seated at the bar. They're weighted down from all their turquoise jewelry and blue eye shadow. "The blonde sells weed and E, and the brunette turns high-class tricks that include bubble baths and foot massages afterward, but spa services will cost you fifty extra."

I blink at him. "And you know this . . . ?"

"I have sources, of course." He points at me with that french fry. "All I'm saying is . . . there were ten violent crimes here in 2019—two rapes, eight aggravated assaults, zero murders, zero robberies."

"What about the island pervert?" I ask. "Louis . . ."

"Moncur," he says. "Okay, so *he's* dangerous. Burglary, carrying a concealed weapon, stealing from old people . . . lewd and lascivious acts. He's on probation, though, and he's registered as a sex offender. I don't think he wants to find his pasty ass back in state prison. But other than Louis . . ." He swirls the beer around the glass. "Catalina is not a place with hard-hitting news. There's no KKK column on the back pages of the *Breeze* anymore. Maddy's screwed."

"Unless . . . she's not," I say.

He pauses before he sips. "What does *that* mean?"

"Since this is a work-related un-date . . ." I pull the island area map from my bag. "Someone left this in my desk drawer." I spread the map across the table, then tap each circle. "Why?"

His brow furrows. "Cuz you're new here. Welcome to Avalon."

"Yesenia told me."

"Oh no." He drops his fork and laughs. "Maddy hasn't warned you about Yesenia?"

"She has, but Yesenia told me that old women are dying every other week. That there's a cannibal—"

"Nope. No. Not the cannibal shit again." Noah tries to keep from smiling and holds up a hand. "Look: Yesenia is *extremely* Catholic, *and* she watches a lot of HLN. Y'know, those *Unusual Suspects*–forensic murder shows? That's a bad combination."

I glare at the compass pendant dangling over his beer. "Doesn't mean that she's wrong."

"True, but people's dogs have *always* gone missing, and where *are* these mutilated corpses and pentagrams burned into hillsides—"

"Pentagrams? What penta—"

"I haven't noticed anything strange," he says. "Believe me, I've been looking for strange, *praying* for strange." He looks up to the ceiling with praying hands. "*Please* let there be strange." He levels his gaze at me. "No strange things here, Coco. As for the map . . . let's see."

He squints at the circled sites. "The rock garden at the botanical garden. This random grove, no idea but bison are probably there. Garden to Sky Summit—I took you up there yesterday. Middle Terrace." He shrugs, then points at Beacon Street. "Your aunt's house is the white rickety one around here, right?"

I take sips of mineral water. "Yes, and it's actually my house, and it needs a lot of work."

"You good with a hammer?"

"I'm good with an index finger, which can tap 'call,' connecting me with people who are good with hammers."

He drains his glass. "You're about to spend a fortune. If I were you, I'd sell."

"Nope. My family—my parents, brother, and me—we were supposed to move in. We went on *Family Feud*—"

"No way!" His grin lights up the room.

"Way. And we won about eighty thousand dollars, and my dad—he commuted from Long Beach to teach high school chemistry here. He was also the tennis coach."

He points at me. "*You're* Coach Weber's daughter? You're *that* Weber? By the way, I was on the tennis team, and your dad helped me get a scholarship to play for Stanford."

"Wow. Yeah. My dad was good at pretty much everything. He wanted us to live here full-time, and so, we had this *Family Feud* money and money from selling our house, and so my parents bought the house on Beacon but . . ."

"But what?" He leans back. "Oh. Yeah."

A heavyset man with a round red face saunters to our table. "Fancy seeing *you* here," he says to Noah.

A brunette bird-steps over to join us and wraps her arms around the big man's waist. She raises a tattooed eyebrow at me. "Noah Bancroft, are you on a *date*?"

Noah's eyes go wide. "No. We're coworkers. Colette started at the paper this week."

He didn't lie. Still . . .

Noah introduces me to the Franks, and the man, Harry, tells me that if I ever need a new cart or scooter, to give him a call.

The woman, Kade, makes a show of exhaling before tapping Noah's shoulder. "Good to hear that it's work related. Mona would be absolutely *heartbroken* if you were taken off the market by an outsider." She winks at me. "No offense . . . Is it 'Colace'?"

"Co-*lette*," Noah says.

Kade says, "Oopsie," and makes a "golly, I'm dumb" face. "No offense," she repeats. "I should've known this is all work and no play." She faux-whispers, "You look nothing like Noah's type." She turns back to Noah, and says, "Miss California was . . ."

Noah clears his throat but doesn't speak.

"Blonde," Harry says.

"The pretty one—her daddy's Silicon Beach. She's a blonde, too," Kade says.

"Our beautiful Mona," Harry says.

"The second coming of Farrah Fawcett," Kade brags.

"I hear they have more fun." I fake a smile. "Maybe I'll go blonde, too. You better tell Mona to watch out."

The couple laughs. "Oh, it's more than just the hair," Kade says.

"Of course it is," I say, smile frozen. "It's brains, too. Again: warn your sweet girl there's a big brain in town."

Once the Franks shamble toward the exit, my smile drops.

"Sorry about that." Noah's cheeks flush. "You're pissed."

I toss sixty dollars onto the table.

He pushes the money back to me. "My treat."

I drop the twenties into his beer glass.

"The Franks," he says, pushing back his hair, "they're the town gossips and—"

"And I don't care who they are."

He smirks. "Oh, but you should. They'll have your business all in the streets."

"Thanks, pal. Wait: Is 'pal' too buddy-buddy? How about 'comrade'? Don't want anybody getting the wrong idea, right?" I stand.

He takes my hand.

I pull my hand back, tuck it into my armadillo shell, and move past the tables.

People everywhere kiss and nibble, sip and Snap. The air cools the closer I get to the exit. My eyes burn with angry tears, and since I can't see, I'm trusting the changes in temperature to lead me to safety.

Cold air fully breaks over me, and raindrops hit my forehead. *I made it!*

Where the hell am I?

Like twenty years ago, I find the Inn at Mount Ada glowing on the hillside, then turn in the opposite direction.

"Coco!" Noah runs to catch up to me.

I keep walking.

He grips my shoulders and turns me around. "It's not what you're thinking."

"No?" I cock my head. "Tell me: What am I thinking?"

"That I'm embarrassed to be with you."

"And why would you be embarrassed to be with me?"

His mouth opens and closes.

"Why would you be embarrassed, Noah?"

Yeah, I'm gonna make him say it.

He sighs. "Because I'm a Scorpio, and you're obviously a Taurus. Because I'm mega-rich, and you *probably* have a regular Amex. Because I require sunscreen even on cloudy days, and you're blessed, unbothered, and highly melanated." He waits a beat. "I saw that on a T-shirt."

I wanna laugh. I own that T-shirt.

"And we *are* coworkers," he says, "which makes this a little . . . *awkward*, but not because you're . . . urban, ha."

Instead of listening to him nervous-babble, I take out my phone and check to see if I need to write five hundred words to announce someone's bake sale.

He squeezes my arm. "Another chance?"

I scroll through my growing inbox.

His body heat comes off as waves, big waves, tsunami. "Please?" He places his forehead against mine.

A shiver crackles through me.

He smiles. "I felt that."

"And you have no idea what to do with it."

"Let me figure it out."

I sigh, then say, "Fine. Walk me home."

16.

My ringing cell phone jars me from rare sleep. The sun is nowhere close to brightening the night sky. I'd been dreaming about eating pasta naked in bed with Noah, with one of my legs around his neck and . . .

Damn phone.

This number . . . I don't know this number, but it's called my phone twice now.

And it's only five thirty.

"Hello?" I croak.

"May I speak to Colette Weber?" An older woman.

"Speaking." I roll over in bed and stare at the ceiling.

"It's Loretta Tucker," the woman says. "I'm Paula's best friend. My daughter told me that you called yesterday or Tuesday or . . . What's time now that Pep's gone?"

I sit up, fully awake now, and scramble for a pen and pad on the nightstand. "I'm so sorry. Yes, I've written Mrs. Paulsen's obituary, and I was just calling for more information. Sounds like she was an interesting woman."

Loretta's laugh is tinkly and bright. "She was a gem. A joy. A hoarder. And I wanted to talk to you before I left for church this morning. Apologies for calling at such an early time."

I turn on the desk lamp and blink as the light startles my eyes. I tell her that Heidi and I talked about Paula's last day alive, that Heidi didn't know who Paula had dinner with that night. "She thinks that it was either you, June, or Clarence."

Loretta clicks her teeth. "Not me—I had robes to prepare that night. And June is pretty gone, mentally, so I doubt that. And Clarence . . . he and Pep fell out over something silly weeks ago. Pep had borrowed a pressure washer last year and misplaced it, and Clarence . . . he didn't want to look for it but didn't want *Pep* to look for it, either. Ridiculous. And now she's gone." She pauses, then adds, "May I sound like a crazy old lady right now?"

"No better time than the present."

"I find all of this strange," Loretta whispers. "From the mystery dinner date and Paula being out late like that to her being found at the rock garden."

My pen slows against the pad. "What do you think happened?" Dread presses inside my chest, and I'm almost whispering now.

"She was lured there."

"By . . . ?"

Loretta exhales, then says, "Well . . . she told me that morning that someone had come around and asked about the house. She didn't know this person—and so this visit worried her a bit. At first she thought it was Hollywood people, the ones who work on that hoarding show? Heidi had tried to get on that show before, but Pep absolutely refused. But then, it could've been the county again, looking at the mess."

"Would she have gone to meet county people at the rock garden, though?" I point out. "Would she get in a cart with a stranger?"

"Never. Okay. So she must've known the murderer."

My nerves jolt. Because she said that word—*murderer*—like I said, "Good morning."

"You think she was murdered?" I say.

"Just like Vera and Consuela. And no one's seen poor Doris since Sunday afternoon."

"Doris . . . ?"

"Ratzenberger."

I scribble that name on my pad. *Who is Doris Ratzenberger??*

"Someone could argue that old women, *sick* women die," I say. "That their deaths aren't strange."

Loretta snorts. "That may be true, but do all old women die at night? Do they all die away from home? Do they all die from something that they hadn't been expected to die from? And why are they all widows?"

Hunh. I grab the map from my bag and open it. "Where was Consuela found?"

"They found her at Bird Park."

On the map, Bird Park is circled.

"And Vera?"

"An abandoned tent at Black Jack Campground."

There's also a circle around the campground.

"Why would she be at a campground alone? She was eighty years old." Loretta sighs. "I shared my concerns with the deputies around here, but none of them seemed worried. So here I am, turning to someone I've only met once—"

"We've met?"

"After . . . everything happened that night, I brought you food and a few sweatshirts, and I kept you company when Gwen couldn't." She waits a beat, then says, "Your aunt and I didn't see eye to eye on many things back then."

Tears fill my eyes. "I don't remember any of this, all that you did for me, but . . . thank you."

"You're a reporter," Loretta says. "Maybe you can find out what's happening around here. It's not normal. And I'm not talking about chupacabras or cannibal satanists. I mean . . . I don't know what I mean, but something's wrong here."

I ask if she has contact information for Consuela's and Vera's families.

She does. "But don't call them right now. I should be the only Rude Ruth in Avalon."

"This is all very helpful information." Her words thud around my head, and I squeeze the bridge of my nose to trap them.

She inhales and slowly lets out the air. "Thank you for letting me say outlandish things so early in the morning. And thank you for not laughing at me. People tend to disregard us old ladies—they think we're only good for sewing robes and making hot chocolate, that we're crazy since we can no longer bear children. But we're smarter than everyone because we don't *have* distractions anymore. No kids. No husbands for many of us. We *always* knew the evil that men did, and we *still* do. Just now, no one believes us."

I touch my heart—feels like it's crumpling beneath my hand. "I believe you."

"I know you do—you're one person I know who has seen the worst of this island. You don't believe the hype, as my grandkids say."

"No, ma'am." Some of the worst call you out of the blue, hurl vulgar slurs, and threaten to burn your house down.

"You be careful, young lady," Loretta warns. "Remember you and I understand what this place did to your family." She pauses, then adds, "That evil is still here. I can feel it."

What do I do with that, at ten minutes to six?

I stare at those water stains on the ceiling.

I stare at my notes.

I turn those words over in my mind.

That evil is still here.

I can feel it.

As for Vera and Consuela, I need to find incident reports. I need to talk to their families.

And Doris Ratzenberger. Where is she? Did a Silver Alert go out? Was a missing person report completed?

Above me, the floorboards creak. Morning news murmurs. Gwen's up.

I close my eyes, not ready to start the day.

◆ ◆ ◆

My phone vibrates.

My eyes pop open—I'd fallen back asleep.

We got another one! A text from Maddy.

Outside, the rain taps at my window. Above me, that water stain darkens to café au lait.

There's a second message beneath Maddy's:

LA County reports 1st COVID-19 Death

I swipe into MESSAGES and tap, **Another what?**

Ellipses bubble on the screen.

While she responds, I groan, then kick off the covers.

OBIT! Felicity Amador!

Lives a block over from Paulsen house

691 Clemente Ave

Talk to Mateo Amador this morning before you come in!

Upstairs, the house smells like coffee and banana-nut muffins. The front door is cracked, and so I slip the chain on and push it closed.

Gwen's voice echoes from the living room. ". . . still here."

What's still here? Who's visiting?

"You know I can't do that," she snaps. There's silence.

She's talking to someone on the phone.

"Who said anything about giving up?" Irritated, she sighs, then says, "Fine. *You* tell me since you know so damn much."

Who's she talking to? Giving up on what?

Once she says, "Bye," I cough to alert my proximity, then stomp up the stairs. "Morning, Auntie."

Warm and aglow with lamplight, the living room feels vibrant with *Good Morning America* on the TV, and even the mismatched furniture looks like it all belongs together. Aunt Gwen, dressed in a mulberry velour tracksuit and a yellow beanie, smiles at me from the armchair. She squints at the phone in her hands. A book of word finds sits on her lap. Her Bible sits on the armrest. All about the Word this morning . . . and a scheme.

"Happy Friday," she chirps, placing the phone on the TV tray.

I kiss the top of her head, then shuffle to the kitchen. I check her pill tub—she's forgotten to take FRI AM, and the GPS necklace is sitting on the counter.

"What's got you up bright and early?" I pour coffee into a mug and add cream and sugar.

"You being here just fills me with energy." She turns down the volume on the TV. "Since you're only gonna be here a few more days, I thought we'd—"

The room turns icy—or is it just me?

"Auntie," I say, perching beside her on the floor, "I live here now, remember? All those boxes downstairs? I shipped those over earlier this month."

She cocks her head, flips through her mind's steno pad, finds that note, frowns, then forces a smile. "That's right. I remember. I made those muffins fresh."

I hold out the pills and the necklace. "You need these."

She blinks at them, and something clicks behind her eyes. She plucks the pills and monitor from my open palm.

"What are your plans for the day?" I ask.

She doesn't hear me. Just fingers the necklace and stares at the jeweled locater.

And for the next ten minutes, I watch *Good Morning America* with my aunt, ignoring the growing water spots and the door pushing against the security chain and the wind whistling past the board across the broken door pane. The mist rolls through the trees and across the ocean and over cruise ships and barges, and I see all North America from the living room window.

The home of Felicity Amador looks like . . . *Indiana*. It's a simple white clapboard house with green trim and a white picket fence, and it sits between two two-story homes. A charming bower of trees leads to a side patio large enough for an umbrella-covered table and chairs. Sure, it needs new paint, new shutters, a trim here and there, but she isn't a decrepit beauty with no money to keep her going. She isn't like Paula Paulsen's house or my house.

A young man with thick black hair opens the door. His bangs cover his right eye, and the scowl on his face is deep—just like mothers everywhere warn, his face has frozen like that.

I'd expected to see trash everywhere, to smell diseased wood and rusty pipes, but no. Just rotten apples, weed, and burned toast. The death metal roaring through the creaky walls doesn't fit with the wicker furniture and floral wallpaper, the porcelain bowls and figurines spaced out neatly in nooks and on mantels. The heat is on, too, and my underarms moisten with sweat.

"You're Felicity Amador's son?" I shout over the music.

He swipes at his dark bangs. "Great-nephew."

"Can we . . . ?" I grimace and twirl my finger in the air.

He taps his phone.

Silence thumps into the house like a dropped barbell.

I almost stumble from the sudden quiet. "Thanks. I'm Colette, from the *Avalon Breeze*."

"Mateo. Hey."

There's no place to sit. Those nice rattan chairs hold boxes that have been filled to the brim—encased coin collections, framed Mayan artwork, silver platters, chrome coffee and teapot sets, a vintage man's fedora . . .

"Moving?" I ask.

"Just getting shit I want."

Like a china set with pink roses. Every twenty-year-old death-metal fan's dream.

"You requested an obituary in the paper."

He snorts. "Uh, no," he says, picking at dry skin on his forearm. "My mom, Linda, did. It's stupid wasting money on obituaries and funerals and shit like that."

My eyes linger on the gem-encrusted jewelry box that reminds me of Versailles. I force a smile. "Is Linda in? I'm here to ask a few questions." I pull out the request form Linda had completed online: birth date (July 26, 1932) and place (Mexico City), family (deceased daughter, Socorro; deceased husband, Esteban Amador), occupation (cook). But I want more.

He shrugs. "My mom lives in Atlanta."

"Is she coming to Avalon for the services?" I ask. "Or have you guys even talked about any of that?"

"Don't know. She hasn't visited Felicity in, like, five years. My family doesn't mess with this island anymore. I was in charge of the day-to-day. I'm the one who found Felicity."

I put pen to pad. "Found . . . ?"

"She had dinner with a friend Wednesday night."

My head lifts. "Dinner with a friend."

"She refused to cook for me, so I had to find something to eat."

"Do you know this friend?" My gut twists like it's being wrung out.

He scowls. "Another oldster, the fuck I know? And so I went to my friend's house over on Sumner. Played some Fortnite. Felicity called. I didn't answer, but she left a voice mail saying that she was going on a ride to her favorite place. Cool. Whatever. I got home around ten, and she still wasn't home. At eleven, I got a little worried cuz she didn't take her meds, and so I got in the cart and started driving around."

My pen whips across the back of the obituary form.

Mateo continues. "She's been depressed cuz her cancer came back."

"What kind?"

"Lung. And so I drove over to the reservoir—"

"I don't know the reservoir," I say. "I'm new here."

He doesn't blink. "No shit. Haypress. It's about three miles away. I drove the old 4Runner cuz it's in the freakin' backcountry, and you're really not supposed to be back there. Anyway, there's this bench she loves, and I saw her lying there, dead."

I'm overheating now, from the heat and from noticing the similarities in Felicity's death to the other deaths. "I'm so sorry for her passing and that you were the one who found her."

He shrugs, gnaws on a cuticle.

"What would you like to mention, then, in the obituary?"

His eyes peek at the boxes. "I didn't really know her. Umm . . . she put up with a lot of shit from the fuckers on the island who blamed her for all the crime. Like we were the only thieves and dealers and shit in Avalon. Umm . . . she was a good cook, too."

"You lived here with her, yes?"

"Yeah, but . . ." His lip curls, and his dark eyes blaze with anger. "I wasn't happy about it, know what I mean? I hate this island. I wanna go back to, like, civilization. Now that she's gone, I can do that."

Does Linda know that Mateo is packing up all the good stuff from this neat little house that's probably worth millions of dollars?

Is any of this my business?

"And when you found her," I say, "you called the sheriff's department?"

"Yeah." He toes the picture books on the bottom shelf of the coffee table.

"Did they question why she was out there? How she got out there? Who drove her there?" I squint at the jewelry box. "I'm sure they had to wonder why an eighty-something-year-old woman was sitting out in the rainy cold on a Wednesday night. Strange, don't you think?"

"Guess so." He grabs the book from the coffee table. Vicente Fernández. "Like I said, I don't fuck around with cops."

"Are they gonna do an autopsy?"

"Cut her open and shit?" He shakes his head. "I think she's getting cremated."

"Did the deputies give you a form documenting all of this?" I ask.

He pulls a folded square of paper from his back pocket.

INCIDENT REPORT

"Mind if I take a picture of this?" I ask.

He's rooting around the coffee table. "You can have it."

"You may need it for insurance and bank accounts." I email the form to my inbox.

"Oh. Then—" He holds out his hand, and I give it back.

"Could you give me a quick tour so that I can see what she liked, how she lived?" Those who may think they have nothing to say usually find their tongues as their feet move. I'm hoping this holds true for Mateo.

He sighs. "Not a long one cuz I have shit to do."

Disgust slithers around my belly. I really don't like Mateo Amador. He doesn't seem to be shaken up over finding his great-aunt dead on a pondside bench.

As we near the kitchen, I spot a business card on the breakfast table. A pretty woman beams at me and announces that she's:

ALESSANDRA VERASCIO, REALTOR, #1 IN AVALON!

My heart sinks as he walks me from the cute wainscot-walled bedroom with its rattan furniture and neat bed to the cute little bathroom, sea foam and white, crocheted toilet paper covers and day lilies. Felicity loved her little house. She loved fresh flowers. There are pictures of Felicity sitting on a red bench near a pond, surrounded by loved ones. And there are gaps on shelves and countertops. It's obvious that Mateo's picked over her things.

Why would she be out on a bench in this weather?

Why was he so quick to take back the incident report?

Why is there a real estate agent's card *anywhere* in this house?

Who *is* this kid?

17.

First of all: Why did I realize just now that today is Friday the thirteenth?

And second: Why am I, one of the only Black people in a small town, trying to follow someone without them knowing?

Am I that stupid?

And next time I try to be inconspicuous, I won't wear a red puffer jacket while trailing a teenager skateboarding to the pier with a box of his great-aunt's china and faux Fabergé eggs.

The haze helps. Not that Mateo looks over his shoulder to see me peeking around the pickup truck, and then the stairway between a spa and a real estate office. No, he keeps rolling on to Front Street. Because why would I want to follow him?

I can't even answer that, not really, but there's something shady about Mateo Amador that's leading me to zigzag from one side of the street to the other, fast walking sometimes and flat-out running other times, stuck between fear and curiosity, which are separated by an isthmus the width of a jelly bean.

My legs ache from scooting and running, squatting and bending. Since my arrival back on Monday, I haven't eaten a proper salad, eaten any fruit, nor slept for more than three hours. The lack of vitamins combined with no sun and no sleep means that my legs *should* hurt and that, yeah, I *should* have scurvy. I'm nauseated, that's for certain, and holding my breath like this makes me dizzier.

I need to better evaluate my choices.

Not now, though. Mateo and I are nearing the harbor.

Mateo skates into the ferry waiting area and stops at the banks of day lockers. He opens one of the larger lockers and stows the box, pays the dollar, grabs the key, then attaches that key fob to a ring heavy with several other locker keys. He texts someone, looks up and around.

I duck, staying behind a cart until I hear skateboard wheels roll away. Then, I scoot over to the locker he'd rented—11224. Is he treating day lockers like storage facilities? What else does he have in here? How can I find out?

I catch my breath at Pancake Cottage on Front Street, a place with high ceilings and white walls—a place that doesn't make me think "pancakes" or "cottage." Even though Gwen made muffins this morning, my soul cries out for berries sprinkled over a short stack of pancakes.

While eating, I open my laptop and type *Mateo Amador* into Google.

Los Angeles County v. Amador, Mateo—subscription required to read the details.

Los Angeles Police Department—Nextdoor. *On February 3, 2020, Mateo Amador, a 20-year-old local transient . . . Located Amador shortly thereafter and arrested him . . .* Another subscription required to access the details.

Mateo Amador Arrest Record Details—Mateo Amador of Los Angeles, age 17, was arrested for Domestic Assault in Avalon, California, on December 25, 2017, by Los Angeles Sheriff's Department.

Previous Arrests: burglary, assault, take vehicle w/o owner's consent.

Domestic assault.

Who did he beat?

I open a new tab and search the *Avalon Breeze* archives and the sheriff's logs from December 2017.

Deputies responded to an assault call on the 600 block
of Clemente Avenue. The informant stated a fight had
occurred. While talking to the informant, the sheriff's
dispatcher could hear crying in the background. Upon
arrival, deputies talked with the victim, who stated she
was arguing with her nephew when he pushed her to
the floor and hit her in the back of her head. A juve-
nile male, 17, of Avalon, was arrested for suspicion of
domestic assault and was booked at Avalon's sheriff
station.

My breath catches.

Mateo was still living with Felicity after he'd beaten her?

This morning, he mentioned that the townspeople hated his family.
Well, kid, maybe they had *reasons*.

And why the hell didn't Maddy warn me that Mateo Amador was
dangerous?

A quick search on Felicity's niece, Linda Amador, turns up a smor-
gasbord of shenanigans, from petty theft to narcotics, public drunken-
ness, and child endangerment.

Petty theft . . . Did she know Gwen? Looking at Linda's birth
date—she's now forty-six—she'd be too young to be a member of
Gwen's crew. Felicity, though, is the right age.

And Mateo . . . he could've killed his aunt.

Over another cup of coffee, I search on Louis Moncur. Burglar and sex
offender, he's a nightmare for the island of Santa Catalina, especially to
Joe and Kristina Elliott, owners of a cottage on Descanso. According
to an article published last year in the *Avalon Breeze*, the Long Beach
residents purchased the home in 2019, with the goal of making it a

vacation rental. Moncur claimed that he was a legal tenant and refused to move out—even though he had no documents to prove that. Moncur stated that he had an "oral lease agreement" with Yasmin and Nick Bongino, the cottage's previous owners. Because of his recent prison release, he couldn't find a job that paid enough to move elsewhere. The article, written by Maddy, quoted Moncur: "I've paid my dues to society. They want me to be homeless and to slip back into a life of crime. It just ain't fair."

Problem is: No one knows where the Bonginos are. They never purchased another new home. They haven't filed taxes. Some suspect that Louis Moncur had something to do with the Bonginos' disappearance, but they can't prove anything . . . *yet*. He was spotted a month ago, near the minigolf course, with a mouth filled with blood.

Right outside Pancake Cottage, Front Street on a rainy Friday in March is the opposite of Catalina Island postcards and travel sites. On this morning, the marina isn't bustling and loud with chunky-heeled young women taking selfies and group pics. No drunk-off-their-asses middle-aged men wearing high straw hats, their wives and girlfriends lugging white Island Threadz bags to the ferry. Even the everlasting putter of golf carts has diminished.

Some touristy stuff is still happening. The banners announcing tomorrow's kite festival and marathon flap above the cobblestone street. Two women in love pose in front of a bronze sea lion. A tricked-out multipassenger Eco Tour Jeep roars by with only four customers in rows of seats meant for eight. Thin rain that causes fender benders and traffic in LA drifts across the island, but weather is only one factor for the quiet. Rumors abound in Pancake Cottage that the second biggest city in the country will be shutting down any day now.

"That's ridiculous," a man says as he peppers his eggs. "They can't *shut down* LA. It's freakin' . . . *LA*, for Pete's sake."

This man has been wrong about so many other things during this breakfast hour. Sir, Drake is *not* the greatest rapper of all time. The New England Patriots *aren't* the greatest football team to ever play in the NFL. And he must not have ever *worn* UGG boots because, sir, they are hella comfortable, even in the summertime.

And so he's probably just as wrong in his "LA ain't shutting down" prediction.

Which means . . . LA *will* shut down.

I search for reviews of Realtor Alessandra Verascio—five stars from thirty reviews. "Phenomenally knowledgeable and helpful," and "A pleasure to work with every step of the way." Recent sales—a house on Canyon Terrace Road sold just last week for $730,000. Looks like Felicity's charming cottage. Back on March 1, another cottage—this island loves that word—sold for nearly $930,000. She averages three sales a month.

A quick look at a few real estate sites for on-sale homes . . . four lots at the Hamilton Cove development, a town house, a duplex, and two single-family houses.

"That's it?" I whisper.

There's nothing to buy here.

"Can I get you anything else?" The green-eyed waitress's name tag says TRACIE.

"Just the check."

Tracie reaches into her apron pocket and sifts through curled slips of paper. "Visiting?"

"No, I just moved here from LA back on Monday."

Tracie smirks. "Why would you do that?"

"Good opportunity."

She lays the receipt on the table. "Like?"

"I'm a writer over at the *Breeze*."

"Cool. So you know Noah."

I smile. "Yeah."

She flutters a hand at her face.

"Right? Hey. Question. Anything strange going on around here? Anything standing out?"

She laughs. "Standing out? Other than you?"

My cheeks burn. "Ha. Yeah. Other than me."

"Nope," she says. "Same ol', same ol'. 'Strange' and 'standing out' would be cool. Not too much of it, though. No one moves here for 'strange.' Oh. Wait. I heard that some campers went missing over in Two Harbors, that some convicted killer escaped from overtown, came on a ferry, and is hiding out in the backcountry.

"I heard that he ate some campers cuz they were easier to kill than the buffalo. I don't know about the eating part, but the missing campers—that's true. They ordered german pancakes the morning they left for the trails." She taps the check. "Pay that when you're ready."

"One more question. What happened at the rock garden last week?"

"Oh, *that*?" She rolls her eyes. "Okay, *that* was strange. The deputies and fire department spent all that time to find out those containers were just these weird backpacks from Norway. The sloshing sound? Water. In. A. Thermos. Not explosives."

And not a woman found dead on a stone bench.

While following Mateo earlier, I'd hidden in a stairway between a spa and a real estate office. That slender white building with the red trim belongs to Realtor Alessandra Verascio. An older couple wearing matching sweatshirts peer at listings taped to Verascio's front window. I glimpse several "For Rent" listings for cottages around the island, and more than one "For Sale" slip for yachts worth more than some people's houses.

I push open the door and a bell *ting-a-lings*. The office is as narrow as a double-wide trailer, and no natural light makes it past those listings taped on the windows. Two heavy desks hide beneath stacks of papers and folders. Older computers live atop file cabinets. A flight of stairs leads up to the second floor.

A young woman with small tight lips and big blue eyes sits at one of those heavy desks. Since I've been standing here, she's typed six thousand words per minute without blinking. A potted African violet wilts on the corner of her desk. A name plate says BIANCA WALSH.

Bianca's eyes dart to me, and her smile comes and goes just as quickly as the words spilling across the monitor's screen. "How may I help you today?" she asks, her eyes back on the screen.

"Is Alessandra in?"

Bianca finally stops typing. There's country music playing softly somewhere in the office. "Ms. Verascio is overtown today. Long Beach, I think. May I take a message?"

"What about . . . ?" My eyes scan the wall. A picture of Alessandra sits atop a picture pyramid of lesser Realtors: Stan Horvitz, Helen Nilsen, and Ziggy Lowe.

"Stan, Helen, and Ziggy are in the field until later today," the young woman says.

The doorbell *ting-a-lings*. Helen Nilsen, cotton-candy-pink lips and black bob sleek and shiny even in this weather, breezes through the door. Her kohl-lined eyes widen with surprise. "Coco!" she exclaims. "You're here. This is wonderful news."

"I'm hoping that you can help me," I say, letting her pull me into an Opium-scented hug.

"Of course, little one," she says. "Anything for Gwennie's girl."

Helen pulls me into a tiny office crammed with awards and fancy-looking certificates, framed pictures of her standing alongside John Wayne and Katy Perry, Ronald Reagan and Taylor Swift. A few frames show Flynn and Maddy, but none taken with Helen and whoever was Flynn's father. She pulls a legal pad from her desk drawer and a fountain pen too ornate to actually write. "We will get a *lot* for your wonderful house. *Millions* of dollars, setting you and Gwen up to live *anywhere* in the world."

I settle in the chair at the front of her desk. "I'm not here to sell my house."

She blinks at me. "That's probably the dumbest thing I've heard today." A beat. "No offense." She laughs.

I blush. "I'd like information on a few houses I hear are possibly going on sale."

Helen holds my gaze, then squares her shoulders. "You want to buy *another* house?"

"Well, it's more like . . . so, I just came from Felicity Amador's house over on Clemente."

"Miss Amador died this week," Helen says. "May her memory be a blessing."

I touch my heart spot. "Yes. So, will the house be on the market soon? Should I contact Linda Amador? Mateo, maybe? Who?"

"To buy? Absolutely not. Those people. They're . . . no, dearest. You come to *me* to buy *anything*." Helen squints at me. "You *know* there's a housing crisis on this beautiful island, don't you? People are absolutely *desperate* and will cut off their *entire* right hand to successfully purchase a home here. Just a warning, as an old family friend: you'll be overbid by thousands. *Hundreds* of thousands. A *million*, even."

My tongue feels thick, pissed at that slight. "What about the Paulsen house?"

Helen rolls her eyes. "That house is a mess. Whoever buys it will have to completely gut it. And there are people who will pay to gut it. Again: I wouldn't get my hopes up."

Like she knows my economic status from just looking at me. Helen don't know that I got a diamond-and-ruby stunner stuffed in a unicorn's ass.

177

"Is Alessandra working that house, too?" I ask.

"Colette," she says, leaning forward. "Are you interested in selling or buying, or are you here just asking questions? I really must start my day, dearest."

I clear my throat. "Guess I'm just asking questions. For now."

She turns and taps her computer keyboard. The screen brightens. "So wonderful to see you. I'll talk to you later, yes?" She grabs the phone receiver from the cradle and smiles her cotton-candy-pink smile. She's done with me.

I take one of her business cards from the holder. "Thanks for your time."

Out into the misty rain I go.

Yesenia Duran is now standing at the plate glass window, pretending to read a "For Sale" announcement for a yacht as big as this island. Without speaking, she beckons me to follow her down a side street and past a charming white clapboard inn.

What's the big secret?

She hustles to a small park beneath a grove of palm and eucalyptus trees. No one else is in the park—no children climb the teal and fuchsia play structures, no moms huddle on benches beneath the redwood gazebo.

Yesenia sits on one of those benches.

I sit beside her. "What's going on?"

She reaches into her jacket and pulls out a manila envelope. "Read these."

"You told me back on Tuesday to watch Gwen," I say. "How do you know my aunt?"

Her lips tremble. "She gave my mom a job at the hotel. We had nothing, and Gwen . . . she was so nice to us." She lifts her mouth into a smile. "Momma couldn't steal worth shit, but she had a great memory."

I look down at the envelope. "And this is . . . ?"

"Important." She holds out the envelope until I take it. And it feels like all of Avalon just saw me take it.

I start to open the flap, but she grabs my hand. "Not here. It's paperwork. Death reports. Hospital stuff, crime things, all involving the women who have died."

I blink at her. "O-kay." I shiver like I'm getting sick.

"My friend," Yesenia says, watching an old woman walk a Pomeranian. "She cleans the sheriff's station. They don't see her, either. She got these for me. We got these for you."

"Me?" I frown. "Why me?"

"Cuz this island took people away from you, too. You know what Avalon does. You know that it's not just this paradise for everybody who lives here." She stands from the bench. "Don't let them keep doing this. I gotta go." She gets up and hurries back down the street.

Upstairs, Aunt Gwen naps in the armchair. Her shoes are off.

She's not going anywhere.

I return to the driveway and turn the key to her raggedy red cart, and the damn thing rumbles on and sends a plume of exhaust into the air. It was perfect yesterday. So now, I have a choice: either I fix up this cart or use my legs or a bike to get around. Noah told me that Avalon law mandates one cart per address. And since the damn thing works . . .

No new buggy for me unless we chuck this one. But all my money must go to the house.

Onward.

According to my Maps app, Haypress Pond is a four-mile trek. I'm not walking four miles in the rain. I'm not a local yet, and the bougie Angeleno that still lives within me *refuses* to walk four miles up hills, between hills, in the freaking rain. That same bougie Angeleno who still *thrives* within me is glaring at the rainy sky right now.

Folks wave at me as I drive past. An old woman walking an old golden retriever, wearing a fur vest and exercise weights around her legs and wrists shouts, "How's Gwennie?"

The fire-engine-red cart with white flames, everyone knows it belongs to Gwen Weber.

"She's good," I shout back to the woman. "Watching TV and doing puzzles."

The woman gives me a thumbs-up. "Tell her that Lucky and I will see her tomorrow. I'm in the senior group training for the marathon and Gwen usually watches my old girl anytime I run." She pats the dog's head.

I say, "Okay," even though I have *no clue* who the hell this woman is.

Quiet envelops me as I putter past the pink hotel and the bright homes that make up the Flats. Down the block to my left, I spot Mateo Amador standing to the side of Paula Paulsen's house. He's holding a plastic shopping bag that looks weighed down with a heavy object. With no carts behind me, I stop and aim my camera phone in his direction. Why is he standing there? Did he know Paula Paulsen? *What's in that bag?*

He spots me.

My heart leaps, and I press the gas, puttering up the hill past the park and gazebo, past the country club, up Cemetery Road—how appropriate. As I drive this thing with its open doors and no windows, I feel vulnerable, antsy, goosefleshed down to my bones. No matter what Noah says, someone *can* snatch me, hit me, shoot me as I drive *and get away with it*. Someone murdered my family and certainly did.

The cart whines as the incline increases. Hillsides of cactus . . . more hillsides of cactus . . . the road curves left, giving way to parking lots filled with trucks, stacked canoes, and a bunch of other men's treasures that all look like junk to me. Directions tell me to continue straight to reach the reservoir, but I can't—a yellow gate blocks access to the trail.

A shaggy man wearing a field coat waves at me from the tower of kayaks. "Where you trying to go?"

"Haypress Pond," I shout over the cart's puttering.

He chuckles. "Can't drive there. Gotta hike or take a tour."

I point at that trail. "So who gets to drive that?"

"Legally? Tour companies, private shuttles, law enforcement, fire . . . conservancy folks, those types."

"Thanks."

He tips his cap, then waddles back over to the kayaks.

Felicity Amador could not have driven her cart here alone. She sure as hell didn't walk.

Instead of turning left to go home, I turn right.

The rock garden sits beneath swaying trees. In the middle of the circle is a boulder the size of a basketball. Someone has placed a small picture of Paula Paulsen and an electric candle on that rock. Smaller stones radiate outward in eight rings, each larger the farther away it is from the center. The bench, slick and gray from the rain, is made from flat slabs of slate, large enough to seat only one person. Just nights ago, that person was Paula Paulsen.

A beautiful, tranquil spot—and it's not easily accessible for a sick old woman.

Yeah, I call bullshit.

Who brought her here and left her to die?

I think about that for a moment and hold my breath as long as I can.

The bougie Angeleno in me is happy that Gwen watches TV instead of walking her dog around town in a fur vest and wearing body weights.

I say a prayer—*Be with Paula's friends and family*—as a headache worms its way between my eyes. Blame the noise and vibration from Gwen's cart and every cart on the island. Even way up here, I can hear those carts buzzing around Avalon. But I also hear the swish of leaves and palm fronds and the echoes of rain falling across the canyon floor.

I sit there on that stone bench, and I breathe . . . and breathe . . . then, I open Yesenia's envelope.

INCIDENT REPORT

Name: Vera Johansen

Injury Description: none observed at scene

Foul Play Suspected: No

At 7:18 p.m., Dispatch received a 911 call regarding the discovery of a dead body at Black Jack Campground. LA Sheriff's Unit 111 (Deputy Peter Santos) was dispatched and arrived at the scene . . .

7:44 p.m. . . . . was directed to the entrance of a green tent on the beach where there was the body of an adult female, who the deputy identified as Vera Johansen . . .

Investigator determined the victim had been dead 12 to 24 hours . . .

There's a death certificate: . . . immediate cause of death . . . cardiac arrest. Underlying causes: congestive cardiomyopathy—17 years, chronic obstructive pulmonary disease—four years.

So Vera Johansen went camping and probably shouldn't have. Too much exertion, too cold out there on the beach. She'd had a heart attack; but even before then, she'd had COPD.

Reading the interview of Monica Murphy, the woman who found Vera Johansen, depicts something different, though. The tent had been there when Murphy's party arrived, and they'd seen no one enter or leave that tent for a day. Foxes and ravens tried to chew their way into the tent because they smelled food. The wildlife diners were starting to annoy Murphy and her friends, and they decided to check out the tent and maybe store the food in a better container. Murphy pulled up the zipper on the tent, and there was an old lady wrapped in a sleeping bag. Murphy then checked to see if the woman was breathing, but she was too hard and too solid to be alive. There wasn't a knapsack or anything in the tent. Just the old woman. Just the sleeping bag.

Okay, so that's strange.

How did Vera Johansen reach the campground way on the other side of the island?

And who left her in that tent?

Why would someone target this old lady?

In the envelope, there's an incident report for Consuela Barraza, and it reads like Vera's.

> 911 call . . . Body discovered at Bird Park at 5:12 a.m.
> . . . Deputy (Cooper) was dispatched to the scene . . .
> Observed a lifeless human body, a woman in her late
> seventies, lying on the ground and partially supported
> by a tiled wall . . . MedicAlert bracelet identified the de-
> ceased as Consuela Barraza . . .

No mention of blood or weapons or anything that could've caused Consuela Barraza to be found dead at a former aviary turned preschool on the first morning of March.

Consuela's death certificate also lists congestive heart failure as the immediate cause of death. Underlying cause of death: coronary heart disease.

Maybe Consuela had taken an early-morning walk, did too much walking, and her heart just couldn't handle it.

There are no other documents in the envelope.

My phone screen is filled with messages, though—somehow I'd turned off the sound, and with the rumbling from the golf cart, I couldn't feel the phone vibrating.

News alert . . . another news alert . . .

My heart jumps.

A Life Alert notification from Gwen's GPS.

She's left the house and is now walking along Metropole Avenue.

The songs of cooing doves make me look away from the phone.

The rain has stopped, and the branches dip under the weight of water.

A family of deer wander close by in the high grass.

My skin burns, and beads of sweat pop along my eyebrows.

Feels like someone's watching me.

"Hello?" I say.

No answer.

I stand and creep around the rock garden.

No one else is here.

Just deer.

Just doves.

Just rocks formed into a circle.

Just me.

18.

Back at home, the grate that leads beneath the house has been fixed, and new wire now blocks that entrance. No creature can burrow there, have babies, and die.

Another change: the front door is not the same front door that I exited this morning.

Handy Andy has been handy.

Gwen is shuffling up the block, bright in her pink raincoat and matching Wellingtons. She's licking an ice-cream cone and looks as though all is right in the world.

My heart flares seeing her just . . . *wander* Beacon Street. "Auntie, why are you outside?"

The smile on her face dies. "Excuse me?"

I hop out of the cart. "You shouldn't be out in the rain like this. You should've called me. Where were you?" I take her elbow to lead her back up the slick, rickety stairs.

She snatches away from me and spits, "Don't *touch* me." Her hot eyes sear my cheeks. "I went out for some fresh air. I can't do that now?"

"Of course you can," I say. "But you can also slip. You can also get lost again. What if that social worker saw you wandering? She could have you taken away—"

Gwen sneers at me. "And you'd love that, wouldn't you?"

"Auntie," I say. "I'm just trying—"

"I made it all this time without you here," she snaps. "I'm not no invalid. And why am I wearing this stupid necklace if you still gotta worry?"

I squeeze the bridge of my nose. "I know, Auntie. I'm sorry. You're right."

She natters on about me taking the cart, about her need to go to the post office, and about her desire for ice cream. She growls about being a grown-ass woman who doesn't get bossed around and just because I decided that this is my house now *blah blah blah.*

I take her reprimands because I deserve it, even if my motivations— keeping her safe and happy—are a value to me. "I'm still at work," I say. "Do you need me to bring you anything?"

She snorts, then makes her way up the stairs.

I watch, wincing every time her foot falls funny. "You need help?" I start to climb the steps, but she glares at me. "I just saw a friend of yours. Fur vest, golden retriever named Lucky. She's in the marathon tomorrow. She says, 'Hi.'"

Gwen makes it to the top landing, entering the house and slamming the door closed.

She didn't use the house key. Did she leave the door unlocked?

Colette, stop.

I store that worry in my back pocket, then hop back into the cart. At least the door is fixed.

My phone vibrates in my hand.

A text from Noah. Buy you some tacos?

Ugh. I wanna make it up to Gwen for being . . . thoughtless? Paranoid? What?

Please?

Goose bumps prick my neck and arms, and I look down Beacon Street.

Louis Moncur stands at the end of the block, staring in my direction. He's just . . . standing there. Doing nothing except . . .

My phone vibrates again with Noah's Please?

I tear my eyes away from Louis Moncur to type back, Sure!

Noah's directions lead me away from the harbor and onto an oceanside road that hugs the curves of the hill on my right side. The air feels softer here. On this road, life is less ordered—the new fences against the hillsides are there to stop rocks from tumbling again onto the highway.

Soon, the Buffalo Nickel is on my left, with a white buffalo painted on a brown wooden door, a cobblestone courtyard, glowing fairy lights, and a red-tiled roof. The cantina sits next door to a helicopter landing pad—and a bird is blasting off right now with its propellors spinning a million miles a minute.

Noah sits at a window booth, sipping water and swiping around his phone.

I tap his arm. "Hey!"

"Hey, you!" His face lights up seeing me, and this time, he slips out of the booth and gives me a long hug.

We immediately order drinks: beer for him, mineral water for me. "And taquitos and ceviche to start," he tells our server, Pedro.

"Thanks for inviting me," I add. "I would've never found this place on my own."

"You don't drink?" he asks. "I noticed that the other night."

"Nope. All the foolish things I do, I do completely sober."

"So, obits," he says, peering at me. "How did a girl named Coco, of all things, start writing obituaries?"

I give a one-shouldered shrug. "Pretty easily—it was the only job they'd give me at the *Times*, first of all. And second . . . I'm trying to figure out my life, even now, and my family's legacy, and no one's helped me with that."

I look up at him and know that tears shine bright in my eyes. "But I can do that for other families, you know? I can tell them a story about something that may have been so insignificant once upon a time— how their dad drank only RC Cola or Grandma fried chicken in that apron—and give it meaning, make it *special*. Help them see that life just doesn't *happen* for no reason. Every decision affects you more than you know."

Noah thinks about that, then smiles. "Yeah, I know." His phone buzzes from the table. He peeks at the screen, frowns, then picks it up.

I pluck a tortilla chip from the basket. "Everything okay?"

He taps out a text. "My dad and a few of my cousins and uncles are stuck in Italy right now. The airports are closing from . . . whatever the hell's going on and . . ." He takes a deep breath and pushes it out. "What have you been up to all day? You weren't in the office, and for a minute I thought you'd quit and sailed back to LA."

Pedro sets our drinks at our hands and a bowl of ceviche in the middle of the table.

"I've been busy." I catch Noah up on my interview with Mateo Amador.

"*That* guy," Noah says.

"You know him?"

"Not personally, but he's always in the sheriff's log."

I sip my bubbly water. "Violent?"

Noah nods.

"Greedy?"

Noah nods again.

"A murderer?"

Noah squints at me. "Some of his closest friends are, though. And I've heard Mateo doesn't appreciate young women telling him no. So, yes, please. Be very careful."

I share my suspicions about the dead woman's great-nephew. "I can't prove it yet," I say. "And I talked to Helen Nilsen—she wasn't any help. And after talking with a waitress and a few other people, I've learned that horrific violence does not happen here."

Noah grunts and swigs his beer.

"How did Felicity's daughter Socorro die?" I ask.

Noah cocks an eyebrow. "According to Linda—"

"Mateo's mom, right?"

Noah nods. "Boating accident. She bumped her head and fell overboard."

I squint at him. "I'm hearing something in your tone."

"Yes."

I pause, then say, "Why?"

"Some say she bumped her head for insurance. But then, she died, and the family got the payout." He lays his hand on top of mine. "Don't go charging in with your battle-ax, asking shit like, 'Did you kill your aunt Socorro for two hundred and fifty thousand dollars?'"

My mouth goes dry. "I'm good at getting information from people, Noah. I'm not green."

"But people here see you as . . ."

"An outsider?"

"You are."

"I've not seen one Black person in the Flats."

"See?"

"I'm probably the only one in your life."

"Not counting tourists and my life *here*, yes, definitely. And probably for everyone else in their non-tourist-related day-to-day. Which is why you need to step thoughtfully."

I roll my eyes.

"Don't ask Mateo. Find other people. Act like you're fascinated by this place, by the type of person who decides to live here. Flatter them for being mavericks. Have a good piece of gossip to share, and they'll feel the need to reciprocate."

"For instance?"

He leans forward. "So you know, I'm working on this obit for Felicity Amador. And they'll say, 'Nice woman, made great soufflés.' And you'll say, 'I hate that she died the way she did.' Their eyes will bulge, and you'll wait and nod with much wisdom. Then, you will tsk and sigh. They won't be able to stand it, and they'll whisper, 'You know, Mateo beat her a few years ago.' And you, being new, will say, 'He seemed so sweet. He's so heartbroken right now.' They'll roll their eyes and say, 'Lemme tell you . . .' et voilà."

I smirk. "That simple."

Our food arrives.

I finish my first taquito in two bites. "Since you've been so generous . . ." I slide the envelope that Yesenia gave me over to him. "You can't say anything to anyone."

Noah opens the flap. "What is it?"

I say nothing as he flips between the papers related to Vera Johansen's body being found at Black Jack Campground.

He shrugs. "I knew about this. She had a heart attack on a camping trip. And?"

I crunch into my next taquito. "If you actually *read* the report—"

"I don't have to." He shakes his head. "Again: old ladies dying. Vera was very sweet and very sick. Always pulling that oxygen tank around like a third lung. Guess it was."

"There was nothing in the tent."

"Meaning . . . ?"

"She had COPD, right? That oxygen tank was her third lung, you just said that. That tank wasn't in the tent. There was *nothing* in the tent. Because that wasn't her tent, and she wasn't camping."

He blinks at me.

"*And* I tried to visit Haypress Pond today," I say. "That's where Felicity was found."

He picks up the documents again. "And?"

"It's inaccessible by golf cart and to regular Joes. I couldn't see it."

"Right." He looks up. "And that means . . . ?"

"Someone drove her there in a car and also had permission to drive the backcountry."

His eyebrows raise. "You're good."

"You have no idea." I crunch into a taquito.

He brushes a crumb from my lip, and his thumb lingers there, and I burn and burn, and I want him to lean forward and kiss me right here in this booth as Bob Marley wails from the jukebox. But his phone vibrates, and his gaze drops to read the text message.

I wait as he taps out a response.

"Sorry about that." He puts the phone down and tries to smile.

"Who is Mona?" I ask.

"I don't know," he says. "Who?"

"That rude couple mentioned her?"

His eyebrows scrunch, then lift. "Oh. Her. Mona's my stalker."

I snort.

He doesn't. "Seriously, she's, like, one more 'show up naked at my house again' away from a restraining order."

"Yikes."

"And I never dated her, never slept with her . . ." He makes a face. "And I know who she voted for in the last election. I wouldn't trust her with a corkscrew, and she wants my dick in her mouth? Nope. Not gonna happen."

I throw my head back and laugh.

He chuckles. "Am I right, though?"

"I knew a guy who was all teeth."

"How far did he get?"

"My mouth, and afterward, it felt like I'd been eating Cap'n Crunch all night."

He explodes with laughter, then raises his glass. "Here's to finding smart people who know how and when to use their teeth."

We toast.

"Okay," I say. "So you know real estate here."

"I do."

"There aren't any houses to buy."

"Not really." He drags a chip through the ceviche. "How is this relevant to obituaries?"

"When I was at Felicity Amador's house this morning and at Paula Paulsen's house back on Tuesday, I saw business cards for 'Alessandra Verascio, Avalon's #1 Realtor.'"

"Paula's house is worth one-point-three million dollars," Noah says, "and it looks like it's been through the war. It's crazy. Old people live in the best houses."

I snort. "You didn't just say that."

"It's true. If Paula's or Felicity's families want to sell, I don't see that as a bad thing. *Mateo* can't afford the property taxes. Linda's way the hell in Atlanta, and she's not coming back here, not after all her shenanigans. A family who can love it and take care of it deserves to buy it."

"Deserves?" I say, eyebrow high, muscles clenched. "Back in the day, there were people on this island who didn't think *my* family *deserved* the house on Beacon Street."

"They were wrong."

"I don't like that word. *Deserves.*"

"My bad." Noah squeezes my hand. "And I didn't mean it like that. Still holding old grudges all this time?"

"Uh, *yeah*." My annoyance flits like a gnat between my eyes. "Murder isn't the same as 'he didn't return my lawnmower' or 'she slept with my boyfriend.'"

"You're right, but . . ." He shrugs. "You're working too hard on this—"

"I just got here," I say, laughing. "And I just dropped a story in your lap." I cock my head. "I mean, where was Mateo or Louis Moncur on the night Paula Paulsen died? I saw Mateo at Paula's. Did he know her? Where are the Bonginos? Did Moncur kill them?"

He drains the rest of the beer, then holds up the empty glass to the bartender. "And eat them? And leave their bones on an altar made from chicken bones?"

"You're mocking me. Don't do that. I don't react well to shit like that." This time, *my* phone vibrates. A GPS notification. "Gwen's out of the house again."

"That a bad thing?"

"She's losing her memory."

"People know her," Noah says, "and they'll make sure she's okay. This isn't LA, Colette, where senior citizens go missing and Silver Alerts blow up everybody's phones."

I watch the pink dot—Gwen—move down Beacon Street. "I should be there—"

Noah takes my phone. "Let's go dancing."

After he pays the bill, we climb into our carts. The sun has set, and the island flickers with light. I follow him back into town.

The Chi Club is steps away from the sheriff's station, in a building with a green awning.

"I know," he says, "it's not the Standard or the Mayan, *but!*" He raises his vape pen, then blows out a cloud of that fruit-scented vapor. "It's all we have."

I've stepped into an eighties movie: there's a dance floor and pool tables, and everything's bathed in fluorescent pinks, oranges, and greens. "No one's here," I say.

No customers sit on stools at the bar. No one hangs out at the pool table.

The bartender tosses us a wave and shouts, "What's up, dude?"

We wander to the digital jukebox and choose six songs for five dollars. Noah pulls me to the empty dance floor.

I wiggle my hips and ass to Cardi B, and he steps back to enjoy the view. Then, he pulls me close, and we rock against each other in time. The vibe slows with an R & B classic, "Knockin' da Boots." Noah shouts, "He-eey," in that old-school way. I slink into his arms, and we slow dance to this slow jam.

He squeezes me and holds me tighter.

I squeeze back and press my body to his.

Our foreheads meet, and we gaze into each other's eyes.

"So should I be worried about that matadora spearing me through the heart?"

"Not at all."

"Should I be worried about stalker Mona?"

He smiles. "Well . . . maybe."

I smile. "Okay."

We dance.

His nose nuzzles my neck.

My skin explodes from his touch.

"Ready to go?" His warm breath gently tugs every hair on my skin.

I can barely whisper, "Yes," before sort of passing out.

He leads me outside.

The cold mist hits me and clears my head some but does nothing for the fire raging through the rest of me.

Holding hands, we walk to the harbor, stopping at the fountain. The slick streets are empty—we have the island to ourselves. We stand there, we rock there, nose to nose as misty rain drifts around us.

"Who gave you this?" I tap the compass pendant around his neck. "A girl?"

"Yeah," he says, "and I'll love her forever."

"Did she give it to you so that you'll be able to find your way back to her?"

"Yep, which is why I rarely take it off. I don't wanna be lost."

I laugh. "Your mom, she gave that to you."

"She did." He smiles. "Have a good time tonight?"

"The best time," I whisper.

He kisses me.

It is the simplest, sweetest kiss in the world.

19.

Noah tastes like whiskey and gummy bears.

Before tonight, I hated the flavors of smoke and wood on a man's tongue. Tonight, though . . . on Noah . . . he is a feast of flavors, and his kisses taste like vanilla, oranges, and candied almonds.

Right there beside the water, we make out like nineteen-year-olds, and I'm now the girl that mothers whisper about, the one letting her boyfriend disrespect her like that in public.

"Come home with me," I say, catching my breath.

Before he can say yes—and his lips are formed to say yes—his phone rings with "Bohemian Rhapsody." His eyebrows furrow.

"Uh-oh," I say. "Your mother heard you were making out on the pier."

"I'm about to get grounded." He pulls his phone from his pocket, and the picture of an older blonde with his eyes brightens the phone's screen. "Sorry, I have to—"

"No need to explain." I give him the "no problem" smile.

"Mom, hey," he says. "Everything okay?"

I step away and give him space. Out on the Pacific, lights burn on barges that carry televisions, fuzzy jackets, and scooters. I check my own phone and find a missed call from Andrea Liszl. She's left a voice mail.

"Colette. Andrea, hi. Seems we're having a hard time connecting. This book, oh my goodness, we have to get going on the manuscript. Listen: I'm flying to the West Coast next week, and I've never been to Catalina Island. Let's say I pop over and we meet in person? Let me know. Talk soon. Bye."

My stomach is a storm now, and I regret listening to this message. Not that the dying mood is all on me . . .

Noah's hand covers his eyes as he listens to his mother shout into the phone.

I don't want to be at the hospital . . . They say I have a fever . . . Come get me . . .

"Hey, Mom." Noah's eyes flick over to me. "Okay . . . okay . . . she hung up." He pushes out a breath, then runs his hand through his wet hair.

I tug the sleeve of his jacket. "Sounds like chaos."

He tries to smile. "She's at the hospital. No one except her nurse is there—"

"Go," I say, shooing him away, feeling guilty about not checking on Gwen all this time.

He takes my hand, then leans in for another kiss. "I'll walk you to your cart."

Then, at my cart, he says, "I should follow you home."

"I live *right there*." I point toward Beacon Street. "Less than a mile away. You're going in the opposite direction."

"Seriously," he says, "The night nurse is—"

"Bohemian Rhapsody" plays from the phone again, and the picture of Elle Bancroft once again brightens the screen.

"She needs you," I say.

"*I* need *you*." He kisses me, and my blood becomes boozy even though I haven't had a drink since June 2001.

But I push him away. "I'm not going anywhere."

One last kiss, and he climbs into his cart.

At the stop sign, I turn right, and he turns left.

Damn it. A tourist's golf cart blocks my driveway. I make a three-point turn, and my shoulders and arms burn from twisting this steering wheel.

There are no other empty spaces on this short block.

Pissed, I putter along until I find a spot a block and a half away. My phone vibrates with a text message from Noah.

Home safe?

No parking on my block

Tourist Airbnb assholes

LOL

You're sounding like a true local already

Let me know when you're home

At hospital now

20.

I open my eyes.

Bright light shines past the pink bedsheet. That light isn't from a flashlight. No—that's light from the sun.

What time is it?

I reach for my phone, and the muscles in my arm creak.

I'm wearing the same sweatshirt and yoga pants from last night. I haven't changed position from last night's "face up to watch flames dance on the ceiling."

My phone claims . . . *That can't be right.* It *can't* be noon.

Can it?

It is the correct time.

I got all this sleep and couldn't enjoy it?

My phone also tells me that I have messages.

From Maddy: You still work here right? Jk Seriously tho the kite fest??

From Noah:

> I had the best time last night

> Didn't think I'd wake up in a hospital waiting room though

My mother has a sinus infection

No virus tho!!

Nothing from Dr. Tamaguchi.
I respond to Maddy's message first.

Ha ha

Working on Felicity's obit

Challenging since my only source of info came from her great-nephew

Then Noah:

Sorry to hear that and sorry that I couldn't make your morning as sexy as you deserve

How's your mom?

I email the literary agent and tell her that, yes, Catalina is lovely but rainy right now and that I'd love to meet her.

But not now. Right now, I need to grab my laptop and bang out a draft of Felicity Amador's obit before leaving the bed. Distractions are waiting for me beyond this mattress.

After completing the worst draft ever written, I drag my bones to the bathroom. All of me aches, but at least I'd danced and enjoyed life. I'd been touched and I'd been kissed.

That achiness washes off me as soapsuds now circle the drain. I brush my teeth, then slather lotion across my body. I feel refreshed and moisturized, ready to attack a second draft of the Amador obituary.

Not a lot of rain today but plenty of mist and haze. The colors of the room change as the sun moves above it all.

The incident report.

I'd taken a picture of the original that Mateo didn't care about at first. Handwritten responses fill the form.

Circumstances: *death*

Decedent: *Felicity Amador*

Clothes: *black slacks, orange overcoat, sweater*

Sudden / apparent heart attack

Place: *Haypress Pond*

The statement from Mateo isn't any different from the story he told me yesterday.

I search the *Avalon Breeze* archives for "Felicity Amador" and find none. I visit social media community boards, and only three people have commented on a post announcing Felicity Amador's death.

Delia Michaelsen: *She made the best cakes and was sweeter than every pastry she ever made. RIP Fel!*

Iris Puchulski: *Oh no when are the services?*

Graham Zoltar: *Her family what losers they didn't deserve her*

I send each poster a message explaining that I'm writing Felicity's obit and if they'd like to share a memory . . .

Graham responds. *Felicity's daughter Socorro was a teacher's assistant in my class and Felicity's niece Linda worked in the cafeteria. Linda and her brother Hector would beat me up behind the casino, then take my bike and ride it around. One time they bent the frame. Felicity told my mother that since the other Amadors wouldn't make things right that she would buy me a new bike. She must've said something to Linda and Hector because they never took my bike again. They took other things but not my bike.*

I sigh—can't really use this memory.

Unless I spin it. *Felicity was a protector of the weak. She wanted to make things right for those in need.*

My stomach growls, but I refuse to leave this room. Food will be my reward. Maybe I'll treat Gwen to a fancy dinner at the restaurant on the water's edge.

I click on the *Breeze*'s calendar of events. *Shit.* The marathon and kite festival. I *kinda* remember Maddy mentioning that my attendance was required. Both events started hours ago.

I text Maddy.

Sorry for screwing up today

I'm just trying to adjust and it's going slow

She's responding—ellipses bubble and stop . . . bubble . . . stop . . .
What is she gonna say, and why is she taking so—
This was a pretty busy day, she texts.

Lot of VIPs and orgs ran the race

Glad I was there to interview and take pics

I know adjusting is tough

Don't let Noah distract you

I'll let it slide today

I answer with thank-you hands and a thumbs-up, and then:

BTW you didn't tell me re Mateo's criminal history

Heads-up appreciated next time

Weren't you a big time crime editor at the Bruin?

Thought you would've researched on your own

Don't think Mateo has anything to do with you being distracted
by Noah tho

IMHO

Her words—and that stupid shrug emoji—hurt. They twist in my gut and in my heart; then they catch fire. Not cool being thought of as a fuckup. I'm *not* a fuckup, but sometimes, I have some fucked-up ways. Fuckups wake up at noon and miss marathons and skip the chance to gush over some tenth grader's Minecraft-themed kite.

As for Noah: he didn't distract me.

In college, Maddy said shit like that whenever I was with a guy and not doing shit for her. I saw *Batman Begins* with one of the starters of UCLA's lacrosse team instead of attending a lecture with Bob Woodward for the second time that week. *You're gonna let dick distract you and keep you earthbound,* Maddy had emailed me. *FOCUS FOCUS FOCUS,* she'd written on a whole pad of sticky notes and then stuck them all over our apartment after I'd gone out for sushi with a reporter who reminded me of Blair Underwood. I mean . . . Bob Woodward or Blair Underwood, and I'm twenty years old. Come *on.*

It is almost four o'clock by the time I complete the obituary's final draft. I then organize emails and place important dates for the coming week into my calendar.

Tomorrow, I will visit the museum and check out the Esther Williams exhibit and then write a bomb-ass article on it. That makes me chuckle. Have "Esther Williams" and "bomb-ass" ever been together in a sentence? I finally open the bedroom door. My sitting room looks golden in the light of the dying day. Grit and flakes capture sunbeams and twinkle like fairy dust.

The light is brightest upstairs. Gwen, wearing a lemon-colored sweatsuit, sits on the couch with a dirty martini and plate of snacks. "The world is ending," she slurs. "We're all gonna die."

The news on the screen: Los Angeles is days away from Safer at Home mandates. Thousands around the world are dying. Scientists wearing bunny suits, care teams wearing protective gear, crowded emergency rooms, weeping families . . .

"We're not gonna die." I grab the TV remote control. "Smart people know things—they got it under control. It's America. Mind if I change the channel?"

She waves a hand and finishes her cocktail.

I find a random basketball game and turn down the volume. "So." I tap her knee. "Let's go out to dinner. Do you feel like lobster? I feel like lobster."

A grin spreads across her face. "And crab cakes. Ooh, and a proper martini."

"Is that a yes?" I ask. "Will you be my date tonight?"

She nods and her eyes sparkle.

"Let's get dressed." I help her stand. "Let's plan to leave at . . . five o'clock."

"You ain't got to tell me twice." She sashays to her bedroom.

I pop back down the stairs, open my laptop, then launch my favorite nineties R & B playlist. First song: Destiny's Child and "Bills, Bills, Bills." I paw through my clothes as nineties divas sing. Sexy black tonight. These pants and this halter top. It's fifty degrees out and misty, but that's what jackets—

Upstairs, glass breaks.

Gwen yelps.

Is she pregaming with another martini—

A thud.

I freeze in place as Coko from SWV sings about rain.

"Auntie," I shout, "you drop something?"

No response.

I pause SWV and listen.

Nothing.

I pull up the halter top and slip on my flip-flops. I shout, "I'm coming," then hurry up the stairs, heart in my chest, hoping that thud wasn't my aunt collapsing.

Gwen stands in the doorway of her bedroom, her eyes shiny with fear.

"What happened?" I ask.

Her mouth moves but she can't speak. She hands me the fireplace poker.

It's like that?

I grip the heavy iron weapon, trembling like I've guzzled too many cups of coffee. My heart flutters from that same caffeine-high except that I've had no caffeine today.

I creep closer to the kitchen. Closer . . . closer . . .

Glass shards sparkle against the linoleum. Cold air blows in through a newly opened window square above the plywood still standing in for the broken bottom pane. My eyes peck over the sharp debris in search of the heavy object that thudded . . .

That. The forty-ounce Mickey's beer bottle beneath the dishwasher. A piece of paper sticks from the bottle's mouth.

What the hell?

After taking pictures of the broken glass and the beer bottle beneath the dishwasher, I grab a pair of latex dishwashing gloves and carefully retrieve the bottle with two fingers, one at the top and one at the bottom.

This is evidence.

I ease the note from the bottle's mouth and grimace as the stink of old beer fills my nose. I use the same care to carefully open the note, and I gasp at the green-inked handwriting there.

THIS HOUSE IS OURS!!!

21.

"Who threw that?" Gwen clutches the bedpost as though it's keeping her from drowning.

I push the hair away from my face. "Don't know, Auntie."

"Why'd they throw it?" she asks, her eyes manic. "What did you do now?"

I don't answer her questions because I've answered three times already, and my responses will never change.

I don't know why they threw it.

I haven't done anything.

"Answer me," she shouts.

My heart leaps into my throat, and I shout back, "I haven't *done* anything."

"Bull," she spits. "You come here—just like you all came here before—and everything goes to shit. You're gonna get me killed just like . . ." She clamps her lips, swallowing her accusation.

She doesn't have to complete that sentence, because I already know what she's thinking. *You're gonna get me killed just like Reggie, Al, and Langston.*

She plops on the bed. "Who they think they are? This house is *my* house."

No, Gwen. This house is *my* house, no matter how many times she says this, no matter how many copies of titles and deeds she steals from my boxes, no matter how many times she breaks a window or throws a bottle, no matter—

"When are the deputies getting here?" she asks.

Light-headed, I lean against the doorframe. "The dispatcher said they'll get here as soon as they can."

She glares at me, accusing me of . . . *what?* Not protecting her? Of surviving twenty years ago? A small part of me remains upright, remembering Gwen's inauthentic umbrage back in the day, the huffing and puffing even though *she'd* been a creator of chaos. And now, it's possible that *she* paid someone to throw the bottle through the glass pane just to scare me, just to hold something over me, just to take back the house that doesn't belong to her.

To make me return to Los Angeles.

Just like twenty years ago, she wants me back in LA.

She's always kept the good stuff for herself, this island included. She found Catalina Island and never wanted to share it with my father and, now, me. This has always been Gwen's way, sneaking in through the cracks and stealing all the shiny things, hoarding trinkets and talismans like dragons hoard runes and gold, then handing the junk off to her partners in crime. I'd bet my life that her BFF's bedroom is bursting with emerald brooches, expensive silk robes, and ornate letter openers.

As we wait for the deputies to arrive, I take more pictures of the broken glass on the kitchen floor, the violated back door, and the Mickey's beer bottle. I retrieve my laptop and bring it to the living room.

THIS HOUSE IS OURS!!!

Who is "ours"?

The people who killed my family?

I search the few digital files I have on my family's case. That night and days afterward, the forensic investigators collected cell phones and charging cords. One fired .40-caliber casing. Keys, bloodstained clothes, different forms of identification, blood . . . no knife.

I search the PDFs of court transcripts.

No knife mentioned being found in those exhibits.

Who found that knife, and where had it been all that time?

Aunt Gwen shuffles to the kitchen, considers the mess on the floor, then shuffles back to her bedroom.

I toggle over to the archives for the *Avalon Breeze* and search the sheriff's log from late June 2001 to the first week of July, since the murders occurred on June 23 . . . except there are no sheriff's logs in those issues. There are no mentions of the murders in *any* issue, and it's like my family came and went like every other family on vacation. The only proof that the Webers lived briefly on this island? The deed to this house.

More information lives in the boxes stacked inside my parents' bedroom.

I stand at that closed door, but I won't reach for the doorknob. I don't wanna step into that space. Right now, my tank is empty.

An hour passes without a deputy standing in my kitchen. From the living room television, a woman's voice reports on the doom sweeping the globe; but right now, I care about only the doom sweeping this island.

Someone knocks on the front door.

A deputy with a smooth olive face and a crew cut, wearing khaki green pants and a long-sleeved khaki shirt, stands on the porch. The name beneath his gold star says P. Santos. He looks at the steno pad in his hands, then looks back at me. "Are you Colette Weber?" A sheriff's department Jeep sits in the middle of Beacon Street.

I offer a grateful smile. "Yes. Thank you for coming."

A minute later, he's standing in the kitchen, surveying the vandalism.

Gwen shuffles in to join us. "You see what they done, Petey?"

"I see it, Miss Gwen." He offers her a hug. "You okay?" There's true concern in his eyes.

"No, I'm *not* okay." She shoots me a glare. "I've just been unsettled lately."

"We're all feeling that, Miss Gwen." Santos turns to me. "Did you see who threw it?"

I shake my head. "I was downstairs getting ready for dinner."

"I was in my room," Gwen adds. "Not expecting none of this."

Santos scribbles into his pad. "Any reason someone would do this? Gwen, I'm asking you more than Colette here."

He knows her, too.

"I don't know *nothing*, Petey," she says, adopting the little-old-lady stoop. "I'm not out in them streets like I used to be." A teardrop rolls down her cheek, and she swipes it away.

Deputy Santos stares at her a second more, then grunts.

"There's a note." I point at the bottle. "The asshole kinda says it." I offer Deputy Santos a pair of dishwashing gloves.

He slips on his own pair of latex gloves, then lifts the bottle as carefully as I did. He eases the note from the bottle's mouth.

THIS HOUSE IS OURS!!!

The deputy's jaw works this way and that. "Do you know who 'ours' could be?"

I shake my head.

He looks to Gwen. She's staring out the kitchen window above the sink.

His shoulder radio crackles and buzzes as he takes pictures of the broken windowpane, the glass on the floor, and the beer bottle.

Blood fizzes in my veins and makes my skin hurt. I close my eyes and try to will the crackles and buzzes and blurps and beeps to stop.

"You okay?" Santos's voice pulls me back to the kitchen.

"Someone followed me home Monday night," I say. "Crept around outside. I thought I was imagining it but . . ." I wave a hand at the glass. "Guess not."

Santos squints at me. "Did you see *this* person?"

How is he intending "this" to sound? Cuz right now, "this" sounds like *he* doesn't believe that someone exists.

"Tall," I say. "Thin build. Wore a dark hoodie."

He's not writing any of this down in his little pad. Why isn't he writing this down?

"Could it be someone you know?" he asks. "Like an old boyfriend or . . . ?"

Like Micah? "I don't know, Deputy Santos. Like I said, he wore—"

"A hoodie, got it." He scribbles into his pad, then pushes out a breath.

Has Gwen told him that I've lost my mind before and that I've destroyed someone's property and broken his nose with a coffee mug? How could *I* be anyone's victim?

Eventually, Deputy Santos pops down the porch steps and hops into his Jeep. He has the beer bottle and note in a paper evidence bag. "You can come in tomorrow to pick up a copy of the report. Add any details you may be forgetting right now." He tosses a wave and rolls back down Beacon Street.

And that's that.

In the kitchen, I sweep and vacuum the kitchen floor to suck up any remaining shards of glass.

Gwen watches me from the doorway, her hand twisting around the neck of her sweater.

"Don't worry," I tell her. "The handyman is gonna replace the door."

Gwen waggles her head. "He's just coming to do what he needs to do."

"*Who* is coming to do . . . ?"

"Harper."

I snort and wrap the vacuum cleaner cord around its handle. "What does he have to do with anything? What does he have to do with this house?"

Gwen purses her lips. "He told me, right before they took him to jail, that he was gonna get me back for all that we did to him. He said that he'd take everything that I loved just like we'd taken everything that he loved—and he knew that I loved this house more than anything."

I shake my head. "Would he risk going to jail after just getting *out* of jail? And the note says, 'This house is ours'? This house was *never* his. He didn't own the house before we bought it. No, Auntie—this has nothing to do with Harper."

But one can never be sure about some things. Like . . . the where-abouts of a recently freed man who'd been wrongly convicted for three murders.

◆ ◆ ◆

Alessandra Verascio, "Avalon's #1 Realtor" and the woman whose business card I found in both Paula Paulsen's house and Felicity Amador's cottage, hasn't called me back. After I order delivery from Mrs. T's Chinese Kitchen, I search the property records for Consuela Barraza's two-story home at 30671 Eucalyptus Avenue. The other dead old woman's three-bedroom, two-bathroom "stunner" was listed by Alessandra Verascio earlier this week.

The dead old woman found in the tent—Vera Johansen. Her classic Catalina cottage was listed by Alessandra last week.

I toggle over to a new tab and search on *Alessandra Verascio*.

Six pages of results. The images offer a shot of the woman on the business card. But then, there's also an image of a willowy brunette striking a folded-arms pose—the caption reads, "#1 Realtor Helen Nilsen." Flynn's mother. A few quick searches tell me that before joining Verascio's company fifteen years ago, Helen Nilsen ran her own real estate company—Helen of Avalon.

But who is Alessandra Verascio?

More search results offer an image of a redhead using big scissors to cut a red ribbon at a hospital opening. There's another image of a brunette holding a Maltese puppy.

Which woman is Alessandra?

I image search the business card photo.

A single page of results.

First hit: *Smiling Latina woman—BUSINESS*.

That's the tag associated with this . . . *stock photograph*.

For $500, I can purchase a large image of this smiling Latina with her arms crossed, or an image of her pointing at something on a computer screen, or an image of her standing at a conference room table. This physical representation of Alessandra Verascio doesn't exist as a real-woman real estate agent living on Catalina Island.

Who's the *real* Alessandra—and why isn't *her* picture on this business card?

More than that . . .

How is it that she's listing all the houses of Avalon's most recent dead?

The Obituary of
Felicity Socorro Villeda Amador

July 26, 1932—March 11, 2020

Felicity Socorro Amador (née Villeda) never met a deviled egg she didn't like.

She owned two chickens, Cuco and Lucy, and a rooster named Cluckle to source her own eggs because grocery store eggs tasted like slick snot. After a fox snuck into her henhouse and killed Cuco and Lucy, Felicity ordered fresh eggs by mail. She believed in Miracle Whip and Gulden's mustard. Kosher salt was the secret to life. So was nutmeg, but not too much. She wore a smock embroidered with the title, "La Reina del Huevo Relleno."

Yes: Felicity was the Queen of Deviled Eggs.

Born in Mexico City, Felicity married Esteban Amador in 1948. Together, they came to America and settled in Avalon, California, in 1950. A skilled builder, Esteban (called a "lovely idiot" by his beloved bride) could build a chicken coop without a plan, and he built the house on Clemente Street with leftover lumber and supplies from the island's construction companies. Together, Esteban and Felicity had one daughter, Socorro, previously deceased. Her beloved niece, Linda, and great-nephew, Mateo, looked after Felicity once Esteban died in 1993.

Felicity loved Tito Puente and Vicente Fernández, Lloyd's caramel apples, and the Haypress Pond. On Sundays after Mass, she'd often ride a private shuttle to the pond to enjoy fruit plates and chicharrones. She'd sit on that red bench with her little portable boom box and listen to Tito and Vicente. After Esteban's death, she bedded many men with Tito's thick silver hair or Vicente's exquisite mustache. Alas, she never made those great men swoon and fall under her spell—and this was her only lamentation in life.

Even after being diagnosed with lung cancer, Felicity continued to teach LA-style salsa at the VFW. She was teaching "On 1" on the Saturday morning before she passed.

Visitation will be held at Saint Catherine of Alexandria at a later date to be announced.

22.

Even though fear bucked through me, sleep *did* come for me tonight. Earlier, before collapsing across the mattress, I took a shower, helped Gwen with her nighttime medications, then grabbed the second fireplace poker and slipped it beside my mattress.

Ted Archer called back. "I don't have the bandwidth to keep track of a free man, Colette, and since he didn't do it, he has no probation officer to report to."

Gwen claimed that Harper vowed to destroy what she loved the most—and Gwen loved this house more than she loved anyone, especially me.

Which meant . . . the vandal *could* be Harper Hemphill.

Great.

I crumpled to the mattress, then, and started snoring almost immediately. But . . .

WHIR WHIR WHIR!

A car alarm.

And now, my eyes are open. I look at the clock on my phone: 1:37 a.m.

The soft globe of streetlamp light shines behind the sheet curtain. There are no creaks, no rumbles, no rustling. Just . . .

WHIR WHIR WHIR!

I crawl over to the window. Was that alarm on our neighbor's Nissan Pathfinder—

Chirp chirp.

Silence.

But what is *that*? *That sound?*

A roar like . . . an airplane but not that big . . . wheels, *skrrr* . . . a skateboard.

Who would be skating at this time of—

Mateo!

I can't see anyone from this window. I just hear wheels on the sidewalk, the patter of feet, the thump of a wooden board . . . Why is he here? Does he know that I followed him? That I think he may be responsible for Felicity?

Back and forth, he goes. Up the sidewalk. Down the sidewalk . . . *skrr* . . . up . . . down . . . thump . . . *skrr* . . . then . . . silence.

I look to my phone.

It's 1:50 a.m.

I creep up to the living room to peek out the window.

Can't see anyone.

I tiptoe back down to peek out the sitting room window.

Can't see anyone.

I return to my bedroom window.

Finally: silence.

I light a lavender candle, crawl back to the mattress, and settle back under the comforter. My eyelids grow heavy again, and I'm thankful that my brain is still determined to—

WHIR WHIR WHIR!

All night, *whir chirp whir chirp* until the Sunday sky turns pink with new sunlight.

◆ ◆ ◆

Deputy Santos hasn't spoken yet.

"I tried to print it online," I explain, "but every link is broken." I hand him another police report. "This one's on the phone call from Wednesday afternoon. Does no one follow up on crime reports around here?"

"People just chalk it up to kids being kids," he says. "Joking around. Harmless fun."

"But this is no joke to me," I say. "And I doubt the person harassing us is a kid."

He studies the newest report and signs it. "I understand—I mean . . . with what happened to your family and everything."

I nod. "As you know, it didn't turn out so good for us the last time a ne'er-do-well visited my home."

"Ms. Weber—"

"Call me Coco." I lean forward. "Back to my original request. All I'm asking for are public documents. The old detective, Delveccio, said that all of his old files are here. And now, you're telling me that no one's been reassigned to the case, which means no one's being brought to justice. Is that okay with you? It's not okay with me. I promise: anything I discover, you'll be the first person I call."

He chews the inside of his cheek. "I . . . umm . . ." His eyebrows crumple. "I was a freshman in high school back then, and Mr. Weber, your dad, he helped me leave this island. Sent me to a few science camps. Told me to get my college degree before joining the police academy so that I could earn more."

He shakes his head as he remembers. "My mom—she wept for weeks, and she kept crying that this wasn't what Avalon was about, that we loved each other here, that one bad seed can destroy everything . . . she never forgave this place for taking your family. She never believed Hemphill did it." His chin quivers, and the pulse points in his temples pop. "I'll find what I can. It may take a moment, but I'll . . ."

A man wearing a plaster arm cast booms into the station. "Santos!"

Santos fixes a smile on his face and shouts, "Be right there, Jack!" To me, he says, "Gwen staying out of trouble?"

I snort. "What madness could she get into at seventy-eight years old?"

"That lady's still got quick hands," he says, eyebrow high. "You know, right before you arrived, she asked me about eviction laws in Los Angeles County. If she could have an unwanted tenant arrested for trespassing."

Tears burn in my throat. "Really?"

He offers a single nod, then bites his lower lip.

I clear my throat, then waggle my head. "Thanks for sharing that. I'm sure she . . . didn't mean it the way it . . . sounds." I clear my throat again—it remains thick and salty with tears because I don't believe what I just said, not really.

"One last thing." I tell Deputy Santos there's a small chance that Mateo Amador may be unhappy that I've asked him hard questions about Felicity's passing. "I think he may have been hanging around the house late last night, riding his skateboard up and down the sidewalk."

"You think Mateo threw the bottle?"

"No idea," I say, shrugging, "but I *did* see him boxing up some of Felicity's things and hiding them in a day locker at the pier. He was also hanging out by Paula Paulsen's house."

"Oh, really? Did he catch you looking?"

I nod. "I think so. I mean . . . it could be nothing, but then again . . . I've learned a lot about Felicity's family. Sketchy as hell."

Santos sits back in his chair. "They were an embarrassment to that poor lady. If it is Mateo, then watch your back and your purse. He's a problem, and I'm hoping that he leaves this island now that Felicity is gone."

Sure: Mateo could've thrown the bottle, but that message—*THIS HOUSE IS OURS!!!*—wouldn't make sense coming from him.

And then, there's Micah—he thought everything I had was his, too. Did he really think my house was up for grabs?

"My ex-husband," I say now to Deputy Santos. "He's angry, very angry with me right now. He may have thrown the bottle."

Santos grabs his pen and pad. "Okay. Describe him."

"Santos," the broken-armed man shouts. "Those kids broke into my vending machines again. This time, I want their heads! No one steals my Cheetos without payin'."

◆　◆　◆

The Avalon Mortuary and Cemetery is located on the same road that I drove trying to access Haypress Pond. The cemetery doesn't ramble on like the memorial parks over on the mainland. On an island, there's only so much space that can be dedicated to burying the dead.

The mortician, Gary Thresher, is a simple man wearing simple chinos and a wheat-knit sweater. His hair matches the color of the land outside, and he keeps the side part as neat and delineated as the DMZ between North and South Korea.

I share that I look forward to working with him. "Since, you know, I'll be writing about the people you're preparing for burial."

We settle at his desk, and he shares the history of burials here on Catalina Island. "There's no more space out back," Gary says. "People are either buried at sea, or their ashes scattered at sea." He squints at me. "Do we know each other?"

I force a smile. "We do now."

"You seem . . . so familiar to me."

I pretend that he probably wasn't on staff the night my loved ones' bodies were retrieved from the house on Middle Terrace. "I've been talking to a few family members while writing their loved ones' obits. I'm learning that a few of the deceased had unexpected deaths."

Gary crosses his legs, takes a sip of coffee. "A lot of deaths across the state, even here. Hopefully this virus won't take more."

I press my hands together. "That's not what I meant."

"Explain?"

"Felicity Amador, for example. She was found not too far from here."

"Haypress Pond," he says. "Have you been there? It's a beautiful place."

I make a sad face. "I couldn't get past those gates."

"You have to be on a tour or . . ." He glances at his watch.

I remember Noah's advice, then lean forward. "Her friends don't understand how she got to the pond," I say. "And then to die of a heart attack? She had—"

"Lung cancer."

"Strange, right? Her great-nephew, Mateo, is heartbroken—he doted on her."

Gary thinks about that and says, "Hmm . . ."

I hold my breath. Spill it, Gary. *Spill all that tea, bro.*

But he shakes his head. "I'm sure Felicity being exposed to the cold and rain didn't help."

"Is it pretty isolated out there?"

"Oh, definitely. I would show you around, but I have a family visit."

The doors clank open, and voices fill the lobby.

He smiles. "May I direct them to you if they'd like something written?"

"Certainly!"

After we exchange information, I hurry past the grieving family and out into the light.

◆ ◆ ◆

Dr. Burke's eyes are redder than the EMERGENCY sign we stand beside.

"Since I'm writing both the obits and community pages in the *Breeze*, I thought I'd introduce myself and—"

221

She holds up her red, chapped hand. "I truly appreciate it, but like I said, I don't have a lot of time to chat. This . . . virus . . . whatever it is . . . it's taking every bit of focus and energy to make sure we're prepared over here. Because it *is* coming, that is, if it's not here yet."

"Old women are dying," I say, "and as I'm talking with their families, I'm finding—"

She holds up another raw hand. "I'm sorry? What was your name again?"

"Colette Weber." I pause, then say, "Felicity Amador's family, they're understandably upset. Her great-nephew, Mateo, especially—"

"Colette," Dr. Burke interrupts, "I wish I could talk longer, but I really need to get back to caring for the living. After this virus becomes a memory, we'll have drinks and queso, but right now . . ." She thumbs back to the hospital.

I nod. "Understood. No worries. Thank you. Be safe."

She walks backward, saying, "If I were you? I'd stock up on food and supplies right now. They're already laying off people at the restaurants and motels. Trust me when I say that this won't be easy."

◆　◆　◆

The newsroom smells of scorched coffee and burned popcorn, and the carpet feels spongy beneath my shoes. The chatter between Harriet the receptionist and Patty the ad saleswoman is music to my ears. But my trash can hasn't been emptied since Friday—I spot the empty bag of cashews and empty water bottle. The trash cans in the kitchen are also filled with last week's trash. Dried coffee rings and spilled salt dirty the countertop.

Where is Yesenia?

"That always happens, right, honey?" Maddy sits behind her desk as Flynn nests in the window with a sketchbook and pencil in his lap. She looks rested today with her shiny gold hair and low-cut peasant blouse.

"People just . . . *disappearing*?" I plop into the guest chair and pluck the Marvin the Martian figurine from his place near her desk phone.

"With everything going on," Flynn says, "she may have risked boarding the ferry."

"Risk?" I say. "Does the ferry sink regularly or something?"

Flynn chuckles. "Not that kind of risk. ICE rides the ferries."

"ICE as in *immigration*?" I gape at him, then Maddy. "Is she undocumented?" I whisper.

Maddy nods. "I think so."

"ICE agents *arrest* people on the *boat*?" I say.

Amused by my reaction, Flynn laughs. "Once they get to Avalon, some people never leave at all because of their status. They don't visit loved ones overtown. They won't seek any medical treatment beyond what our little hospital can handle. Because if they do, they risk deportation. Yeah, they're trapped."

Pressure builds against my eyes, and I want to explode. "Folks are *okay* with that?"

Maddy shrugs. "Some are. Some aren't. I've tried to help Yesenia any way I can, but there's only so much I can do. Except now, I need to hire someone else. Anyway . . ."

Flynn closes his sketchbook. "Guess that's my cue." He stands and stretches, then pecks Maddy on the cheek. "Heading back to the house. See ya, Coco."

We watch him amble out of the office and down the hallway.

Maddy then smiles and winks at me. "So . . . you and Noah went out Friday night?"

I blush. "We did—but it wasn't planned. He tell you?"

She shakes her head. "A waitress over at the Buffalo Nickel did. How did it go? Not that I'm encouraging my employees to hook up, but then you're not just my employee."

My blush spreads to my neck. "We had fun. Danced. Drank." I pause, then add, "Made out a little."

"Yes!" Maddy high-fives me. "*And* then?"

"And then . . . nothing happened. His mom is sick—she was admitted to the hospital."

Glee drains from her face. "She's okay, right?"

I shrug. "We haven't talked again because . . ."

I tell her about the Mickey's bottle and its threatening note shattering our door window.

She blinks at me. "No way."

I show her pictures that I took.

"Who is 'ours'?" she asks.

"Don't know. Whoever it is also called Gwen and me back on Wednesday. Threatened us after I turned down his offer to sell the house. Said he'd burn it down with Gwen and me inside. *That* wasn't Micah—I know his voice."

"And the sheriff's department—"

"Deputy Santos came over, and this morning, I went to see him. He thinks it's a kid playing a joke . . ."

Maddy grabs a legal pad and pen from her desk drawer. "May I write about this?"

"Umm . . . I really don't wanna draw attention to us since, y'know . . . this may be the person who actually killed my family."

Maddy scoffs. "That would be stupid."

"Because . . . ?"

She starts writing across the pad. "It just is, Coco. You're still looking at this with LA-UCLA communications eyes. Is Avalon crime-free? No. We had a small drug bust just yesterday. And back on Wednesday, someone hit a parked car and fled. And then, when the cruise ship passengers come . . ."

I say nothing and stare at my knees.

"What's wrong?"

"Those dead old women—"

"C'mon, Coco. The two-legged chupacabra serial killer?"

"You told me to gather evidence, and that's what I'm doing."

Maddy sinks in her chair.

"Hear me out. *Please.*"

She looks at her phone's clock. "Three minutes. The mayor's gonna be here in ten."

I pull the area map from my binder and point to each circled site. "Isn't it strange that old women—*widows*—are straight . . . *dropping* at landmarks? And then, there's the houses. Every house—Felicity's, Paula's, Consuela Barraza's, and Vera Johansen's—is being listed by Alessandra Verascio. And after just a few basic searches, I discovered that Alessandra Verascio isn't the woman on the business card." I show her the stock photograph on my phone. "And Helen—"

Maddy bristles. "What about Helen? What does Helen have to do with this? You're not pulling *her* into your little crime-conspiracy-dead-old-ladies-chupacabra-satanist thing, are you?"

I hold out my hands. "No. Of course not. I'm just saying the photographs—"

"So now it's weird to use stock photographs?" Maddy asks, smirking.

"Have you ever met Alessandra in person?"

Maddy rolls her eyes. "Of course I have. Colette, this is crazy—"

"Right. Hard crime supposedly doesn't happen on this island utopia. Of course, I know firsthand that's bull. There *is* a story here, Maddy. There *is* danger here—for Gwen and me, and for any sick old lady with a dead husband and property."

Maddy pulls at her lip and studies me. "I understand where you're coming from, but . . ." She stands from the desk. "And I *want* good stories. I *need* good stories. But this . . ." She waves at the map. "I can't risk publishing something that can't be validated. I have no money for lawsuits, and I'm trying to keep the paper afloat as is. While I'm hella intrigued"—her phone vibrates and she peeks at the screen—"it's not your job to do investigative reporting. You missed a whole weekend of community shit, but now, I'm supposed to be okay with you—"

"Maddy!" A woman with a silver-blonde bob and an easy smile fills the office with her girls' school headmistress vibe and Free People style.

Maddy smiles and says, "Your Honor."

She doesn't introduce me to the mayor.

Guess that's my cue.

Back at my desk, I check email.

Obituary request for Saul Arkanos.

Stay at Home order issued in Los Angeles.

"Hey, Coco." Maddy walks over to me as the mayor talks with the receptionist. "I'm about to be inaccessible for a few hours—the island's shutting down."

My pulse jumps. *"What?"*

"You look terrified. It's gonna be fine."

"This isn't good, Maddy," I say. "Any woman Gwen's age is already in danger—"

"Sweetie." Maddy crouches beside me. "I'm not shocked that you're personalizing this. You do that, which makes you an *astounding* writer. Centering yourself, getting the reader to see life through your eyes, but you need *proof* that something is happening. Boss hat on now . . ." She takes a deep breath, holds it, then slowly exhales. "Please settle down, okay? So much is happening, and we all have our beats, right? Folks are looking to *your* beat to feel . . . *safe*. To have some type of *normalcy*. I need you to focus, okay?" She squeezes my arm. "Boss hat off. I love you—you're like my sister, you know that. Don't be mad. Wish me luck with this press conference. We're about to piss off a lot of people." She kisses my cheek.

I watch my friend and the mayor hustle out the doorway.

Maddy's telling me to drop it.

She did that back when we wrote for the *Times*—I wanted to investigate the monster killing homeless people, but she thought there was no story there. And then she scooped me.

This time, Maddy admitted that there may be something there, but she wants proof first. A *lot* of proof. And for me to do my job or go.

Fine.

I'll do it all.

23.

During that last summer trip here with my family, we took a guided tour around the island. Our tour guide, Fran, noticed that Langston ate tangerines throughout the trip, and she found a bag to carry his peels. At one point, she told us about the goats of Catalina—how the missionaries had brought them over from the mainland to the native Gabrielino Indians in 1827, how the goat population thrived and ate everything it could, and how the goats practically obliterated all ground cover that kept the plants and trees viable, destroying the land so much that in 1990, there'd been a great goat hunt that aimed to kill three thousand goats. "Those goats stripped the land," she said, "and threatened native species, like the now-endangered Catalina fox."

As we stood near the botanical gardens, Langston spit a tangerine seed into the dirt. Fran lunged for that seed and slipped it into the bag. "We can't have outsiders propagating," she explained. "See: there are no citrus trees on Santa Catalina. If one were to grow, what would happen? It would wreck the ecosystem of the entire island. Just like the other outsider trees—eucalyptus and palm trees. We'd have to kill that tree, no matter how much we all love fresh orange juice. It would be for the best. We must do everything we can to protect this very fragile, very *special* place."

That's why the deaths of these women bother me.

People who go crazy about an orange seed falling into the earth are totally ignoring the possibility that there's a "bad seed" killing the island's senior citizens. Or the possibility that a "concerned" citizen may be killing people that they believe are "bad seeds."

Right now, Yesenia, Paula's friend Loretta, and I are the only ones concerned about these deaths. Unless this is how they roll on Santa Catalina. I *am* an outsider, after all.

◆　◆　◆

The rain has stopped, and the thick, still air is so gray that the sea cannot be separated from the sky. The mayor announced during the press conference that ferry service will be limited to twice a day—and only for essential trips like doctor's appointments.

I text Andrea Liszl, the literary agent, and she immediately responds. Oh that's too bad

Let's Skype then

I really want to talk to you, Colette

True crime is in and you have one of the most compelling stories out there

And my partners are starting to question since we agreed to move forward

Ugh. Micah. And I should've . . . so many things. Like having him arrested for impersonating me. Ah, but love, effing love.

Skype is a great idea, I text Andrea.

Maybe together you can help me outline

I think that's my biggest obstacle

Where to start!

Where has Handy Andy gone? He replaced one door and left the worst for last. My irritation quickly ebbs because Aunt Gwen has baked a lemon pound cake and it's sitting on the countertop, so golden, so perfect. There's a note written on a piece of paper near the cake plate.

Gone to dinner with friends.

My phone vibrates, not with a text from Andrea but from Micah.

SIGN. THE. PAPERS.

GIVE. ME. MY. RING!!!

I cut a thick wedge of cake and grab a bottle of Topo Chico from the fridge. I guzzle that bottle and grab another. The water sluices through my belly and spreads into my veins. Between that and the buttery cake, my earlier irritation dies. I trudge to the living room with my snack. The *Family Feud* theme song plays from the television, but Gwen isn't sitting in her armchair.

I eat my slice of still-warm pound cake and sip sparkling mineral water between bites.

Name something snowmen might have nightmares about.

The sun.

Dogs peeing on them.

Drought.

The cake and water settle my mind, and all of me feels as floppy as a beach hat.

And yet . . . and yet . . .

◆　◆　◆

Dr. Tamaguchi's voice mail tells me to leave a message. After the beep, I talk. I don't ask for her to call me back because I just want to . . . *talk*. About Gwen. About the house. About Micah. About my heart.

Name something that won't let Colette find peace.

Micah Patton.

A busted-up house.

A murderer left uncaught.

Down in my bedroom, I paw through the folder of important stuff and find that big manila envelope that contains divorce papers.

If he's asking for the papers, he must not know yet . . .

Name a question a wife asks her soon-to-be ex-husband, who, legally, isn't her husband?

Why did you leave?

Did you ever love me?

How did you come to hate me so hard?

Is it because I stayed with you despite your envious, mean spirit? Is it because I stayed after you hit me that one time and I forgave you and explained it away because you'd been frustrated, and I didn't want to be alone, that I was terrified of being alone? Is it because you knew, some-how, that I fantasized about poisoning you—I knew how to and came so close to doing, but I didn't do it, and that was one time, and I never had that fantasy again and instead broke your nose with a coffee mug?

Therapy over the last twenty years—and especially the last year—still hasn't led me to remember Micah's inciting comment. I remember snapping and swinging the coffee mug in my hand. I don't remember anything after that. That mug connecting to Micah's face. The crack of his nose beneath the porcelain. What Micah described as my glee at having broken his nose. No one believed that I'd disassociated in that act of violence—*zoned out* as Gwen would describe it—not even my own attorney. But no one could prove that I was faking it, either.

During a session last year, Dr. Tamaguchi reminded me that my trauma from 2001 influenced my life with Micah. "Today, right now," she said, "how do you feel about your relationship with your husband?"

That afternoon, I ripped twenty sheets of tissue as I talked. "He was so kind," I told her, "and he laughed easily. He wants me to stay in therapy, and he wants me to talk it all out. He used to go with me every year to put flowers on my family's graves, and . . . and . . .

"He was talented, and he . . . didn't know how to give up. He refused to give up on me, on us, and . . . and . . . I wanted him to be happy. I wanted people to see his talent, to rein in his energy and direct it onto the screen."

After my tribute, Dr. Tamaguchi sighed, then said, "If this is gonna work, Colette, if the judge is going to believe you, you gotta tell the truth."

Stunned into silence, I could only shake my head and wonder . . . *How did she know?*

Because what is the truth? That I'm *not* sorry for hurting Micah even if I can't remember all that he said that night. And I'll never be sorry for hurting Micah because he said something so . . . *extreme* that I lost my mind.

He'd always been spoiled and egocentric, always demanding that I checked with him first on groceries, birth control, streaming options . . . on more than one occasion, he spat that I sucked at life, spat, *Your family really did fuck you up.*

I was always surprised that I never found myself either holding a steak knife to his throat or waking up with my apartment on fire . . . with me in it.

My life with Micah was a Sisyphean triumph, a patina of lies, fear, and lust stitched together like Frankenstein's monster.

It's over now.

We're over now . . . not that I ever trusted us to start, at least before the eyes of California.

My hands shake and the divorce papers vibrate like a hummingbird's wings. My signature at each *X* is just as manic.

There. Done. Happy?

As for the unicorn . . .

Moe isn't on my pillow.

I look in the space between the wall and the mattress.

She's not there, either.

What's that?

I cock my head to hear . . .

Whirring.

Though I'm far away, I can tell that it's the stand-up mixer.

Is Gwen back from dinner and baking another cake?

I swipe at my cheeks. When did I start crying?

Pans and silverware crash to the kitchen floor.

"Gwen?" I shout. "Everything okay?"

No answer.

I dash up the stairs.

Gwen's bedroom door is closed.

I open that door.

No one's there.

I creep into Gwen's room.

Name something that might make you think your house is haunted.

Somewhere outside this bedroom, the floorboards creak.

Oh, shit, *that* would make me think my house was haunted.

In the kitchen, the stand-up mixer growls.

Oh, shit, and *that*, too.

All of me feels twisty and tangled and so very tired.

My gaze skips around Gwen's bedroom. Where is that fireplace poker?

Perfume atomizers . . . cigarette cases . . . stereo speakers . . . an emerald brooch and matching clip-on earrings . . .

I grab an antique-looking letter opener that used to be mine from the nightstand.

My phone . . . is downstairs somewhere.

I take a deep breath and tiptoe to the door.

My footsteps sound like cannon fire.

Applause—that's right. *Family Feud* is still on.

That buttery-vanilla scent of Gwen's pound cake greets me steps away from the kitchen. And then, I smell wine. I see flour first, though, and that's because flour has drifted into the small entryway. Once I step into the kitchen, I see that flour is now all over the tile floor. The mixer is mixing, but there's nothing in its bowl. Spoons and forks lie against the floor, but knives line the countertop. The pound cake that Gwen baked is now smeared against the cabinets. Red wine drips from the stovetop.

I wince and my legs go damp, and I crumple against the doorway, and for a moment I can't see any of this because of the tears in my eyes.

How . . . ?

I open my eyes as my heart lurches in my chest.

The kitchen door is . . . *locked.*

I stumble to the front door.

The chain slide isn't on. The dead bolt is unlocked.

Did I not lock the door? Did I miss sliding on the chain?

I whirl in place, trapped between the kitchen door and front door.

Gwen.

Did *she* do this?

That lady's still got quick hands. That's what Deputy Santos said this morning. He also mentioned that she asked him about eviction and trespassing laws. *Unwanted tenants,* she said.

Is *Gwen* really trying to make me leave?

Squatters—because that's what Gwen is—do shit like this.

They vandalize.

They terrorize.

They gaslight.

My attention is drawn to the refrigerator and to the magnets there.

A rainbow. Disneyland. An old high school picture of me. Beneath that picture of me . . .

The envelope that Gwen mentioned putting on the refrigerator.

It takes every muscle in my body to reach the fridge, to lift my hand and pull that envelope from beneath that high school picture of me.

I read the handprinted words there . . .

The Obituary of Colette Sienna Weber

Colette S. Weber-Patton of Los Angeles, California, is no more.

She was a writer and an orphan—but none of that matters now because on Thursday, March 19, 2020, she tumbled off the bluffs near Two Harbors Camp and crashed into the Pacific Ocean. Her battered body was discovered stuck between the rocks. We take comfort in knowing that the only living survivor of the Weber family struggled to survive even as water filled her lungs, even as her ribs and teeth clattered around her broken body. We take comfort in knowing that she died in agonizing pain.

Colette joins her deceased loved ones in Hell, including trouble-maker and loudmouth Reginald Weber; failed attorney who couldn't persuade her husband to stay away from Paradise Alyson Weber; and overrated wide receiver who caught a knife in his neck Langston Weber.

Colette should've stayed in Los Angeles.

We will not miss her.

In lieu of flowers, we ask that you instead dance on that bitch's bones.

24.

She didn't know the angry man yelling at her father out on the front porch, but his red face, his bugged eyes, and the spit on his chin made her want to laugh. Dad, smirking at this fireball, stood nose to nose with this loser like a boss. His only "tell" of being moments away from exploding? The way those papers in his hands had tightened into a cone. Strong tennis hands that could punch the screaming white man in his face; second-year medical school dropout hands that would know how to fix that angry man's face afterward.

It was too pretty outside to be so angry.

Colette left the chaise and returned to the dining room to grab more potato chips.

The day had started off awesome—the aroma of barbecue from the grill, the view of the Pacific Ocean and the town of Avalon, the promise of both . . . but now, this stranger's pissy attitude and stank-ass cologne had spoiled the potato salad, and not even the new Missy Elliott album could fix her mood.

Between replays of "Get Ur Freak On" and "One Minute Man," Colette heard the stranger insult her father. *Cheater. Bastard. Underhanded motherfucker.*

After one more "motherfucker," she hit PAUSE.

Dad growled, "You really need to step the hell away from me."

"Or?" the man yelled.

She didn't hear Dad's response, but she knew that it wouldn't be a chemistry teacher's measured retort. Her father's life experience growing up on Nicolet Avenue in the Jungles would soon eke out just as it did anytime his spades partner prematurely reneged or anytime someone—like *this* guy—didn't watch his tone. Whatever Dad said, though, made the fireball leave.

Time for more chips.

◆ ◆ ◆

Mom, sporting her favorite denim shorts and pink bandanna halter top, paced the patio with folded arms.

Dad watched her with weary eyes. "C'mon, Al."

She snorted. "Don't 'c'mon, Al' me. I changed my mind, Reggie. Fuck this island."

Colette looked up from her burger and copy of the latest Harry Potter.

"You're gonna let *him* dictate where we can and can't live?" Dad yelled. "Are you kidding me right now? And you can't change your mind—the house in LA is sold, and all our shit is here in the house that is now ours."

Gwen tended the grill, moving pieces of chicken to a plate. Like Alyson, she wore denim shorts and a tank top. She grabbed a bottle of Heineken from the cooler, then said, "I agree with Al. I don't think y'all should—"

"No." Dad pointed at his sister. "You don't get a vote."

"But I'm the only one who knows what it's like living here." Gwen took a pull from the beer bottle, then adjusted the six necklaces around her neck.

"We've had this conversation," Dad said, scowling at Gwen. "You don't want us living here cuz it'll mess up your own shit. People will find out that your real name isn't Rose—"

"It *is* Rose," Gwen shouted.

"That's your *middle* name," Dad countered. "They'll find out that you've stolen from every client that you've worked for. That your apartment is filled with other people's shit."

Gwen slapped her hand against the grill cover. "You know what, asshole?"

"Stop," Mom shouted, glaring at the siblings. "I don't care about y'all's drama. And I don't care that we've had this conversation, Reginald. I still care about being one of a handful of Black people living on an island that's racist as fuck, a place where, back in the day, Black people couldn't even *ride* the ferries to get over here.

"And I still care about bison roaming wherever the hell they want. And I still care about these eucalyptus trees sucking up all the water and workers being exploited and the cost and . . ."

Mom stopped pacing and squeezed the bridge of her nose. "Yes. It's beautiful over here."

"And it's safe over here," Dad added.

"For *whom*?" Mom asked.

"Two of El's friends were shot and killed in *one week*," Dad shouted. "You're telling me that's safer than—"

"Why aren't there more Black people here?" Mom asked, arms out.

Gwen muttered, "She's right, though."

Dad rolled his eyes at his sister. "Since when do you agree with Alyson so much?"

"Answer the question, Reginald," Mom said. When he didn't respond, she chuckled. "*Exactly*. And *that's* why I want to keep my Black ass in LA."

But it didn't end there. Between ribs and chicken, beer and peach cobbler, Mom argued to move back to Los Angeles—she now wanted to deal with the devil she knew.

For the first time *ever*, Gwen agreed with her—living in Avalon was a bad idea.

Dad didn't care—it was ultimately his responsibility to look for the best solution. Also, he didn't want to keep commuting every day to Avalon, and he wanted to be principal of a high school, and the big white house on Beacon Street was his dream house.

Colette grew tired of the bickering, and by three o'clock, her lips stung from too much sun and too many Doritos. Her head hurt from playing music at 100 to drown out the adults' arguing. Her eyes burned from too much sunshine and from reading too many words on a page.

Somehow, the argument shifted its focus and . . .

"I'm tired of cleaning up after you," Dad shouted at Gwen.

"I'm tired of you crowding me," Gwen shouted back. "If you'd just leave me alone, you wouldn't have to do shit for me."

Dad muttered, "You were useless on *Family Feud*—"

Mom gasped and clamped a hand over her mouth.

Gwen's eyes darkened as her lips trembled.

Colette gaped at her family. She wanted to offer them cool drinks or warm cobbler or . . . or . . . but she didn't dare move.

"I'm sorry, Gee." Dad spread his arms and met the eyes of the women keeping him from his dream. "I'm doing this for you, Al, and for you, Gwen, and for the kids. I'll be around more to help out because I won't be commuting. We'd be saving more money, too. I'm tired of the back and forth. You are, too, Al." When Mom sighed, he turned to his sister. "Wouldn't you like a place of your own? The first level is *perfect* for you. We'll fix it up real nice—"

"I'm not living on the bottom like somebody's maid," Gwen huffed.

"You *are* somebody's maid," Dad spat. "Them people up the hill, you clean their houses every week."

"Ohmigod, Reggie," Mom said, shaking her head.

Gwen's eyes hardened into shark eyes. "You slope-headed, goo-gly-eyed son of a bitch."

Those words punched Colette's gut and sickened her. *All his fault.* Maybe *he* could live here alone, and she and Langston and Mom could stay home. They didn't need him. He was here most of the time anyway, staying at Gwen's or in a hotel on late nights.

In tears, Gwen left the patio and rushed out the front door.

Colette followed her aunt with a handful of napkins.

Gwen sat on the back bench of her red golf cart, smoking and crying. She snatched napkins from Colette's hand. "You here to spy on me?"

Colette shook her head.

Gwen blew her nose and muttered, "Fucking Reggie" and "Unbelievable" as she dried her face.

"I hate him, too," Colette said.

Gwen curled her lip. "Cuz he ain't bought you a BMW? Cuz you don't have the latest Louis Vuitton?" Gwen smirked. "You know I'm messing with you—don't get all emotional."

Colette winced—anytime envy splattered against her like that, her skin burned like it had been scraped against asphalt and cleaned with 90 percent alcohol. Still, she tried to smile even though she knew Gwen hated her straight white teeth and bright eyes. "It'll be fun living together once we get used to . . ."

"Used to . . . *what?*" Gwen snarled.

Before Colette could answer, Gwen's cell phone rang. She glanced at the screen and smiled, then answered with a lighthearted, "Hey."

"You do it?" A man's voice rumbled through the speakers.

"Hold on." Gwen shambled down Middle Terrace Road.

241

Colette stayed put and pretended to be interested in her MP3 player.

"I'm done. Come over tonight," Gwen said, her hand playing in her hair. "Cuz we're running out of time . . ."

Running out of time to do what? Colette wondered.

Gwen giggled. "It needs to happen *now* . . . before I chicken out."

Who was she talking to?

And . . . chicken out?

Colette shivered. Gwen was breaking the Weber rule. *Never do your family dirty.*

Gwen was actively planning . . . *something* with . . . *who?* And what was this plan?

Colette kept shrugging as her mother peppered her with these questions. Alyson Weber, Esquire, never accepted a story on its face.

"Her talking made you feel some kind of way?" Mom asked from her lounge chair.

"Yeah. Like before." Before: overhearing Gwen lie to the school principal's wife about Dad not being interested in the vice-principal position. "But not as bad," Colette added now, her tinge of guilt growing blanket size.

Mom said, "Okay," then peered out to the town and sea before dipping back into her Stephen King novel.

That's it? Usually her mother acted immediately, getting Colette's grade before the day ended, or having Langston's jersey number switched to "12" because he was *always* 12. But now . . .

Sometimes Gwen was right about her mother—Alyson Weber *was* a Jimmy Choo–wearing bougie intellectual tyrant.

Simmering, Colette plopped into the other chaise longue. She'd become the opposite of her mother. Pledge red and white instead of pink and green. Become a writer instead of a lawyer. Maybe even—

"Gwen!" Mom's voice cut into Colette's rebellion planning.

Back in the kitchen, her aunt stopped rustling the Doritos bag and came to the patio door.

Mom left the chair and reached Gwen in two steps. "What are you doing?"

Gwen blinked at her sister-in-law, then shifted the pack of cigarettes to her left hand. "What are you talking about?"

"Coco heard you planning something with your boy," Mom said.

Gwen's gaze moved past Alyson and landed on Colette, now frozen in the lounge chair. "So you got your little spy working hard today."

Colette whispered, "I'm not a spy—"

Mom whipped her head back at Colette, and said, "Go!"

Colette stumbled past the women, now watching her with hard eyes. Heart pounding, she hurried down to the first floor and found Langston reading *Discover* and watching a baseball game in the TV room.

"This sport is boring as hell," he announced.

She slipped on her Vans, then grabbed her phone and bag—not a Louis Vuitton, just a denim purse she'd found on sale at the Gap.

"Where are *you* going?" he asked, futzing now with his L BOOGIE bracelet.

"To mind my business," she spat. "Leave the kitchen door unlocked."

"What you gon' give me?"

"My Foot Locker gift certificate."

"Deal."

"Don't forget," she said, pointing at him.

He smirked. "Go mind your business."

Up top, Gwen and Alyson argued about who-knows, and their words blurred the farther Colette got from the house. Too cool and too bright and too perfect for her head to be this stormy. The video game arcade was just a mile away, a twenty-minute walk she'd done twice now with Langston. She'd be alone this time. Good: she needed space, she needed quiet, she needed to find the light again.

The arcade was packed and loud with laughter and *pewpewpew* and *wakawakawaka* and *"Finish him!"* The kids who'd ignored her back on that first day on the island now hunkered near Galaga. Colette could see their acne flares from her spot in the entryway.

Colette chose to spend her money on Street Fighter. She played only the girl, Chun-Li, and always beat the other seven main characters. Soon she saw the reflections of pale faces in the glass as she beat the first of the final four bosses.

"You're really good at that," the cute blond boy said.

Colette's grip tightened around the joystick. She didn't take her eyes off Chun-Li kicking Vega's ass.

"Dude," a kid with oily hair said, "she's gonna beat your score."

"Bullshit," Cute Blond said, concern in his voice.

Colette beat his score—fifteen minutes, 1,125,000. Her hand cramped as Cute Blond—Dylan, she remembered—high-fived her.

"We're gonna go ride around in some carts," Dylan said. "Wanna come?"

"*Your* carts?" Colette asked.

A sunburned redhead rolled her eyes. "No. You just get in and turn the key."

"So . . . someone *else's* cart." Colette's chest tightened. "Stealing."

"Yeah, but not really," Oily Hair said. "We're not going anywhere except . . ." He spread his arms. "Absolutely nowhere."

"And you won't get in trouble?" By now, Colette had followed them out of the arcade.

Dylan laughed. "Hell yeah, we will, but it won't be anything serious. Just kids joyriding around the island. Not like we're doing drive-bys."

Colette knew, though, that *when* they were caught, she would probably be penalized more than the blond and blistered island kids. Her mother always said, *Make better choices, Colette,* and now, here she was. Choosing wisely. You *go*, Coco.

"*Or,*" Dylan said, "you can stay here and keep playing Street Fighter all by yourself." He smiled at her, and her stomach oogly-googlied like she'd read in Nora Roberts romances.

She had another choice: return to the house of unhappy adults and be miserable yet another night in Avalon.

She stood there in the arcade entryway, alone, thinking about the right choice.

"Colette." Dylan had returned. "We'll do something else. Stealing carts is stupid. I know what we can do." He cocked his head and held out his hand. "It'll be fun. Promise."

25.

"You think that this is a joke? That me dying by cliff dive on March 19 is funny?"

"I'm not saying that," Deputy Santos says, his hands up. "I'm saying . . ." He rubs his neck, chomps his gum, then slowly exhales.

I'm pacing and waiting for him to decide his next steps, because I know mine.

Find this person, this monster, before he pushes me off a cliff in four days.

Gnats have descended into our house and now dance over the puddles of spilled red wine. The sun has already dropped behind the hills, and now, I'm surrounded by the forest and creatures that chirp, snort, and creep.

Deputy Santos waggles his steno pad. "Yes, this obituary is a little unsettling."

I stop pacing long enough to say, "Glad we're in agreement," then start pacing again.

"Here's what I'll do. I'll send a patrol over a few times a day, just to be a presence."

"Okay." When he doesn't continue, I stop pacing again. "And?"

He's now writing in his pad. "And . . . *what?* There's nothing else I can do more than what I'm already doing."

"Which is . . . ?" I screech. "What's happening to address the vandalism? The phone calls? You said you were going to find public documents . . ."

His jaw clenches. He wants to pop off at me, but he's holding it all in.

Once Noah arrives, though, Santos pulls out his phone and takes pictures of the messy kitchen like it's brand new. "We're doing the best we can," he tells me. "But we're shutting down the island and preparing for the worst with this virus. I'd appreciate your patience."

I fold my arms and search the wet sky. "You're placing me on hold, then."

Santos scratches his eyebrow. "There are more immediate concerns."

Noah gapes at him. "Really?"

The deputy backs down the porch. "Where's Gwen right now?"

I throw up my hands.

"Well, lock up," he says. "Don't let strangers in, and stay away from high places."

The kitchen smells like a bakery and a nightclub because of Deputy Santos's cologne.

"Sounds like it's up to us to find this guy," Noah says. "And to find him before Thursday." His eyes are bright as sunshine, and stubble darkens his jawline. A whole two days have passed since I've last seen him, and my eyes can't stop pecking at his shoulders and that hair and the faint pulse in the center of his clavicles.

"You know almost everyone here," I say. "Who's good for this?"

He leans back against the refrigerator. He squints as he thinks. "Well . . . I mean . . . there's your aunt—it's obvious Gwen doesn't want you here."

I snort. "Yeah."

"And there's Mateo Amador, but this seems too clever for him. There's . . ." He cocks his head, then clicks his teeth. "No one. Seriously. We have drunks and potheads and assholes with short fuses. We have middle managers who think the world needs their zip lines and bison tours. We have bored, freckled ladies who make jewelry and candles and soap . . ."

"But you don't have any Hannibal Lecters?"

"No evil geniuses live in Avalon. Whoever's stalking you"—Noah holds up a finger—"isn't necessarily a genius. Angry, yes. Greedy, that's for certain."

"And he's heartless," I add. "Who terrorizes sick, old women and an orphan?" I wait a beat, then add, "He owns a car because he's going into muddy backcountry. *And* he's been on the island long enough to have a permit to own a car."

"Ooh, that's a good one," he says. "But that's still eight hundred people or something. I can probably get that information somehow."

"He found my phone number." I finally tell him about the threatening phone calls.

Noah gapes at me. "You can't be serious. Who . . . ? Why . . . ?"

I close my eyes and try to remember anyone who held my gaze too long, but I see no one. "He's plain, easy to miss because there's nothing spectacular or memorable about him."

Noah tousles his hair. "Can't be me, then. I'm spectacular *and* memorable."

I say, "Ha," as tears pop in my eyes.

But then, why couldn't it be Noah? He's always "with his mother" anytime shit goes haywire. He harassed bison, which, yes, still niggles at my mind. And his father is a beast—to his wife, to other men's wives, to other men, to the earth and its wetland creatures. Noah comes from a family made rich by building and restoring vacation resorts, and what is Catalina Island since William Wrigley bought it? One big vacation spot.

But I don't feel . . . *evil* pulsing from him.

So many villains, so little time.

A teardrop rolls down my cheek, and I swipe it away. "This is so messed up."

"Yeah," he says. "Come here."

I slump into his arms, and my heart rate slows from his touch. "How's your mom?" I ask.

"Better. Just wish my father was here. She keeps asking about him."

"Sorry that she's having a hard time."

"And I'm sorry *you're* having a hard time." He lifts my chin and smiles. "It's gonna be okay. Let's do a project, like . . . cleaning that backyard tomorrow."

"After cleaning all of this?" I survey the messy kitchen. "I'm thinking something simpler like . . ." My head drops—it's too heavy to think.

Noah squeezes me tight. "How about the garden—it's small. We'll wear protective clothing and cut back some of our good ol' deadly solanum wallacei. We'll carve out a writing nook or something in that space. Not like we can do much of anything for the next two weeks."

"Let's start with this." I wave my hands at the kitchen.

I don't want Gwen to come back home and see this mess. Even though, *Gwen* could've made said mess. My heart pops admitting this, and shame burns like lava in my belly.

But Gwen isn't a writer—she could've never written that obituary . . . unless she's partnering with somebody. Someone like Noah . . .

No. No. No.

I tap PLAY on my "clean up" playlist, and it's true: many hands *do* make light work. Noah and I sweep and mop, swipe and trash, and I turn that possibility over in my head—*maybe Gwen and a friend are trying to get me out of the house*—as Rihanna sings about umbrellas.

Parts of me keep saying no, and other parts of me: Yeah, it's possible.

I teach Noah how to wobble, and now, he's wobbling to every song that plays, including Rick James and Teena Marie's "Fire and Desire." He makes me laugh, and that's what I need. He takes my hand and kisses it—that's what I need, too.

I lead him down the stairs because I need more than a laugh and a kiss on the hand.

◆ ◆ ◆

We sprawl across my bed and listen to the house creak and hiss. We watch shadows made by the candles dance across the ceiling. Every now and then, his eyebrows form into one. His muscles also tighten, and for a moment he stops breathing.

"I'll be your quarantine buddy," he says. "But only because we've exchanged germs."

I mock pout. "Ugh. That sucks."

The stitching for one of my hair extensions feels loose from being trapped beneath my body and Noah's. My skin feels scratchy and hot, like someone is watching me and judging me.

Noah tugs my hair. "You okay?"

My skin flushes. First, because my track is loose and his hand being so close worries me, and I have no idea where a bobby pin is to hold it in, and I don't want tonight to be the night I have to explain Black women's hair culture to a white guy. And second, what would Mom say right now about me being in bed with a man I've known for less than a week? Someone that I just suspected of threatening me and vandalizing my home?

Noah scooches down on the mattress until we're face-to-face. "Talk to me, Coco."

I swallow, try to smile, but I fail. "It's . . . I haven't . . . maybe . . . my judgment . . . sometimes I rush things."

"Micah would want you to be happy," he says with a confident smile.

I shake my head. "No, he wouldn't. Not at all."

"C'mon, Coco—"

"We've been . . . *extreme* toward one another, and sometimes it feels like he's here, watching me, and . . ." I sit up and point toward the level above us. "The attack tonight feels pointed and angry. I haven't been here long enough for someone to be so angry that they break into my house, bust up my kitchen, and write my obituary."

Noah blinks at me, not sure what to say.

I blush, then say, "You're probably very much regretting being in my bed right now."

"No. It's just . . . you think *Micah* could've done this?"

My resolve crumbles, a sandcastle during high tide. I blurt, "Yes," then hide my face in my hands.

"Colette." He kisses my arm, nuzzles the crook of my elbow. "We'll find out what's going on, okay? *Together.* For now, though . . ." He kisses me.

I close my eyes and tingles zigzag through my veins.

"Let's live in the present," he whispers. "Who knows what's about to happen with this virus. There may be *zombies* overtown right now."

I whisper, "Yeah. Zombies." I kiss him and kiss him until I can hardly breathe, and I'm so loud in loving him that I can wake the dead.

◆　◆　◆

What?

My eyes pop open.

. . .

Darkness.

The candle's been snuffed out.

Soft breathing—that's Noah.

A dark shadow creeps beyond the bedsheet and in the small garden off my bedroom.

I squint at that shadow.

It's not a deer, not any creature that can move through the night-shade horizontally. It's a vertical being, someone who doesn't fear the wild poison twining around their head. Someone who belongs . . .

Terror climbs my spine and looks for a place to rest.

Noah sleeps beside me with his lips slightly parted.

The shadow moves left, then stops. Darkens as it moves closer to the window.

I ease from beneath Noah's arm.

Noah turns over and sinks back into sleep.

The shadow moves to the back of the house, in the direction of the kitchen door.

I sweep my hand beneath the mattress and grab the fireplace poker. Naked, I creep over to the window and count . . .

One . . . two . . .

I push aside the curtain.

The flowerpots. The garden hose. The darkness.

I grab my phone and squint at the bright screen. I find MICAH in my contacts, then type:

STOP IT!

PLEASE!

BEFORE SOMEONE GETS HURT AGAIN!!

Not three seconds pass before my phone vibrates with a response.

MESSAGE FAILED TO SEND.

26.

The wind tore across her face and stung her eyes. Any other time, especially this late at night, she'd wear a scarf for protection against the weather. Cuz if she didn't, she'd get sick as a dog. Living this long on the island, she should be used to the rain, the cold, and the wind—like driving a cart instead of a car or paying almost four dollars for lettuce or seeing tourists everywhere, except for this moment, when she needed a crowd.

Right now, the misty rain felt icy, and anyway, a scarf wouldn't matter—she couldn't move her arms to wrap that scarf around her head. The blood in her veins felt slow, clumpy. The world before her twisted and shimmied, and she glided through the air like an eagle.

Moonlight brightened behind the racing clouds . . . whispering, someone was . . . the sparkling moon . . . man in the moon . . . the world . . . blurry . . . her memory . . . slipping away . . .

She wasn't on the ground. She floated with the clouds, and the clouds groaned beneath her. She'd closed her eyes, but they'd snapped open since she'd slid into this . . . into this—

Moving, she was moving.

She didn't really feel like taking a trip. Her stomach hurt, and her mouth was dry, and what were those black beetles crawling everywhere?

"I change my mind," she whispered. "Take me home."

No response from the glowing circle to her right left up down . . .

"You hear me?" She didn't hear her. Were her lips even moving?

The middle of her body cramped and twisted, and the goo deep within her burned.

"I gotta go real bad," she said, unable to clench and hold it all.

The cloud wheezed and made the stars bigger . . . brighter . . . reds and whites and . . .

Tears filled her eyes.

So beautiful.

The glowing circle bobbed until it was behind her. So nice since she couldn't move on her own. Her bowels splatted against her underwear, and her eyes snapped open, and she was now sitting on . . .

The glow . . . was gone.

Where am I?

In and out . . . heavy eyes . . . hot heart . . .

So many times before this, she'd wished she was dead, and now, she was dying.

I want to live. I don't care about houses or . . . or . . . I wanna make things right. Bake cakes. Please let me go home.

Hot heart, burning . . . burning . . .

Now I lay me down to sleep, I pray the Lord my soul to keep . . .

Her family . . . they stood right there on that star.

She saw them, clear as day.

"Haven't seen y'all in a while," she called out.

No more aching heart.

"I'm so happy to see you," she shouted.

And that was the truth.

She drifted over to them, joy bright on her face. She linked arms with her loved ones and looked down on Avalon, the city she loved.

"Ready?" her brother asked.

She shrugged. "Guess so."

He tapped the gem around her neck.

She studied it, pressed it between her fingers until the gem glowed, a beacon in the night.

He gazed back at the city beside the sea. "Raging . . . blank . . ."

"Raging . . . bull," she said.

"Good answer," he said, smiling. "Good answer."

27.

Monday, March 16, 2020

On this first morning of Safer at Home, there are no ferries breaking across the ocean, no schoolkids or parents hustling with backpacks
and lunch boxes from the Flats to the elementary school. Paper signs
at beaches, the pier, and the port announce CLOSED UNTIL FURTHER
NOTICE. Heavy mist shrouds Paradise as Noah and I walk past rows of
unrented golf carts. Way out there on a rocky outcropping, one man
fishes alone in gray waters.

"This is freaky," Noah says, his words muffled by the bandanna
covering his mouth.

I pay the server for our coffees and bagels, then peer at the nearly
empty street behind us.

Crackling pressure weighs across my shoulders. "We should get
back home." My words sound garbled behind my own scarf.

Something wicked this way comes.

Like this street is peppered with hidden mines. Like a phantom
clutching a butcher knife lurks behind every shadowy corner. But the
obituary didn't predict death by explosion or stabbing. Pushed off a cliff
high above the Pacific Ocean—that's how I'm supposed to go.

And Micah . . . I'd tried to text him again and again, but the number no longer works. And then, my phone died. He could reach *me,*

but I can no longer contact him, especially since I forgot to connect my phone to the charger. I'm stumbling in the dark as he watches me stumble.

Maybe Gwen's cooking breakfast now, and maybe the house smells of crispy potatoes speckled with onions or coffee cake with cinnamon crumbles on top. Maybe. Hopefully.

Noah isn't talking much—he feels it, too.

Back at the house, I open the front door and sniff.

No breakfast smells.

No morning TV shows.

Just heavy silence.

"She still asleep?" Noah whispers.

"Guess so." I don't like seeing the kitchen still clean, nor do I like seeing that tired armchair empty or the television screen dark.

Something wicked . . .

"Maybe she decided to relax and stay in bed." Noah finds a plate in the cabinet for the bagels. "So much going on with the break-ins and the . . ."

My heart sags as I accept that Gwen was right. I *did* bring madness back into her life. I even blamed her *for* the madness. Hunh. I am the freakin' . . . orange seed. Here I am, thinking we'd be a normal family this morning with fresh bagels, hot coffee, and crispy potatoes. Forgetting that I haven't experienced "normal family" since June 2001. Foolish fool.

"I'll go check on her." I steal one last kiss from Noah.

"If you want crispy potatoes," he says, "I'll make you crispy potatoes."

"Is there anything that you *can't* do?"

"Nope. And I do everything *splendidly*, as you recently discovered." He winks at me, then opens the fridge.

My limbs go weak, remembering his bare muscles and the way my thighs burned from his stubbled cheeks.

I duck first into the bathroom and grab two bobby pins from the jar on the countertop. I pin the loose extension to the braid beneath, satisfied now that I won't leave a trail of Indian Wavy in my wake.

Down the hallway I go, stopping at Gwen's closed bedroom door. I knock. "Auntie?"

No answer.

I open the door.

Not a lot of light moves past boxes stacked in front of the windows.

"You feelin' okay?" I step closer to the bed . . . the *empty* bed.

A flare shoots across my heart.

Gwen isn't in bed.

Gwen isn't in the bathrooms . . . the laundry room . . . the backyard . . .

"She's not *here*," I tell Noah, tears burning in my eyes.

Noah peeks in my parents' bedroom . . . then Langston's bedroom . . . then the room that was supposed to be mine . . .

No Gwen.

He takes my hand. "Maybe she went out on her morning walk. She has a routine."

I close my eyes and imagine Gwen moving through the house over the last week and . . .

"Pills!" I dart back to the kitchen.

Gwen's daily pillbox sits near the bread box.

I gape at the white pill, red pill, yellow capsule—all pills for Monday morning. *Today.* "She didn't take them." I open Sunday evening's slot. A white pill, a red pill, and a yellow capsule. "She didn't take these, either."

Blood pushes to my face as I dust devil through the house, dead phone in my hand.

I stop in my step. *The unicorn.*

Down in my bedroom, I tear the linens off the bed and shake out the comforter.

No unicorn.

I look beneath the dresser and in the closet and through boxes . . . No unicorn.

"Ohmigod." I drop to my butt.

Did Gwen take Moe and leave?

That lady's still got quick hands.

"Colette," Noah shouts from the living room.

I trudge up the stairs. Gwen stole Moe, which means she stole the ring.

"Didn't you say she had dinner out last night?" Noah asks.

I nod and shift from one foot to the other. What if Gwen's in Long Beach *right now*, hocking my ring?

"Maybe that's where she is." His eyes twinkle.

My lips stay as slashes across my face, and I spit, "What?"

He waggles his eyebrows. "Maybe she has a boyfriend. Or maybe she had, y'know, a one-nighter. Why wouldn't she need that kind of comfort, too?"

I blink at him, then rush back down the stairs. I paw through my bag and find the lithium battery used for quick charges.

The battery itself has only 30 percent juice, but that's not enough to fully charge a phone so dead that it won't even light up as I connect it to the charging cord.

Who was Gwen's partner in crime back in the day? She stole countless tons of shit from hotels . . . *Who did she work with?*

"*You* called *me*," Noah continues. "Maybe dinner turned into . . . *more*. I mean . . . Gwen's pretty hot for an eighty-year-old."

Why is he still talking?

That slash on my face straightens. "Still not a good answer. She should've let me know."

"Maybe she did," he counters. "Your phone's dead."

"Oh. Yeah."

"And she's an adult," he says. "Let the old lady get laid before the zombies come."

"She hasn't had her meds," I say.

"She missed one day, Colette." He takes my hands and kisses them. "I'll make crispy potatoes, and then, we'll start on the yard and—"

"What if she went back to LA?" I ask.

"No ferries in this weather and with the shutdown," he reminds me.

Gwen's still here in Avalon, which means the unicorn and ring are, too.

"It's gonna be okay," Noah says.

It *can't* be. And now, a wasp's nest of worry buzzes in my head. *Something wicked this way . . .* I know dread—I've lived with it almost all my life. It wouldn't let me live normally back in 2001, and it will never let me live without it today.

"I need a car," I tell Noah. *"Now."*

I'd hung out with Flynn a handful of times before he and Maddy married. He'd pay for dinner and crack a few jokes, none at my expense nor Maddy's. He was smarter than he seemed but kept his thoughts to himself.

And he's doing that now as he sits behind the wheel of the old Jeep Wrangler.

The wet air smells clean—not many gas fumes from golf carts. The clouds scrape the tree lines, leaving behind trails of silver rain.

Maddy and Noah are obvious in their thinking. They're exchanging glances that say, "Coco's cuckoo" and "Coco's gone 'round the bend." But I'm not overreacting. Yes, Gwen is an adult who's moved just fine around the island without my help. Yes, Gwen could've turned to a boyfriend during this trying time—between my barging into her home and the acts of vandalism, to this mysterious illness consuming the world. I can't blame Gwen for seeking respite from someone not named "Weber."

"But this isn't that," I tell the group.

Noah says, "Understood," as he buckles his seat belt.

My phone is now at 11 percent, still not strong enough to box against island dead spots.

"Thanks for coming," I say, tapping Maddy's and Flynn's shoulders. "I couldn't search for her in a freaking cart."

"Anything to keep you sane, my dear," Maddy says, squeezing my hand. "We were out taking pictures of Avalon in this new era of pandemic." She pulls her damp hair into a ponytail, then slips on a UCLA sweatshirt. She finishes her breakfast burrito in three bites, then pulls long sips from her berry smoothie.

I've interrupted their day.

"How about . . . the library?" Flynn suggests. "She volunteers there sometimes."

Noah nods. "I've seen her there a lot lately."

"There and Dee Dee's," Maddy says.

"Dee Dee. That's her best friend, right?" My face burns—I don't know any of Gwen's favorite places, nor have I met any of the people she loves. There was supposed to be time for that.

"Dee Dee used to be on Gwen's cleaning crew at the hotel," Maddy explains.

"And she drove one of the tour company shuttles," Flynn adds.

"How do you guys know all this?" I ask.

"My mom volunteered at the library, too," Maddy says.

"My mom drank at a lot of hotels around the island," Noah adds.

"And *my* mom drank with *his* mom," Flynn says.

"We're like a family here," Noah says. "I told you that, Colette. You can't keep any secrets on an island."

Gwen isn't at the library, though. Another CLOSED DUE TO COVID-19 flyer is taped to the entrance.

No one answers the front door of Dee Dee's sea-green cottage.

"Maybe they're together," Maddy suggests.

I clench my hands and stare at the trio of garden gnomes along Dee Dee's front porch. Even though it's fifty-five degrees, my shirt sticks to my sweaty back.

Noah places his hands on my shoulders. "Don't think the worst, Coco."

I snort. "You saw the kitchen last night. You read the obituary—"

"Obituary?" Maddy asks. "Huh?"

"Someone's threatening us," I explain.

"What?" both Flynn and Maddy say.

"Not *exactly*," Noah says as he activates his vape pen.

I cock an eyebrow. "Colette S. Weber is no more because she tumbled off the bluffs near Two Harbors Camp and crashed into the Pacific Ocean?"

Flynn laughs. "Seriously?"

I don't laugh and meet his eyes in the rearview mirror.

Noah blows raspberry-scented vapor into the air. "I'm saying . . . that's a threat against *you*, Coco, and not Gwen."

Maddy's eyes ping-pong between Noah and me, but they linger on me. "But Gwen could still be in harm's way, Noah. Collateral damage from whatever Coco's done—"

"I haven't *done* anything," I snap. Even if Micah *did* send that threat, I'd *still* say that because I've done *nothing*.

Maddy swallows her response and trains her eyes on the fast-moving fog.

I'll be more present for Gwen, I promise. Just let me find her and I'll be there for her.

And just like that, I've moved from wanting Gwen gone to wanting Gwen back, just like I had with Dad so long ago.

Maddy is first to break the silence. "We should get back to the office. Noah, the article's due on the—"

"Wait." I hold up a hand, close my eyes, and picture my aunt . . . in the armchair, martini glass in one hand, vienna sausage–Ritz cracker sandwich in the other . . . cracker crumbs on her lips . . . the space between her shoulders . . .

"Blinking," I say. "She has a thing . . ." I snap my fingers and scrunch my face to remember. "GPS necklace."

Flynn's and Maddy's eyes widen.

My phone chimes—the battery is now 25 percent charged. The screen brightens. I've missed news alerts, emails, phone calls . . . but no notifications from Life Alert. I tap into the voice-activated app, then say, "Find Gwen."

There's a text message sent from Gwen around eight o'clock last night.

Still at dinner

Someone left a letter for you on porch

I put refrig

Yes, and I saw that letter.

Gwen's little pink dot now spins on the app's map.

"Good," I say, exhaling, "it still works."

Gwen's avatar turns as I orientate myself. "There." I point northwest.

"The trails?" Flynn asks.

"Nuh-uh." Noah zooms in. "The airport."

"How did she get to the airport?" I ask.

"Dee Dee has the shuttle," Maddy says. "Maybe they went to breakfast."

Flynn rubs his neck. "That's a thirty-minute drive."

"It says it's nine miles away," I say.

"Yeah," Maddy says, "but it's dirt road most of the way, and it's been raining and . . ."

"Are you gonna take me," I ask, "or do I need to walk? I don't care either way, I'm going up there."

Flynn grips the wheel of the Wrangler. "I'll take you, Coco."

Maddy looks at her watch, then up to the misty sky. She sighs, then pulls a thick brick of a phone from the glove box. "Always carry a satellite phone in this weather if you're going to the interior," she tells me.

I nod even though I have no plans of traveling to the freaking forest in the rain.

The pink dot brightens and enlarges as the Jeep trundles and skirts, revs and rolls the closer we get to Gwen. Trees and earth and grass shimmer from the heavy mist, and the air becomes wetter and thicker as we slip higher into the clouds.

My head hurts the higher we climb. "What the hell is she doing up here in this weather?"

"The bison burgers at the airport are pretty bomb," Flynn says.

Up, up, up into the interior. Dark shapes move slowly from pasture to pond.

Maddy points. "Bison. Be careful, babe."

Flynn says, "Yup."

The fog and mist blanket the world, and I can't hear anything, not even the Jeep.

That little pink dot—that's all I care about, that's all I want to see.

I should've kept my phone charged, and I shouldn't have invited Noah over and—

"Is that her?" Flynn slows even though we haven't reached the airport yet.

A bright-red jacket sits abandoned in the dirt.

I hop out of the Jeep even before it comes to a stop. Ice crackles across my chest as I run to the jacket and find the GPS necklace in its pocket.

No Gwen, though.

Maddy's satellite phone buzzes.

"Maddy, is Colette with you?" It's Deputy Santos.

Maddy toggles the radio. "Yeah, Pete. She's here."

"Tell her . . . tell her that we found Gwen."

28.

Back down the hill we drive, the Jeep whirring and revving, slipping and rolling. Damp and scratchy, I keep reminding myself to breathe, to think the best, to hold out hope. Deputy Santos hasn't said *how* they found Gwen nor what her condition was when they found her. Just to come to the park only six minutes from the house on Beacon Street.

On Friday, Yesenia and I sat beneath that park's gazebo and talked about dead women . . .

Noah holds my hand as Flynn drives us back into town. But I can't feel his touch—I'm numb to everything. My phone vibrates with missed messages: Deputy Santos, AT&T, and a text from an unknown number.

Are we having fun yet?

Noah says something but I don't hear him. This text message is louder than his voice.

Who is this?? I text back.

The response: Free Msg: Unable to send message—Message Blocking is active.

"What the *fuck*?" I cry.

Noah pulls me closer, and I'm number than before. He coos at me, and his comfort rolls off me and into the fog.

Micah's messing with me again.

It's okay.

She's okay.

I'll be okay.

But up at the park, there are three sheriff's Jeeps and yellow tape strung from here to there and *no*, it's *not* okay.

Squawking police radios disturb the quiet typically found on Avalon Canyon Road in the middle of the school day. After pronouncing my aunt dead on arrival, EMTs have already draped a white sheet over Gwen's body and wait for the mortuary van to arrive. Less than a mile away, the Chimes Tower tolls the noon hour.

I can't feel my face.

I'll wake up any minute now . . .

Any minute . . .

The van arrives, and the nice man I met back on Friday takes my aunt away.

Grief floods me, and I collapse on the sidewalk, cratered by tears and sobs that come like breathing, and I can't stop myself from crying just as I can't stop myself from breathing.

I'll wake up . . .

Wake up . . .

WAKE UP . . .

Noah huddles over my broken body like a storm break, and he whispers, "I'm here, it's okay, it's okay," over and over again.

This island stole my parents. This island stole my little brother and best friend. And now, this island has taken my aunt, the last of my family. And now, I am truly alone.

No, that is *not* okay.

I will never, ever be okay ever again.

◆ ◆ ◆

Too much light in the sheriff's station. And it's too quiet. And there's too much air that makes my skin stretch, and I remember that line from *The Lord of the Rings*, when Bilbo Baggins expressed that he felt like butter scraped across too much bread. Yes, there's too much of everything even though I'm sitting alone in Deputy Santos's cubicle.

Deputy Santos extends his condolences again, then offers me a cup of coffee.

Hand shaking, I accept the cup and watch the dark, hot brew slosh at the rim. Would serve me right if it spills and burns my fingers.

Santos sits beside me instead of behind his desk. "Colette . . ."

I close my eyes. "It wasn't a heart attack. No. And how the hell did she get up there? And who brought her back down here?"

He spreads his hands. "Are there unanswered questions? Yes, I'll admit that—"

"And Felicity Amador," I continue, "she was found at Haypress Pond with vomit dried on her chin, too. So was Paula Paulsen at the rock garden."

"Ms. Amador died of a sickness related to cancer," Santos explains, "and salmonella just pushed it over the edge. Heidi confirmed that Paula refused to throw out old food. I mean . . . you visited that house."

Gwen wasn't nearly as bad as Paula Paulsen with hoarding . . . because she was a thief, not a dragon. And she insisted on eating lots of canned meat. If she'd eaten poisoned food, it was because someone *fed* her poison food.

"And," Deputy Santos is saying, "we can't forget the virus. Folks are dying, especially the elderly."

"No. No, that's not . . ." I shake my head and the motion makes me queasy.

"Gwen must've gone out for a drive again—" the deputy says.

"Her golf cart's at home."

"She must've asked someone to drop her off," Santos says. "Didn't you mention Dee Dee? Maybe *that's* who Gwen had dinner with—"

"That was a guess. She was still alive at eight o'clock. She texted me about that threatening obituary, that it had been left on the porch. She's the one who put it on the fridge."

He makes a note in his steno pad.

"And why did whoever it was leave her there on that bench in the rain?" I ask.

Santos grins. "Have you *met* your aunt?"

"*Excuse* me?" I snap, frowning. "That supposed to be funny?"

His smile crumples. "Apologies. Point is: there are millions of reasons why. We just have to find them out. I don't think there's anything nefarious going on. This isn't LA. Things are—"

"Different here, yeah." I slap my hand against my knee and slosh more coffee onto the linoleum floor. "Everybody keeps saying that," I shout, "and that would be fine if my house hadn't been broken into twice now and if I hadn't been threatened with being pushed off a cliff to my death. I've reported all of this to you, and nothing's happening, and you told me that you'd help, but you haven't helped, and no one's listening, and now, my aunt . . ." I sip air again.

Santos takes the coffee cup so that he can hold my hands. "I *am* listening. And I'm looking for those old case files, and I have questions out to our Robbery and Homicide Division—it all takes time, okay? You said you received a threatening call last week. That number should be in your history."

I fumble for my phone and swipe up . . . up . . .

There it is!

I recite that number to Deputy Santos.

"Okay. Talk to me. What else?" He waggles my arms. "I've asked this before: Anyone suspicious hanging around the house? Just . . . throw out some names, descriptions. Let's figure this out, no holds barred. Who's been at the house?"

I take a breath, another breath, and I massage my temples and think. "The handyman Gwen hires every now and then. He just hung a new front door for us."

Santos releases my hands, then grabs his steno pad. "Name?"

"Not sure of his real name, but I know him as Handy Andy. I guess that's what's on his business card."

Santos pales, frowns.

"What? What's wrong?"

"Handy Andy," he says. "Describe him for me."

"He's . . ." I shake my head and clamp my lips. Last time I described someone, he'd been wrongly accused and jailed for nearly two decades.

Sensing my reluctance, Santos takes out his cell phone. He swipes . . . swipes . . . taps, then holds up a picture. "Is this Handy Andy?"

The man in the photograph is round, Mayan brown, and gold toothed.

"No."

"He's the handyman Gwen usually hires. He's my uncle. This is Andreas Cisneros, a.k.a. Handy Andy."

"But . . . *no.*"

"He died about three weeks ago," Santos says, "on vacation in Puerto Vallarta."

So who is the man . . . ?

"Describe the guy you saw at the house," Santos repeats. "I'll probably know him, and I'll ask him questions, and we'll figure this out."

"He's a white guy," I say, voice shaky. "I know that for sure. He's tall—taller than me, at least. His eyes . . ." Blue? Green? Gray? "I don't remember. He wore a baseball cap."

"What color was the cap?"

I close my eyes, and the memory of him bobs and weaves. "I'm sorry, I can't remember."

"Okay. Anyone else at the house?"

"No." I pause, then ask, "What if fake Handy Andy killed my aunt?"

Santos holds my gaze. "Well, we need to be certain, right? I don't wanna arrest someone for murder when they were simply looking for work. I'm sure you understand that, given the recent . . . *developments* in your family's case."

My skin stings from that verbal pop, but I nod because yeah, I understand.

Santos lets me sit in his cubicle for as long as I need. He's going out to look for a tall white guy calling himself "Handy Andy."

I pluck my cup of coffee from the desktop and sip.

What happened to Aunt Gwen?

Who took her to the airport and then left her at the park to die?

Who was the man who fixed the grate on the side of the house and replaced the door?

If Santos can't find the answers, then . . .

I must.

29.

Another deputy offers to drive me home, but I want—no, *need*—to walk. The mist and cold air force me to breathe, to look up and around, to be reminded that I'm still alive.

And I don't know how to feel about that.

I head east, away from the station, away from the house on Beacon Street. The beachfront is still deserted, and only two kayakers paddle in the harbor. A golf cart rumbles behind me and toots its horn.

Frank, the man who picked me up from the ferry parking lot and dropped me home a week ago, waves at me.

Did he know Gwen?

Did he *kill* Gwen?

Just cuz he smiles, wears a straw hat, and tells great stories doesn't make him innocent.

"How you doing . . . *Colette*, right?" He grins at me. "Getting settled in? Wondering what took you so long to move here?"

I say, "Ha," because I don't feel like talking about my failed week in Avalon.

"You win the game yet?" he asks.

"Not yet," I admit. "Not even close to winning."

"I told you what to do," he says, faux serious, pointing at me.

You have to stop and face your demons before you can win the game.

Tears spring in my eyes. "I *am* getting a little bloody in the battle."

"You gotta stay strong," Frank says. "Running—"

"Ain't gonna make it go away," I complete.

And it hasn't.

"Give you a lift?" he asks. "No charge."

I shake my head. "Don't know where I'm—"

A skateboard clunks against pavement.

Mateo Amador is watching me from his spot across the street. He scowls there, banging his skateboard against his knee and the sidewalk.

"Actually," I say to Frank with a forced smile, "could you drop me at the hardware store? I need to pick up a few things."

"Can do! And I'll even drive you home afterward." He pulls up his mask. "I'm bored outa my mind since we're now shut down."

Mateo Amador keeps his gaze trained on me as Frank drives past.

I'm running away.

Again.

◆　◆　◆

The small hardware store doesn't have any surveillance cameras for purchase or even the jankiest security systems in stock. The clerk, a bubbly man wearing adult braces, tells me the quickest he'll have something in from overtown is . . . he taps the computer keyboard . . . two weeks *at least.*

On the internet, a fourteen-piece security system comes with a Wi-Fi router, two indoor cameras, two video doorbells with cameras, two keypads, and eight contact sensors. Digital Pinkerton guards standing sentinel throughout the house. Two weeks, Monday, March 30—that's how long whole-home protection will take to arrive. That's way past my death date. Still, I tap PURCHASE NOW and leave the safety of the hardware store for Frank's cart.

We putter around the streets of Avalon. Mateo no longer glowers from his spot. The sidewalks are empty, the sky gray. It's not too cold, but I'm still shivering. Fog rolls through my head like it rolls over the hills. One thought blinks past that murk.

I am truly an orphan now.

Salmonella poisoning. Absurd. But then again, I have no idea what Gwen ate last night. We haven't eaten dinner together since . . . since . . .

When *was* the last time I laid eyes on Gwen?

Back on Saturday, the night someone threw the beer bottle through the kitchen window.

I didn't see my aunt that next morning—I assumed she was just sleeping heavily. And then, later on, she left the note about dinner with a friend.

What kind of "loving niece" am I?

The house on Beacon Street feels . . . *flat* without the smells of boiled vienna sausages and spilled olive juice. The house feels . . . *dead* without the constant cheering from the *Family Feud* studio audience and the scoreboard dinging and donging. The floorboards don't even creak as much as I move from room to room.

You wanted the house. It's yours now, free and clear.

Happy?

And how do you hold a funeral during a pandemic? Two weeks—that's how long Safer at Home is supposed to last. Can Gwen wait that long? Can *I?*

At the hardware store, I'd grabbed six bouquets of fresh flowers.

Gwen loved fresh flowers. Once we returned to Los Angeles, she'd keep our tiny apartment filled with bouquets. "Always put beautiful things around you, girl. Even if they eventually go in the trash."

We'd find flowers at the farmers' markets in Culver City, Baldwin Hills, or Westwood, or we'd go downtown to Flower Mart. Vendors would give Gwen one free flower, and she'd give that to me to hold, and by the end of our trip, I'd be holding a chaotic bouquet that made my eyes cross.

Now, I find vases—crystal, china, glass, most with "Property of" tags that don't name my aunt. I place the arrangements of roses, lilies, mums, and carnations around the house, then vacuum and load full trash bags into the big black bins.

Between chores, I check the locks on the front and back doors and peek out the windows.

To his word, Santos has sent a patrol car to Beacon Street, and a deputy sits in a parked Jeep in front of my house. In the distance, Mateo Amador skates in the middle of the street, not daring to come closer, not with a sheriff's deputy parked there.

Even with the flowers and the clean floors, the plug-in air fresheners and fancier wood covering the broken door panes . . . those panes are still broken, and wood now lives where glass was. And the pipes still rumble, and that ceiling water spot is still darkening and . . . I'm still three days away from my death date, and I don't know why I'm supposed to die or who will push me from that cliff.

Now that the house is cleaner, I search for the unicorn again.

Moe is not in my bedroom, nor is she in my closet.

Gwen must have taken her.

Someone's knocking on the front door.

I hurry up the stairs and look out the peephole.

It's Handy Andy. Except "Andy" isn't his name. He's wearing a cardigan sweater and a smile as sad as the sneakers on his feet. "Hey, there."

My eyes burn holes into him. "Your name isn't Andy."

"Never said that I was *the* Handy Andy," he says, blue eyes—*blue!*—twinkling. "I was under his employ, and sometimes it's just easier for people to remember the company name rather than individuals, y'know?" He chuckles. "Everybody that works at Apple is Steve Jobs to me, and every Nike sneaker is an Air Jordan, ha ha."

"Who *are* you?"

He holds out his hand to shake. "Call me JR. I've known Gwen forever, and when Andreas, Mr. Handy Andy himself, died a few weeks ago, I took over his customer base. I'm one of the volunteer patrol guys around here, and I especially watch out for the elderly. Comes from being in a law enforcement family, protecting's in my blood.

"After Miss Gwen took her second dive into the harbor, well . . . it was in my heart to keep an eye on her until you got here. And since I was waiting, this house needed a few things fixed. So . . . no harm, no foul." His hand is still out. "Handy JR doesn't roll off your tongue, does it?"

I sigh and shake his hand.

He drops his head. "I'm so sorry to hear about Gwen. She was a hoot. It must be so hard for you right now. When I stop to think about it . . ." His eyes cloud with tears, and he looks away. "Nah, I won't think about it. Gwen and I, we were pretty close."

He looks up at the house's blistered fascia, the swollen planks on the landing, the termite dust soaked into the grooves. "What's next then? With the house?"

I toe the splintered wet wood. "This place needs a *lot* of work. It's two months away from becoming a death trap."

"But she's beautiful, though," JR says. "I remember when the paint was so white and bright that you could see it from the harbor. And the landscaping . . . *meticulous.*"

I remember my family's first house tour. The view of the harbor from the front porch—Mom loved that the most because it reminded her of that view of downtown LA.

"The expense of keeping up a house on Catalina is a bitch," he says, nodding. "The ocean and salt? Relentless. And if you don't do a lot of construction or have an endless stream of cash, repairs can get away from you."

I glare at the wobbly staircase. "Yeah."

"I'd love to buy her from you. I'm handy with a hammer. I promise to bring her back to her former glory." His smile is joyful, and his heart will pop any minute now.

For a moment, cheer breaks through me like wild stallions, and I almost blurt, "A million dollars as is," but I don't blurt a price. Dad blurted out a price when Everett and Owen offered to buy our house back in View Park—they restored it as promised, and then sold it to an investor who gave no fucks about its history. And now, I run my hand across the banister and stare out at the view my mother loved. "Let me think about it."

He nods, shrugs. "Sure, but what's there to think about?"

My expression freezes. "*Sir.* I found my aunt dead on a park bench just three hours ago. May I have a moment? *Please?*"

He blushes and holds up his hand. "Apologies. I didn't mean . . . of course. Sorry. I'm so sorry." He backs down the rickety steps. "If you need anything fixed—"

"I asked you to fix the back door, remember?"

He nods. "And I told Gwen that afternoon when I hung this new one that the hardware store is out of doors, out of all the big items. The barges aren't coming in cuz of whatever's happening with the virus. I'll scrounge around my garage and a few of my friends'. Maybe somebody has a random door they don't need."

"Didn't know you'd told Gwen—she didn't mention . . ." I clasp my hands and dip my head in humility. "Thank you for fixing *this* door, though. I appreciate it. Really."

"No problem." He waves, then totters down the street, waving to people in golf carts and chatting with an old lady walking a Chihuahua. He walks south until the fog and clutter of candy-colored houses claim him.

A million dollars as is for Dad's dream house.

I'd come here to quasi-kick Gwen out because this house belonged to me, and now, here I am, thinking about selling it.

But I'm thinking about selling it to start over somewhere else like . . . a place not sticky with my family's blood.

No longer able to carry this grief, I crumple onto the porch and weep, and I weep until gulls stop their swooping and swirling, and the heavy orange moon calls them home.

30.

. . . unless I'm lowballing, and a million dollars is too modest a selling price for this house.

The house groans and creaks around me. Crickets chirp in the walls. A cold draft wraps around my ankles and slips past my skin to settle in my bones. The lights flicker because the electrical system hasn't been updated since President Bush stood before that aircraft carrier's MISSION ACCOMPLISHED sign in 2003.

To be honest . . .

This house is a trap.

But it's *my* trap, and I'm not running away from it again. It belongs to my family, one of the only Black families to own property on Catalina Island. I wasn't taught to run, and yeah, I have—and my life hasn't manifested in the way I'd dreamed by running, either.

Frank the taxi cart driver is right.

After I change the damp sheets on my bed, I wander up the stairs to the quiet second level. Aunt Gwen's armchair remains empty, and her big Bible and last martini glass sit there on the TV tray. Cracker crumbs line the rim of the glass.

The lamps in the living room burn bright until I switch them off. I wander to the kitchen and shiver—wet, cold air slips past the weak plyboard substituting as the door's windowpanes. The dead bolt I'd purchased from the hardware store ages ago sits on the counter.

Sadness swirls around me, but I am out of tears. For now. Another failure.

Damn, Colette.

Aunt Gwen is gone.

As I wander the house, turning off lights, that thought stays with me.

Aunt Gwen is gone.

I grab the picture of my family from the mantel, then stand in the doorway of my aunt's bedroom. In the dark, I can't see anything except shadows of those stacked boxes.

So much to do.

Back down in my bedroom, I hunker on the edge of the mattress and text Noah. I want to be with him tonight, but he hasn't responded to my messages.

Hey, just checking in again

Hard being here without her

No ellipses. No READ or DELIVERED receipts.

Where is he?

Maddy's gone quiet, too—she hasn't responded to my **U AROUND** message.

Should I call Micah and tell him?

Gwen had always thought that he was trash, and *he* always thought that *she* was trash.

My aunt is dead, I text as a peace offering and parley.

My phone buzzes immediately with that **Message: Failed to Send** response.

A few of my former coworkers text that they want to send food, too, but need my address. All their texts say:

You are not alone!

Wrong.

I *am* alone.

And despite Deputy Santos's belief in this island and the unwavering goodness of the people here, Santa Catalina is still hosting a killer. I'm not going crazy. I'm not seeing things that aren't there. Gwen was kidnapped, poisoned, and abandoned.

Who did that?

Is it the same monster who claimed Paula, Felicity, Vera, and Consuela?

Above me, the floorboards creak. Like . . . someone's walking, that kind of creak.

I look up to the ceiling and hold my breath. My cheeks turn icy, and the breath in my chest does, too.

Because there shouldn't be anyone walking. I'm the only person in the house . . .

Right?

I spring to my feet as though I've been jabbed in the ass. I clench my jaw almost as tight as I clench the phone, so hard the side buttons dent my palm. I hold my breath—not even my heart dares to make a sound as I listen . . . listen . . .

Crickets.

And crickets inside the walls chirp faster . . . *fasterfaster* . . .

The floorboards creak again.

The crickets hear it, too, and stop their chirping.

I grab the fireplace poker from beside the mattress and take a step . . . take a breath . . . another step . . . another breath . . . I creep up the stairs . . .

No strange lights rove the walls. No weird smells drift through the air.

Up ahead, Gwen's bedroom door is still closed.

I creep to the kitchen, my armpits stinging with sweat.

The kitchen is clean. No mess.

I swing back to the living room.

No one's sitting in Gwen's chair or on the couch.

At the front door, on the floor . . .

A white business-size envelope.

Another condolence card?

Another coupon for truffle fries and a cocktail at Luau Larry's?

I grab the envelope and tear open the flap.

What the *hell*?

My heart jolts, and I tighten my grip on the poker before throwing open the front door.

Streetlights glow on the ratty golf carts parked along Beacon Street. No one is shuffling down the block or leaning against a post. There's no one I can point to and shout, "You there! Did you leave this note?" But their eyes are on me right now. I know this is true.

I shout, "Fuck you," to the phantom, then slam the door. I take deep breaths to stop shaking, but I can't stop shaking and the letter rattles in my hand.

This time . . .

Colette Sienna Weber of Los Angeles, California, is no more because on Thursday, March 19, she was killed by a stampeding herd of American bison in the hills of Santa Catalina . . .

◆　◆　◆

The fog covers everything now as it rushes down Beacon Street, late for an appointment to blanket the world. It hides the phantom who is keeping me from sleeping. The fog crushes my sense of safety and control and keeps me pacing near the mattress instead of sleeping on it.

Death by stampeding bison.

Anxiety is a bubble bobbing in my gut and keeping me from settling anywhere.

The clock on my phone claims it is 2:16 a.m. but that can't be right. I don't sweat like this at 2:16 in the morning. The way I'm panting and chewing the inside of my cheek? This is not 2:16 a.m. behavior.

Bison. In two days.

The floorboards creak—that noise keeps me from closing my eyes, keeps me from trusting that these walls and the goodness deep within the people of Avalon will keep me safe from harm.

I pick up that picture of my family, then kiss it and set it on the floor beside my phone.

How have I handled sleeplessness without having a man in my bed? I close my eyes and picture Los Angeles Colette unable to sleep. What did she do?

Oh. Yeah.

Late-night TV. *The Golden Girls. Cheers. Seinfeld. Living Single. Martin. King of the Hill. Law & Order.* Anything with Guy Fieri. In between Sam and Diane's bickering, Kyle and Maxine's bickering, and some cook in North Carolina making exquisite and glistening pulled pork, my eyes would droop, and sleep would come.

But there is no TV down here. My hot spot is already smoking from all its labor, and with the poor electricity, nothing fully charges anyway.

I have no TV friends to put me to sleep. Just memories. Just creaking floors.

Okay. So I will tackle the electricity immediately—use every penny I have and call that agent to get *more* money, just so that I can have television and reliable internet around the house. I will call Handy JR first thing in the morning.

I lumber to the bathroom. I open the medicine cabinet and grab the NyQuil—but then, I think twice about self-medicating. I'd fall asleep—but then, if I went to sleep, I wouldn't be alert, and then . . .

Crap.

I set the bottle back on the shelf, and I close the medicine cabinet.

In the mirror's reflection, Gwen stands behind me.

I shriek and I feel the color in my face drain.

"Maybe this time," she says, smiling, "when you close your eyes, you won't wake up."

I spin around to face her. "Why are you doing this?"

But there is no Gwen in the mirror.

There's only me. And I am alone.

Still.

31.

Noah's eyebrows furrow—he doesn't know *what* to say. He reads the obituary again and squints at this newest threat of death. "Stampede?" he says again. "Are you kidding me?"

I pull a raisin out of the bagel Noah brought. My brain is both spongy and stiff from hearing sounds that I told myself that I didn't hear. My muscles ache from living a lifetime clenched. My eyes are puffy and bloodshot from crying and not sleeping, from crying and nightmaring. Somehow I managed to grab snatches of sleep, and the next time I opened my eyes, rain was pounding against the windows, and most of the morning had passed.

Noah clears his throat now, and whispers, "I'm so sorry. I wish . . ."

"No," I croak. "You have your own family drama."

His mother had taken a bad turn and he'd arranged medevac to fly her to Torrance Memorial Medical Center. Because of new virus protocols, he couldn't join her on the chopper.

Unless . . . maybe . . . he was with Gwen and . . . no, he was with *me* that night.

"If I find out who's sending these," I say, pointing at the obituary, "then, that may lead me to whoever killed Gwen. But who would kill Gwen?"

Noah drops the threatening note, then stares at the boxes stacked around the living room. "How about . . . the people she stole from?"

I snort. "That could be . . ."

"Anyone," we say together.

Whoever purchased the wet bar double jiggers and matching bottle opener. Whoever wore the Confederate flag bikini. Whoever owned the Sony Walkman, baggies of weed, and baggies of Oxy. It could be the entire housekeeping staff at one Avalon hotel after they'd been questioned for hours because someone—*Gwen*—had stolen a jar of expensive face cream.

"A Kickstarter murder?" Noah asks, eyebrow high.

I throw up my hands. "I don't know. Maybe she slept with someone's husband."

"And an eighty-year-old scorned wife put Gwen in a car, drove her to the airport in the rain, changed course, and drove her to the park instead, left her there, then wrote an obituary and slipped it beneath the door?"

I nibble my bagel. "Dee Dee: She has a tour van, right? And a husband?"

"Wife." Noah cocks his head. "She never called back, did she?"

This time, Dee Dee *does* answer the door to her sea-foam-colored shotgun house. Her name is Letizia. "But people here couldn't pronounce it," she explains, "so I just say, 'Call me Dee Dee.'" With her helmet of wiry silver hair and face as creased as an old road map, Dee Dee tries to smile past the tears in her eyes.

I wait as the woman blows her nose, using that time to study the dusty purple minivan parked at the curb.

One last nose blow and Dee Dee turns to Noah. "How's your momma? I heard they took her overtown last night."

I stare at the woman's strong-looking hands. Did those hands hurt Gwen? Her back—curved and a little humped. Could she carry Gwen to a park bench?

"You and Gwen were best friends?" I ask, not sure if I'd just interrupted a conversation.

Both Noah and Dee Dee gape at me—yes, I'd interrupted their conversation.

My throat tightens, but I cough it out and then find a pen in my bag. "I'm gonna try to write her obituary today, so anything you can tell me . . ."

Dee Dee rests against the doorframe. "She was my best friend. We came here, what, thirty years ago? Worked together as maids ever since. We'd take our smoke breaks together. Go out on double dates together . . . *steal* together. Ha ha!" Her eyes brighten and she winks at me. "C'mon." She beckons us to follow her inside.

The living room is as big as a child's playpen, and every inch of space is crammed with photos, candles, and papier-mâché masks. A love seat and an armchair are the only furniture pieces around a small coffee table.

Dee Dee brings us Diet Cokes and a photo album to the coffee table. The old woman sits on the edge of the armchair, then lights a Newport. She hums as she flips through the album. "Ha!" She jabs her finger at a photo. "Our biggest heist, and I use the term 'heist' loosely."

She's pointing at a diamond-and-sapphire bracelet. "Belonged to this awful, *awful* woman who treated us like slaves. Called us every racist name in the book. Left her bloody panties on the floor. Coughed in our faces."

Dee Dee's lip curls. "So we stole her bracelet. Gwen fenced it overtown—her boyfriend knew a guy, and with the money, we bought . . ." She turns to a picture of her and Gwen on mopeds. "These!"

Noah laughs. "My mother talked about that woman. Sharon Mikolos. Her husband owned race cars or something. She was—"

"Were you and Gwen together two nights ago?" I blurt, interrupting again. I turn to Noah. "Sorry, I just . . ." Panic tastes like Listerine and cinnamon bagels.

286

Dee Dee takes a long drag from the cigarette and swipes at the tears slipping down her cheeks. She blows smoke to the yellowed ceiling, then says, "Gwen was supposed to come here for dinner and play a few hands of spades with some of our old crew, but she canceled on me. Said she had a date with a longtime love."

"Who would that be?" Noah asks. "A local?"

Dee Dee shrugs but averts her eyes.

"You *do* know," I say.

She squints at me. "You putting that in the obituary, too?"

My face warms. "If it's relevant, yes. It would be a roll call of lovers for one of the most colorful characters in Avalon."

Dee Dee peers at me through the smoke. "That may be true— Gwen being a colorful character—but I don't know who this longtime love would be."

And if I did, I'm not gonna say.

Noah doesn't speak much as he drives me to the newsroom.

"Are you gonna say something?" I ask.

"No one's gonna tell you anything if you keep . . ."

"Keep *what*?"

"You have to ease your way into the conversation—"

"I'm not some cub reporter—"

"But you aren't an investigative reporter, either." He stops at an intersection, pausing long enough to look at me. "The people here drive you crazy, I know that, but they're not gonna confess and bare their souls to you if you keep throwing loaded questions at them."

My skin and spine tighten, and I fold my arms and twist as far away as I can from him in the front seat of a golf cart.

He sighs, then hits the gas.

I don't talk again until Maddy finds me in a conference room.

"You didn't have to come in," Maddy says, tapping my head.

I shrug. "Your internet connection is stronger than my hot spot."

Maddy laughs, then pecks my forehead with two kisses. "Use whatever you need, okay?"

Noah slips into the room with a cup of coffee and his laptop.

Maddy points at him. "You taking care of her, right?"

His eyes flick at me. "Trying my best."

I say, "And I'm grateful."

I am.

I sit across from Noah with a blank legal pad. "So . . . where do I start?"

He tells me to call Gary at the mortuary, the pastor at Avalon Community Church, and a whole list of people to invite for Gwen's memorial service.

Gwen volunteered at the library and played bingo. Each year, she made lemon pound cakes for the high school senior prom, and she donated blood and plasma twice a year. The owner of Buffalo Nickel knew that Gwen loved Ritz crackers and vienna sausages, and he'd make her an uptown version of that anytime she stopped by for lunch. Her friends included Dee Dee, Jerry over at the conservancy, Arnold over at the beach club, and retired concierges, front-desk clerks, banquet stewards, and hospitality crews employed between 1963 and 2015.

There won't be a luncheon afterward, not with this virus, and I'll send pictures for a slideshow to the mortician and also pick a few Bible verses, a hymn . . .

After hanging up with Ruben (who used to be a security guard back in the day), I push away from the table, rush to the emergency exit door near Maddy's office, and stumble up the emergency stairwell to the outside deck.

Rain comes down in ribbons, and out on the ocean, a cruise ship sails, homeless and forced to roam until some official in an office in Washington, DC, or Long Beach lets them dock.

Noah finds me standing in the rain and huddles behind me.

I rest my cheek against his arm. "Everyone's shocked that Gwen's gone. She may have been forgetting things, but she was healthy. Ruben told me that she did tai chi three times a week, and that she could 'grasp the bird's tail' like nobody's business, whatever *that* means."

Noah stares at the slow-moving boat out on the Pacific. "Maybe you're right. Maybe someone *is* watching you. I mean . . . we just met a week ago, but you don't strike me as a woman who imagines things for shits and giggles."

I kiss him, tap his compass, then swipe a raindrop from his eyelashes.

"None of this is natural," he says, "no matter how much Santos keeps saying it. For some reason, there's a beast targeting old women in Avalon." His eyes widen. "That's his name. The Beast of Avalon."

I manage a tiny smile. "Good one."

"I'm gonna go full steam on this, okay? Let's agree that this won't be a competition between you and me, who scoops who and all that. We just need to find this fucker—*together*—and we need to stop him. Balls to the wall."

Micah lived like we were in competition, and he even had a leaderboard to track our wins. I'd resisted, but he insisted, and once I lapped him after winning a Grimmy, after I was interviewed for a documentary on obituary writers, Micah refused to take down the leaderboard. He started actively hating me then, and wrote on the board, "Coco won a stupid award no one cares about" and "We met the widow of some washed-up, now-dead movie star."

We were a couple—when one succeeded, the other did, too. At least that's how I'd been raised. That's how my parents' marriage had worked.

Back downstairs, Noah commandeers a tiny conference room, called that only because the landline telephone takes conference calls. He finds index cards, a battered corkboard, and pushpins. I provide the area map of Avalon that someone left in my desk drawer a week ago.

As soon as I pin the first card—*Vera Johansen found in a tent at Black Jack Campground*—Maddy, pale and glassy eyed, appears in the doorway.

Noah freezes. "What's wrong?"

Maddy's mouth moves as her brain searches for words. Finally: "They got Yesenia."

◆　◆　◆

Pacing the conference room, I say, "But how?"

Maddy shrugs.

"I've never seen an ICE agent here," Noah says, shaking his head.

"They weren't *here*," Maddy says. "According to her husband, she was on a ferry."

"Why?" I shriek. "They patrol the ferries."

"Maybe she needed to visit a bigger hospital," Maddy suggests. "Maybe she needed . . . I don't know, Colette. I *do* know that she's in custody."

"Are we gonna try and get her out?" I ask.

Maddy holds up her hands. "What am I supposed to do? She's here without papers. I can't force the government to let her stay." She frowns at the corkboard. "I don't even wanna know what that's supposed to be." She turns on her heel and wanders back toward her office.

"What now?" I ask Noah.

He shrugs. "No idea."

We sit like that for a moment until he says: "I'll ask our family attorney to look into it. He knows people." He taps out a text, then *swoosh*, it's handled for the moment. "Okay. Back to the Beast of Avalon. Next." He makes a card for Consuela Barraza—found dead at Bird Park—then pins it to the board.

I use the large whiteboard to create a timeline—Vera first and Gwen last. My phone brightens with a number I'd called hours ago.

It's Ida the nail technician.

"My sweet Gwennie," the old woman says between whimpers. "I was at dialysis when you called."

"I'm so sorry to share this bad news." I give Noah a "be right back" finger and make my way up to the deck again.

There's a break in the rain, and the air smells fresh and salty.

"How did you know Gwen?" I ask Ida.

"We've known each other since 1985," Ida shares. "We did tai chi together, and Gwen had stopped by last week. I've been under the weather, but she was okay. Her mind was slipping a little, and she took about six pills a day for her heart."

I've heard this many times now about all the dead women. *Her* [body part] *was slipping, but she was okay.*

Ida starts weeping into the phone. "I'm scared outa my mind, Colette. Someone's killing all of my friends—"

My heart thuds once, *hard*, in my ears. I stop pacing—Ida thinks so, too?

"And this virus is taking my people overtown," Ida cries. "I just don't know what to do. I just don't know how we're gonna make it."

I say nothing as the old woman cries, prays, and cries some more. What can I say? I couldn't even save my aunt, who'd slept yards away from me.

Ida's call is followed by a call from Jerry over at the conservancy. "I know Ida thinks some conspiracy's afoot, but Ida also believes we didn't land on the moon. We're *old*, Colette, and old people are good for dying. We don't have any monsters hunting us, not here on Santa Catalina. If we're supposed to be scared of something, it should be birds. They aren't real, y'know. They're surveillance drones made by the government."

◆　◆　◆

Maddy sips her Buffalo Milk, winces, then twists in her patio chair to shout at Flynn. "This tastes awful."

Through the screen door, Flynn shouts back, "Deal with it! I'm the only restaurant now open in Avalon."

Maddy and Flynn's saffron-colored house sits on the edges of Avalon. A 1970s version of a Victorian, the house's white shutters don't close, but there is a wraparound porch, a steep-pitched roof, gingerbread trim, and aluminum siding.

"You haven't touched your cocktail," Maddy says to me. "It's not *that* bad."

"I'm serious," I say. "I don't drink."

"Still?"

"Especially now."

"So when you hit Micah with the coffee mug . . . ?"

"Sober."

"Vandalized his . . . ?"

"Sober."

She gapes at me. "It's okay to have a *little* sip."

I smirk at her. "What is this? An ABC Afterschool Special? You gonna offer me angel dust next? PCP? Premarital sex?"

Maddy throws her head back and says, "Ha! Hey, beloved husband!"

Flynn pops into the doorway. "Yes, my darling."

"This one's still on the wagon. Virgins, please."

He cocks his head. "That a joke?"

"Nope," she says.

A minute later, Flynn returns with a virgin Buffalo Milk. "Basically, it's a milkshake."

"Thank you very much," I say, then stare at the ribbons of chocolate syrup swirling through my mocktail.

"May I be truthful?" Maddy doesn't wait for my response before leaning toward me. "I understand the initial shock and sadness of losing Gwen but . . ." She winces, then whispers, "You hated her, Coco."

I sit up in my wicker chair, rigid and horrified. *"What?"*

Maddy nods. "You told me how she always embarrassed your father, how your parents always had to bail her out of jail. That she always blamed you for what happened up on Middle Terrace. That she didn't even show up for your high school graduation or get you a graduation gift. That she practically stole the house from you."

I take a long glug of the mocktail, seeking liquid courage from stupid amounts of sugar and fat. "Gwen didn't come to graduation because she was under house arrest."

Maddy snorts, then sits back in her chair. "And the other things? Stealing flowers from Flower Mart and making you carry them?"

"They gave her those flowers," I say. *Right?* "Okay, yes, you may be right," I say, "but they . . . I . . . that didn't mean someone had the right to kill her."

Maddy sips, then gags. "Ugh. Too much vodka. Anyway, I don't think someone's out there intentionally killing old women. Sorry. I know Noah's come up with a nifty name, and you all have string on a board going here and there like we're in an episode of *Mindhunter* or whatever, but . . . people don't get killed here."

I frown. "Come again?"

"With the obvious exception," Maddy says, blushing.

I glare into the wild backyard.

"But I didn't invite you to my home to talk about work." She holds up her glass. "Let's toast to Gwen. Here's to that sexy, sticky-fingered bandit!"

We toast, then sip, then slip down in our chairs.

"We should pitch a limited series about her," Maddy says, chuckling.

"There was no one like her," I choke out.

Maddy looks over to me.

"You'll be okay," she says, taking my hand. "You're a survivor."

I squeeze her hand and try to smile. "Not so sure about that."

"I'm here, 'kay?"

I nod. "Thank you."

The patio door flings open, and Flynn, all muscles and wavy red hair, joins us with an amber drink in hand. "Try this."

"What is it?" Maddy asks, holding the new cocktail to the light.

"You said you wanted me to try and make Negronis, right?"

Maddy laughs. "Is that the magic in this glass?"

"Yep. I followed the directions on YouTube." He disappears back into the house.

Maddy sips the Negroni.

"Better?" I ask.

Maddy coughs. "Than what? Gasoline and urine? This is the worst drink I've ever had."

A Black man wearing a hoodie and white sneakers jogs past the house.

I gasp.

"What's wrong?" Maddy asks.

The man jogs north, toward Beacon Street, and I watch him run into the fog.

Maddy waggles my arm. "Coco."

I whisper, "That . . . was Harper Hemphill."

"The guy who just ran down the street?"

I gape at my friend. "You saw him, too?" I swallow to push against the need to vomit.

Maddy nods, then stares down the foggy block. "Yeah, I saw him."

Harper Hemphill is here in Avalon.

32.

As I burst into the lobby of the sheriff's station, Deputy Santos is gnawing on a chunk of sourdough bread smeared with enough butter to baste a Christmas ham. He wipes his mouth with a napkin, then says, "I received your invitation to Gwen's memorial. Thursday, right—"

I grab the counter like it's a life raft. "He's here. I just saw him, and so did Maddy."

Maddy and Flynn had tried to convince me to stay, and then, they'd tried to run after me as I drove off in Gwen's cart, but who can stop the wind? I raced past dark, wet trees through the dark, wet streets, my mind a snarl of fishing line.

Deputy Santos is now cocking his head—I'm not making sense.

He says, "You saw . . . *who? Who's* here?"

I look over my shoulder. "Harper Hemphill. Maddy saw him, too, and I wanna make a report, take out a restraining order, I don't . . . I can't . . . What if . . . ? Revenge—he's angry, I don't blame him . . . they tried to force me to say it was him—"

Santos holds out his hands. "Okay, okay, stop. Take a breath, Coco." He then snaps his fingers in front of my manic eyes. "Listen. Hey! Breathe . . . breathe . . ."

I listen to his instructions, taking sips of air, then pushing that air out . . . then, taking another breath in . . . out . . . until finally, my mind clears.

Santos squeezes my shoulder. "Good. Let's talk this out, okay? I'm here to help. Promise. You're not alone, Coco. Okay?"

I whisper, "Okay."

The station is empty, and walkie-talkies and police radios crackle, and I catch snippets about a house party on Marillo Avenue.

Santos leads me to his desk, a place of organized chaos with stacked-up file folders, unbound reports, a framed picture of him with every Avalon VIP, and that plate of sourdough bread and clam chowder. He pulls up a form on his computer, then taps the keyboard, ready to fill in the blanks. There's a small cut on his chin from shaving, and the crystallized blood looks like dragonstone.

Behind me, the entry door opens, and cold air washes over my neck and shoulders.

Santos looks past me and smiles. "Gimme a minute."

"No rush. Just catching my breath." That's a Black man's voice.

I twist in my chair to see this rare bird, then whirl back around, and my brain pops, and all I can think is *shitshitshit.*

Santos squints at me. "What's wrong?"

"That man. That's him, that's Harper."

I peek back at the man now leaning against the counter and tapping on his phone.

"How old do you think that guy is?" Santos asks.

"What?" I ask, annoyed, because what does it matter?

"Harper Hemphill was accused of murdering your family in 2001, correct?"

"Yes." I squeeze my eyes shut and see sixteen-year-old Colette hiding in that closet.

"When he was arrested," Santos is saying, "Harper Hemphill was fifty years old. He'd be about seventy today." He nods to the man leaning against the counter. "He's nowhere *near* seventy. Colette, I know that because he's a visiting deputy that comes from overtown to work a few hours a week."

I whirl around in my chair again. "But . . . but . . ."

He's tall. He's strong. He has wavy black hair beneath that hoodie.

"You're imagining Harper as he was the last time you saw him," Santos explains. "In 2001, not the seventy-year-old man he'd be today."

Huh?

The last time I saw Harper Hemphill in person was during his first appeal back in 2010. Years have passed since then. This man—*any* man I thought was Harper . . . could have never been him. They're all too young.

Santos prints out a document. "Here it is, in black and white. According to the warden, Hemphill is still in Central California—Santa Maria, to be exact. Some of his buddies got him a job at a vineyard."

"I'm sorry," I whisper. "I just . . . I don't . . ." I drop my head in my hands, and guilt drowns all my words, all my apologies.

"With all that you've gone through," he says, "back then, and right now after losing Gwen . . . it's PTSD, Colette. I'm amazed you're functioning."

But am I functioning? Blaming every Black man with wavy hair and a mustache of being a mass murderer is not functioning.

My eyes fill with fresh tears—I'm relieved that Santos has confirmed that Harper Hemphill is faraway, but I'm sad that I'm still wrong and broken and very alone.

"As far as looking into Handy Andy—" Santos continues.

I sit up in my chair like a trained seal. "He says his name is JR. He seemed nice. He's helping out at the house. He also made an offer to buy it."

"And you . . . ?" Santos asks.

I shake my head.

The deputy considers me for a moment, then points to the report in my hands. "Read that anytime you need a reminder that Harper's not gonna come over here and ruin the last years of his life on you. Not that he can even get over here. No ferries. No toilet paper. No cans of Lysol. I mean . . . they closed Disneyland. The world has turned upside down."

◆ ◆ ◆

After leaving the station, I called Noah and asked that he come to the house. Then, I dived into busywork. Three hours later, the grime on the shower tile is gone thanks to heavy-duty cleaner, a scrub brush, and Noah's sheer determination.

Light bulbs—I changed them.

Cobwebs—I cleared those, too.

The bedsheets that I ordered last week are now available for pickup at the post office.

With the windows washed, tomorrow's sunlight will spill into the house, and the lower level will especially feel livable, and maybe I'll stay down here instead of moving to the rooms on the upper level. Maybe I'll rent those empty bedrooms. It's not like they're haunted, it's not like anyone *died* up there.

But to rent that top level, I need money to fix . . . *everything.*

As Noah naps on the couch, I open my laptop and notebook. I drag family pictures into a folder for Gwen's memorial. I google a list of hymns, finding a few that sound familiar. Then, I open a blank document and start Gwen's obituary. I wrote notes during my conversations with Dee Dee, Ida, and the rest, and they now swirl across these Moleskine pages.

Gwyneth Rose, I type. *A beautiful name for a thief.*

After writing that first draft, I start another project: the synopsis for *Lost in Paradise*, the title that I came up with for the true-crime story.

"What are you writing?" Noah's hand slips drowsily into my hair.

My pulse jumps, and I close my laptop, hoping that Word will autosave. "Just . . . nothing." I clamber beside him on the couch, then kiss him and snuggle. My heart pounds—I'm gonna do it, I'm gonna write this story . . . that is, if I make it past Thursday.

I *will* make it past Thursday, fuck that noise.

Once Noah's fallen back to sleep, I slip out of his arms and peek out the window.

A sheriff's Jeep is parked across the street.

Thank you, Deputy Santos.

I slip back to the floor, then open my laptop again and start an email.

> Hi, Andrea. We've had difficulty connecting but please know that I've been thinking about the book and my family's case. Even though the idea came out of deceit by my ex-husband, there's still something worth telling. What is Stan possibly offering, advance-wise? I've attached a brief synopsis and an outline that will need your expertise. The case continues to evolve, even now. A lot is happening. Looking forward to working with you and hearing more.

With book money, I can make major home repairs, starting with the electricity and . . .

I sink against the couch, feeling wrung out. My eyes flick over to the dark television and those stacks of boxes. Gwen's loot. Her dragon treasure.

I will memorialize her on Thursday, March 19.

March 19 will be just another Thursday.

Trust and believe . . .

The Obituary of Gwyneth Rose Weber

January 7, 1942–March 15, 2020

Ingredients for a splendid afternoon in the life of Gwyneth Rose Weber: sliced vienna sausages dolloped with yellow mustard atop Ritz crackers, a dirty martini (vodka, not gin, and pimento-stuffed olives), and *Family Feud* playing on the television. On Sunday, March 15, Gwen joined her favorite game show host, Richard Dawson, at the studio in the sky. By now, he's kissed her cheek and called her "darling." Right now, she's glowing like she's won a new car.

Gwen had sticky fingers and wasn't ashamed of it. A skilled thief, she was known throughout Santa Catalina for her small-stakes heists, taking random possessions of Avalon's most obnoxious tourists: the Confederate flag tiepin of a self-identified Klansman, the cigarette lighter of a domestic abuser, the bejeweled brooch of a spoiled and aging beauty queen. "So many villains, so little time," Gwen always said. She utilized her days in jail to plan for her next campaign of banditry.

"I am not Robin Hood," she claimed once. "I take from the rich and I keep what I take because I *am* the poor." Then, she laughed, tapped out a Newport, and lit it using the wife-abuser's lighter.

Never married, Gwen found lovers according to the season. Winter boyfriends were like chili and stew, muscular and hardy. Summer lovers were lean, but satisfying, sirloin steaks and coleslaw. She received five marriage proposals over her seventy-eight years and five rings that she sold for jaunts to Vegas, bottles of top-shelf vodka, and loans to friends around Avalon.

Gwen was not a biological mother, but she helped raise her only niece, Colette, after tragedy took the lives of Gwen's younger brother, Reginald; his wife, Alyson; and their son, Langston. Gwen taught Colette to always take what's hers, to always keep a Swiss Army knife in her purse, and how to make the perfect lemon pound cake. One of Gwen's only regrets: never stealing anything during her days as a maid at Four Seasons Beverly Hills.

The service to say goodbye to Gwen will be held at Avalon Community Church on Thursday, March 19.

In lieu of flowers, Colette asks that you donate to Friends of the Avalon Library.

33.

This morning, the newsroom looks narrower than usual. The jar of gummy bears on Noah's desk is nearly empty now, and I can see almost every drop of rain rolling down the storefront windows. I can also smell the onion on Maddy's breath since she's nearly standing on top of me in this curiously cramped office space.

"The Saint Patrick's Day Karaoke Party was canceled last night," Maddy says, her lips now an angry gash across her face. Her head looks tiny above the gray cowl-necked sweater.

"I thought everything was supposed to be closed," I say, studying Vera Johansen's incident report. "Was it Saint Patrick's Day yesterday?"

Maddy plucks the incident report from my hands. "I don't know, Coco. As the community events editor, you're supposed to know. Twenty people showed up at El Galleon for an event that didn't happen."

My face burns, and my feet ache in the Doc Martens boots. "Again: social distancing is supposed to be the law of the land now. I mean . . . should we be in the office?"

"Of course we should be in the office. We're keeping people informed." Maddy reads the report, then frowns. "What *is* this?"

"An incident report from the sheriff's—"

"I *know* that," Maddy snipes. "Why are you reading it? We didn't get a request for Vera."

I blink at her. "What is up with the tone?"

"Her family came up with four hundred dollars for an obituary?" Maddy probes.

I swallow, then say, "I'm paying for it."

"*Why?* And why are you reading an incident report? *I* do the sheriff's log."

"I'm trying to figure out how poor Vera died, *why* she died, who left her out there in that tent. She didn't have an oxygen—"

Maddy holds up her hand. "Stop. Colette—"

"I know, but listen—"

"No, Coco, no." She places her hands, prayer-style, against her lips. "I understand: Avalon is hella boring, but *you* agreed to take on the community events section. Yuck, church picnics and bingo and karaoke parties. But now you're stealing police reports—"

"I didn't *steal*—"

"—for your serial killer investigation."

I run a hand over my mouth to calm down, then say, "First of all, I didn't steal police reports. Second, my own life is on the line right now—"

"Was that Harper?" Maddy asks. "The man you saw last night?"

"No," I say, blushing. "Just a visiting sheriff's deputy."

Maddy's expression softens, and she takes a showy deep breath. "First: sorry for sounding crazy. I'm . . . *ugh!* I'm so freaking tired." She lets her head fall back, then pushes a breath out. Then, she looks back at me. "Seeing things is normal after a tragic death." She takes another breath, then reaches to brush hair away from my face. "Listen: maybe you should take a few days off—"

"No!" I shout. "I'm fine. I'll do better. The karaoke thing . . . that was just a slip, especially since everything is supposed to be shut down anyway. I assumed that the restaurant had already canceled. *And* the notice must've come in on Monday because I worked on the week's calendar back on Sunday. We found my aunt on Monday, and I've had to deal with the mortuary and the church and . . . and . . ."

"If there *is* a serial killer," Maddy whispers, "Noah and I will handle it. Okay? This is what we do."

Noah and I? When did *that* happen?

"I've started writing an article," Maddy continues, "and it's pretty good for a first draft."

First of all: *Started?* When? Does Noah know this? He's been with me almost every day now, and he hasn't said a word about *any* of this.

Second of all: Pretty good for a first draft? Hard disagree. Maddy's writing is basic, the words equivalent of white IKEA furniture.

A tornado is now spinning in my head, and I can barely hear Maddy say . . .

"Maybe you can give it a read-through—"

"May I ask a question?" I say, interrupting her Billy-built words. "When . . . did you decide to join in the writing of this?"

Maddy scoffs. "I'm the editor in chief and publisher of the *Avalon Breeze.*"

I blink back at her. *That's it? And?*

Maddy smiles. *Yep, that's it.*

"Wow."

"I mean . . ." Maddy leans against my desk and scans Vera Johansen's incident report again. "You're right—something weird *is* happening here. And we're supposed to be collaborators, right? If you're worried about the byline, your name's totally going after Noah's—"

"No, it's fine," I say, giving her the fake smile I've inherited from my ancestors. "I like collaborating. And I totally get what you're saying. I'm just . . . I'll keep my finger on the pulse of Avalon—"

"I'm not saying don't write this—it's important if you think it's important."

"Right, I get it—"

"Just . . ." She smiles. "Write the other stuff, too. Like the hike this weekend over at the conservancy—it's still happening since it's outside. Folks can social distance."

I say, "Yay."

Maddy's cell phone chimes from her back pocket, and she answers on speaker.

"Maddy, this is Jim." He sounds breathless, like he's caught in a wind tunnel.

"Hey, Jimbo." Maddy whispers to me, "He flies helicopters." Back to Jim: "What's up?"

"I'm at Buffalo Springs Reservoir," Jim says. "You better get up here."

"I'm in a meeting right now. Can it wait—"

"No," he says, "you gotta come now. They just found a body."

I text Noah that Maddy and I are en route to another death site, but he took a rare ferry ride early this morning to see his mother at the hospital in Torrance. He's on the ferry returning to Avalon right now.

The rain is coming down in drifts, lighter than it's been all morning. Wind whips my face as I ride in the back seat of Flynn's Wrangler. Maddy's hair flies loose in the wind, and Flynn's new-growth beard in training is beaded with water.

"Noah coming?" Flynn asks me.

I shake my head. "He's with his mother."

Flynn cocks his head, squints at Maddy. "I thought I just saw him at the coffee shop."

Maddy blushes. "Don't think so."

My eyebrow lifts. "Can't be him."

Flynn forces a smile, and says, "Probably some other guy." He clears his throat, then guns the Wrangler.

Probably.

A sheriff's helicopter soars over us and disappears behind the hills of the backcountry. The streets are clear—everyone is safe at home.

Except for the poor soul we're about to meet a half-hour's drive away and a stone's throw from Catalina Island airport.

"We drove here back on Monday, right?" I ask, gripping the door handle.

Maddy nods. "Yeah. Searching for Gwen."

We reach the island's interior, where the deer and the buffalo roam.

For the second time since my arrival, police radios squawk, filling the natural silence of this rugged place. The thunder of helicopter rotors pushes at my eardrums. Even in the cold, I'm overheating, shivering too much now.

Who will we find this time?

The stink of decomposition slams over the Jeep, and Flynn, Maddy, and I wince. Bolder than the radio's squawks, louder than the helicopter rotors, the reek of death overpowers the musk of bison and the dank California chaparral.

My stomach twangs as Flynn parks along the dirt road. Maddy and I slip PRESS passes around our necks and hop out of the Jeep. Flynn stays put in the driver's seat and analyzes his starter beard in the rearview mirror.

Deputy Santos holds out his hands to stop our progress. "Far enough." His face is the color of dishwater. His lips quiver, and the vein about his left eye twitches. The yellow sheriff's raincoat makes him look like he's been playing in his daddy's closet again.

"Where?" Maddy asks, scanning the hillsides.

There is the airport almost lost in the clouds. There is a herd of bison far enough away. There is the reservoir, sparkling and gray. And in the tufts of long green grass, there is a bare foot, gray and stiff, toenails painted cotton-candy pink. There is a leg covered in buffalo-print pajama bottoms.

"Who is she?" Maddy asks, steno pad and pen ready.

"Doris Ratzenberger," Santos says.

Maddy's eyes bug. She turns to me. "She's been missing for more than a week."

"Folks thought she went overtown without telling anybody," Santos adds. "She'd been taking classes over in San Pedro to learn Tongva, her native language. But it looks like she's been out here for a while. We didn't see her back on Monday when we were looking for . . ."

"Gwen," I say.

"Oh no," Maddy says, dropping her head. "Poor Doris."

I rub my friend's back.

"She was my seventh-grade English teacher," Maddy says.

Santos nods. "Mine too. The medical examiner and Norris are on their way," Santos says, walking back toward the drop site.

"Sean Norris," Maddy says to me. "He's a detective from overtown." To Deputy Santos: "How do you know this wasn't a natural death?"

Santos turns to look back at us. "Doris was seventy-eight years old and blind in one eye. She didn't get here by herself." He holds my gaze. "Someone left her here to die."

34.

The chairs in the Beast of Avalon war room are all turned this way and that, like the occupants left in a hurry. The fluorescent lights make Maddy and me look craggy and jaundiced. Damp as the outdoors, we pull off our sweatshirts and we each open our laptops. She yanks her hair out of its scrunchie, then tousles it. The loose extensions on my scalp hang heavy, and now, I need more than these two bobby pins.

Noah joins us. He's on the phone, and his mother is speaking so loud that I can hear their conversation. Mrs. Bancroft is talking about the goats in their backyard, in their kitchen, and outside her hospital room.

Noah plops into a chair and rubs his bloodshot eyes. Unlike Maddy and me, Noah looks crisp in his thermal shirt and jeans—he's walked between the raindrops all his life. "Mom," he interrupts, "I need to get the goats out of the pool, okay?"

Mrs. Bancroft's laughter sounds like tinkling bells. "Okay, darling. Tell Aunt Jessica that she needs to come visit. We can do jigsaw—I found a good one. Two thousand pieces."

After coaxing her to hang up, Noah tosses the phone on the table. "Aunt Jessica has been dead since 1995."

I say, "Hmm." And I still wonder if Flynn saw Noah in the coffee shop or if he'd been at Torrance Memorial with his mother.

He shrugs. "Wish my father was here to help, but when does he ever pick up the pieces?"

"I don't think he *meant* to get stuck in Italy," Maddy says.

Noah cocks an eyebrow. "Between covering the virus and Doris being found and all the ringing phones and copy machine noise, this place almost sounds like a real newsroom."

"It's *always* been a real newsroom," Maddy says, ice in her tone.

"Sure." Noah plucks a copy of Doris Ratzenberger's incident report from the desk. He leans over to me and asks, "You okay? You're more quiet than normal."

"I'm tired. A lot on my mind."

Too much. And now . . .

Doris Ratzenberger, who was last seen by her neighbor LuAnn on the evening of the ninth—LuAnn's security camera caught Doris shuffling down Descanso at 5:32 p.m. Another camera—Bobby Garrett's—recorded Doris in the passenger seat of a cart traveling south on Third Street around 5:37 p.m. The old woman wore buffalo-print pajamas and a black windbreaker.

"She didn't show up for her knitting circle on Tuesday," Maddy says, "but with social distancing, all the rules of people checking in and showing up have changed."

Noah flips to the next page. "Who found her?"

"Hikers," I say. "Actually, their chocolate Lab Rufus found her. He found one shoe on the road and the other shoe one hundred yards away." I wait a beat, then ask, "Do bison just . . . *charge* like that?"

Noah shakes his head. "And Doris was a conservationist. Bison were her babies. She just wouldn't start a stampede."

"Someone else disturbed the herd," Maddy says, nodding.

I flip through the report. "Doris had a broken back and neck, but the medical examiner—just eyeballing since she hasn't done the autopsy—believes that probably happened postmortem by the bison."

"Are those hikers still on the island?" Noah asks. "Will Santos give us their names?"

Maddy makes a note on her pad. "I'll ask."

"Anything else?" Noah asks. "Stab wounds?"

I shrug. "Not sure yet. But they think that she's been out there for over a week. Again: How does a two-hundred-year-old blind woman reach the Trans-Catalina Trail on a Monday night?" I grab the marker and circle Buffalo Springs Reservoir on the area map.

"The Beast got another one," Noah says.

Maddy hesitates before she nods.

"And you're fully on board with this?" Noah asks her.

Maddy says, "I told you Tuesday: one hundred percent."

Alarm snags my heart. *"Tuesday?"*

"I took the draft you and Noah started," Maddy says, pulling the story up on her laptop. "I punched it up a little. I told you that. I'm revising it to include Doris now, but it's almost ready to go."

As she taps at the keyboard, I glance at Noah—*What the hell?*—but he's glaring at the incident report he's read twelve times now. What else hasn't he told me?

"May I read it before the rest of the world does?" I ask.

Maddy flushes, still writing. "Simmer down. I was planning to."

"Before or *after* you dinged me for not reporting on canceled karaoke night?"

Noah holds up his hand, then rubs the bridge of his nose. "Can we stop before we start?"

Maddy swallows her words and continues to tap at her laptop keyboard.

A moment later, my inbox pings. I open the draft and try to control my breathing as I read *my* words beneath *Maddy's* byline. My anger turns liquid, and it feels like I'm moments away from drowning.

"The byline. I told you that I'd fix it," Maddy says, reading my mind. "Don't worry."

Woman found dead at Buffalo Springs Reservoir is the sixth victim in three weeks on Catalina Island

The sixth victim in three weeks has been found on Catalina Island.

Hikers spotted Doris Ratzenberger's badly decomposed body off the Trans-Catalina Trail and near Buffalo Springs Reservoir, known for its sparkling water and the bison that find rest there, around 8:30 a.m. on Wednesday, sheriff's deputies say.

The hikers had no reception on their cell phones at that site and hiked until they reached the airport.

The county medical examiner may investigate the cause of death in this case.

Two days ago, Gwyneth Weber was found dead on a bench at the park on Avalon Canyon Road. She was seventy-eight years old.

On Thursday, March 12, Felicity Amador, eighty-nine years old, was found dead on a bench at Haypress Pond.

Paula Paulsen, seventy-eight years old, was found dead on Saturday, March 7, at the rock garden near the botanical garden.

Consuela Barraza, seventy-nine years old, was found dead on Sunday, March 1, at Bird Park.

Vera Johansen, eighty years old, was found dead on Monday, February 24, at Black Jack Campground.

The sheriff's department immediately stated they did not suspect foul play in the women's deaths.

"We don't believe there's anything nefarious in these discoveries," Watch Commander Michael Vexelman said. "There haven't been murders on this island in recent memory."

Prior to this month; the last homicides on the island were the unsolved murders of Reginald Weber, Alyson Weber, and Langston Weber. One of the victims of these most recent events—Gwyneth Weber—was the sister of victim Reginald Weber.

Rumors of a serial killer stalking Avalon have led deputies to conduct extra patrols around the town. Some residents have even started to refer to this phantom as the Beast of Avalon.

Anyone with information about the victims is urged to call Avalon Sheriff's Department Crime Stoppers Hotline.

❖ ❖ ❖

The digital version hits the internet first.

Two minutes after the article posts, the phone lines blink, and Noah, Maddy, and I gather in her office and scribble tips into our notepads.

He's been creeping around a lot and late at night.

People are wearing masks now, but this guy's been wearing masks since February.

Mateo Amador . . .

Mateo Amador . . .

I saw him lifting weights—he's never done that before.

Louis Moncur killed the Bonginos and he probably killed Doris!

He bought a shovel from the hardware.

There's a scratch on his cheek.

There's a weird smell coming from that house he's squatting in.

Louis Moncur . . .

Louis Moncur . . .

One call isn't a tip.

Maddy stares at the number blinking on her desk phone and whispers, "The mayor."

Noah whispers, "Shit," then slips down in his chair.

I say nothing and hold my breath.

Maddy hits the speaker button. "Your Honor."

"Madeline, how *could* you?" the woman shouts. "This article is irresponsible and inflammatory. No killers are living on this island. Never have. Never will."

"Except for the person who killed my family," I whisper to Noah during the mayor's tirade. My bitterness and anger and exhaustion make my heart thrum, and maybe I will explode and end us all.

After she gets off the call, Maddy's phone rings again. This time, it's the president of the chamber of commerce. "What are you trying to do? Destroy our businesses? People won't come if they think folks get murdered here."

"Folks *have* been murdered here," I say to Maddy. "Have they forgotten?"

My family history is being erased—*again*—in real time.

Deputy Santos calls. "I wish you would've worked with me instead of publishing—"

"The truth?" Maddy pops back. "Nothing in this article is inaccurate."

"Yeah, but—"

"People have a right to know," Maddy says.

"That their neighbors are dead? They know that already," Santos counters.

"That someone is out there hunting old women and leaving them all around our island," Maddy says. Her third line brightens, and she frowns at the phone number on the display. "You should get back to work. I gotta get this—the mayor's calling again."

Poor Maddy.

I wander up to the deck.

Out on the ocean, the rain darkens the world. Here on land, the rain simply drifts, and it feels good on my face. I'll never stop seeing that withered foot or Gwen's waxy face, nor will I ever forget the smell of old death that has now joined my memories of new death. I've seen too much in my thirty-five years, and too much of it is death.

And everything today—even with the tips rolling in—has not brought me closer to identifying who plans to kill me tomorrow.

Mateo Amador. Yes, he may be responsible for his great-aunt's death, but I'm a *stranger* to him. He has no reason to push me off a cliff.

My phone rings.

"You come here and all shit breaks loose." It's Deputy Santos.

My head pops back as though he's punched me.

"What's the endgame?" he asks. "You trying to destroy this place because you think we killed your family? You trying to make sure that no one vacations in Avalon ever again?"

I bury my head beneath my arm. "You think that I'm *killing* people for revenge? That I sacrificed all these women, including my aunt, to prove a point? Innocent women—"

"Innocent?" he spits. "Your *aunt*? It may look cute now that she's dead, but she was a thief, a menace to society—"

"Cuz stealing bangles and a tiepin is the equivalent of murder and kidnapping?"

"Gwen brought trouble to this island—"

"The one Black lady—"

"And now, here you are—"

"The other Black lady." I push out a breath—I'm alive, but I can't feel my face, my feet, my fingers. "Look, Deputy *Santos*. You may have forgotten who you are, but we can have that conversation another time. I am not Tippi Hedren and this ain't *The Birds*. Vera, Doris and Consuela were dead before I came. Doris went missing the day I arrived. And if you think you did me favors for not arresting Gwen, then fuck you, I didn't need those favors."

"Now that she's dead."

I snort. "You've been on this island too long. Do you really believe that all these deaths were accidental or natural?"

He doesn't respond. His breath sounds ragged, though.

"Exactly," I say. "Erase my family all you want. Pretend that we never existed. But know that you and everyone else who tries that will fail. I'll make sure everyone knows our story. And since *you* won't warn the people of Avalon, we will. We *must*. Our job is to tell the truth—"

"Even if our economy—"

"What good is the economy if everyone's dead?" I screech. "We can't look away from very real danger just because y'all—"

Dead air.

He hung up.

By the time I reach my desk, the city fathers have already lobbed their first formal attack against the *Avalon Breeze*.

Maddy, grinning, waves it in her hand. "They're demanding a retraction."

She high-fives a reluctant Noah and holds her hand up to me—and I pretend that I don't see it, leaving her hanging. "Good work," she says anyway. "We're in the big time now."

If I'm gonna die tomorrow, I want to go out with a bang. "But dinner first," I tell Noah while flipping the burgers on the grill.

Noah opens a bottle of Pellegrino. "I don't think that's funny." He fills our glasses, then takes a pull on his vape pen.

Our puffer coats protect us against the wet, chilly air. The moon sends that milky light between gaps of clouds. Somewhere on the island, a dog howls and a radio blasts Bananarama's "Cruel Summer" over and over again.

"I'm doing everything just to keep it together." I force a smile. "This is me keeping it together. See? Pretty good, huh?"

He hands me a glass of fizzy water.

"Bohemian Rhapsody" plays from his phone. Back from overtown, his mother called as we roamed the grocery store—she needed him to get the goats off the hill and then search for Barney, the family dog that died twenty-five years ago.

"I can't with her." He studies his vibrating phone. "And I used to love 'Bohemian Rhapsody.' I should change my ringtone."

I raise my glass. "Here's to living in a fantasy and escaping from reality."

We toast, and as soon as I move the burgers off the grill, Noah sweeps me off my feet. He carries me to the chaise longue.

I straddle his hips, and his lower half immediately reacts. "Seems like I've turned that frown upside down," I purr, running my hands down his chest and stopping at his zipper. "I have new bedsheets. Wanna break them in?"

He says, "Later," then kisses me as though I've saved his life.

And maybe I have.

The sun set hours ago, and an evening chill pulls me from sleep—some of the best sleep I've had in months. Naked, I'm slick as a seal from the fog now blanketing the backyard and beyond. Those flecks of happiness still smolder inside me, and just *thinking* about Noah kicks embers into my veins.

Noah still sleeps beside me, also sated from food and folly in the backyard.

I reach down to the deck for my sweatshirt—

What's that?

Rustling leaves . . .

A huff of air.

Deer?

I sense eyes trained on my bare back, and I look over to the fence and the trash bins . . . stacked cinder blocks and . . . I can't see past the trees and the tall grass. Behind me, a loose screen shivers in a window.

Noah shifts in the chaise, runs his hand up my spine. "You okay?"

I whisper, "I hear something."

"Deer. They roam. It's all good." His hand drifts down to my ass, then drops. In a moment, he's asleep again.

I watch his chest rise and fall with each—

That.

Sounds like . . . a muffled sneeze.

That's not deer.

I tremble, but not because it's cold. I hold my breath as I listen and look.

There's a spatula on the grill. There's Noah's rhythmic breathing. There's a steel watering can in the grass and wind moving across the island.

I grab the big grilling fork, then slip on my flip-flops. I shake Noah awake.

He turns over, drapes his hand over his eyes. "Um-hmm?"

"Someone's here," I whisper.

He sits up as though he's been shocked. "What? Where?"

I point to the side of the house, then whisper, "We need to check . . ."

Buzzing fills my ears as we creep to the side of the house.

Closer . . . closer . . .

Cigarette smoke mingles with wet dirt and ozone. But I don't see anyone.

Noah keeps moving.

I catch my breath first. Then, I lick my lips, squeeze the handle of the big fork, and slip into the shadow of the house using my phone's flashlight.

Go . . . go . . . keep going . . .

No one's here, and this side of the house runs as wild as the woods behind it . . .

Wait.

Noah shines his phone's flashlight on the ground.

Footprints . . . new footprints . . . footprints too big to be mine.

He shines the flashlight up the side of the house, then stops.

A palm print on the window.

He moves the light from the window and back down to the wet earth . . .

A cigarette butt, its tip still orange as it dies in the dirt.

35.

Whose footprints are those?

Whose cigarette?

Noah can't answer these questions, nor is he trying to.

Because we have a bigger mess on our hands.

I'd left the backyard to grab a plastic bag from the kitchen to hold that cigarette. And I walked into . . . *chaos*.

Toothpaste now covers the cabinets. Coffee grounds dirty the countertops and the walls. Crumbled Ritz crackers and the fresh flowers I bought back on Monday lay scattered and trampled across the linoleum floor. *LEAVE NOW* is smeared in ketchup on my cabinets.

I can't see much of the mess past the veil of tears in my eyes. I've bit my tongue, and now, the taste of blood mixes with bile. "And you didn't hear *anyone*?" I ask Noah. "You didn't *see* anyone?"

"Coco," Noah says, "you were sleeping on top of me the *entire* time."

I swipe at my face with the arm of my sweatshirt and shift the phone to the other ear. "Santos isn't answering."

He's ignoring me. Typical boy weirdness.

As Noah pulls out the broom and dustpan—I've never swept this much in my entire life—I retreat to the living room and find my purse on the couch. I grab the tub of Advil to combat the buzz saw screaming in my head.

Down at the front door, I glimpse a folded note on the dingy floor.

COLETTE is written in thick black marker, and this handwriting matches the handwriting on the other obituaries I've received.

> Colette Sienna Weber is no more. On Thursday, March 19, she drowned in Buffalo Springs—

Someone tugs my elbow.

I whirl away.

Noah stands there holding an empty paper towel roll. "Where do you keep the—"

I sneer at him, then wave the note. "Is this you? Are you writing these?"

He blinks at me. *"What?"* He pales as he reads the new threat. "No, I didn't—I'd never . . . Colette, we've been outside all night. *Again:* You were in my arms *all night.*"

I can only stare at him.

His skin colors pepper red. "I can't believe you actually just asked me that. Why the hell would I threaten you? How could I be with *you* while also vandalizing your kitchen and . . . *No,* I'm *not* doing this." He pauses, then says, "Is it your ex? Didn't you say he's gaslighted you for years and . . . ?"

I open my mouth to respond, but my will deflates.

"You should call him," Noah says. *"I'll* talk to him."

Half-heartedly, I text Micah, knowing what the response will be— and it's immediate.

Message failed.

I tap the phone icon and it rings . . . rings . . . rings . . .

Voice mail picks up. "The number you have reached—"

I tap END CALL, then hide my face in my hands. I count to one, two . . . seven . . . twelve . . . and the first sob breaks from my chest.

Noah pulls me into his arms. "I'm sorry. We're gonna catch him. I promise."

What good are promises?

Dad promised this island would be safer than LA.

Mom promised that she'd change Dad's mind about moving here.

Gwen promised to be kinder to me.

Micah promised to love and cherish me until the end of time.

Each promise broken.

Noah will break his promise, too. He just doesn't know that yet.

Elle Bancroft was seen wandering near the Chimes Tower. On the phone now with Noah, she sounds confused and diminished.

With the stranger's cigarette now in a bag, I sit beside Noah on the couch, and my heart breaks as the home nurse, now on the phone, tries to calm down his mother. "I thought your dog died twenty-five years ago," the nurse shouts from the receiver.

Noah sighs. "He did. I'll be there in a minute."

I place my head on his shoulder. "This is all too much."

"Yeah." He kisses the top of my head. "It's gonna be okay. The world is a trash fire right now, but we're gonna be okay. Promise."

My ears burn because there it is again, that word. *Promise.* A signpost that shit is about to go off the rails.

But this time, I'll prepare. My death date is hours away, and so is Gwen's memorial service. Since my security system is stuck on some slow train from Timbuktu, screw it, I will create my own version. I have no training in these arts—just a solid knowledge of *Home Alone.*

I can't make ice to cover the stairs, but I *do* have gallons of vegetable oil.

Let them slip and break their effing backs.

I don't own any Micro Machine cars, but I *do* find in Gwen's boxes a Star Wars LEGO set and glass Christmas bulbs that can be crushed and sprinkled throughout the house.

May their feet bleed and little shards of glass wiggle into their veins and up to their heart and then cut that heart to pieces so they death-drop to the floor.

Telephone cables: great for double Dutch and perfect for trip wires. And concussions.

Knowing about the can of hair spray and a cigarette lighter doesn't come from *Home Alone*. No, I saw that makeshift blowtorch in *The Long Kiss Goodnight*.

Fire is a bitch.

The fireplace poker and the crowbar now live next to the toilet and living room couch. I'll carry the machete everywhere I go.

I will *fucking* . . . slice and dice and slam and chop whoever the hell wants to come off in here without my permission.

"Try me," I shout to whoever's listening.

I place the baggie with the stranger's cigarette on the mantel, then take pictures of every trap I make, just to keep track—especially the trip wire at the top of the staircase.

The bogeyman exists, and he's come here too many times now. On his next visit, he'll leave with a bloody wound—that is, if he's still able to walk.

I don't have a lot of free space to move around, but I don't need much. Anyone visiting will assume I'm losing my mind—and maybe I am. I'm too tired now to sort mania from caution. Feels like sawdust is clogging my pores, and now I can't get enough oxygen.

Gwen's memorial service is tomorrow.

Will I have the mental strength to attend?

Will I make it through the night?

Will the Beast of Avalon find me alone?

Will he try to snatch me from the church so that he can push me or drown me like he forecast in those obituaries? If he tries and fails, I'm done with this house, with this island. A million dollars as is. I'll leave for good, and I won't regret one single thing.

And that's *a promise.*

36.

Do my neighbors hear the banging?

It's after midnight, and I'm hammering another floor rug to cover the window I'd already covered with a bedsheet.

I lift the rug and peek out the window one last time.

Only darkness.

I finish driving the nail into the window frame, then drop the hammer to the floor, then drop to the mattress to sleep. Weariness rolls over me and weighs me down . . . but . . .

◆ ◆ ◆

Sleep won't come.

It's 1:38 a.m., and I'm staring at pictures I'd taken of the booby traps. I've crept upstairs three times now, sidestepping LEGOs and crushed candy-colored bulbs. On this fourth trip, I've stopped to stand in the hallway of closed bedroom doors.

Langston's bedroom. Mom and Dad's bedroom. My bedroom.

I pace, even though three steps back and forth down a hallway edged in crushed glass isn't much of a pace. A few times I reach for the doorknob but then snatch back my hand.

◆ ◆ ◆

It's now 2:50 a.m. according to the radio clock Gwen keeps in the upstairs bathroom.

I stare at the now-ordered shelves—I've tossed old and expired medications, twisted tubes of ointments, and empty lotion bottles.

Clean-freak insomniac.

That's a vibe. Except is this clean?

The grout is clean. So are the windows.

Does any of this count as home improvement?

Sleep tries to take me standing here at the bathroom sink.

And I don't fight it.

I grab towels from beneath the sink and climb into the large tub, being careful not to slice myself with the machete. My limbs grow as heavy as my eyelids.

My phone vibrates once . . . then it vibrates again.

I pull the phone out from beneath the towels.

A text message from a number I don't know.

You don't know me

But I know you

WATCH OUT FOR NOAH

◆ ◆ ◆

On the morning of Gwen's funeral, the State of California officially announces statewide closures—stay at home for all those who aren't essential workers. Avalon Community Church will allow a small gathering of fewer than twenty people—I don't think Gwen has more than twenty friends still alive. As for the weather in Avalon: clouds stack one on top of the other, ready to burst, merge, then burst again. The rain will never stop falling from the sky.

Watch out for Noah. Why? Is Noah the Beast of Avalon?

I texted the sender of that insanely timed message, but I've received no response so far. I stayed hunched in the bathtub all night—the safest room in the house, Dad always said—not sleeping and shrinking with every groan, creak, and tap.

The booby traps kept me on that cliff of sanity—at least I'd hear death coming.

My transformation into an armadillo is nearly complete.

Now, at seven on a Thursday morning, the air smells of breakfast: vienna sausages and yellow mustard. My family's episode of *Family Feud* loops on the living room television. I'm curled in Gwen's armchair, my hand cramped around the machete, and my ankles throbbing from twisting them to avoid injury from the traps around the house.

My phone needs charging—I've lived my life through this rectangular block in my pocket, and it's now dead, and I need to grab the charger from downstairs. But I'm not moving from this armchair.

My stomach growls, and I've only had the will to microwave cans of mechanically separated chicken-beef-pork sausages and nibble Ritz crackers.

I want to stay in my house and hide.

The Stay at Home order says I can.

But I need to say goodbye to Gwen one last time.

The black turtleneck chokes me, but at least it fits. My black slacks are too big. I grab my now-charged phone from the kitchen counter and an umbrella for the one-block walk down to Avalon Community Church. Sore and tired, hungry and thirsty, I move like I'm carrying a bison on my back.

The stalker is probably watching me trudge down Beacon Street, and he's probably thinking, *Too easy.*

Gary the mortician offers me a paper face mask. "Some folks that planned to come had to cancel," he says with soft eyes. "Social distancing is now the law of the land."

A lilac urn sits on a bier at the end of Avalon Community Church's center aisle. A large, framed picture sits beside the urn. Gwen was a dead ringer for Nichelle Nichols, the actress who played Communications Officer Uhura on the starship *Enterprise.* In this picture, my feisty aunt wears a miniskirt and holds a cigarette, its cloud of smoke billowing around her head. So glam. So sexy.

I haven't found plans she may have left behind for her burial, but most locals choose cremation since there's limited space for plots. Does Gwen want to be sprinkled into the sea or taken overtown and to Glendale, where Mom, Dad, and Langston lay?

No idea.

The few mourners in attendance settle into the pews, the lower halves of their faces covered with masks, bandannas, and scarves. I take the front bench. Five minutes before the start of service, Noah slides into the pew and sits beside me.

Watch out for Noah.

Maddy and Flynn slip into the pew behind me, and both squeeze my shoulder.

A brunette with bright-red lipstick sits alone in the last pew.

Helen Nilsen, Flynn's mother. New lipstick, same face.

A man wearing a battered fedora sits four benches back.

I don't know him.

A woman with cottony silver hair and bright-orange acrylic nails sits near the entrance.

Is she Ida the nail technician, and is the man in the fedora Ruben the former security guard?

Deputy Santos stands near the entrance to the sanctuary. Is he also checking out the small gathering for suspects?

Dee Dee sits on the first pew on the other side of the aisle. She blows me a kiss, then dabs her wet eyes with limp tissue.

Who's at my house right now, squeezing tubes of toothpaste onto toilet seats? Who's picking red and green glass from their elbows and rubbing their twisted ankles?

The minister, a plump man with gray button eyes that match his robe, talks about the meek, the poor, the jailed, and the orphaned.

My eyes close more than once, and sometimes I cover my eyes with my hand to make others believe that I'm overcome with grief. I'm also overcome with exhaustion and hunger.

The service is short—prayer, obituary, a ten-minute eulogy, the saddest a cappella rendition of "It Is Well with My Soul," a slideshow of twenty pictures and then, mercifully, benediction.

It is not well with my soul. I'm supposed to die today, and I'm not okay with that.

❖ ❖ ❖

I clutch Gwen's urn to my chest and start my way home.

Noah trudges beside me.

Maddy offers lunch.

I decline.

Watch out for Noah.

What does that mean, though?

I will ask him, but not right now.

Sasha, the owner of Café Metropole, meets us at the front door. She's brought bags loaded with foil containers. "There's Cobb salad, barbecue chicken sandwiches, Cubanos, salamis, and cheese . . ." Even though half her face hides behind a mask, Sasha's dazzling blue eyes express sadness. "That should get you through the rest of the week—*oh!*

There are cookies, muffins, and a cheesecake, too. Gwen loved sweets. That lemon pound cake she used to make? Delicious!"

"Thank you so much." I sound like wheat, thin and scratchy. I shift Gwen's urn to my other hand as the kind woman navigates back down the slick, rickety steps.

Noah picks up the bags of food.

I take one of the bags from his hands. "I just wanna sleep. I was up all night."

"We'll figure this out, okay?" He waits a beat, then says, "I'll make sure Santos sends a patrol by, too. Wanna eat sandwiches and watch a movie, or . . . ?"

Besides the obvious reasons, I don't feel like explaining the LEGO blocks, the crushed ornaments, the vegetable oil on the back steps, and the machete.

I shake my head, then sigh. My tongue turns icy, and fatigue tendrils around my brain. "I just . . . can't deal right now."

Disappointed, he nods and says, "Ah."

I try to smile. "Would you like a salad and a sandwich? I have plenty."

He pokes through the bags and finds a Cubano and a Caesar salad. "What about breakfast tomorrow? I'll cook."

"Sounds good."

He kisses my forehead.

Watch out for Noah.

Will watching him be the last thing I do before sailing off the cliffs above Avalon?

◆ ◆ ◆

The house is how I left it—none of the wires have been tripped, and none of the ornaments have been crushed extrafine from someone else's shoe. I place Gwen's urn on the fireplace mantel, then go downstairs to change into sweats and a T-shirt.

Eating a barbecue chicken sandwich and countless cheese cubes makes me feel solid again. I watch *Maury* on the living room TV and continue to grab food from the bag—cheesecake and a giant oatmeal raisin cookie. A woman with long red acrylic nails and a bad weave sits across from Maury Povich as three men do the "I'm not the baddydaddy to little Sinnamin" dance across the stage.

Someone knocks on the front door.

I peek through the peephole: it's Helen Nilsen and her fire-engine-red lips.

She tells me that she just wanted to stop by and offer her condolences in person.

"Thank you for attending Gwen's service today," I say. "I know it was weird, with the pandemic and masks and . . . no lunch."

"No time like the present." Helen Nilsen leans forward, clearly expecting to be let in.

I don't budge. I know that rule about vampires at the threshold.

Rebuffed, she rocks back on her heels and offers me that weird smile. "Don't know if I told you, but Gwennie and I go way back. She'd clean out the houses that I'd sell. She was wonderful at her job."

Gwen *did* clean the hell out of a house—and half of those houses' contents now live in boxes crowding my hallways, the living room, and Gwen's bedroom.

"Before she passed," Helen Nilsen continues, "we were talking about this house. I told you that, didn't I?"

"No, you didn't." I cross my arms. "And what did you two talk about?"

"It was way too much for her. The pipes need replacing. The roof—just a wreck. The wood and the termites, my goodness. At her age and income level, she couldn't afford repairs."

I lean against the doorjamb. "Uh-huh."

"She told me that she wanted to sell. And so . . ." Helen holds out her hands: *ta-dah*.

I squint at her. "And you're here now . . . ?"

"To express my condolences, like I said, and to fulfill Gwen's wishes."

A chill clenches my heart. "*First* of all, this house wasn't Gwen's to sell. It's *my* house—my parents left it for *me. Second*, her ashes haven't even cooled down yet, and now you're here, telling me *what?*"

"I'm so sorry," Helen sputters, red faced. "I didn't—"

"Get the fuck off my porch." I take a step back and slam the door.

The wood creaks and heeled feet tap back down the steps.

I stomp through the house—but it's only a short march because of the booby traps.

How dare *she.*

She—Gwen. She—Helen Nilsen.

"She had no right," I tell Dr. Tamaguchi's voice mail. "She . . ." A sob bursts from my gut that I force into a scream. "I'm sick of people taking advantage of me. I'm sick of having fucking . . . *manners* and trying to avoid pissing people off because I don't want them getting angry enough to kill me . . ." I take a deep breath, but my head hurts so much that I can't see, and I squeeze my eyes closed. Is Helen going to tell Maddy that I disrespected her, and will Maddy fire me as a result? Do I even care? Not caring fills me with even more anger.

I throw cookies and sandwiches at the television, then plop on the couch. "I'm so tired, Dr. Tamaguchi . . . I don't know if I can do it."

"*It*"—what is "it"?

I don't know what "it" is, and I end the call with Dr. Tamaguchi's voice mail. Then, I sprawl out on the couch and cry fully and completely, from the tips of my toes to the ends of my hair. Grief makes its way out of my body, and I'm crying tears that I didn't shed back in 2001. Tears that have collected in my reservoir are now bursting like tsunami, one wave after another . . . after another . . .

. . .

A hard rap on the front door makes me sit up from the couch.

I've cried myself to sleep again.

My phone says that it's a little after two, and a court show plays on the television. The machete is still nestled beside me between couch cushions. Glass ornaments are still sharp. Telephone wires are still taut . . .

. . .

And I'm still alive.

Another knock on the door.

I peek out the peephole.

No one's there.

I open the door and cold, wet air kisses my face.

A vase of white lilies sits on the porch. Its little envelope is addressed to COLETTE.

Did Noah send flowers?

I pull the card from the envelope . . .

YOUR TIME HAS COME.

ARE YOU READY?

37.

The beautiful white lilies aren't so beautiful now, especially since they (and the vase) now live in the big black trash can beside the garage. That notecard, though, sits on the living room coffee table. Hours have passed since the bouquet arrived on the front porch, but my hands still shake, and they won't stop trembling long enough to take an unblurred picture.

YOUR TIME HAS COME.

ARE YOU READY?

Did Helen Nilsen leave this?

I *did* slam the door in that bitch's face; then I'd told her to get the fuck off my porch.

Or are the flowers a gift from Mateo Amador?

Or Micah?

So many villains, so little time.

My mind whirls as I listen to Deputy Santos on the other side of the phone.

"Could be a prize—" he's now saying.

"A . . . *what?*"

"Like a getaway," he says.

I plop on the living room couch. "Are you telling me that I shouldn't feel *threatened?*"

"We don't know *what* the intent—"

"Are you being willfully obtuse?"

"Excuse me?"

"Someone wants to *kill* me." My voice breaks as I hunch over my knees. "My aunt is dead. So are five other women since late February. Why? And why *me?* I don't fit the Beast's type. I'm healthy, I'm thirty-five years old, and I'm not an islander, and after just living here for eleven days, I still don't qualify as a local." I pause. "Mateo Amador. Where is he? Why haven't you—"

"Mateo's been in jail since Tuesday. For burglary."

A light snaps off inside me. "What about Louis Moncur?"

Deputy Santos sighs. "We're looking for him right now. He assaulted a woman last night in her home. So . . ."

There's nothing more to say.

After ending my call with Deputy Santos, I open the door to Gwen's bedroom like an usher opening the doors to a theater. Drama and rococo shenanigans everywhere—from the stacked boxes to the bedposts covered in silk bathrobes. The air smells of cloves and wood and oily, pressed hair. Baubles (some stolen, some purchased), tangled necklaces, jeweled earrings, and bracelets with broken clasps spill from the mahogany jewelry box and over the edges of the bureau. A bottle of Shalimar perfume has tipped over and dried on a rose-and-gold Hermès scarf. My browsing triggers a music box that now plays a sad song by the Carpenters.

The Ark of the Covenant could be hiding in this bedroom. Amelia Earhart's airplane, too. But I'm not looking for those things.

I'm looking for . . .

"What the *hell?*"

Moe the Unicorn is under Gwen's bed—and her stitches have been ripped apart.

I shove my shaky hand into her stuffing and . . .

The ring is still there and scrapes against my fingertips.

I hold the ring to the light and those precious gems twinkle. Yes. Still here. Still perfect.

Gwen . . . a thief until the end. As Mom used to say, *A jackrabbit gotta jackrabbit.*

I stuff the ring back up Moe's butt and resume my search for . . .

That.

Gwen's cell phone is still in her jacket's inside pocket. Back on Monday, I'd just tossed the jacket in her bedroom, shocked and exhausted after finding my aunt dead on a park bench not far from my house. The rhinestone-encrusted phone case captures the room's light, and it still isn't as gaudy as the vintage emerald brooch and clip-on earrings I also find in that jacket pocket.

Oh, Gwen. Whose shit did you pinch before you . . . ?

Wait. Really. Whose shit *is* this, and does it belong to the murderer?

Months ago, I deactivated the phone's passcode when Gwen started forgetting things. Now, I swipe up and past an old photograph of Gwen and actor Billy Dee Williams taken during the jazz festival at the casino just a mile away.

Gwen's digital photo album is open to a picture of teenage Gwen and my teenage father riding matching mopeds at the Santa Monica Pier.

My breath sharpens, seeing their beautiful young faces, their joy so bright and dazzling. Riding mopeds had been one hobby they both shared.

I'll print these pictures later, but now, I press the HOME button and swipe to MESSAGES. There are more than one hundred unread texts—from me, Ida, Sarah, Marvin, and HIN.

The last messages from Sunday afternoon have been read.

Auntie, where are you? From me.

Are you coming tonight? From Dee Dee.

Auntie, just let me know you're okay.

We're on for tonight? From HIN.

Gwen had responded to HIN. Yes, can't wait 😊 🕯️ ♥

"Tonight"—that was Sunday night.

And who's HIN?

I parkour over the booby traps to reach the living room coffee table. I grab Gwen's swollen phone book and flip through the pages in search of "HIN."

Dee Dee, Jerry, Ida, Jack, Laurel, Seamus . . .

No HIN.

Gwen had talked to someone on an unknown number for seven minutes.

Was *that* HIN?

I scroll back through the older texts—no other texts from HIN. However, I do find more messages sent between Gwen and Dee Dee.

She all moved in now? From Dee Dee.

Gwen responded. Yes ugh

You still don't want her there?

No!!

She just like Reggie

Always forcing themselves into places they don't belong

He always got in the way

He dead because he didn't listen to me

Dee Dee responded with: You could've been rich if he'd let you sell all that

Maybe I can get Coco to sell it all on eBay

She not good for nothing else

Except taking things away from me

And the text exchange back on Sunday . . .
So what it worth, Dee Dee texted.

Nothing he say it's not real ruby not real diamond

Wow you telling her?

No I'll let her think her little ring is worth something ha ha

Poor Colette, Dee Dee texted.
What? Not worth . . . ?
Yeah. Poor me. Bamboozled again. My stomach turns, and the urge to vomit washes over me. My future was supposed to be kick-started with this ring.
What if Gwen's appraiser is wrong?
No. Just thinking about the provenance of this ring . . . Getty gave it to one of his many, *many* mistresses. He was a notoriously cheap man, and the mistress probably knew that he was a cheap man, and she kept the ring for its history. She gave it to Micah and me not because it was worth millions, but because it was one helluva story.

And my aunt. Would she have really sold *my* stolen property without telling me?

As I look around her bedroom filled with other people's stuff . . . yeah, she would've, and she and Dee Dee would've bought mopeds and crystal bras or some such nonsense.

"Fuck you, Gwyneth. You, too, Dee Dee." I fall back on the living room couch.

Those text messages make me sick, "too much bacon" kind of sick. A familiar feeling when it involves life with Gwen.

I push out a breath, then swipe the phone screen over to MAPS.

37714 East Whitley Avenue—that had been the last address Gwen entered, but she never pressed START.

It's a thirteen-minute walk heading toward the harbor, then turns back to a home that overlooks the Flats. On the map, it's right above Beacon Street—the owners can probably see my house from their front porch.

I parkour back to Gwen's bedroom and spot on the nightstand a small desk calendar from the ASPCA. The square for March 15 is filled with Gwen's cursive. *Dinner with HIN.*

I tap the unknown number on Gwen's phone, and it rings . . . no answer. No voice mail.

Hunh.

While it takes thirteen minutes to walk to 37714 East Whitley Avenue, it takes only five minutes to drive. It's still March 19, my death date, but this "HIN" is probably the last person who'd been with Gwen. Maybe the same person who wants to push me off a cliff.

This can stop right now.

My skin feels so tight that I can sense my blood rushing through my thin veins.

I hide the unicorn in the back of my closet, then call Deputy Santos. He's at the marina, according to the desk deputy, dealing with a man on a boat who claims to have a bomb on board. I leave a message that

I'm going to a house on 37714 East Whitley, that Gwen had planned an evening with someone named "HIN."

I call Maddy—her voice mail picks up.

I call Noah—no answer.

Shit.

I pace in the small space free of booby traps, then try calling my friends again.

No one picks up.

I leave both the same message I left for Deputy Santos. "Meet me outside of 37714 East Whitley. That's where Gwen was going that night before we found her. I'm on my way there right now."

I grab my Swiss Army knife and the machete and pull on a bright-white sweatshirt and my most reflective sneakers. *Please bring me back to this house.* Then, I creep past the booby traps and out of the house.

Moonlight slips like spilled milk through the clouds. The rain is just mist now.

I slip into Gwen's cart and turn the ignition. The engine sounds like a tank.

I'm the only cart on the road, and my pulse booms as I follow Whitley Avenue westward, upward, my eyes trained on the dark streets ahead. The higher I climb, the nicer the homes. Red brick and flagstone, ceramic tiles and Mediterranean white paint. Squat palm trees and eucalyptus trees and hillsides without any homes at all.

I reach the end of Whitley and the beginning of Las Lomas. The house I'm seeking sits back from the street, its facade modernized with whitewashed stucco. The windows look out to a hillside of eucalyptus trees. A light shines behind a narrow frosted window.

The land around me brightens: headlamps.

Is that Maddy's Jeep?

No—a Toyota truck sweeps past me.

There are no streetlights up here.

It's so dark.

It's so cold.

Back to the house.

No one moves behind that frosted-glass window. No cars are parked in the driveway.

Who lives here?

I slip my hand into my pocket and clutch the Swiss Army knife. I pull out my cell phone again to call Noah. I keep my eyes trained on that single light as I—

A rough hand clamps over my mouth.

Every nerve in my body strains, and even with that hand over my mouth, I scream.

38.

My head swims and throbs with sharp pain, then dull pain, sharp . . . dull . . . sharp. I'm moving—the cart vrooms instead of rattles. Maybe I'm not in a cart—the dashboard seems too . . . big. Smells like old milk in here and stale breath and . . . I can't move—I'm strapped in. I swipe at the buckle, but my fingers can't find the release.

The driver wears a baseball cap, a gaiter, sunglasses, and a dark jacket. He (*he!*) grips the steering wheel with strong, bare hands. Strong *pale* hands.

We're going up up . . . up . . .

He pulls me out of the vehicle, then throws me to the ground.

Blackness swims between gaps of night sky and wispy clouds.

I open my eyes to see that milk-spill moon. The earth sponges beneath my hands.

I try to rise but he hits me, and I lunge forward, stopping only when my head hits something hard and unmoving. I'm now seeing two of everything—a stump, a stump, a tree, a tree, the moon, the moon, the man, the man, and darkness that goes on forever, forever.

I smell musk, chaparral . . . I hear grunts and snuffles . . .

My heart jolts.

Bison!

Another blow to the back of my head sends me face-first into the dirt. Light dances before my eyes. I cry out as I fall onto my stomach—something jabs me . . . *my Swiss Army knife!*

"It's *your* fault," he shouts, pacing. "*You* drove off the tourists. *You* made the island dangerous. You didn't have to come back here. Your family—it's their fault everything went wrong. You stole that house from good, honest, hardworking people. You didn't have to come here. Why didn't you listen to Gwen?"

His foot strikes my shoulder. Then, he raises his fist.

I lift my hands to protect my head, then grab his arm to stop the coming blow.

He dips toward me.

I scrape my nails somewhere against his bare skin, then dip my hand back into my hoodie pocket for the Swiss Army knife.

He kicks me again.

The world swims again.

He yanks back my hair. "Since you won't fucking leave this island, I'll—"

I swing my knife hard, missing his face and striking the collar of his jacket.

He rears back, then freezes.

I scramble backward and hold out the knife. I taste blood and dirt.

There's lowing and the sound of hooves beating the earth. Herd on the move.

The man pulls a hunting knife out of his back pocket, then steps toward me.

The earth rumbles beneath us—the bison are nearing.

The man advances toward me as I step back, back, back, trying to see more details . . . tattoos or scars or . . . or . . . but I can't see anything beneath his hat, past that gaiter . . .

A bison snorts, and my attacker and I both look toward that stampeding herd.

The moon shines on the big male bison with bright-white horns, leading the others.

Tears swell in my throat. It's March 19. *Trampled to death.*

My attacker rushes to the truck—*it's a truck, this is a truck.* He makes a quick three-point turn and speeds into the dark.

Cold air and fear and the stitch in my ribs from his kick make it hard for me to breathe.

The world rumbles beneath my knees. I can try to run, or I can stay and let fate decide.

Shit.

I wince as I stand. I wobble, then gain enough strength to run toward a small grove of trees. I scramble up into the V of a tree trunk and branches and hold on as best as I can.

The bison are so close, I can feel the heat from their bodies. I watch them run, one after the other after the other . . .

After waiting hours, days, weeks, the world slips back into silence.

I climb down from the tree, then run down the dirt path that takes me back to Avalon . . .

Maybe.

◆ ◆ ◆

The deputy on duty can only blink at me with wide eyes, then blink at Peter Santos.

Officially off duty, Santos—his hair free of gel, dressed in track pants and a hoodie—taps the younger man on the back, and says, "Thanks for getting it started." To me, he says, "Wanna look this over?" He holds out the printed copy of the statement I just gave the rookie.

My head hurts and my eyes aren't working. My skin feels cracked, and my hair feels like straw. The moon still reigns, I know that, and the world is still dark. The digital clock on the wall reads 1:11 a.m. I was up there, out there for . . . *two hours?*

"So you just wandered . . . ?" Santos asks.

"Until I spotted light," I say. "I saw the casino—I used the casino's light as a guide."

Twenty years ago, I used the light from the Inn at Mount Ada.

Santos peers at my face. "He left something behind."

I reach for my cheek.

Santos grabs my hand. "Whoa! Don't. Looks like he left a bloody fingerprint."

My eyes widen. "Ohmigod, really?"

Santos leans in more, then says, "Yeah. I see ridges."

"Check my fingernails, too. I scratched him."

Something in his eyes shifts as he gazes at me. "We'll get him, Coco. And thank you for providing that cigarette butt—that will be really helpful in identifying this creep."

"That's it?" I shout.

He blinks at me. "I don't know what you mean."

I point at him. "You didn't believe me. I told you—"

"And I listened," he shouts back. "And I sent patrol units to watch the house. Do you not see what's happening here? We're in a once-in-a-lifetime pandemic. I'm being stretched beyond . . . beyond . . ."

His hands whirl around his head. "You want an apology? Fine. I'm sorry. I'm sorry for trying to take care of everyone on Avalon *and* you, especially. You called it. I fucked it up. My bad. Okay? Is that better? You feel good now?"

I snort. "Absolutely. All is right with the world because you said 'sorry.' Phew. I can sleep now. Thank you."

A woman deputy leads me to a smaller room and swabs beneath my fingernails. Another deputy slips tape across my cheek to collect the fingerprint. The deputy swabs my face for DNA, then hands me an LASD sweatshirt in exchange for my hoodie they keep as evidence.

She says, "Let's take you to the hospital."

I shake my head.

"Your ribs could be cracked," she counters.

I say, "Maybe."

She blinks at me.

I blink at her. Failure swells in me like the oceans. Why did I leave my house of traps? Why did I leave LA? Why did I try with Micah? Why did I pursue journalism? Why did I leave the house on Middle Terrace twenty years ago? Why did I survive? Why am I here?

After the evidence collection is complete, Santos and I sit knee to knee at his desk. "I'm sorry," he says, deflated. "For real, this time. I'm . . . trying. I'll do better. Sincerely."

He holds out his hand for me to shake.

I take it, then nod.

"Now for the hard part," he says. "Describe the person who attacked you."

I take a deep breath in—my torso flares and rattles. Cracked rib just like the deputy suggested? I release that breath through clenched teeth. "He was masked."

"He?" Santos asks.

"The voice was definitely male," I say, nodding. "He wore a light-colored gaiter with something like a bright circle printed on it. He wore a baseball cap—"

"Which team?"

I close my eyes to picture the cap, but I can't see a logo. "Don't know. When I pulled at the gaiter, I saw a scar that started . . ." I place my finger on the side of my throat.

Santos nods as he writes. "Good, that's good. Anything else?"

I shake my head—I taste tears on my lips.

"Did you get a good look at the car you were in?"

I close my eyes again. "It was a truck, and there was something round hanging from the rearview mirror. And it was quiet—didn't strain going up the hill. Gearshift on the steering column . . ."

Santos squints in the distance, then scribbles into the pad. "Did he have an accent? Did he have a limp? Tattoos?"

I shake my head.

"Why were you up on Whitley?" Santos asks. "You left a message saying that you were going there but not why."

"Gwen." I reach into my second pants pocket—I still have Gwen's cell phone, now at 7 percent charge. I show Santos the maps app. "It was the last address she entered—and I think it's connected to texts . . ." I show him the texts. "To someone with the initials HIN."

Santos frowns. "Mind if I . . . ?"

I give him the phone.

"I'll have a deputy retrieve your cart," he says. "You'll have it by the morning. And we'll look into this address. See who lives there."

"Thank you."

"Let's get you to the hospital, okay?"

Sure.

"And Colette," he says, "I *will* catch the Beast of Avalon. That's a promise."

Promise. That word.

This time, though, I brought DNA evidence. This time, I can't possibly accuse the wrong man again, right? Because . . . *science.*

Right?

39.

The red-faced deputy didn't speak to the sixteen-year-old again that night. He *did* share her description with the other deputies. Black guy, six feet tall, mustache, wavy black hair.

Colette shivered and wrapped the wool blanket she'd been given tighter around her shoulders. She saw blood everywhere—on the golf carts, on the curbsides, on the sidewalks, and on the grass, splattered across the dawn-kissed sky.

What if they don't catch him?

She wanted to ask Aunt Gwen that question. Her aunt now paced and smoked, ignoring the deputy asking her questions. Gwen's eyes skipped from Colette to the hills to the cigarette between her fingers.

What if he comes back for me?

Because he *had* to come back, right? In every slasher movie, the monster *always* returned for the last girl.

Police radios squawked and cameras clicked as deputies and crime scene technicians worked and collected. Neighbors wearing robes and sweatshirts crowded Middle Terrace Road, their pale faces horror stricken, their mouths agape. They all gawked at poor blood-soaked Colette, now perched on the ambulance liftgate. They shook their heads and whispered—Colette could hear their headshaking louder than their whispers, and she wanted to scream, *This isn't our fault!*

She didn't scream, though—she'd never speak again.

"They got him!" This from a straw-haired deputy.

Gwen stopped in her step.

Other deputies fist-bumped and said, "Fuck yeah," and "We don't fuck around."

Colette should've grinned and fist-bumped, too. The monster couldn't get her now.

"Where was he?" the red-faced deputy asked.

"Behind the inn, hiding in the hills off Wrigley. He wasn't doing no hiking in them fancy kicks he had on."

A troop of deputies marched down Middle Terrace Road. In the middle of their huddle was a tall Black man with wavy hair and white Air Jordans. Handcuffed. His eyes were puffy, his lips were puffy, and blood glistened in his eyebrows.

Colette jolted, sat upright on the ambulance liftgate.

Did he change clothes?

There was no blood on his light-blue track pants or his bright-white Jordans.

Colette was bloodier than *this* man.

And the monster she'd glimpsed from the closet wore black and had a beer belly.

The deputy who'd asked for a description . . . Where was he?

Hands covering her mouth, Gwen watched the officers lead the man to a squad car.

The man looked at Gwen, then gave her the smallest headshake.

Did they . . . *know* . . . each other?

Forensic investigators continued to search the house on Middle Terrace, collecting blood and fingerprint evidence. They found a beanie that Colette confirmed didn't belong to anyone in her family. They found cell phones. They didn't find weapons.

After being examined by Avalon's only trauma physician, Colette was released into Gwen's care. Deputies dropped the Weber women at Gwen's tiny apartment on Tremont Avenue, a space filled with multicolored throw pillows, potted plants, vinyl record albums, men's watches, women's handbags, an entire tea service. Her aunt shuffled to the bathroom and closed the door. Over the noise of running shower water, Colette heard Gwen weeping.

Exhausted, Colette didn't move from her spot on the couch. She closed her eyes . . . listened to the drumming in her head quiet . . . quiet . . .

Gwen stormed out of the bathroom. Hands clutching the neck of her bathrobe, she stood over Colette. "You sure you saw *him* in the house?"

Colette hesitated because no, she'd said *patio*.

"*In* the house?" Gwen demanded.

"*At* the house." Her voice hurt. "On the patio. I saw . . . he . . . wearing all black."

Gwen glared at her. "Did one of them deputies threaten you? Tell you what to say?"

Colette's spine curled. Because the red-faced deputy *had* told her to tell him about the Black man or he'd arrest her for obstructing an investigation and for being an accessory to murder. *Because you all know each other,* he'd said.

Gwen grabbed Colette's arm. "Did they threaten you?"

Tears filled Colette's eyes. "He said . . . I told him that . . . two people . . . I . . . I . . . I'm scared . . ." She hadn't seen the red-faced deputy again, but she'd told another deputy that another man, one with a beer belly and dressed in all black, had been standing over her brother.

Gwen's eyes goggled. "What did he *say*? Focus, girl!"

Colette shook her head. "Nothing. He didn't . . . nothing."

"You telling the truth?" Gwen snarled, her face inches now from Colette's. "I'll leave your little ass here if you're lying to me."

Colette shook her head. "I'm not lying. Please don't leave me. Please don't." Her pleas turned into sobbing, which turned into high-pitched shrieks that shook the walls and tore at her heart, her throat, her soul.

Gwen tried to soothe her and pulled her into a hug, shushing her, rocking her.

Colette tried to stop shrieking, but she couldn't stop shrieking, even as her aunt shushed her, even as the living room crowded with strangers. She would never stop screaming. She wanted to leave this island, she wanted to go home.

The next morning, Colette opened her eyes, hoping that she'd been Dorothy and that her mother, father, and brother would be standing beside her bed—"What a nightmare you were having" and pancakes for breakfast.

No.

Pillows and other people's property surrounded her. A cottage-cheese ceiling sparkled above her. Gwen stood on the patio with Dee Dee, and both women were smoking.

The blood—that had happened. The cops and the lights—that had happened, too. So . . . not a dream. Her family was gone forever.

Colette turned over on the couch, and warm tears slid across her nose and cheeks and into the funky throw pillows. Maybe, if she prayed hard enough, she'd fall asleep, and God would decide to keep her soul this time . . .

But He didn't.

Three days later, Colette sat in a taxi cart and watched as Gwen eased suitcases down the steps of the house on Beacon Street. The furniture had arrived days before the murders, and now, it sat in the house, wrapped in plastic, waiting to be lived on, slept on, dusted, and crowded with pictures and clay pots from South America, and bouquets of fresh flowers.

Gwen and Colette rode to the harbor in silence.

The world had the audacity to continue. Girls her age stumbled around town wearing wedges and tank tops, wanting to be seen and touched and worshipped, concerned only about being a Paris or a Nicole or an Aaliyah and reading Harry Potter and watching *Buffy* and . . .

"I'll come back for my things," Gwen told Colette on the ferry ride to Long Beach.

Colette's things and her family's things remained boxed in the bedrooms of that house on Beacon Street.

"You can't go through life not talking," Gwen said on that first night at Residence Inn.

Colette bit her lip and turned over in the twin bed across from her aunt. She wanted to talk, but this room was already too loud with the roar of traffic and police sirens, the clink of bottles, and raucous laughter from men living in the park next door.

She was eventually forced to talk to the therapist ordered by children's court and to the attorneys who asked her questions during the murder trial of Harper Hemphill. After all, Colette was the only person alive who saw the man at her family's vacation rental on Middle Terrace.

Before she took the stand in *State of California v. Harper Hemphill*, that red-faced deputy found her outside the ladies' bathroom.

"You're a brave young woman," the man whispered to her. "Just tell the truth and Harper Hemphill can't kill you. Promise. You don't wanna be looking over your shoulder for him forever, do you? Looking for him . . ." He paused, then added, "Or for me, right?"

Colette shook her head. No, she didn't want to see either man ever again.

No one asked her about the man wearing all black, the one with the beer belly.

Harper Hemphill was found guilty of three murders and was sentenced to life in prison.

But Colette never stopped looking over her shoulder.

40.

Maddy doesn't comment on the telephone trip wires or the LEGO blocks or the crushed Christmas ornaments. She just helps me over the traps and helps me settle on the couch.

The ER team at Avalon's only hospital found no major injuries—just cuts, swollen places, and a bruised rib.

Maddy came to drive me home.

And now, I wait for my friend to return from the lower level with a clean T-shirt and boxers, thinking about nothing and everything. Like: Where is Noah? Why hasn't he responded to my texts? Yes, it's three thirty in the morning, but why isn't he *here*? There is never a *right* time to be ghosted, but he's gonna do it right *now*?

"I'm not surprised," Maddy says with a mischievous grin. "He's been a little distracted lately, and not just because you two are hanging out. He's late on delivering his next article. Like he's cheating . . . on *me*, ha ha. Something's off." She pushes out a breath, holds up a bottle of rubbing alcohol, then tosses me sleeping wear. "Enough about Noah. This may sting a little. The nurse says we gotta keep even these little cuts clean. Don't wanna go back to a hospital in a pandemic, right?"

I wince—from her observations about Noah and from the alcohol-soaked cotton ball she's now dabbing on my face.

"You should order curtains," she says, "instead of nailing rugs to your windows."

I grunt. "I *have* curtains, but I don't have the time to hang them. You know with people vandalizing my house and my aunt dying, but sure. Curtains." And right now, I still taste blood and dirt, and my head pounds as though someone kicked it. Guess someone did.

"Sorry," Maddy says. "I didn't mean anything by it."

I close my eyes and bite my tongue.

"I still don't get it," Maddy says. "Who'd *do* this to you?"

"Whoever wants me off the island," I say. "He was very clear of that. First, he blamed the paper, then said that I shouldn't have come back here, that my family messed everything up—"

"Your *family?*" Maddy cocks her head. "A newcomer wouldn't know jack about your family. If they *did* know, they wouldn't care."

"Right. Who'd hold a grudge against the Webers after all these years?"

Maddy slows her dabbing as she thinks. "A grudge that would lead to kidnapping you and trying to kill you in the backcountry."

"To die like Doris Ratzenberger," I say. "Broken by bison."

"But the Beast of Avalon didn't leave living victims."

"This guy didn't *plan* for me to live," I say. "He had a knife as long as my arm."

Maddy sits back on the couch. "We need to figure out this grudge thing. Your dad—when he was a teacher here, did he fail a football player or something?" She chuckles. "I remember when Noah and a few of the tennis players lobbed firecrackers at the bison. Your dad found out, and he wrote them up. Community service for two months."

I blink at her. "Noah mentioned the bison, but not . . . I mean . . ."

"Your dad was tough," she says, "but he was cool. Fair. Did you keep all his records?"

I motion to the creaky walls and drafty ceiling. "They're in the house somewhere."

Noah didn't mention the punishment he'd received—and that my father had given it. Why not? Would he wait all this time for payback? And payback for what my *father* did to him and his friends? Worse: Would he kill my family because he was made to pick up trash after school for two months?

"Have you ever gone back to see the house on Middle Terrace?" Maddy asks now.

"No. I've been trying to work up the nerve but . . ." I shake my head.

"Look for those records," Maddy instructs. "Teacher-parent conference notes, evaluations . . . I bet all of this is related to his job. I can help if you want. Catalina may present as utopia, but some folks here can be racist as fuck."

I snort. "Okay, Malcolm."

She blushes. "Sorry. I know you're aware."

"Who was commander of the sheriff's department back then?"

Maddy shakes her head.

"I don't remember, either, but again . . ." I motion to the house. "I'm sure all that information is in a box somewhere."

"Santos is useless," Maddy spits. "Don't go to him." She looks at her watch, then claps her hands. "You don't smell them cuz of your swollen nose but . . . cookies are ready!" She ducks and creeps past the booby traps to reach the kitchen.

I change into the T-shirt and boxers. "You hear anything about Yesenia's case?"

Maddy shouts, "Nope," from the kitchen and returns with a plate of chocolate chip cookies and two mugs of tea. "Did you know that she was a mule for one of the big drug cartels? Sinaloa or Zetas or whoever? Back in the day, before her family snuck over the border and came to the island. She married the resident drug dealer here, and he's legal, so they can't deport him."

I gape at my friend. "*Yesenia*, our cleaning lady? She risked every-thing to give me those incident reports on Vera and Consuela."

"*See?*" Maddy says, pointing a cookie at me. "Stealing reports. Being in the country illegally. Associated with drugs. Shit just caught up to her, Coco, and *that* has nothing to do with the Beast of Avalon."

I gobble three cookies. The Advil PM caplets are kicking in, and I want to sink into the couch cushions and sleep until Sunday. "Anyway, I thought you hated beards."

"Huh?" Maddy dunks a cookie into her tea.

I motion to my face. "Flynn and that sad creature he's growing on his chin."

Maddy rolls her eyes and makes a raspberry. "His pandemic beard. *Anyway*." She nudges my knee, keeping me from drifting to sleep. "You should write about what happened tonight."

My eyes pop open. "Nuh-uh."

"Coco—"

"I'm not about to sensationalize—"

"That's such a subjective word," Maddy says, mug to her lips. "Aren't you writing about the murders of your family?"

"I'm *trying* to write about that. I keep putting it off, but I wrote a synopsis and outline, though."

"Are you writing it for *free*, or will a publisher be paying you?" Maddy sips from her mug, eyebrow high.

My face burns.

Maddy smirks. "Thought so. And that's not sensationalizing, right? You're . . . sharing your story and being compensated for your efforts." Maddy grins. "I'll help you, if you'd like."

I sink back into the couch cushions. "All I want is to make it to tomorrow and the next day." My arms weigh as much as a battleship. My back and thighs, arms and abs, still scream even as the pain dulls. There are crushed Christmas ornaments still cracking in my head.

Quiet—that's all I want. I haven't experienced more than a handful of true quiet moments since June 23, 2001.

The Beast of Avalon—I didn't awaken him by coming here. He'd already killed Vera, Paula, and Consuela before I'd arrived.

So what did those women share with my family? With *me*?

◆ ◆ ◆

My eyes pop open—according to my phone, it's 6:16 a.m. on Saturday morning. Almost three full hours of sleep. The Advil PM effects have already worn off, and even though my eyes burn, I can't close them again. My sleep is like a summer night in Alaska—brief and barely restorative.

Maddy made a fire before I finally drifted to sleep and smashed herself into Gwen's armchair, where she's now asleep.

Wood in the fireplace still crackles as I turn over on the couch. My joints sound as brittle as the smoldering logs. Micah built great fires, one of the few things he enjoyed doing for us. We'd sit by the fire, and we'd read funny tweets to each other, and play Never Have I Ever.

Micah . . .

Thinking of him chases away all the lingering medicated sleepies. If we'd truly been right for each other, I wouldn't be here right now. It wasn't like we *never* loved each other. He always told me that I was the bravest person he knew. That I was pretty—no, *beautiful*—and that my beauty left him breathless. He admired how I connected with people on a personal level, wanting folks to feel *seen*, to be *remembered*.

"It's not you, it's me." Words he never said.

So . . . *why* weren't we together?

It's time to understand those reasons, to finally read his last letter.

I find it on the bureau top in my downstairs bedroom. The envelope still has its tiny rips, and it still smells of peppermint gum and gardenia lotion. *Here we go.*

I pull out the folded letter, feeling Micah's words push against the paper like braille. I smile—he lacks so much, but at least he has perfect penmanship.

Colette.

A lovely name for someone so miserable and selfish. Throughout our marriage, it was all about you. Even as I'm far away from you, it's STILL all about you. Your pain. Your job. Your refusal to live and go out and BE NORMAL. I thought I could help you. I was wrong. You were exhausting and unavailable and I am CONVINCED that you've given me some kind of cancer that will grow and spread. If I had to do it all over again, I'd run away from you the moment we met at that alumni mixer. Give me my ring. SIGN. THE. PAPERS.

I sip air as though his words punched me in the throat.
Selfish?
Who made me feel bad for not making six figures, which would've been enough to pay for more than a year of voice lessons, and so I sold Dad's vintage Timex to cover the cost?
Miserable?
Who forgave Micah after he had multiple affairs with women *and* men? He didn't love these people, he said. Casting couch requirements, he claimed. He wasn't even an outstanding whore because he *still* didn't land big roles.

And he was lazy. If shit didn't swing his way, he didn't do anything beyond what was required. Steve Buscemi was a firefighter before he found fame. Hugh Jackman taught PE and performed as a party clown. Sylvester freaking Stallone cleaned lion cages at the Central Park Zoo.

But for some inexplicable reason, Micah expected the world simply because he was a beautiful Black man with turquoise eyes.

No, Micah never hit me again after that first time, but his simmering malevolence was asbestos and carbon monoxide. No one knew that he'd changed the passwords to our banking accounts without telling me. No one knew that he pretended to be me and pitched my story of family murder and planned to keep some of the advance after forging my signature on the contract.

The divorce papers don't go into this detail—and with this being a no-contest separation, there's no opportunity to air any of it out in court. Maybe we can go on *Divorce Court* or . . .

I can't contest a divorce. We aren't legally married, so there's that, too.

Too many times in my adult life, I *did* want to die. I'd curl into my armadillo ball and pray that someone would just end me like they ended my family. And yeah, I didn't like going out, and I didn't drink, and I didn't like living with my chest open and unprotected, but there was a *reason.*

And he knew that reason!

And here I thought I'd read last words about what could've been . . .

Why am I shocked?

It was right there, even on our first date when he expected me to pay. *Women always pay my way,* he told me.

I just didn't *want* to see it because I wanted to be safe. I wanted stability. I wanted another family to replace the family I'd lost. I boxed with Micah because at least I had a boxing partner.

Selfish! That was the word Micah hurled that made me lose my mind. I remember now! I'd planned to visit my family's grave last year on their death date. Micah, though, had scheduled a coffee date with a potential new manager, and he wanted me to drive him so that he wouldn't be stressed out. I told him to catch an Uber or drive himself—I'd planned to go straight from work to the cemetery. By the time I got home at nine o'clock that evening, he'd worked himself into a bitter lather. We argued, back and forth, louder and louder until he said . . . he said . . .

You're such a selfish bitch.

Then, the coffee mug I was holding swung through the air and connected with his face.

Whatever we'd had as a couple collapsed that night . . . along with the bones in his nose.

And now, even though these divorce papers are void—you can't end something that never started—I sign my name anyway in every spot required.

I initial there.

I sign there.

Then, I shove it all in the prepaid envelope and seal it.

I feel nothing.

It's time to make big moves, and to find out all that I've refused to see.

It's time to explore this house.

◆ ◆ ◆

Maddy's still sleeping.

As weak sunlight pushes through the mist and warms the house, I open the door to the bedroom that would've been mine. Back then, I wanted my room to look like Cher's room in *Clueless* with the pink-striped wallpaper, the zebra-print armchair, the three-mirror vanity. These windows look out to the hills, now shrouded in fog. Moving boxes labeled "Coco's Stuff" are stacked against the walls. Dust and cobwebs cover the top boxes, and I swipe it away, then pry off weak packing tape.

A tasseled desk lamp, hats, stuffed animals, every V. C. Andrews novel ever published, photo albums, shoes . . .

My hot-pink Motorola beeper!

None of these boxes contain case files—they reached Avalon weeks before the murders.

I clip the pager to the waistband of my shorts and scuffle next door to what would've been Langston's bedroom. His windows also look out to those foggy hills. His moving boxes are just as dusty as mine but plastered with Raiders stickers. Inside: his beat-up copy of *H2O: a Biography of Water* by Philip Ball, three skateboards, gold chains, baseball caps, a periodic table poster signed by Bill Nye the Science Guy, two pairs of sneakers . . .

I find his favorite Raiders sweatshirt—it no longer smells of Calvin Klein Eternity, just dust and disintegrating cardboard. His boxes arrived the same time as mine. I wrap his sweatshirt around my neck.

Pausing in the hallway, I cry some. What would Langston be right now? A wide receiver for the Raiders? A biochemist *thisclose* to a cure for breast cancer? A father?

The windows of my parents' bedroom look out to the harbor—it's the ocean view that convinced Mom life here would be as picturesque as that sparkling sea. Several boxes march along walls that would've been painted sandy-beach brown. One container—a blue plastic tub—stands out from the others. Mom always stored important stuff in this tub.

And that's what I find now: bank statements, life insurance policies, outdated passports, copies of the house titles and loan papers for the house in LA and this house on Beacon Street. My parents put all the *Family Feud* money down along with hundreds of thousands from the sale of our Los Angeles house. Our Realtor was . . . Alessandra Verascio. Her business card is clipped to the loan papers.

There is also a second business card from Kate Bushwell, Realtor, with a folded sticky note stuck to its back. The note is filled with Dad's handwriting. *Aly, this is the seller's agent. She's willing to work something out on the DL. I'll call her tonight.*

Work something out? And working it out secretly? Hunh.

Rachel Howzell Hall

After pawing through other boxes, I carry the blue tub back to the living room—it's the only container in my parents' room not filled with clothes, shoes, desk sets, jewelry, and hats.

Back in Gwen's bedroom, I search those boxes near the closet. I find heavy onyx-and-marble trinket boxes, fancy-shaped bars of soap, quilts, ribbon candy stuck into a single clump, postcards, envelopes . . . envelopes stamped with fat red letters have been bundled together.

STATE PRISON GENERATED MAIL.

The sender: Harper Hemphill.

Did he send Gwen threatening mail?

From December 6, 2002, two months after he was convicted for the three murders.

> Gwen, you KNOW this is all a lie. You let me stay in here all this time when you knew I could've never done this. I HATE YOU. That bitch is a liar! She's a liar! Why are you doing this to me? I'm dying in here. I didn't do it! You KNOW THIS! I got proof! You know I do!

What proof? Why didn't his attorney share it during the trial?

I carry this box into the living room. Looking through it, I find loose stacks of pictures: Gwen at the racetrack, Gwen and Harper on mopeds. Gwen and Harper in different photo booths . . . *kissing* in different photo booths.

My throat tightens, and my mind scrambles to unscramble what I'm seeing.

Gwen and Harper . . . *dated?*

What?

As my pulse thunders in my ears, I find a cache of letters sent from "Harper Hemphill, Booking No. 33XIP, Terminal Annex, Los Angeles, CA."

362

March 3, 2001

This not going to work babe. It is obvious he isn't listening to you. If he gets it then it's over. Kiss your little enterprise goodbye. Reggie got a big mouth and he don't back down from a fight. He just like you in that. He'll be outnumbered over there and that ain't good.

April 22, 2001

So what now? Scare him to death then? Stop acting that way. I agree with you. Nothing good will come from him being there.

May 6, 2001

I don't get it and I saw *Gaslight* a long time ago. That's the plan? Scare him, make him think that Al, Coco, and El are in danger and then what? He supposed to say fuck it, I don't want this house no more? And then, you and Dee Dee and everybody go back to your little enterprise? I don't get it but I'm not as brilliant as you.

May 28, 2001

I miss you too. If you think this will work then it will work. You picking me up from downtown? The warden releasing everybody around noon. I can't wait to talk to you face to face. I never wrote these many letters in my life. I can get with the plan but no tussling. I'll just kick a few things around and make it look like Oh shit!

I can't come back here not even for a beautiful woman like you. Jail ain't no joke.

PS: I want In and Out.

Every hair on my body stands straight. My breath . . . I can't breathe. Like . . . a car has slammed into me and all my insides are just . . . just . . .

Gwen and Harper planned to scare us off the island. To make it look like a break-in. Mom would've freaked out. Dad would've shrunk back. We would've returned to Los Angeles.

Maybe Harper had arrived that night, planning to just kick over a few chairs. But my family . . . they'd already been dead. He saw the blood and the chaos, and he ran just as he testified, believing that if he called 9-1-1, he'd be arrested for the murders.

No wonder Gwen felt guilt afterward. No wonder she'd cared for me without pushback.

I clamp my jaw, pushing back the need to scream, to throw all of this into a pile and strike a match . . . I crouch over until my face hides behind my thighs, and I scream then, and the sound gets lost in my skin. I clench tighter and tighter until I'm curled knees to chest.

My wrecked body tires, though, and my arms loosen, and my legs loosen, and I'm now lying flat on my back, twitching.

A slice of sunshine lights the TV screen. Light speckles on the carpet. None of it is as bright as the fire burning in my brain.

My stomach growls. There are sandwiches and muffins from the café. I'll wake up Maddy. We'll eat, and then, I'll search the house for more information.

I stand and stretch, and my weary bones click-click-click. I scoot and duck to go to the bathroom.

Maddy's still sleeping in the—

What's that?

Someone's slipped two flyers—one marigold, one blue—beneath the front door.

Special City Council COVID-19 Budget Impacts

TODAY!

Watch on Facebook Live, Channel 3, on our website

And the second flyer, the pretty golden one, the message there . . . takes my breath away.

The Obituary of Colette Sienna Weber

Colette Sienna Weber of Los Angeles, California, is no more. She left this world on Sunday, March 22, 2020. The woman didn't heed any of our previous warnings. That is why Colette was taken to the highest point on Santa Catalina and shot in her fingers, toes, and then knees, living agonizingly long enough to suffer until one final bullet between the eyes ended her for good.

We warned you, Colette.

You fucked around—and you found out.

41.

That's it.

I'm done.

I'm outa here.

"What?" Maddy says, trailing after me through the house. "Will you slow down and talk to me?"

I whirl around to face her. "Please leave."

Her face crumples. "I can't leave you now—"

"I need you to go. I have things to do—"

"I can help—"

"No!" I shout. "Go. *Please?*"

Tears pop in her eyes.

I take her hand. "I'll call you later. I need to do a few things. *Alone.*"

After I walk her to the front door and watch her putter away in her cart, I slam the door.

It's time.

I sweep away all the booby traps, then race down to my bedroom. I shove all my things back into a suitcase and duffel bag, packing as frantically as I'd packed during those days after my family's deaths. Three extensions in my hair have separated from the thread holding them to my corn rows—another part of me coming undone. I can find only three bobby pins, and I stick them near the braids closest to my left ear, to my crown and near the base of my scalp.

Raggedy bitch, that's who I am, down to the hair on my head.

The need to weep bobbles in my heart, but I refuse. No more tears spilled over this place.

Fuck Avalon.

As I pack, I call Helen Nilsen. For $1.5 million as is, she can have this house *today*.

But Helen isn't answering.

I careen through the house, grabbing as many documents as possible, including the envelope containing the divorce papers and as many of my parents' records, family pictures, and Gwen's case files as I can carry. I throw out clothes just to be able to take Harper Hemphill's letters to Gwen; then I grab the unicorn stuffed with the ring.

I'll pay Flynn's mom or Alessandra Verascio or who-the-hell-ever to pack up all my family's stuff and ship it to a storage facility back in LA.

The Realtor still isn't answering, though.

Micah made living in Los Angeles difficult, but it wasn't downright *dangerous*.

Maybe I won't settle back in LA.

There's Santa Barbara.

There's Honolulu.

Vegas.

The world is mine.

A sheriff's deputy found Gwen's golf cart up on Whitley and parked it in my driveway. Since then, though, someone has parked their rental cart to block my driveway again, and now, I can't back out.

I'll walk.

Backpack on, duffel bag slung across my body, and hands pulling two rolling suitcases, I start my two-mile walk to the harbor. My body still stings and wobbles—less than twenty-four hours ago, a man, and then bison, nearly ended me, and I walked the island for hours. I don't have any energy—I never warmed a sandwich or muffin for breakfast.

The sun came out earlier, but now, it slips back behind clouds. My breath puffs from my mouth, it's that cold, and the wheels on the suitcases are the loudest sounds on the island.

Is the Beast of Avalon watching me right now and smiling his terrible smile?

Tears made from moving so fast whip off my face. I hate running, but what else should I do? Especially since the Beast *did* keep his promise. I survived, but only because—

I stop walking.

No ferries are docked in the harbor. That's right—limited schedule. The ticket booth looks dark. According to the sign, it will open in ten minutes.

I huddle near the shuttered souvenir shop and take in the scene.

Gray water. Empty pleasure boats. No aromas of fried fish or pancake batter. No one taking selfies. No one fishing on the pier.

A woman wearing a Catalina Express polo shirt ambles from the parking lot over to the office. Her mascara has clumped from the mist. She sees me and frowns. "No ferries today. One of the captains is sick."

A sob burbles beneath my fragile calm. "So . . . when . . . ?"

She shrugs. "No idea. I just came in to be here if folks had questions. Maybe tomorrow."

I'm trapped.

I need to leave Avalon.

How, though?

I roll my bags back to the souvenir shop and sit on a low wall. I kick over a piece of luggage, then bend until my face hides between my knees. I scream into my thighs, my rage rumbling out of me like the bison that nearly trampled me.

Seagulls drift from the cloudy sky to land on the wooden posts across from me.

I have nothing to offer them.

More gulls land on posts and on the wood-planked walkway. They watch me and wait.

◆ ◆ ◆

I'm trapped—but I'm also in America. There *has* to be someone I can pay for passage. How much does a private charter cost?

"By sea or by air?" Maddy's eyes haven't left the computer screen, not since I came whirling into the newsroom looking like a hobo with bags and raggedy hair.

"Either," I say. "I don't care. I just wanna leave." It's almost half past twelve.

Time keeps on slippin', slippin' . . .

Maddy finally stops and looks at me. "A turboprop starts at around fifteen hundred dollars. A private yacht, around two hundred dollars an hour—and remember, it won't go as fast as the high-speed ferry. So you're looking at around six hundred to a thousand dollars, depending on the conditions."

"I don't have that kind of money." I let my suitcases drop and stare at Maddy's uneaten cream-cheese-schmeared jalapeño bagel. "May I? I'm so freaking hungry."

Maddy says, "Help yourself," and returns to clicking on her computer. "I don't know what to say right now. I don't want you to go—the monster shouldn't win—but I can't blame you for wanting to get the hell off this island."

I chew the bagel, more interested in food than anything my friend is saying.

Maddy grins at me. "We're actually getting tips—people are freaked out and turning on boyfriends and husbands. Somebody thinks the Beast is the main tour guide over at the zip lines. Best of all, the *Times* wants to syndicate the story, so if you stay, I'll need you—"

"Maddy, stop it," I shout, dropping the bagel back on the desk. "Somebody's trying to kill me. People are *dead*. There's a killer loose on the island."

"I know this," she shouts back.

"And you're *cool* with it?"

"Hell no, I'm not okay with this. I'm just as triggered as you, but what am I supposed to do, Colette? I'm doing the only thing I know how, and that's writing about it. Just like you write about it even if it comes out differently." She sits back in the chair. "This is what we *do*, Coco. We're reporters. We can't *run* from danger. If we run, who's gonna tell the world to beware? Is it dangerous work? *Yes. Absolutely.* But that's my job. No, that's my *calling*."

The cream cheese sours in my mouth. "Even with death breathing down your back."

"This is an opportunity of a lifetime. To catch a monster and end this once and for all. Wanna talk about legacy? I want you to write that I go down with the monster's head in my hands. *That's* the first line in my obituary."

I scowl and roll my eyes. "But that ain't gonna be the first line in mine. No, ma'am."

She stares at me with soft eyes, accepting my answer even if she thinks it's a crappy one. "I don't know anyone with a boat or helicopter. Noah probably does, but he's not here. He's still overtown."

I take deep breaths that pull at my bruised rib. "I haven't seen him since he walked me home after Gwen's service."

Hunh.

Watch out for Noah.

"He said his mom took a turn for the worst," Maddy shares. "They medevaced her back to Torrance." She pushes her smoothie toward me. "Stay with Flynn and me. We'll protect you, and we'll feed you, and I promise that we'll help you figure out next steps with all of this. The house, the job . . . Harper. All of it. Okay? Will you let me help you?"

Nope.

I trust *me*.

If someone's gonna come through for me, she's gonna be me.

My luggage still sits by my desk. I have two choices: return to the harbor and search for a boater sailing to Los Angeles or . . . stay.

But I won't be stuck here forever.

I'll die by push, by bison, or by gunshot. For me, there is no forever-living in Avalon.

I need to make a levelheaded plan.

That will be my first order of business.

I march out of the newsroom and to the sidewalks. My legs burn and ache, but not as much as my back. My bones rub against each other as I limp to the post office and slip the envelope with the divorce papers into the mail slot. Seagulls circle overhead, bright against the cloudy sky. The town looks ghostly, with stabs of hot-pink and yellow paint against the gray.

Noah still hasn't texted. Why hasn't he responded?

Is he really with his mother?

Everything okay? I text.

Maddy told me about your mom

I'm finding a way to leave this island

No ellipses.

His lack of response makes me sick.

All the storefronts are dark. None of these businesses are essential— no one needs wafty Stevie Nicks skirts or boat-print ties, three-wick soy candles, or handcrafted journals. One window brightens against the gloom. The hanging tire-shaped sign above the door says,

McIn-TIRES Bikes

I stare at that sign of a bicycle against a setting sun. Light blue . . . orange circle . . .

So . . . familiar.

A shadow moves inside the shop.

I duck, then creep over to look in the window. I can see only his back, but a man is lining up a row of bikes. A kerchief hangs from his belt loop. His index finger is wrapped in a bandage, and new scratches run along his right forearm.

Orange circle . . . light blue . . .

That's him!

I rush to the sheriff's station, ignoring all pain as I burst through the doors.

The desk deputy looks at me with weary eyes. He's the same guy who took my statement last night, three nights ago, when was that, what is time? "If you're looking for Santos," the deputy says, "he's out on a call right now."

My eyes skip around the station. No one's standing at the dispatch monitor. No one's standing at the copier. "Can someone else . . . ?"

"I'm the only one here right now," Deputy Nguyen says. "I'll pass Santos the message as soon as he gets back."

I release the edge of the reception desk and back out.

That kerchief . . . the orange circle set against the light-blue sky. Those scratches . . .

My mind crackles—my brain is imperfect and exhausted, and that means I can be wrong.

But the scarf . . .

Those scratches . . .

The bandaged fingers . . .

I'll need to stay until I talk to Deputy Santos.

And really: What other choice do I have?

I can't go home, not now. Now that I know my attacker—the Beast of Avalon—is *lit-uh-ruh-lee* half a mile away from my front porch. He can probably see everything that I do around the house. But I need proof. I need—

DNA!

We have DNA!

Sheriff's deputies took swabs of that fingerprint on my cheek and fingernail clippings.

But what if his prints and DNA aren't in the database? Other than my accusation, what can I show Santos that will *make* him question this man in the bike shop?

I need to research the *Breeze*'s archives.

I race back to the newsroom. My phone buzzes with a text from Noah.

I'm back

On my way over

I tap the phone icon, and before Noah speaks, I blurt, "I'm at the office."

"Why? You should be resting."

"Just come here," I demand.

Heart racing, I hurtle into the newsroom, startling Gabriella, the new cleaning woman. "Sorry," I say to her, smiling weakly and scrambling to my desk.

I never answered Noah's question.

Why?

Because I'm tired of running, I'm tired of being scared, I'm tired of looking over my shoulder and not breathing, not sleeping, not loving myself, not living fully. The answers are just over there, lost in the mist, still not close but not a life's journey away.

Who is the man in that bicycle shop—and how are we connected?

"I'm not running," I whisper. "Not anymore."

The room smells like sunshine and lemons, and its brightness and hope make me look up from the desk.

Gabriella's humming as she sprays a can of air freshener toward the ceiling.

I know this song that she's humming.

And *yes*, I *will* survive.

42.

January 12, 1944, was the first mention of McIn-TIRES Bikes in the *Avalon Breeze*. "The Avalon PTA expressed appreciation to Avalon merchants . . ."

There's also an advertisement from 1947: Get a new Roadmaster bicycle for only $39.95.

> Still located on Metropole Avenue. We also rent wheelchairs and strollers! Free maps of the island! Rent, Sales and Repair!

But I can't find anything about who actually *owned* the shop.

I push back from the desk and twist in the chair.

Still humming, Gabriella pushes a vacuum cleaner up and down the hallway.

Outside, the light turns to creamy sherbet—the sun finally pushes through the mist to shine, if only for a second or two.

Sometimes, that's long enough.

I open one of my stuffed suitcases. All the case files from Gwen's box and Mom's blue plastic tub are crammed together. I grab a battered manila envelope fat with documents, then dump it all onto my desk.

Stapled reports . . . crinkled and faded receipts . . . so much stuff . . .

I grab a ream of legal-size documents held together by a binder clip, then flip through.

My breath whooshes from my mouth. *The sale papers for the house on Beacon Street!*

I flip and scan the legalese and notary stamps, pausing at my parents' inked initials. Strong and right-leaning *AW*s for Alyson Weber and light upright *RW*s for Reginald Weber.

I reach the final page of signatures.

There's Mom's signature.

There's Dad's signature.

Credit card statements . . . invoices . . . a business card for a moving company . . . a business card for an electrician . . .

Back to the pile.

Initiating Case Report.

I don't think I've read this document.

Occurrence from: 6/21/2001 23:58

Occurrence to: 6/21/2001 23:58

Reporting LEO: Fisker, Alex

Backup LEO: McIntyre, Carson

I search on *Alex Fisker.*

The first result is an obituary. Fisker died by suicide on January 3, 2002. I remember him—he had straw-like blond hair and big teeth. He didn't speak to me that night. He focused on the crime scene, made sure the techs did their jobs, made sure neighbors left statements.

"Carson McIntyre"—is he related to the McIn-TIRES Bikes family?

I type that name into the search bar and gasp. The crew cut. The red face. The scowl. He was the deputy who told me to not lie, the one who threatened to arrest me. Other search results include an article about the bike shop being handed down from generation to generation, about Carson McIntyre receiving a commendation from the City of Avalon for his service as a law enforcement officer and business owner. There he is, riding a homemade float on the Fourth of July. There he is, winner of the "All You Can Eat" pancake contest. There he is, celebrating his fiftieth anniversary with his wife and best friend, Carol Tatum.

"You look like you're about to explode."

I startle and look up. "Oh. Huh?"

Noah's standing over me, unshaven and rumpled in his T-shirt and jeans. "Damn. What happened to your . . . ?" His eyes skip from my face to my neck. "What happened to you?"

For a second, anger pulses through me, but just like that . . . I jump up from the desk and hug him. My heartbeat pounds against his.

"Where have you been?" I ask, sitting again. "I figured we were done."

Noah pulls the chair from his desk and plops into it with a heavy sigh. "First: I didn't ghost you. Second: I'm trying to figure out what to do with my mother, and my dad is still with his mistress in Italy and can't be bothered as he allegedly shelters in place."

I sneer. "Love in the time of corona."

Noah rubs his face, then looks at me, bleary eyed. "Sorry for not communicating. My mother hid my phone—I found it in her dresser drawer along with her pills and the TV remote control. She hides stuff when she's not running away from the nurse, and damn, I miss you." He kisses my hand, then rubs it against his stubbled cheek. "I'm gonna ignore the suitcases. I refuse to let you go. You will not leave me. We are gonna adventure together and write cool-ass, balls-to-the-wall stories together."

"If you want me to stay . . ." I grasp his face in my hands. "Help me with something first."

"Anything."

I catch him up on my assault in bison country, the visit at the sheriff's station, the fingerprint on my cheek, the scratches I'd left on my attacker, trying to leave Avalon, then walking past McIn-TIRES Bikes and seeing the man who attacked me.

"Then, I started reviewing crime scene reports from my family's case," I say, motioning to my desk. "And I saw that one of the officers on the scene that night was Carson McIntyre."

Noah says, "Okay," then brushes hair away from the cut on my forehead.

I shake him. "It's the deputy who threatened me as a kid."

"Okay," Noah says, nodding. "And?"

"And . . . that's when *you* walked in."

"Interrupting all your Nancy Drew shit."

"He could be the monster who killed my family," I say. "The same monster killing the old woman in Avalon."

"Except that . . . Carson McIntyre died last year."

"What?" My heart shrivels.

"Yep. Cancer. He was going around the island, making amends and apologizing, actually saying 'thank you' and being . . . *nice.*"

He gives me a sad smile. "He wasn't just a jerk to you. He was a very angry man. He was very protective of this island, and he absolutely hated outsiders who decided to settle on this island."

"Outsiders." I twist in my chair as I think. "And if Gwen—*an outsider*—ran a burglary ring, the last people McIntyre would want moving here would be her ratchet family?"

Noah gives me gun fingers. "Why would one of the original, mainland transplant law-and-order families be okay living in paradise with folks who don't look like them?"

"But he still could've done it twenty years ago," I say.

"There's also . . ." Noah leans on his knees and steeples his fingers.
I squint at him. "There's also . . . *who?*"
"Mikey, a.k.a. Carson McIntyre, Junior."
"Who's Carson—"
His phone chimes from his pocket.
My phone vibrates on the desk.
"It's Maddy," Noah says, peering at the bright screen.
Our boss is texting us.

A break in the case!!

We're at Helen's house

Come ASAP!!

As we walk to Noah's cart, he leans in for a kiss. I close my eyes
and try to enjoy the bubble drifting around my chest. My mind drifts
instead.

The last obituary I received predicted that I'd die on Sunday,
March 22.

But that ain't today.

43.

At the stop sign just yards from the newsroom, I press SEND on the email containing scans of the newest documents I've read on my family's case. I smile at Noah, feeling lighter. "I told my attorney everything that's happened, and that if he doesn't hear from me by Monday, then he knows something's wrong."

Like . . . I'm dead, that kind of "something's wrong."

Noah rests his chin on the cart's steering wheel, then stares out to the deserted streets. He takes a deep breath, then says, "I . . . need to tell you something."

"Okay."

When he doesn't speak, my heart jumps. "You're married."

He snorts. "Oh, hell no. It's worse . . . maybe."

I squint at him. "Dude, you're scaring me. What is it?"

He takes a deep breath, then pushes out: "I'm wearing a hidden recording device. And I've been wearing it since the first time we met."

"A . . . *what?*"

"A hidden camera."

"What? Where . . . ?" I look at his wrist, his hair, that . . . "Compass," I say, pointing at the pendant hanging around his neck.

He holds up his hands. "Except for the times you and I were in bed and on the couch and in a patio chair . . . I'd never—"

"Nuh-uh." I hop out of the cart on numb legs. "No. Fuck that." I can't feel my face. Millions of pinpricks of light swirl before my eyes. I'm walking, but I don't know how I'm doing that.

"Colette," he shouts. "Wait."

I spin around to face him. "You're just another liar. Just like Micah."

"No," he says, blocking my path. "Coco. Let me explain. It's not what you're thinking. I'd never—"

"Betray my trust like that?" I ask, gaping at him. "I don't even know . . ."

My voice is cracking, and my face is flushing, and if I had a coffee mug in my hand . . .

"*Why?*" I ask. "Why did you lie to me? Why are you recording me?"

"I'm not just recording you, though," he explains. "I'm capturing *everything*. My mother's decline. Conversations with my father. Meetings with people around the island. I'm recording everything as it happens. Your return to Avalon. The murders. The investigation. And it'll all go into a documentary—"

"I don't care," I shout. "You've lied to me all this time."

He reaches for me, and says, "No—"

I slap his hand away. "You're not interested in *me*. You're interested in my *story*."

"*Both,*" he says. "Colette, look—"

"Watch out for Noah," I say, squinting at him. "Someone sent me a text saying that, and I couldn't understand . . . now, I get it."

He turns red. "I'm not trying to get over on you. I didn't want you to know because . . ."

I nod and smirk. "I would've said, 'Fuck you,' to exploiting me? Like you exploit 'the Other' all around the world? Like I'm some kind of freakin' curiosity?"

He clasps his hands around his head. "It's not like that."

"The hell it ain't." I point at him. "We're done. I'm fucking over it. I'm over you."

"I'll show you what I have so far," he says. "You'll see that I'm not . . . that it's not . . ." He squats and rubs his face with his hands.

We say nothing as the mist swirls around us.

Both of our phones vibrate.

It's Maddy again, telling us to hurry the hell on.

I rub my temples to ease the pounding in my head. "Where is it stored?"

"Where is what—"

"The freaking video. What if something happens to you? You get gored by a bull or someone pushes *you* from a cliff. Where does it go?"

"I've set it up that you and my editor will get an email that I've already scheduled—if I don't change the date on the send, it gets sent automatically."

"Does Maddy know?" I ask.

"No," he shouts. "And don't tell her, okay?"

I snort and stomp to his cart. "You have no say over what I can and cannot do. Take me to Helen's."

Bastard.

Noah drives up, up, up, and I let my mind wander in a fog. So much has happened since I arrived back on March 9, and in a few minutes, we will be one step closer to formally outing the Beast of Avalon. This time, the right man will go to jail.

"What are you thinking about?" Noah asks over the cart noise.

"All the houses and streets look the same," I say, my eyes moving from house to house.

"That's not what I meant—"

"Fuck you, Noah." I face him, then lean toward the dangling pendant. "Did you get that? I'll say it louder, this time with more feeling. *Fuck. You.*"

A bright wind pushes at the cart while fog softens the sound of the engine. I can barely make out the lights of the casino that way or the lights of the Inn at Mount Ada that way. My body aches—I haven't taken any painkillers in several hours, and now, the pounding I received pulls at my weary body.

Noah parks and tries to take my hand before we climb out.

I snatch away from him again, still pissed. He was supposed to be a part of my "Happy at Last" plan. I was supposed to go adventuring with him.

And now, I walk alongside him, unable to look at him—to some house, any house. They all look the same, especially at night in the fog.

This one, Flynn's mom's house, smells like cinnamon and coffee. Vases filled with fresh flowers sit on flat spaces. Sleek furniture—leather and glass—crowd the type of Persian rugs that no one buys because they're too damn expensive.

How will Helen respond to me, the one who told her to get bent before slamming the door in her face? Maddy hasn't mentioned that confrontation, so . . . maybe Helen chalked it up to my grief and exhaustion.

Maddy hugs me. "You look like you need some coffee cake and a drink."

I chuckle without humor. "You have no idea."

Maddy looks at Noah, looks at me, then smiles. "Oh no! Did we have our first lover's tiff?" She threads her arms through both Noah's and mine. "Tell me all about it over dessert."

Flynn and his mother work blenders.

Maddy says, "Flynn, say 'hi.' These two wacky kids are mad at each other."

He waves. "You'll figure it out. Virgin, right, Coco?"

"Right," I say.

"And you know Helen," Maddy says, pointing to her waspy-waisted mother-in-law.

"Nice seeing you again." Helen gives me a knowing smile—*I'm being nice, but I didn't forget.* "Condolences, again, Colette. Gwen was a special woman. She actually stole my emerald earrings and brooch. Could you be a dear and find those for me? Give them to Maddy."

I say, "Sure."

Nope. There's a reason Gwen pinched from Helen, and I'll honor that theft.

Maddy, Noah, and I settle on the veranda that overlooks the town. Helen and Flynn come out with trays of coffee cake and white blended cocktails drizzled with chocolate.

"For you, a high-end virgin Buffalo Milk," Helen says, handing me a glass. "The *enhanced* one contains top-shelf vodka. Both versions have a little more half-and-half than what restaurants use. I used to be a bartender a very, *very* long time ago."

I thank her, then take a quick sip of my mocktail. It's sweet. Too sweet. Makes-my-teeth-hurt sweet. And it tastes funny in my cut-up mouth.

Maddy waits for her mother-in-law to return to the kitchen, then claps her hands and says, "So: good news, Coco. Santos stopped by your house, but you weren't there, so he found me at home. He arrested Carson McIntyre Junior tonight."

I gawk at her. *"What?"*

Maddy nods. "His fingerprint matches the bloody print on your cheek. He was already in the system for DUIs."

"So, he's in jail?" I ask, taking a longer pull of the mocktail.

Maddy nods. "Indeed, he is. And Santos told me some other things as well."

"Like?" Noah asks.

"You probably know that Mac Senior was the deputy in charge of—"

"My family's case," I say. "I didn't, but today I found his name on a report."

"But wait, there's more," Maddy takes a deep breath. "The night your family died, the crime scene techs collected evidence. Evidence that would've pointed to McIntyre *Junior* as the man who committed the murders—your *family's* murders."

The red-faced man yelling at my father.

"But Mac Senior," Maddy continues, "destroyed fingerprint evidence, destroyed DNA samples, and hid the knife."

I nod. "And since I'd already identified Harper Hemphill as the man I saw at the house that night . . . they went with that."

"Back in November," Maddy says, "Mac Senior knew that he was dying, and he anonymously sent the knife to Harper Hemphill's team. His wife knew and spilled her guts to Santos tonight."

I cover my face with my hands.

Noah rubs my back.

My mind spins with Maddy's words, with my own descriptions that were too twisted to fit a narrative, too twisted to convict an innocent man.

"Do you have a picture of Mikey?" I ask, sitting up.

Maddy finds a picture on her phone.

"Ohmigod." My stomach feels slick, and I wobble forward onto my knees.

"So you recognize him?" Noah asks, eyes big.

That salt-and-pepper hair. Those bright-blue eyes . . .

I nod, then whisper, "I thought he was Gwen's handyman."

"What?" Noah and Maddy shout.

"He called himself Handy Andy," I explain. "And then he said his name was J. R. He replaced the doors and . . . and . . . J. R. *Junior.*"

"He's been in the *house*?" Noah asks.

My head spins, and all of it—exhaustion, hunger, fear—slams into me, then drops me, and the world darkens at its edges. I allowed a murderer to come within my gates.

Right there, he was right there all along.

I want my aunt back. All Gwen wanted in life was to steal from awful people, to watch her TV shows, and to drink martinis and eat sausages and crackers.

My hands. I can't feel my hands or my feet. My heart . . . is it beating? I can't feel any pounding in my chest, in my throat, in my head. I can't feel anything . . . at all.

44.

Cold from the stone ground beneath me settles in my bones. My damp hands push against that hard floor. In the gloom, I spot wine bottles in cubbies and more wine bottles in cubbies, bottles, bottles everywhere. I blink, and my eyes crunch like dry leaves, and my stomach feels hollowed out and fuzzy.

Where am I?

I close my eyes.

So tired.

. . .

. . .

I open my eyes.

I'm on my back now, a flipped beetle. Same hard, cold floor beneath me.

A moth dances around the light bulbs in the wrought iron chandelier.

I wince and turn my head. Spikes pierce my eyes and behind my ears.

"Hey." Noah fills my vision—he's kneeling beside me.

I try to move, but those spikes now travel down my spine. "What happened?"

"We don't have a lot of time," Noah says, worry in his eyes.

A steady hum in my head makes it hard to hear.

"I've been working on something," Noah's saying, "and I need to tell you . . ." He looks over his shoulder.

I squint—at him, at the dusty bottles in those eternal cubbies, at the wrought iron chandelier . . . "What? I don't . . ." I push up from the stone-slabbed floor.

There's a small table with four dark wood chairs. There's a small sink . . .

"This is all about real estate," Noah whispers.

"What is 'this'?"

"And this is all about money," he continues. "They want the house on Beacon Street."

Pain pounds against my temples. "I tried calling Helen or Alessandra or whoever."

"Right. Yeah." He shakes his head. "Forget that. They want you to sell it for twenty thousand dollars."

I stare at him, then laugh as I push onto my knees. "Is this a joke? It's obvious that I'm not ready for this conversation. And I wanna keep the house. It's my family's house."

He closes his eyes. "Just sell. *Please.* Other people . . . they've turned Helen down—"

"Well, *yeah.* Especially if she's lowballing. Where's Alessandra—"

"Dead," Noah blurts. "She's *been* dead. They killed her a long time ago."

"Huh? Wait—'other people'? Other than Gwen?"

"Paula Paulsen—she met with Helen. And so did Felicity, Vera, Doris, and Consuela. All widows, all old, all vulnerable. I knew something strange was going on, back when Vera disappeared, but I couldn't figure it out, not until you came. I left you that map, hoping that your fresh eyes would see . . . and you *did* see and . . ." He stands and holds out his hand. "You passed out, and they carried you down here, and I followed, thinking this was a bedroom, and . . . we need to get out of here. Just say yes, okay? To whatever offer they make, accept it."

My stomach wobbles as I try to stand. "You keep saying 'they.' Who is 'they'?"

Somewhere, a door opens. Somewhere, feet tap against steps.

Maddy rounds the corner at the end of a short corridor. "Yay! She's up."

Noah backs away from me, then taps his compass.

"Did you ask her?" Maddy asks Noah.

Noah says, "I haven't had a chance. She just woke up."

"Ask me what?" I say.

"Are you going to sell the house to my mother-in-law?" Maddy asks.

Flynn rounds that same corner and stands behind Maddy. "He tell her yet?"

Noah pales. "No."

My throat tightens as I look at Noah, then Maddy. "Tell me *what*?"

Noah's eyes swell with tears. "The Beast of Avalon."

I nod. "It's Mikey, right?"

Flynn says, "That's funny."

"Colette, honey," Maddy purrs. "Flynn and I . . . *we're* the Beast of Avalon."

I blink at Maddy, then at Flynn. I shake my head to clear it, then manage, "I don't understand . . . *What?*"

Maddy snaps her fingers in front of my face. "Pay attention. We don't have time."

"Did you know that back in 2001, Mikey bid forty thousand dollars above asking price for the house on Beacon Street?" Flynn asks. "The owners told him that he was the highest bidder."

I shake my head—I didn't know that.

"But then," Maddy continues, "your father gave the selling agent, Kate Bushwell, a very *generous* bonus, which then pissed off an already unstable man, who then learned that the house on Beacon was no longer his."

"And that's why Mikey came to Middle Terrace that day," Flynn concluded.

I nod. "I remember he screamed at my dad." Tired of the noise, tired of Gwen's glares, I left the house and walked into town.

"Then, Mikey came back later that night to do more than scream," Maddy says.

Flynn points at me. "You all swindled your way onto this island with that under-the-table deal. If you'd just stayed where you belonged, everyone would still be alive. Kate. Alessandra. Your family." He pulls out a gun from the small of his back.

"No!" Noah and I shout.

I lift my hands. "I'll sell Helen the house." I turn to Maddy with wild, feverish eyes. "And I'll help you write the book series, the podcast, the teleplay . . . a publisher already wants to pay me millions right now. Can you imagine? One of your cowriters is the survivor of *two* Avalon serial murders? You'll make a killing."

Flynn squints at me. "So, what do we need Noah for?"

Maddy says, "Nothing."

Flynn says, "Good." He points the gun at Noah and pulls the trigger.

45.

The jarring bang of a single gunshot rocks around the room of stone and glass.

Noah falls back against the wall with a sickening thump.

I'm dreaming.

None of this is real.

EEEeeeee . . .

I can't hear anything except for a steady *EEEeeeee* . . .

Maddy, my friend . . .

Noah, my lover . . .

Flynn and Maddy . . . serial killers.

Maddy's mouth is moving, but my ears still ring with *EEEeeeee* . . .

I squeeze my eyes. *Wakeupwakeupwakeup* . . .

Seconds pass . . . minutes . . . hours . . . lifetimes . . .

Hot breath warms my ears and pulls me from sleep or shock. "Did you know that Gwen called suicide hotlines for years?"

I shrink away from Maddy, whose breath hits my face. That, combined with the pungent, sickening smells of wine, sulfur, and firecrackers, makes me gag. "We need to get a doctor—Noah . . ."

"Could die? Yeah, he could," Maddy says, nodding. "On Sunday night, Gwen told me that she felt immense guilt for dating Harper. For scheming with him to scare your family back to LA, and . . ."

She leans even closer. "Did you know that Paula Paulsen's house was worth $1.3 million? After she died, Helen purchased the house for $112,000. Felicity Amador's house was worth $735,000. We purchased that house for $112,000."

"You killed them for . . . houses?" I ask.

"There's a housing crisis on Avalon, don't you know?" Maddy says, wide eyed.

"Gwen and the others?" Flynn shrugs. "They were gonna die anyway. Cancer, heart disease, dementia. And Paula was filthy. Felicity brought criminals to the island. Vera was annoying but not as much as Consuela. Gwen was a thief."

Maddy nods. "But! They all died peacefully. We prepared lovely last meals—"

"So my aunt came *here*?" I ask, voice weak.

HIN . . . *Helen Nilsen.*

"Rib eye, lobster . . . she thought Helen wanted her to stage a house, just like she did back in the good old days. Gwen drank her third Buffalo Milk before she realized she was a dead woman. None of them tasted the nightshade in their Buffalo Milk."

"The berries from the deadly plant taste sweet," Flynn says. "Mixed into a cocktail heavy on Kahlúa and crème de bananes, they never tasted a thing."

"Everyone loved the obituaries you wrote," Maddy adds. "Flynn and I tried to be as personal in the obituaries we wrote for *you*, but I've never been as good a writer as you."

My heart thuds once, hard. "You wrote . . . ?"

Pushed from a cliff.

Trampled by bison.

Shot point-blank in the head.

"Noah?" I find him slouching near the sink—he's pale and still. Not much time. "I'll do whatever you need—just call 9-1-1."

"Too late for that," Maddy says.

My heart bobs in my chest. *Please let him survive, please.*

"Don't you wanna know if Noah knew?" Maddy asks.

I lift my head even though it weighs more than a boulder. "Does it matter?"

Maddy gasps. "Of *course* it matters."

"Our intrepid reporter," Flynn says, standing over Noah and me. "He knew something was up, and he was chasing it." He nudges Noah's thigh. "Sad to see you go, bro."

Maddy wags her finger at me. "I told you to look out for him."

Maddy texted me?

Maddy pulls me away from Noah's side. "And Gwen . . . at least she won't have to call any more suicide hotlines. After we got her all cozy in a blanket, Flynn drove her up to the airport. But then, he chickened out and left her at the park. He always had a soft spot for Gwen."

"That lemon pound cake was fire," Flynn says, nodding.

Maddy claps her hands. "Okay. So. You end here."

I say, "No, wait."

"Helen is gonna buy the house on Beacon with or without you," Maddy continues.

"No problem at all." Helen's voice echoes from above.

Flynn grabs me from behind and clamps his hand over my mouth.

"Detective Santos," Helen continues, "it's so nice for you to stop by. We were just about to open a bottle of wine. Madeline," she shouts. "Flynn. Bring up a second bottle, will you?"

Maddy flushes. "Sure, Helen."

I try to force my lips apart to bite Flynn's hand.

His grasp is too tight.

"Go up there," Flynn hisses at Maddy. Then, he squeezes my face tighter . . . tighter . . .

The room gets grayer, my knees weaker.

Grayer . . . weaker . . . weaker . . . and then I . . .

◆　◆　◆

I wake up on my back, a stunned beetle again.

Still on this stone floor.

For how long?

I groan, and my head spins as I pull myself to my feet. I stumble down the short hallway to find a flight of stairs that leads up to a door. And, I discover, a *locked* door.

I *must* get out of here.

Flynn will kill me just like he killed . . .

I gaze back at Noah, at the blood splattered against the wall, the blood gathering beneath him. Where was he shot? I can't tell because all of him hides beneath bright crimson.

The pulse in his neck is weak against my fingertips. He's still alive. I lift the pendant from around his neck, then run my fingers along his face. Fighting tears. I slip the compass over my head.

Okay. *Think.*

Who knows that I'm here?

Anyone out today—*Is it still today?*—saw me carrying luggage to the dock. The woman at the ferry office would assume I'd successfully escaped the island.

Santos came to my house, but I was already gone.

So . . . no one.

If I want to live, I need to find a way out.

I dart around the cellar in search of a weapon.

There is a candle in the center of the table. There are bottles of wine in cubbies . . .

I pull out a drawer.

Cheese forks, sauce spoons, and . . . *that!*

◆ ◆ ◆

What did they slip in my mocktail?

Nightshade?

Most likely.

But I took only a few sips.

I didn't die.

I was supposed to die. Just like Gwen. Just like the other women.

I settle into a corner of the cellar. How long have I been down here? I don't have my phone, so I can't tell. I try to keep my eyes moving to stay awake, but the rest of me . . . prickling legs . . . numb face . . . eyes closed . . . eyes open . . . sleeping now when I haven't been able to sleep all this time.

The door clicks.

I startle, so awake that I can see next Thursday. I touch my key to freedom that is now nestled behind me. I close my eyes and fake a light snore.

A hand jostles my shoulder. "Wake up." It's Flynn.

I part my eyes, but just barely. I've never been this close to him. In this light, his skin looks cracked—that scraggly beard covers still-healing scratch marks, his preternaturally white teeth are fanged, his haircut is severe, like those worn by the men who'd marched on a Virginia college campus holding store-bought tiki torches.

I settle into a different position, coughing to hide any noise I make behind my back.

Flynn reels back. "Cover your mouth—"

I tighten my grip around the neck of the wine bottle in my right hand, then tighten my grip around the corkscrew in the left. *Go!* Cabernet Sauvignon has a nice weight, and the bottle connects solidly against the side of Flynn's head.

He goes down to his knees.

I hit him again, harder this time, and break the bottle against his skull. Then, I plunge the corkscrew into his neck.

Blood spurts like champagne from a bottle and mixes with the 2018 Cab.

Flynn doesn't move even as blood and wine puddle on the stone floor around him.

I tiptoe up the steps with the slippery corkscrew in my hand.

The door is unlocked.

I push the door open a little . . . then, I push it open a little more . . .

Light glints off the fridge . . . the blender still contains sleepy-time night-night drink.

"She really needs to do something," Helen says. "We can't afford to miss tourist season."

"What good is money if you're too dead to spend it?" Maddy asks.

A door!

"How are we supposed to pay bills, then?" Helen asks.

"I have a business plan—"

I hold my breath as I twist the doorknob.

Click.

I slowly . . . slowly . . . pull open the door.

There are two high-pitched beeps, and then: "Kitchen. Door. Open."

Security system.

"Flynn?" Maddy shouts. "Everything okay?"

I throw open the door and race out into a black hole filled with trees, wild nightshade, and the forever dark. The light from the kitchen breaks up some of the gloom, and I run up the hill because they would assume that I ran down.

Santos was here, but . . . When? How long ago?

My legs burn as I hike up . . . over . . . up . . . over. I reach the bluffs that overlook the Pacific Ocean. The roar of crashing waves down below keeps me from hearing my thundering heart.

There is a yellow sign.

CAUTION FALLING ROCK

There is a red-and-black sign.

DANGER
NO TRESPASSING
STEEP GRADE

Both signs show a stick figure—me—tumbling off a mountainside.

There's no place to run—I need to turn back.

And then what?

If I return to Beacon Street, Maddy and Flynn (if he's still alive) will find me there.

I turn back to the bluffs.

How high up am I? How steep are these hillsides?

"Climb down and find out," Maddy shouts from behind me.

I whirl around.

Maddy holds a flashlight. The rest of her hides in shadow. "Sorry about Noah. You have such a hard time finding love."

I swallow spit thick with dirt, sedatives, and fear.

"He wanted you to be his little travel buddy," she says. "You two were so cute."

I touch the compass and peek behind me.

"Do you know what today is?" she asks. "Sunday, March twenty-second, and here we are."

I peek behind me again. Crumbling land . . . jagged rocks . . . cold white water . . .

"You won't survive that." Maddy is moving closer, and the flashlight beam is growing larger. "C'mon, Colette. Everything's changed, and so let's think this through. You lost the game, okay? There's nowhere to go. No one can help you. You're wearing Noah's compass, but sweetheart, you're lost, and there's only one way out of here."

I shudder, hold my bloody hands over my eyes to block the flashlight's glare.

"I'm blaming all of this on Noah," Maddy says. "He *is* the son of a greedy land developer currently having an affair with a senator's wife. No one likes colonists and adulterers, right?"

My muscles coil at the thought of picking my way down the hillside. But if I have to . . .

"Say you try to fight me," Maddy's saying. "Say you survive. How will you explain what you did to Flynn?"

"Self-defense," I shout, stepping back.

And Noah's compass now dangling around my neck has captured *all* of this.

Use your enemy's hand to catch snakes.

Maddy shines the light at her own face. Her blue eyes shimmer with tears. "Your Honor, Colette lost it. She was jealous of Flynn, and—" A sob escapes her chest. "She *killed* him in cold blood." She cries to the night sky, then stops as suddenly as she started. Then, she curtsies.

Is the camera around my neck capturing this performance?

"Who do you think America's judicial system will believe?" Maddy asks. "Me, a hardworking small business owner? Or you, the angry Black woman whose lies wrongfully imprisoned an innocent Black man? The angry woman who came to Catalina Island to kick her old suicidal auntie out of the only house she's ever known? Someone who broke her husband's nose with a coffee mug? They won't relate to an unlikable female character."

Something shifts inside me that sends me hurtling into Maddy Swenson.

Maddy, caught off guard, screams as my hands wrap around her neck.

Wind blows at my back.

Maddy tries to twist from under me, but I'm a vise.

I ignore the pain ripping through my body, and I squeeze harder . . . harder . . .

The blow to my ear makes me release her neck. I duck as the flashlight swings in the air.

Maddy grabs my arm, bringing me on top of her, then grabs my hair, and I hear the thread tear from my extensions as we roll . . . and we roll . . .

Sea air and sea mist meet us, and Maddy stops rolling at the cliff's edge. She gapes at the ocean below.

I bite her hand.

She cries out and lets me go.

I scramble away from the edge.

Maddy grabs my boot.

I kick her once and knock her even closer to the precipice . . . then, I kick her again . . .

The third kick is the hardest, and she tumbles over the edge of the cliff. She tries to scramble forward, but her hands slip over crumbling rock and dirt. She tries to scoot up, facedown in the dirt, but more earth crumbles beneath her. She tries to swing her leg up to gain traction, but she overshoots, and her momentum pulls her back and sends her plummeting down . . . down . . .

The land beneath my hands also crumbles, and I slide down the steep bluff.

I stop my descent by grabbing a root jutting from the slope . . . and then, I grab another root, and another . . .

My lungs scream for air as I slowly . . . slowly . . . pull myself back to solid ground.

There, in the light of the flashlight, a small deer nibbles wild grass. She sees me, cocks her head, stops chewing, and then bounds into the darkness.

EPILOGUE

July 2020

As the new editor in chief of the *Avalon Breeze*, I should be writing about revised dining guidelines and updating the island's weekly positive test results—nine on my last check.

As a homeowner, I should be overseeing the crew ripping out mildewed drywall in the bathrooms. Somehow, a few new doors fell off the back of a barge and showed up on my porch, along with a crew of six bored men.

As a memoirist, I should be writing about the month before the Webers settled in the rental on Middle Terrace, and our last trips and dinners with friends. My agent, Andrea Liszl, and I worked the treatment until I couldn't stand to see my name. Then, she sold the book, the TV and film rights, and foreign rights.

Since then, I've rebuffed Micah's pleas to reconcile.

We just needed a break Coco

You know you miss me

You can't live without me

And where's the ring??

Oh, Micah.
The ring is worthless, I finally text back.

Not a real diamond or ruby

The story though is priceless

No time passes when he texts back, Fuck a story

Stories ain't worth shit

Stupid rabbit.

How many people died on Avalon, all for a story?

As a journalist, I should be explaining the schemes between the McIntyres and Nilsens to buy up the island—and do it by killing, if needed. But for now, I'm in possession of Noah's hidden camera and holding it over the heads of both families—and the Swensons. They think I'm gonna keep it to myself, that I won't share with the world just how they've rotted Avalon. *They* are the invasive species, far worse than a throwaway tangerine seed. But I never agreed to *not* talk. I *am* Reginald Weber's daughter. I *am* Gwyneth Rose's niece. They *will* go to jail. Flynn (who survived), Helen, and anyone else involved.

Carson McIntyre Junior spotted me at his arraignment and made great effort to send spit in my direction. Bail revoked.

He'd been caught by Santos not just because his prints matched the print on my cheek, but because Santos caught him using a key to enter my house. He'd planned to vandalize, just as he had been doing all that time. Squirting toothpaste, spilling coffee grounds, and throwing flour and beer bottles. That was his cigarette butt that I'd found in the dirt.

After Maddy's private memorial—I wasn't invited, but I hadn't planned to attend the funeral of a serial killer—and after checking up on Noah recovering in the hospital in Torrance, I drove my aunt's cart up to Middle Terrace and sat in front of that vacation rental that changed my life. I tried to cry, but by then, I was too exhausted to find a tear to shed.

◆　◆　◆

Tucked between Los Angeles and San Francisco (and 206 miles from Catalina Island), Paso Robles is known for its almond orchards, hot sulfur springs, and more than forty wine grape varieties, from Cabernet Sauvignon to Viognier. With more than two hundred wineries, Paso Robles could offer an old man a new start. And while none of the wineries are open for tastings, there is still grape cluster thinning to do, and leaf trimming and pest-control monitoring . . .

According to my attorney Ted, Harper Hemphill worked at a winery known for its Bordeaux and Rhône-style wines and for the boxcar and caboose next to its tasting room.

And now, I'm here.

A friendly-faced man wearing a floppy straw hat meets me in the winery's dirt driveway.

"We're closed, ma'am," he says, standing more than six feet away.

I remove my mask. "I'm here to see Harper."

The man looks over to an old rickety shack with peeling white paint and fading green trim. "He expecting you?"

I take a deep breath, then push it out. "Don't think so. Please tell him that Colette Weber is here to see him."

The man shuffles over to the shack.

A gray cat hops onto a picnic table and runs its pink tongue along its paw. The wind rustles the lavender bushes, and I inhale deeply, hoping for on-the-spot organic aromatherapy. My pulse races and revs, and I can very well have a heart attack before speaking to Harper Hemphill.

Dr. Tamaguchi agrees—making amends is an important part of my therapy. Ted, always thinking like an attorney, thinks my visit can open me up to a lawsuit.

They are both right.

I close my eyes now and focus on slowing my heart rate. Back in LA, my hairdresser replaced old hair with new extensions, but she braided my cornrows too tight, and my scalp pulls with each deep breath.

"Coco?" The man wearing dusty jeans and a chambray shirt is stooped, and no longer six four and 210 pounds. He wears a green baseball cap over his brown head.

Tears swell in my eyes. "Harper?"

"What you doing here?" He offers me a cold bottle of water.

I accept the gift, not ready yet to offer him mine—a check to help him start his new life and a fresh-baked lemon pound cake, Gwen's recipe. Instead, I square my shoulders, and say, "We have a lot to talk about."

Colette Sienna Weber

[DRAFT]

Colette Sienna Weber of Los Angeles, California, left this world on [insert date]. She loved her family hard and missed them even harder after their deaths on June 23, 2001. [Mention Aunt Gwen—come up with something positive since I can't right now.] She remained in Avalon, California, for [insert #] years, inheriting a house filled with silk robes and jeweled baubles, dusty throw pillows, and a phallic-shaped cactus she named Rambo. Almost everything in that house on Beacon Street (including the cactus) was stolen property.

Preowned, Colette liked to say.

Unauthorized recycled and reused, she'd say on her chattier days.

She served as editor in chief of *Avalon Breeze* for [insert #] [months/ years], an unexpected twist in a life filled with unexpected twists. Over the course of her leadership, she [list my accomplishments]. A Grimmy Award–winning obituary writer, Colette wrote the final words for the extraordinary people and the everyday citizens—CEOs, mistresses to billionaires, small-heist queens, and old ladies who simply wanted to live their lives on Paradise.

On [date], she met the love of her life, [name]. He worshipped Colette and ensured that in her final days she [insert something fun].

She married [name] for his [insert good traits] and insisted that he [do this thing—he'll be interesting, so it won't be too hard to come up with something]. Together, they sailed to the Galápagos Islands, skied in the French and Swiss Alps (okay, he skied, and she sat by a fire with glasses of the finest bubbly waters and a book), and sunbathed on countless beaches. She found peace and love with [name].

Colette was born on April 25, 1985, to Reginald and Alyson Weber, fire and ice, sea salt and smoky paprika. She was big sister to Langston "L Boogie" Weber, the star wide receiver for the Crenshaw Cougars, two-time science fair winner, and the best brother in the world. They were taken from her too soon.

The Webers are now together again . . . except for Gwen. They are no longer interested in sharing a mansion in the Kingdom with Gwen.

Colette is survived by [who's left??].

Visitation will take place on [date and time] at [place] with the funeral and burial at [place and location].

To Colette's chagrin, there are still only [insert #] Black people living full-time on Santa Catalina Island.

ACKNOWLEDGMENTS

I am writing these acknowledgments on the Monday after Thanksgiving 2022. On Sunday evening, I said goodbye to my writing partner of fourteen years. Lucky, our family's golden retriever, gave so much love to David, Maya, and me. She served as a sister and another daughter, as the household Kong-catcher and prime peanut butter lover. She nudged me awake every morning at four thirty. After taking her out to pee and feeding her (and as she got older, also giving her estrogen and painkillers), I'd settle at my writing desk and she'd settle at my feet, and together, we'd write stories. Except for my first book, Lucky has helped me complete every story I've written since 2008. This morning, Lucky isn't snoring at my feet, and my heart is broken. Thank you, Lucky Hall, for being my ride-and-die at zero dark thirty every day. I love you, Ducky-Bucks.

Thank you, Jill, for always looking out for me. Your continued guidance and advice through these years . . . I couldn't ask for a better agent and friend.

Jessica and Clarence, you both are incredible editors, and I appreciate your advice, guidance, and sharp eye. Thanks to all my team at Thomas & Mercer. My stories—and my writing life—are so rich and wonderful with you standing with me.

Thank you, Kaytee Canfield, PhD, for sharing your expertise on Catalina Island. Your dissertation, and then, our conversation and emails, helped provide the background I needed to fully realize this story on page.

Thank you, Letty, for that incredible golf-cart tour of Avalon. I couldn't write fast enough to capture all your incredible stories and experience. Everything that I learned from you that afternoon can be found in these pages, and if I got something wrong, it was due to my own mangling of words.

To my writing friends, I love y'all for loving me. Keep writing great stories and coming up with new tricks. You know I love figuring out your tricks!

Thank you, readers, for supporting my work, for reaching out with positivity and excitement. I have the opportunity to share my stories because of you!

To my parents, Nate and Jackie, and siblings, Terry, Gretchen, and Jason, you will always be inspiration for every story I write. You will forever be my perfectly imperfect family.

Maya Grace, my love for you is boundless and you, too, are not here as I write. I'm glad that you're thriving in your first year of college—I miss you, though. You still serve as my muse and my delight, and now that you're experiencing another part of life, I will sap you of all your experiences as a college student in post-COVID America.

David, what can I say? No engagement ring commercials show the life after the "I do's." We've experienced so many highs, and right now, we're in the valley of loss. I'm glad that we're battling together, side by side, co-op playing this video game called Life. I love you, and I appreciate everything that you've done for me, for Meatz, for GusGus and Major, and for our golden girl, Lucky. Can't wait to live the Royal Caribbean, dancing on white sand, watching food being flambéed-part of our empty nest experience.

ABOUT THE AUTHOR

Photo © 2019 Andre Ellis

Rachel Howzell Hall is the *New York Times* bestselling author of *We Lie Here*; *These Toxic Things*; *And Now She's Gone*; and *They All Fall Down*; and, with James Patterson, *The Good Sister*, which was included in Patterson's collection *The Family Lawyer*. A *Los Angeles Times* Book Prize finalist as well as an Anthony, International Thriller Writers, and Lefty Award nominee, Rachel is also the author of *Land of Shadows*, *Skies of Ash*, *Trail of Echoes*, and *City of Saviors* in the Detective Elouise Norton series. A past member of the board of directors for Mystery Writers of America, Rachel has been a featured writer on NPR's acclaimed *Crime in the City* series and the National Endowment for the Arts weekly podcast; she has also served as a mentor in Pitch Wars and the Association of Writers & Writing Programs. Rachel lives in Los Angeles with her husband and daughter. For more information, visit www.rachelhowzell.com.